The
Talk-Funny
Girl

Also by Roland Merullo

Fiction

Fidel's Last Days

American Savior

Breakfast with Buddha

Golfing with God

A Little Love Story

In Revere, in Those Days

Revere Beach Boulevard

A Russian Requiem

Leaving Losapas

Nonfiction

The Italian Summer

Revere Beach Elegy

Passion for Golf

The
Talk-Funny
Girl

a novel

Roland Merullo

Crown Publishers
New York

Copyright © 2011 by Roland Merullo

All rights reserved.
Published in the United States by Crown Publishers,
an imprint of the Crown Publishing Group,
a division of Random House, Inc., New York.
www.crownpublishing.com

CROWN and the Crown colophon are registered trademarks of Random House, Inc.

Library of Congress Cataloging-in-Publication Data
Merullo, Roland.
Talk funny girl : a novel / Roland Merullo.—1st ed.
p. cm.
1. Self-realization in women—Fiction. I. Title
PS3563.E748T35 2011
813'.54—dc22   2011003328

ISBN 978-0-307-45292-4
eISBN 978-0-307-45294-8

PRINTED IN THE UNITED STATES OF AMERICA

Book design by Donna Sinisgalli
Title page photography by Emily Lahteine
Jacket design by Nupoor Gordon
Jacket photography © Ocean/Corbis

10 9 8 7 6 5 4 3 2 1

First Edition

for
Shaye Areheart

Author's Note

Although this story grew out of a chance encounter in a Vermont convenience store twenty-five years ago—a glimpse into the hidden world of New England's rural poor—the people described here are creatures of my imagination. While the places where some of the main scenes are set bear a resemblance to certain old New Hampshire mill towns, they are made-up places and should not be confused with those actual towns.

Many people helped with this book, and I would like to express my gratitude to them. First thanks, as always, to my wife, Amanda, for her unflappable love and optimism in the face of the persistent uncertainty of the writing life and the quirks and moods of her husband. My inexpressible gratitude to her, and to Alexandra and Juliana for the gift of their presence.

It is a huge favor to spend hours reading a manuscript and offering suggestions. I am grateful to Craig Nova, Peter Grudin, Jeffrey Forhan, and Amanda Merullo for their time and care in doing that. Thanks to my neighbor Joe Miraglia for passing on some of his extensive knowledge of New England's natural world; to Paul Wetzel for his expertise about the New England woods; to John Recco for his knowledge of stonework; to my agents Marly Rusoff and Michael Radulescu for their consistent support, hard work on my behalf, and sound advice;

to Anne Pardun, Sarah Stearns, and Jackie Hudak, my three therapist sisters-in-law, for insight into the intricacies of family psychology; to Shaye Areheart and Kate Kennedy for their wise editing and their belief in this book from start to finish; to Aja Pollock for her wonderful copyediting job; to Tim DeChristopher, master stoneworker, for his help with the technical aspects of cathedral buildings; to the late Alan Schiffmann for his courage, support, and good conversation. Any mistakes or omissions in these pages belong to me, not to these generous friends.

I would like to offer a last word—not of thanks but of empathy—to boys and girls like the fictional Marjorie Richards, wherever they might be. May the busy, self-important adult world someday see you as the full souls you are.

The more people have studied different methods of bringing up children the more they have come to the conclusion that what good mothers and fathers instinctively feel like doing for their babies is the best after all.

–Benjamin Spock

Our children are not individuals whose rights and tastes are casually respected from infancy, as they are in some primitive societies. . . . They are fundamentally extensions of our own egos and give a special opportunity for the display of authority.

–Ruth Benedict

Prologue

I am a grown woman now, married and raising children, and happy enough most of the time. Underneath that happiness, though, showing its face every now and again, is a part of me still connected to a time when I was a girl living with her parents in the New Hampshire hills. That girl was not treated well, and when anyone is hurt like that—especially a child—the hurt burrows down inside and makes a kind of museum there, with images of the bad times displayed on every wall. Some people try to forget the museum exists and keep their mind occupied with drink or drugs or food, or by staying busy with work, or they chase one kind of excitement after another, while the memories fester there in the dark. I understand all that, and I don't lay a judgment, as we used to say, over any of it. Some people use their own hurt as an excuse for hurting others, or for soaking in self-pity, or for a sharp anger that knifes up through the surface whenever something reminds them of what happened long ago. Some people spend their lives trying never to do what was done to them.

I have all those impulses in me—anger and self-pity, the urge to hide, and, sometimes, the urge to hurt. But there is a stronger, warmer part of me, and some courage and kindness, too, and a stubbornness that makes it hard for me to give up on things. I've been lucky to find a loving husband and to have children with him, but even when the people close to you are caring and good, there are going to be times when they say or do something that throws open the museum doors, pushes you in there, forces you to look.

My children are eleven and eight now, their lives different in so many ways from the life I knew at that age. I had fear instead of dreams. I was so much tougher than they are, and paid such a high price for that toughness. Enormous as it was, I couldn't have found the anger inside me with a flashlight and magnifying glass, but their anger is right there on the surface and they know—sometimes too well—how to express it. There have been times when things they've done or said, or forgotten to do or say, have flung me back into the past—it happens to every parent, I think—and I reacted in ways they were confused or hurt by, ways I'm not proud of. Sometimes this has happened with my husband, too, a man who wrestles with his own demons. If I could close down the museum for good, or rip the pictures off the walls and burn them in some kind of healing ceremony, I would do that. But something my husband showed me a long time ago has given me a method of wearing away at the foundations of the trouble, little by little, year after year, the way water erodes stone. As part of my own healing, I decided, not long ago, to open the doors and windows of the museum and let the light in. I returned to the place I was raised, only twenty miles from where we live now, and I walked the roads and went into the buildings, and talked to some of the people I recognized and who remembered me. "Mom's own private history project," the kids called it, but, of course, they had no idea what I was really doing. It was more than a history project and had nothing to do with nostalgia. It was my way of trying to stand up to the worst memories, eye to eye, so that they wouldn't send their poisons, through me, into my children.

The events I'm going to describe here happened more than twenty years ago. I was a different person then, the demons so much larger in my world. While I don't pretend to remember conversations exactly, I do remember the spirit of them. Strange as it may seem to readers in the main stream of society, I really did talk that way, and the people around me really did behave that way. Though the pain of my upbringing made me stronger, I can't say I'm grateful, and I would never wish anything like it for any other child on this earth. At the same time I don't let myself feel much self-pity. Hard things happen to people— that's the nature of the world—and, horrible as that can be, I believe there has to be some purpose behind it all. The question isn't *Why did this happen to me?* but *What do I do with it?* The past shouts at you, the ugly words or actions echo down across the years. You're walking through the museum with headphones on, listening to all that, your children and husband nearby, the world asking you to grow up, clean up, straighten out, pass on something good. What do you do?

One

There are a lot of places I could begin the story, and a lot of ways I could change a few details and make it easier to read. But I'm after the truth here—the truth is what heals you—so I'll just begin where it seems right, on my seventeenth birthday, and tell the story as it sits in my memory.

On the day I turned seventeen I went looking for a job. I was close to finishing tenth grade then, a year behind where I should have been. Classes let out just before lunch that day. I remember pretending to myself it was in honor of my birthday, but it must have been for a teachers' meeting or a conference or something like that. I remember it was warm for April in middle-north New Hampshire and that I stepped out the school's front door into sunlight and saw the buses lined up in the driveway, engines grumbling, yellow fenders marked with mud. I should have just walked into town, but I needed time to get ready for what I had to do, and so I stepped onto my bus with the other kids, sat with my friend Cindy, and rode all the way back to the corner of Waldrup Road, near where my parents and I lived. Because I didn't want to go home first, I hid my backpack in the trees there, tried to gather up some courage, and then set off on foot back toward town along highway 112.

At that time of year the river that winds beside that two-lane country highway was swollen with snowmelt, and the leaves from the previous fall were matted and damp on the road shoulder. I went along in my hand-me-down pants and sweater and tied-back chestnut-brown hair and made a promise to myself that I wouldn't go home without having found a job. The night before—it was their way of acknowledging my birthday—my parents told me I had to get what they referred to as "full-pay work." I'd worked "part-pay" for as long as I could remember: mother's helper and babysitter for other families that belonged to Pastor Schect's church, and then cleaning the grease racks and sweeping the floor at Emily's Dough Nuts until the chain doughnut shop came to the town and sent Emily's out of business. All the money from those jobs went to my parents, who did not work for either full or part pay. My mother bought the food and cooked. My father cut our stove wood, fished the stream behind our house, and sometimes was able to sell the skins of animals he trapped in the woods in late winter. Every month he received a disability check for back troubles he didn't suffer from. But all that together wasn't really enough for us to live on, even the way we lived, so they told me it was time to find real work. If I had to quit school in order to help support the family, my mother said, I wouldn't be the first person in the world to put up a sacrifice.

The blackflies hadn't come out yet—still too cold for them—and the trees hadn't gone into bud or blossom. Set along the north side of the road stood two small wood-frame houses. When I returned to make that walk again, on the same date in April, those houses were still there and had worn-out American flags flying from their front porches, snowmobiles in the yards, one rusted car, one pickup, a bow target left over from hunting season. Just as they had years before, lumber trucks rumbled down out of the hills loaded with ash, pine, hemlock, and oak, and the sound echoed in the valley where the river ran. You could still feel the hard fist of northern New England winter in the hills to either side. I liked being outdoors, though, I've always liked it. And, as a girl, I enjoyed that walk especially, because, in the same way school did, it made me feel connected to the world of people, the more-or-less sane, more-or-less normal world.

On that birthday walk into town the first place that offered any chance of work was C&P Welding. It has long been out of business now, but in those days it was housed in a low, cement-block building close beside the road, with a gravel lot out front. I knew I shouldn't have, but I stopped in there—out of spite, I think, to upset my parents and to show I wasn't afraid of the owner, Cary Patanauk, a snake of a man. There had always been some unexplained trouble between Mr. Patanauk and my father. Though I hadn't really met Mr. Patanauk before that day, I'd seen him a few years earlier in the church we attended, and I'd heard about him often enough. I knew his nephew at school. The Patanauk name was a kind of curse word in our house, and it's probably a mark of how foolish I was then, how naïve in certain ways, even at seventeen, how angry deep down inside, that I set foot in that building at all.

There was an old-fashioned metal knocker on the door. In my mind I can still see the coppery shine where people's fingers had rubbed away the blue-green tarnish. I lifted the knocker and let it fall. No one answered. I waited, knocked again, thought I heard a voice, and pushed the door open. Inside, there was a mess of gas cylinders, metal parts, and tools, and Cary Patanauk stood at a wooden table mending what looked like a tractor axle. The room smelled of oil and acetylene. Mr. Patanauk closed down the blowtorch, lifted the welding mask, and looked at me.

"I come for a try for paying work," I said into the sudden silence, because that was the way I spoke then, with a private, mixed-up grammar that belonged to my father, and to his father, and to me. Even my mother started to talk that way after she'd been married to my father for a while. My kids think I'm joking when I reproduce that speech now. No matter what I say, no matter what their father tells them, they think that, at the very least, I must be exaggerating.

Mr. Patanauk's eyes went from my face to my chest and back to my face again. "You come for a try for paying work?" he mimicked.

"Yes. I could."

"You could what?"

I looked away from him. Beside me hung a calendar, notes scribbled on some of the days and, on the top half, a mostly naked woman holding a welding torch across her middle.

"You could what?" Mr. Patanauk said a second time. I looked at him and noticed that he hadn't shaved in several days. His pants were held up with suspenders.

"Any of a thing for pay."

He watched me. "Your father and granddad talks of a that of a way, too," he said in a voice as mean as smoke. There was a kind of vapor surrounding him, a nastiness, a vulgar stink; the words seemed to slide out of that.

"I have a good liking for work."

"I could give you lots of jobs," he told me after thinking about it for a few seconds. Across the skin of his face crawled a kind of purplish hope, or need, and it was mixed in with the sense that the world owed him a debt. You could feel the anger in him, too, a quarter inch below the surface. The way he used the torch seemed angry, the way he shut down the flame, the way he stood with his arms drooping. "There's a lot of things you could do for me," he said, out of that anger. "But you'd have to not say a word about it to your crazy old man or your mother."

"I couldn't not say on them."

"Good money for it, you know, and you might have some fun."

I shook my head.

"You wouldn't even have to talk right. You wouldn't even have to talk at all."

I had, then, the nervous habit of bending my lips in between my teeth and biting down on them. I did that. I shook my head. We were standing probably fifteen feet from each other.

Mr. Patanauk let his eyes run over me one more time, top to middle and back again, then with a jerk of his head he nodded the mask down over his face and fired up the torch, and after a few seconds I realized the conversation was finished and I turned and went out the door.

A quarter mile beyond the welding shop stood a brown shingled house with a sagging roof and a sign out front: 112 STORE. It's still there, though it's been fixed up now, and painted a lighter color, and they sell, along with a few groceries, toiletries, and lottery tickets, used CDs and movies from a table at the back. It was the place my mother shopped when my father wouldn't drive her into town. She complained that prices were unfair at the 112, and she made up for that by stealing things in small amounts—a can of baked beans, a box of tampons, one of what she called the "fold-papers" she liked to read. The young owner of the store then, Mrs. Jensen, never caught her in any of those thefts, or maybe only pretended never to catch her, and always treated me with a reserved country kindness. No doubt she had some idea what went on in our family, but probably she felt—as most people felt in those parts and still do—that what happened in our house wasn't any of her business, that it was part of life, that I'd survive it the way so many other children did. On that day she greeted me with a pleasant voice and when I asked about work she told me things were slow just then, money was tight all around. But I could stop back in a few months if things seemed to have turned a little for the better. She looked at my sweater and pants and sneakers. "Are you hungry, Margie?" she asked. "I have some muffins I made this morning and they're not going to sell. I could give you one, and some milk if you wanted."

"I'm for thanking you, but no today."

"You sure?"

I nodded, stomach empty. "Today's a day for to finding work."

"Well, good luck then."

———

Next along the route was Warner and Sons Gravel and Stone, where Zeke Warner took my name and said they had nothing there for seventeen-year-old girls unless they happened to know how to drive a dump truck, but if something came up he'd be sure to get in touch. Did I have a phone number I could leave?

"We aren't to have one," I told him. "Pastor Schect isn't liking for us to have on a phone or the TV or to curse."

"Well, the not-cursing's probably a good idea. I know your aunt Elaine. I'll contact you through her if something comes, or I'll mention it to your father if I see him at Weedon's. Okay?"

I thanked him and went along.

On that afternoon I walked all the way into town and back, just under eight miles. Fourteen or fifteen places of business I made myself step into—Art and Pat's Diner, the Sewing Shop, the chain doughnut place—and the answer was the same in all of them. It was a bad time for the country, especially bad where we lived. Along the Honey River, which ran through town and fed the Connecticut, the concrete of the bridge abutments had broken away in places, showing rusting reinforcing rod. There were men in old clothes and dirty hats fishing from the span. On the street corners there were knots of kids my own age—some of them turned and looked at me as I passed—smoking cigarettes and spitting, dressed dark and shabby, slanting their eyes around as if any minute somebody in a car with out-of-state plates would drive up and hand them a small package of delight. The paper mills and machine shops—industries that town had been built on—were closing, one after the next. People were losing their houses, and a sucking quicksand of debt was forming along the banks of the river where the factories had been. Who was going to have extra money to pay a seventeen-year-old girl?

Even used to walking as I was, that trip exhausted me. In the cold dusk I found my backpack behind the beech tree and set off on the last leg, down Waldrup Road. By then it was almost dark. The tree trunks were black and the stream was loud and I had to stay near the edge of the road where the mud wasn't deep. I saw our mailbox, tilted at a crooked angle on its post, and then, beyond my father's stacks of stove wood, a square of yellow light that was our kitchen window.

My mother was sitting on the counter with a bottle of cheap wine beside her and a mug of it between her legs. The ceiling light made shadows near her eyes. "Damn better say you found something, you Majie," she said. She and my father were the only ones who called me by that name, MAY-gee. No one calls me that now.

My mother took a drink from the mug. I watched the muscles work in her thin neck and her legs jiggle as if small animals inside the jeans were trying to break free. Her hair, dark as used motor oil, had fallen loose and hung down along the sides of her jaw. She had full lips like I do and a straight small nose and pretty green eyes buried in the shadows and in webs of wrinkles. If we had a little money and she fell into a certain mood she'd buy herself a bottle of Hammonds Rosé and sit for half a day on the counter or the couch, her shoulders hunched and her eyes cast down, and she'd drink her way through most of the bottle. There was something methodical about the way she did it, something brutally efficient, as if she was feeling her way back, decision by decision, across an unlit landscape mined with regret. There was something quietly terrifying about her when she drank; her regret had a murderous quality. People told me then, and have told me since then, that my mother was very attractive as a girl and grew up in a family that wasn't desperately poor. She had a stepsister—my aunt Elaine— seven years older, and a stepfather who worked in a hardware store and had one wife and then another who died young. After the second of those deaths—my grandmother's—a kind of wildness broke loose from inside my mother. Against the advice of every relative and friend, she started riding around with the man who would become my father, Curtis John Richards. Curtis John was known for swan-diving from the top ledge—sixty-five feet—into the quarry and climbing up into the treetops during thunderstorms. He scaled the trellis of the railroad bridge at night to mark his initials there in gold paint. *C j R,* you can still see them. He struggled in school, and had a father who taught him how to fight and drink and chew tobacco and not much beyond that. He pronounced his last name as if it were French Canadian—it wasn't—and that probably seemed exotic to my mother. He had a motorcycle, which she loved, and a future painted in the bleakest of northern New England colors, which she couldn't see. He was twenty-six. My mother married him a day after she turned sixteen and no longer needed her stepfather's consent. She didn't speak about it very much, but from the one-or-two-line comments she passed down to me over the years, I understood that she liked being married, at least in the early going. In that part of America, in those years, among the girls she called her friends, it counted for something to be able to say the words "my husband" and to show off a real gold ring. In the warm weather, she and Curtis John liked to go riding in the hills. When it was cold, she told me, "We drunk and screwed."

Having a child had not been part of their plans, if they had any plans, and once I was born, what little chance they had for a prosperous, peaceful life seemed to evaporate like river splash on hot stone. My mother was nineteen and a half when I came into the world. She didn't like to get out of bed in the night to mix formula. She didn't like people telling her to give up cigarettes. She didn't like changing diapers, or making regular appointments with the pediatrician, or taking the stroller to a place where there were sidewalks and meandering around with other young mothers, discussing the joys and troubles of parenthood. She hated having to give up the motorcycle rides, and she didn't appreciate the change in her sex life that having a baby in the house brought on.

At the time I was born, my father had work in a small plant that made hand tools. His parents had never lived together; his mother died when he was ten. After that, his father, Dad Paul, raised him in a three-room apartment above the gas station, taught him about trees and ropes and female anatomy, took him on rides to Montreal. From the start Dad Paul liked my mother—he had "a big side of him," my father used to say—so as a grand present to mark the birth of a grandchild he gave his son and daughter-in-law his four-room "camp" on twelve acres in the woods. The camp had been used for hunting and was not much more than a cabin, poorly insulated, cold in winter, but out of sight of any neighbors, and the privacy suited my father. His own father's gift was something he mentioned, with great pride, dozens of times over the years, even long after Dad Paul had been sent away.

We moved into the camp just before I turned one. When I was two, my father's place of work closed down. After a few weeks, he found, at a lower salary, a job in another small plant where they made plastic picture frames and TV remotes. And then something happened—what, exactly, I've never been able to find out. There was some kind of trouble, an accident or a fight. My father told me once that he'd taken a fall and hurt his back, but I don't think that was the true story. After a long stretch of legal squabbling and a series of consultations with doctors, the company let him retire on what he referred to with some pride as "part but permanent disable." In order to keep the checks coming, he had to pretend to be physically unable to do any kind of work, so he stayed in bed for a few weeks, carved himself a cane to use when he went out in public, and parked in the handicapped spaces whenever he thought he could get away with it. After the accident, though, if that's what it was, trips to town became rare for him; except for a couple of friends he'd had enough of people by that point in his life, and he preferred to spend his time alone in the woods, coming home only to eat dinner and sleep. Once every few weeks we'd all go into town, or we'd go to the quarry for a swim on very hot days, but for the most part my father kept himself away from other people.

"Mister Warner told he might have a work to give," I said to my mother. I set the backpack down at my feet.

She squeezed the mug between her thighs and made a drunken, pinched-eye face I'd seen before, hundreds of times. It was an expression that promised nothing good. "Might?" she said hoarsely.

I nodded and looked away.

"Look on me in my eyes, you Majie you. . . . Might?"

"Probly will. Next week he could of."

"You lie maker. Probly dint even go."

"I went."

"Your dad in't gonna like that *might* you said."

"Where is he?"

"Fishin' the bridge. *Might* in't gonna work for him today, give at his mood, I'll lay cash money."

"He'll to know I went."

"Light in a ciggo for me, Majie."

"I don't like to light in, Ma. I'm tired. I—"

"Light in or I'll go douse ya, no matter how big you think you are now. I can still take you, too, I'll show you some time on that."

"I don't want being doused. I don't want fighting."

She made a witch's laugh, a sound with little sparklers in it, alcohol and smoke, a ribbon of meanness winding it up in a bow. "God douses the bad," she said. "Light in one then, girl."

I went to the cupboard where she kept the carton of Primes, took down and opened a fresh pack, tapped out a cigarette, and lit it for her, pulling the smoke into my mouth and blowing it out as quickly as I could. Cigarettes tasted like dirt to me—I hate the smell of them even now—like the dust raised from cars passing on Waldrup Road at the end of summer. My mother watched me smoke, one puff . . . two . . . three . . . then reached out a hand that was thin and shaking and let me pass the cigarette over to her. She kept her eyes on me while she drew a deep drag. She held the smoke as long as she could, shot it out her nostrils, and smiled. "Pa might douse ya, though."

"I don't want to being doused. Call on Mr. Warner if you can't believe me. Call on Mr. Patanauk."

"Hah. Your father would cut me on up if I even spoken the man's name. Fricken chainsaw me. And don't to give mouth, girl you."

I waited to see if she had anything else to say, then went into my room and lay facedown on my sagging bed. I closed my eyes and thought, for the millionth time, about finding a way to leave. But, beyond a few coins in my pants pocket, I had no money. How would I run away? Hitchhike? After what had been happening in those hills then? I thought of Aunt Elaine, and the one time I'd tried to run away, and what happened afterward. I thought of the birthday gift she'd just sent, and was surprised and happy that my parents had let me keep it. I fell asleep thinking about that and was awakened by my father's knocking.

The door was open. He knocked on the casing, as he always did, in bursts of three. *Rap. Rap. Rap.* Again. Again. Again. He stood there staring and knocking until I sat up, rubbed my face, and walked over to him. Without saying anything, he took hold of my ponytail and marched me through the main room of the house, where the table had been set for supper, and out the door. Full darkness had fallen by then, but my father went across the yard without a misstep. "Three douses, three douses," he chanted quietly as he went. And then: "For be the lazy girl not to finding the job, three douses, she say."

"You don't to have to, Pa. I did and tried hard."

"Have to is not wanting to. God say. Your mother say. Pastor say penance for keeping children on to the good."

When I started to speak again he tugged once, hard, on my hair. My father was small but very strong. It made no sense to try to get away. When we reached the stream he turned me with his hands on my shoulders and made me stand facing the house, arms at my sides. He took a metal bucket he kept there for that purpose, filled it three times, and three times poured the water—cold as ice at that time of year—over my head. I forced myself not to make a sound. When it was finished, he tapped me on the shoulder and I hurried across the dark yard and back into the house. I shut the bathroom door, wrung out my clothes, and took a hot shower—five minutes on the small plastic timer my mother had found at the dump and my parents kept on the back of the toilet—then I dressed in the new pair of flannel pajamas Aunt Elaine had mailed me as a birthday present, and a pair of thick socks. I said a prayer for forgiveness, wiped up the water on the floor, hung my wet clothes over the shower curtain rod, and went and sat with my mother and father for the blessing.

My father hadn't had any luck fishing, so that night we had the last of his venison sausage, canned beans, two slices each of white bread, and lemonade made from powder. My parents talked a little—about money, about how high the stream might get with the melted snow. I listened. When they told me to, I stood up and cleared the table, then went into my room and closed the door almost all the way and did my schoolwork. I liked the work. I remember, at that point, we were study- ing how people in Africa lived, and I liked reading about the types of food they ate, and the way the families would sit around a fire at night telling stories. Mr. Anders said some of them lived in tribes, the way the Indians had lived in America, and although they didn't have cars and television, they spent a lot of time with their families and out in nature and some of them had happy lives.

When I'd stayed in my room as long as I thought my parents would allow, I walked back out into the main room. I could sense they were in a different mood—which usually happened after they'd given me a penance. It was the way they sat at opposite ends of the couch, my mother, half-sober by then, reading a fold-paper, my father staring at the floor, as if lost in a pleasant memory. They raised their eyes to me and had nothing bad to say. I went to tell them good night. My mother kissed me on the mouth with her smoky, winey breath. My father didn't touch me, but he looked into my eyes and seemed to be wondering if there was any lasting hurt from the dousing. In the lamplight I could see a few short bristles of gray mixed into the brick-colored hairs of his beard. He said, "Tell a prayer for us and for Pastor Schect on your knees in there now, girl."

So I went into my room and did that, ran my hands over the soft cloth of the birthday pajamas, and in a few minutes I was asleep.

TWO

On Sundays we drove to the "Lord of God's House," as my mother and father called the Assembly of the Good Risen Christ. The Lord of God's House was a Quonset hut on the grounds of a private airport that still exists, in West Ober, Vermont, half an hour northwest of our town and on the other side of the big river. The assembly was presided over by a man who called himself the Reverend Pastor Schect. Among his other ideas, Pastor Schect believed it was sinful for girls and women to wear a dress or a skirt into the Lord of God's House. So on that Sunday, as always, I put on my corduroy pants and a clean white shirt with a collar. My mother set out plates of eggs and toast. We had breakfast, then climbed into my father's pickup and made the drive to West Ober with the cab full of cigarette smoke and my left leg bent up under me so it wouldn't be in the way of the shift.

When he wasn't changing gears, my father steered with the middle finger of each hand (he was missing the index finger of his left hand from a chain saw accident) and watched the road with such intensity that I sometimes glanced over to see if he was even blinking. It turned out that his check had come the afternoon before, which was the reason he and my mother had been up late, drinking and making noise in the bedroom.

My father didn't like the interstate. Too many fast cars, he said. Too much police. But I think there was something else involved—a premonition, a superstition, a sense that the big highway was connected to a world that would never respect him, a world in which he existed only as a clump of country dirt, "a possum piss," as he would have put it. We passed through the north end of our town, crossed the river on a covered bridge there, and then instead of going up the entrance ramp we took the old two-lane highway that ran north-south. I looked at the bare cornfields as we went, at the gray river that moved in and out of view behind them. There were farmhouses set at a good distance from each other, the barns red and the silos silver-topped, sometimes a small herd of dairy cows in a field. One of the farms was where a young girl, not much older than I was then, had lived before she'd been taken. Two other girls had disappeared in those parts over the previous eighteen months. Some people said they'd run away, but the families didn't think so, and the police didn't, and none of the girls had ever been seen or heard from since they disappeared. The whole area lived under a blanket of fear because of the disappearances. You'd see parents waiting at bus stops with their fifteen-year-old daughters. You saw more state police in the town. Some people had started locking their houses for the first time in generations, though my parents never went to that extreme.

As it passed through West Ober, the highway curved east, the speed limit dropped from fifty to thirty, and I studied the houses by the road there—the steep slate roofs, the covered porches. I wondered what the rooms looked like inside, and what it felt like to have neighbors, and if there were certain kinds of things people didn't do in the privacy of their family life because there were other people close by. On the mountain behind the houses I noticed strips of white still showing on the ski trails.

Downtown West Ober has now become a low-key tourist destination, with bed-and-breakfasts and a few art galleries, but at that time it consisted of a white clapboard church, a two-pump gas station, and a grocery store. Beyond it were more houses set close together, the yards slightly larger. When we'd gone past that stretch of houses, my father turned left onto a paved road, and half a mile up that road, he turned right, onto airport property. It is one of the only places I have not been able to make myself go back to.

On that Sunday we climbed out of the truck and walked past two rows of small propeller planes, some of them tied to stakes in the earth. Years earlier, my mother, who liked machines and mechanical things—motorcycles, knives, guns (which my father wasn't allowed to own because of some previous legal trouble we couldn't speak about)—had let me go up and touch one of the propellers to see how sharp it was. But someone had seen us and told Pastor Schect, and he'd said something about it during the service—the worship of machines being just another of the devil's tricks. That embarrassed my father, and from then on he'd forbidden us from going near the planes.

The metal door of the assembly scraped open. Inside the Quonset hut, twenty rows of folding chairs had been evenly arranged on the concrete floor. There were more than a hundred chairs in all, as if Pastor always hoped for the day when his reputation would spread and the multitudes would arrive. On that morning three dozen or so worshippers sat in small clusters among the larger patches of empty chairs. They were country people like us, dressed in plain clothes, a sense of hard physical work hanging over them, and most of them lived, as we did, in a granite-and-pine world not reported on in the newspapers and not seen on television, in a pool of thoughts outside the main current of thought, in wood-heated houses and trailers and cabins where a newsletter called *True Home and Country* appeared in the mailbox twice every month. I have never been able to find out how my mother and father first learned about *True Home and Country*—from one of my father's friends at Weedon's Bar, probably—but once we started to subscribe to it our life changed. In my early years I remember some trouble in the house, arguments, a little violence, but good times, too, some sense of normal family life. I didn't go to school then, but I was occasionally allowed to play with other children. And then, about the time I turned nine, the newsletter started coming, we began going to services at Pastor Schect's, and it was as if a metal bucket was set upside down over the three of us. More and more, my parents pulled away from any connection with other people. More and more, they depended on the words of Reverend Pastor Schect for guidance, and the good times we'd had—at the quarry, fishing the stream—shriveled up and died as if there was no longer enough air or light or water to keep them growing.

On a typical week there would be half a dozen children at the service, ranging in age from babies to teenagers. I was often the oldest. Once we stepped through the door of the building, children were not allowed to speak. When I passed close by one of the other kids, I noticed that many of them smelled like tobacco smoke—as I'm sure I did—and in their faces I could see something else that was familiar, a species of alertness, as if they walked through their days on early-winter ice, with thin spots they couldn't see, places where they could fall through and travel, that fast, from the cold to something worse than cold.

There were no hymnals—Pastor Schect didn't believe God wanted people to sing—and no cushions on which to kneel. My mother and father and I found seats toward the middle, a safe distance from anyone else. We had been in our places only a minute or so when Pastor stood up from the first row of chairs and walked to his homemade plywood pulpit. He was on the short side, like my father, somewhere in his forties, I'd guess, and he had wavy hair he dyed black, and thick eyebrows and thick lips. His eyes were rarely still. As he did every Sunday, he wore a suit and tie with work boots, a combination intended to make him appear at once linked to the people he served and superior to them. Though he quoted it often, he didn't ever read from the Bible during services. Now and again he'd lift the Good Book high into the air, or tap it with a finger, or point at it with a trembling hand, but I never saw him open it. At times, I had the sinful thought that he couldn't read.

The congregation rose to its feet. Pastor Schect eyeballed us for a few seconds then gestured for us to be seated. He took hold of the sides of the pulpit and began. "Sinners and hell-seekers, say," he almost whispered. His voice was high-pitched and raspy. Then he repeated the phrase more loudly, so that the words echoed off the metal ceiling and seemed to come around behind you and take hold of the skin of your neck. "Sinners and hell-seekers, say!" he yelled. "God is disappointed in you to the point of abscondenment, say." He paused and lifted his face to the rounded ceiling. He drew and released a breath, pressed his lips together for a moment, then opened his mouth and shouted, "I want the hell-bound children up here front of me now! All the devil-some children!" Nudged by our parents, all of us who were old enough to walk left our seats, formed a line, and shuffled to the front of the church. It was a ritual we had participated in before, and we knew how it would begin but not how it would end. "You are the worst of all sin-ners!" Pastor Schect shouted at us as we stood in a ragged row a few feet in front of the pulpit. "The very worst! Do you know it now?"

I kept a sad expression on my face and nodded. The younger chil-dren glanced over and did what I did.

"Because you don't listen on every word, every single word, say, of your parents who brought you unto this world! God watches you every second, you know. Every second! Every time you disobey the substitute gods of your household, your sacred mother and father, you stab another knife in the cuts in Jesus's hands and feet, you drive a long arrow into the womb in his side, say! Suffer the little children, the Good Book tells!" He lifted the Bible and glared into our faces one by one, his cheeks shaking and his unblinking eyes skipping over us as if we were pickets in a fence and he was riding past, trying to get an accurate count. With his other hand he pounded on the top of the pulpit. "Do you know it now?!"

We nodded again and looked down.

On that day, Pastor Schect let us wait a long time, let us know he was deciding what our punishment might be for the week, which one of the many penances he might choose from—to be administered there in the church, or later, at home, by our parents. And then he must have felt a rare tenderness for us, because he pursed his lips and shouted, "Go from me! Sin no more!"

"Sin no more!" the adults all said together.

We returned to our seats. Pastor Schect took a few seconds to calm himself, walking this way and that, shaking his head in disappointment. After a time he abruptly stopped moving, looked into the faces before him, and swept into the main part of the service, a sermon-talk that rambled from the biblical plagues to various whoremongering degenerations and illethal government officials who populated the cities of our troubled land. He went on and on, making up some words and mispronouncing others, casting the net of his disapproval over boys who listened to music, and girls who showed their legs and rode bicycles, and politicians who took our money and led us down a path to spiritual ruin. Some weeks he talked for more than an hour and a half, his voice rising into a shriek, his arms waving wildly so that one or two of the inexperienced younger children made the mistake of giggling and were hit. He paced back and forth at the front of the church. Windmilling his short arms, he screamed out things like "What happens to sinner is that sinner die and transcend down through the bottom of the grave to hellfire, say, and inside hell he is chewed on by rats, and burned up by fire, and froze up hard in ice, and then burned up again and he is forced to survive in his own filth, say! His own uncommunicated lusts! His own blood passion! He rot like sliced-up meat, say! Like deer gut buried in leaves and left! And all that time the fire keeps to burning him up, say, burning him up for wicked transmagressions, unblessed sex and other disobediences, that he committed in this life!"

When Pastor came to the end of what he had to say he stopped as suddenly as a radio going off. He wiped the sweat from his throat with a huge white handkerchief that he pulled from his back pocket like a magician, he touched the Bible once in a gesture of reverence, then he returned to his seat taking big breaths as if he'd just finished a race. The families waited a moment to be sure he was through, then we all filed out and formed a line on the right side of the church. We went up and put money—no coin allowed, say!—into a woven reed basket (it was said to have come from Egypt) at Pastor Schect's feet, and we all made a small bow to him. Sometimes I'd see a five- or ten-dollar bill there, but my father and mother always gave one dollar each, and always folded it twice in half so that the number couldn't be seen.

That day, as we sometimes did after the check had come, we drove straight from church to the special brunch at Mimi's in Ober. All you could eat for three dollars and ninety-nine cents, a smorgasbord of eggs and bacon and potatoes and oatmeal, with sticky buns and hot chocolate for dessert. We always sat in the same booth in the back corner—if it was occupied, we waited for it—and ate until our stomachs hurt.

On that Sunday, after his third plateful of food, my father wiped his mouth with the paper napkin, looked at me across the table, and said, "That Zeke Warner said on me down Weedon's that you go there Monday after school has done. His place to work. He might to have some kind of job in for you, girl. You might to bring some money for at last."

I nodded in a restrained way, then went up to get another cup of hot chocolate so my parents wouldn't be able to see the expression on my face.

Three

The following Monday after the school bus left me off, I hid my backpack behind the beech tree again and made the half-mile walk to Warner and Sons Gravel and Stone. I felt as though two large hands were pulling at me, one from each side—on one side was the moment when I walked into my house without a job and looked into my mother's and father's faces; and on the other side was another moment, a dream, something I was trying not to let myself think about.

I was a fairly tall girl, but the tires on the trucks in the Warners' parking lot came up to my shoulders. I could hear loud engines at the back part of the complex of buildings. I could hear the sound of crushed stone rushing down a metal chute, and I could smell diesel smoke and stone dust. Inside the building, two stocky, round-faced men took orders over the phone and wrote them on sheets with carbon paper between. There were no girls working there that I could see. In contrast to Cary Patanauk's shop, with its naked-women calendars on the walls, the Warners had put up an old framed photo of President Reagan—just retired then—and nature photographs, still ponds reflecting hillsides in foliage season. I hadn't noticed them on my first visit. I stared at the colors and tried to make myself calm down.

One of the men told me to sit in a chair and wait, and I tried to keep my posture good and not let my eyes wander around. I guessed—I hoped—that they were going to offer me some kind of position in one of the small offices. Filing. Answering the phone. A real job. My parents would be happy. Pastor Schect would be pleased if he heard. I wouldn't be doused anymore, or boyed, or hungered. There was even a fantasy, hiding behind the legs of the dark figures that populated my inner world in those years, that I would be able to lift my parents out of the life they lived, a life that seemed so much more meager than almost any life I saw around the town. I would be able to buy my father new work clothes and a real fishing rod, my mother a new blouse and shoes. Or I would escape into a different life altogether. For as long as I could remember, my dreams had circled around the same image: a house near town with a tidy lawn on which a black and white dog ran and jumped, a clean car sitting in the driveway. Grass on the yard instead of stones and dirt and piles of cordwood; neighbors instead of trees. In my fantasy I was always dressed in a light-colored skirt and a new summer jersey; I was playing with the dog, tossing a ball or a stick. I was a different girl, and this girl's mother, who was a different mother, who looked something like Aunt Elaine but younger and thinner, came to the door and watched me for a few seconds and then called out, in a musical voice, that there was cider and chocolate-chip cookies on the table. Was I coming in, or did I want to wait until Dad got home from work?

Though I had no idea where the image came from—I had sneaked a few minutes of TV, twice, at Aunt Elaine's, and a few times at Cindy's, maybe that was it—I'd been picturing myself in that imaginary house for as long as I could remember. As I grew older the picture evolved—there had been swings and a slide in the yard once; now those were gone. Still, familiar as it was, whenever I became aware of having this dream, I tried to make myself stop. I had learned to take my hopes by the throat and choke them almost, but not quite, to the point of death, though I found, on that day, sitting in the warm office with men laughing quietly, pictures of ponds and the former president on the wall, and the prospect of an actual job awaiting me, it wasn't so easy to do that.

After a long time, Zeke Warner called me into one of the small rooms. He sat at a desk that was covered with piles of forms and envelopes, and he looked more frightening than on my first visit. His big head and oval face hadn't been set against a background of hope then. Looking at the mess of papers on the desk, I had an urge to tell him what a good worker I was, that I could make the desk neat, could sweep out the office and dust the file cabinets. I could chop wood, if he wanted, to fill the stove in winter. But the words never made it as far as my lips. After a few seconds Mr. Warner looked up and smiled, but when he failed to ask me to sit down I could feel the sides of the house of hope starting to slump and sag against each other, the imaginary mother disappearing behind the door, the dog running off. Mr. Warner searched for a minute, and then, from beneath the overlapping layers in front of him, he pulled a scrap of notebook paper on which something was printed in blue pen. He held it out to me, in a kind way, but also slightly distracted, as if he had more important things on his mind. "This fellow," he said, "is looking for a helper. Somebody he can train. I know your family a little bit, your aunt Elaine and I are friends, did I tell you that the other day? I know about your dad and granddad. I liked the way you walked in here and asked for work. That took courage. So when this fellow came asking, I recommended you like you were the queen of England. Make sure you call him, okay? Don't make me look bad."

"Okay, yes," I said. My hand was trembling when I reached it toward him and I was afraid he might see. "I have a thank you for it very much."

"I know you do," Mr. Warner said. "And don't look so worried. You'll do fine. I can see the worker in you."

"I want to be it."

He smiled and dropped his eyes back down to his desk, a signal that I should leave. I whirled around clutching the slip of paper and hurried out of the office. A huge black cloud puffed up around me. The words "Somebody he can train" rang in my ears like something my mother would yell in one of her moods, the kind of thing you might say about an animal. I wasn't going to be working at Warners' then, but for a strange man I didn't know. I had an image of the man putting me in traces like a plow horse, training me to haul loads of stone up a hillside. I went out past the drivers and clerks in the main room, out past the dump trucks with their huge tires, and I walked all the way back to the bus stop thinking that now I would surely run away again. Whatever the consequences, I would run. I had the backpack. Aunt Elaine would give me a few dollars. I would go to the Greyhound station in Watsonboro and take a bus to Montreal or Montpelier and find a job as a waitress there, or in a factory. I walked a tar road between two cold ideas: run away, or go home right then with news that the Warners hadn't given me a job after all. I would be doused, or boyed, or given the hunger or the face.

It wasn't until I reached the beech tree and retrieved my backpack from its hiding place that I actually calmed down enough to look at the slip of paper. It read "MR. IVERS" in a neat hand. There was a phone number. I stood still. I had twenty-five cents in my pocket. My parents had given it to me reluctantly, only because the teachers told us to carry twenty-five cents in case we could make a phone call and report the person who was kidnapping girls, or in case we were kidnapped ourselves and escaped and needed to call the police. I fingered the coin, then made myself turn around and walk back up the highway as far as the 112 Store. I took my backpack with me for comfort. I slipped the quarter into the pay phone at the side of the building, dialed the number, and said to the man who answered, "Could Mister Ivers be there to talk?"

Four

Only a week or so before my birthday, a fourteen-year-old girl had disappeared from a town on the other side of the river in Vermont. She had gone to visit a friend. On the way home, her bicycle had gotten a flat tire (the bike was found soon after her parents reported her missing; the police decided she must have tried to hitchhike home when that happened, rather than making the long climb back on foot so late in the day). I had heard the story from kids at school and the details from my friend Cindy, and I'd listened to Pastor Schect say it was payment for the girl's sins, and I'd thought about her a hundred times. As I'd done with the other disappearances, I went into the school library after lunch and read about the victim in the newspaper and stared at the picture of her face. But I felt that I knew this girl better than I knew the others. I knew she'd been tired, worried about what her parents would do if she arrived home late, that she'd heard a car approaching and, without thinking, had held out her thumb. The car had stopped, she'd gotten in, and the man had driven her down one of the dirt roads that snaked through the hills there, killed her, and buried her in a place no one would ever find. In rare better moments, to keep the terror of it from my mind, I wondered if it could have been a boy who'd stopped, and the girl had liked him and run away with him, and they'd gone off to somewhere

like Mexico or California, and she was refusing to call her parents because she hated them and wanted them to worry. Someday she might
come back, I told myself, and maybe the other girls would come back,
too . . . but I knew it wasn't so.

"This is Ivers," a man's voice said over the phone line.

"This is I'm Marjorie. Mr. Warner told I could to call you. I am
ready on to work."

There was a pause, and then the man said, "Can you drive over
here for a quick interview?"

"I'm seventeen just now," I said. "But I don't can't drive." I held
the phone very tightly and listened. The man didn't say anything. "But
nobody works for so hard as me. Nobody does."

"That's what Mr. Warner said."

"What kind doesn't to matter. Different kinds I did before. Nobody can."

"It's an apprenticeship."

"All right. I do that kind."

I heard the man make a small laugh and I felt like I'd become a
little girl again, a little girl trying desperately to say the thing her daddy
wanted to hear. The top part of the phone was pressed against my ear,
and I had a hand up over my other ear so the noise from lumber trucks
and tractor trailers passing on the road wouldn't cause me to miss a
word. "I'm at beside the 112 Store on the road that goes for to town."
I swallowed. "In a little time I . . . my mother and father want that I'm
home then. But I can to walk in town for it and see you."

"I'll come pick you up there. We can drive over here and look at
the job site and then I'll bring you home and introduce myself to your
parents. I have a black truck. I can be there in eight minutes."

I squeezed the phone. "All right," I said. And then, "I have hair the
color of brown and a backpack."

There was another small laugh. The man was shy, or he was a
trickster, I couldn't tell. I had the thought that I should ask him to give
me his license plate number so I could pass it on to Mrs. Jensen in the

store. That was something the teachers talked about in school. But it would ruin any chance for the job, I was sure of that, so I said only, "I'll to stand right against the road waiting."

"I'm eight minutes away," the man said a second time, and it sounded to me as if he'd known I would call, that he had something all planned. Maybe he'd seen me go into Warners' looking for work and had gone in there after I left and made up the idea of a job as a way to get me into his truck.

But it seemed to me that I had very little to lose then, so I stood out next to the road with the backpack against my right ankle and waited. In northern New England, in spring and fall, there is a warm stretch of the day that lasts from about late morning until middle afternoon. The nights are still cold, and the cold stays on for a few hours even after the sun has come up; and then, when late afternoon arrives, you can feel the cold reaching toward you again, as if the night is marching back down the river valley, chasing off the weaker soldiers of the sun. While I waited, I could feel the night coming. Even pushed down in the pockets of my pants, my hands were cold. The cars and trucks had turned on their headlights. Every time I saw a set of lights come around the bend in the road, half a mile to the west of where I stood, I would think it was the man in his black truck, and a cool tickling would run up the muscles of my back. He was going to train me. Train me to do what?

I saw a pair of lights, then the dark fenders and roof. The driver flashed his lights, waited for a car going in the opposite direction, then looped into the lot and pulled up so that I was a few feet from the window. The man—Mr. Ivers he was pretending to be called—slid the window down and leaned his face out. He was only a little older than some of the boys in school. His face was not exactly the face of a white man—square cut, the skin either tanned at the wrong time of year or light brown to begin with, a pair of thick spectacles over eyes I couldn't yet get a read on, the curly charcoal-colored hair tied back in a short ponytail. For an instant, I thought I recognized him, or at least that he reminded me of someone I knew. From what I could see of the neck and shoulders, and part of his forearm near the hand that held the wheel, he was stronger even than my father.

"Marjorie?" He pushed the glasses back up against the top of his nose and I could see his eyes then. They were green eyes, strange against the light brown face, and in them, and in the way he spoke my name, he seemed to me, even from that first minute, like a shy boy. Or like someone pretending to be a shy boy.

He held out his hand. I hesitated. I stepped closer and shook it.

"Come on. Get in. So I can take you to see the work site before it gets too dark."

I looked at the windows of the store, at a person, a woman, going up the steps there. Beneath the woman's weight, I could hear the sound of the steps creaking, like a series of small screams, and then the loud bang of the door. For a few seconds, in my imagination, I was the girl on the other side of the river, deciding whether or not to get into the stranger's car. I wondered if the sight of the woman going up the stairs would be one of the last things I would ever see. There were ways of playing tricks, of saying you knew somebody when you didn't really know them. My aunt had never mentioned Mr. Warner as being a friend of hers, and no one I knew had a friend who wasn't white, no one at church, no one in school. Someone had said that the person who was making the girls disappear was a black man. I looked back at Mr. Ivers, at his eyes behind the glasses, his big shoulders, the tanned skin in mid-April. I looked into the bed of the truck: a steel rack for carrying lumber. Concrete blocks. Rope.

He said, "If you want, I can let you take my license number and call your folks, or leave it with the people in the store."

It was either a trick or it wasn't. He was either a good man, shy, different, or he was the devil come to take me. I thought of what it would feel like for this man to change his mind about offering me the job, because I didn't trust him, because I didn't have the courage to get into his truck, and then for me to walk down the highway in the dark and turn onto Waldrup Road and go home, and what it would be like to go into my house and tell my parents things hadn't worked out.

I tried to do what I often did—look past the features of a person's face and in through their eyes and come to a decision about what they wanted from me. If they would hurt me or not, and how badly. I hesitated another second, then grabbed my backpack, walked around to the far side of the pickup, and climbed in.

The man asked me to put my seat belt on, something my father did not ever do. As I clicked the buckle in place I noticed there was a loop of wooden beads hanging from the stem of the rearview mirror. For strangling teenage girls before you dumped them in the woods, I thought. I ran my eyes over the new upholstery and the carpet at my feet, and over the dashboard, looking for blood. Without saying a word the man pulled out onto the highway, and he went along there on the smooth pavement, turning the truck easily with one hand as the road wound, keeping his eyes forward. Trying not to let him see, I looked at the curly ponytail, at the glasses, at his square face.

"You're afraid," he said.

My right leg twitched. "I'm not having afraid of anything."

He nodded. "I'm only going to take you into the center of town, show you the work site, tell you what I'd expect, ask you a couple of questions, let you ask me a couple of questions, and then drive you straight home."

"I can do walking."

"I wouldn't let you walk," he said.

"I want it. I make a lot of walking. I'm strong."

He didn't answer. By then it was almost dark beyond the windows, just the last shreds of light hanging above the hills, lights on in the houses, a broken string of lights coming at us on the other side of the highway. "Why do you talk like that?" the man asked after a minute.

"I don't talk for bad now."

"No, it's just . . . different."

"We talk like the same for everybody," I said, but I knew it wasn't true and I looked away from him and out the window and pressed my lips hard against each other. It was something I'd heard so many times before, for years and years. During all those years, there had been meetings with school counselors, with principals, with speech thera-pists. They all ended up saying, "You can speak correctly, we know you can from your written work, Marjorie. So why don't you?" It was from not going to school all those years when I was young, they said. It was something I could change, it was important to talk like other people, important for doing well in school, going to college, getting a good job. Almost every day some of the other kids would make fun of me, calling me "the talk-funny girl," or greeting me with strange forms of hello in the hallways ("to hi to you in of Margie!" was a favorite). Most high school kids would have tried to change, I know that, would have tried desperately to fit in. But I had a lot of my father in me then, the same woundedness, the same fierce stubbornness, and I believed that if I changed, if I came halfway out to meet people, they'd only make fun of me anyway and I'd be whipped and ridiculed at home. The best strategy was to burrow down deep into myself, to stay different, to keep a distance. I knew our speech was odd, obviously, but it had been natural to me for so long that, really, I preferred the sound of it to standard American English. I hadn't gone to school until I was nine, and for those first years I'd had one or two occasional playmates but no television or radio to learn from. My parents never read to me from children's books; they barely spoke themselves and were so removed from society that, like some tribe living in isolation, they'd evolved their own dialect. They were mocked, too, my father especially. But, like me, he used it as a kind of protective barrier between him and other people, a way of avoiding questions and probing conversations, of keeping strangers at arm's length. He had learned that trick from his own father, Dad Paul, and I had learned it well from him. Until I was seventeen and a half, being the talk-funny girl was a soft, ugly cushion I held close around myself in every human interaction.

We crossed the bridge over the river; the metal grating hummed under the truck tires. I looked down at the waterfall and the mills there on both banks, redbrick buildings as long as downtown, with boarded windows and weedy parking lots and graffiti all across the lower floors. My grandfather, Dad Paul, had worked in one of those buildings for a little while before going to pump gas at Zeski's and then, later, being sent upstate, and I remember wondering if somehow this was a trick he'd organized from prison. He would have met some bad people there; he might have mentioned he had a granddaughter who needed work; he might have told them my name and where I lived.

Mr. Ivers—who looked to me, with his weightlifter's arms and shoulders, like the kind of man who might have been in jail once—turned the truck left onto Main Street. Some of the shops had lights in their front windows. A line of cars and pickup trucks stood at the traffic signal, waiting for it to change. Three blocks south of the strip of stores he pulled to the curb and cut the engine. "Here it is," he said.

"Where?"

"This is where I work."

"It's not at anything."

The man laughed his shy laugh again and looked across the seat at me. He hadn't driven me into the hills, at least not this time, not yet. There were lights reflecting on the lenses of his glasses and I couldn't see his eyes.

"This used to be St. Mark's Episcopal Church."

"I know it."

"The old boiler exploded, did you know that, too?"

"There was a fire at it. Everybody knows."

"The fire destroyed the timbers, the crossbeams inside," he went on in what seemed to me a nervous voice. "They held the walls up from falling away from each other. When they burned, and the cables burned, and the rafters of the roof started to burn, the roof fell in and the walls fell outward. The explosion had already blown away part of the base of one of them. The people who owned the church had been trying to save money by not insuring the building for what it would cost to rebuild, and so when this happened they couldn't afford to rebuild it. They paid somebody to come and knock down the broken walls and cart away the roof. That's as far as they got. Then they ended up moving the congregation to Walpole, and sharing a church there, and they've been trying to sell this lot ever since."

"When I was two grades ago they had it this way."

"Right. It's been a while. I bought it at the end of last month."

"Why for?"

"Because it was inexpensive, and it has that little building off in the back, that wasn't damaged too badly. That was the rectory. It's inhabitable, more or less."

"You want for making it so you live there?"

"I'm going to build a cathedral here, what I call a cathedral anyway. I designed it myself and I'm going to build it myself and use it to show people what kind of work I can do. I have some money. I'm going to have a business here in this town, building walls and stone houses and doing repairs."

I looked at the piles of stones, the weeds growing out of them as if there were green-haired spirits hiding half-underground, the streetlamp casting a light over all of it and against the two-story box of a building at the rear. The man was making up a story. Who bought a church and lived in it? Who did that?

"Did you ever have a big dream for your life?" he asked.

I shook my head and kept staring at the rubble. If he let me go I was going to carry a lie home to my mother and father. I never lied to them, almost never, because they had a miraculous instinct for secrets, fibs, and tricks, and they would penance me if they thought I wasn't telling them the absolute truth. But this time it made no sense to tell the truth. Why was I late for supper? Because the man from Warners' had told me to talk to this other man who was buying the blown-up church and building a new church over it. I went with him alone in a truck to see. We stayed there a long time while he talked.

"Well, this is my dream for myself," he was saying. "To design and build a cathedral, a place of worship, but not ordinary worship. A place of peace, not rules. A place you can go and be quiet and be left alone and not need a priest or a minister or a rabbi to dial God's number on the phone so you can talk with him. Come on, let's get out and do a quick inspection."

I didn't want to leave my backpack in the truck, but when I started to pick it up the man reached over and put his hand on it. "Leave that," he said, and I felt the cool sparkles go up my back muscles again.

He got out, and I got out, too, and followed him across the sidewalk and onto what had been the church's front lawn. Some of the larger debris must have been carted away—the roof, the burned wood—but there were piles of rubble everywhere, stones of different sizes, chunks of concrete, a few pieces of metal and wood. Weeds growing out of it all. The man was lying or he was crazy or both. It was cold.

But I walked up the front steps and followed him, using the light from the streetlamp to keep from stepping on the rubble in a way that would make me fall.

"See this?" Mr. Ivers tapped his work boot near what had been the back end of the church. He raised his eyes to the street for a second and I thought he might be looking for a police car, waiting for someone to come and chase him off church property. "The floor here is in good shape, except over there where the boiler burst up through it. The foundation is about eighty-five percent solid. I'm going to clear this rubble off and build a cathedral on the solid part of the floor. It won't be as big as the church, at least to start with. I'm going to do it in sections."

"With all just your own hands?"

He made his small nervous laugh and I didn't know then if he was tricking me or making fun of me or if he was a good man and just shy. There was something in the laugh, and in him, that was different from any person I had ever met. In the light he looked older than he'd looked at first, and not as dark, and I tried to examine him without letting him see. "A long time that's to take."

"Exactly. And I'll need a helper. You came very highly recommended . . . unless you think a girl can't do the work."

"She can do."

"Do you have any skills?"

I looked at him. I knew what the word meant, of course, but I never thought of myself that way, as having skills.

"Can you do anything special with your hands?"

"I have . . . I know to take out a fishhook with one hand out the mouth of it. My dad showed. I can to chop wood. Clean up good. A little cook."

"That's it?"

He seemed then almost to be mocking me. He was a big man, four or five inches taller than my father. Big shoulders, big arms, but thin in the middle, as if a child had been putting together a toy figure from two kits and had mismatched the muscle man's arms with the little boy's body. "Nobody can does work harder of me."

"Than I."

"Nobody does. You won't be sorry if you ask me for the job."

"It's not a job exactly, it's an apprenticeship."

At those words—"not a job exactly"—I felt something drop out of my insides. I thought about how long it would take to walk home from there, about my backpack in his truck, about my mother's voice.

"Why you made it for me to come here then?"

"A paid apprenticeship. You can learn the trade of stonemasonry."

"To pay?"

"Right. I pay you. Except indirectly."

I looked at him. I heard cars passing behind me on the street.

"You'd get money every month, through your aunt."

"How are you to know her?"

"I met her at the hospital a long time ago."

"She works at there even still."

"I know. I'll pay her. She'll pay you. I'll give you a two-week trial period, and if you can keep up, I'll guarantee you a job as long as we're both still alive. How's that for a good deal?"

I had been starting to think he wasn't a bad man until he said "both still alive." There was something not right about him, and as good as I was at reading people, understanding their motivations within a few minutes of meeting them, there was a dimension to this man that puzzled me. The mix of strong and shy, of manly and boyish, the idea of building a church for himself—who had the money and time to do that? And it seemed strange and wrong not to be paid directly; with all the work I'd done in my life, I'd never had a job like that.

But when he talked about his cathedral, a tone came into his voice that didn't sound like anything evil. For a few minutes it had seemed he would let me work, and pay me regularly, and not hurt me, and then he said the part about being alive. If my aunt Elaine really knew him, she'd never mentioned it. No one named Ivers. No one with a ponytail. No one with part-dark skin. I looked at him. I was accustomed to my father moving all the time, shifting his weight, playing with the stump of his missing finger, his eyes running over every object within view, his head tilting right and left as if he was trying to shake water out of his ears after a swim in the quarry. I was used to my mother's smoking and the constant twists and secret messages of her mouth and lips. But this man was standing as still as an oak tree, studying me, and in the shadows his face gave away absolutely nothing.

"Want to give it a shot?"

"I'm not knowing yet."

He lifted his eyebrows, surprised. "Why don't you think about it, then? And if you want the job, come here tomorrow after school and we can start. You'll have to wear boots, though. You can't do this work in sneakers or shoes, too dangerous. If I don't see you, I'll assume it wasn't right for you and there will be no hard feelings."

I looked at him. "I have boots only for the snow kind."

"Well you'll have to buy some then. Steel-toed."

I nodded, and could feel the warmth running beneath the skin of my face.

"Now I'll drive you home."

"You didn't say what money."

"What do you mean?"

"What money you are paying me for, you didn't tell."

"You'd work three afternoons a week for two hours, at first. Monday, Wednesday, Friday. And six hours on Saturday. Twelve hours a week to start. I'd pay you a hundred dollars."

"In a month?"

"A week."

I looked at him.

"That's a little more than eight dollars an hour. I'd nudge it up as you learn the trade, and in summer you could work more."

The legal minimum wage then had just been raised to three dollars and eighty cents. At Emily's Dough Nuts, I had been paid two dollars and fifty cents an hour, cash money. I looked at him. I bit down on my lips. I put my hand up and took hold of a small fistful of my hair behind my right ear, tugging against the roots but not too hard.

"You think about it," he said. "I'll take you home."

"Just to the 112. Then I could walk to home for there."

"Fine."

We rode back along the highway without speaking. I kept replaying everything he'd said, and every few hundred yards I turned and looked at the side of his face. I wondered if there were any seventeen-year-old girls in the world who made eight dollars an hour, or if it was just part of his trick, an impossible promise like that.

When the truck pulled into the lot and stopped and I had my fingers on the door handle and the backpack on my lap, I said, "If I want for the work I come on tomorrow when school has done."

He turned to face me, the lenses shining in the light. "I believe I understood that, yes. Tomorrow after school, with steel-toed work boots. You can buy them tonight. The mall is open until late. And if I don't see you, that's okay, too."

He held out his hand and I shook it, feeling the calluses there. I thanked him and got out and waited until he'd driven away before I showed what direction I would walk in. By the time I'd gone along the dark, cold stretch of highway and down Waldrup Road and turned in at my house and seen that my father's truck wasn't in the driveway but my aunt's car was, I had already made up my mind.

Five

Once a month—twice a month on those occasions when they had a little extra money—my mother and father would disappear for a night and a day. This usually happened not long after my father received his disability check—which arrived in a gray envelope with the olive green check visible in the window and the name of an insurance company printed in the upper left-hand corner. If my mother hadn't gotten there first, it was one of my jobs to fetch the mail from the mailbox at the end of our short dirt driveway. I'd pull down the squeaking metal door of the box, take whatever I found, and bring it inside. Sometimes there were bills—property taxes, electricity, a reminder about an old unpaid dentist visit—which sent my mother into half-hour spells of muttering. On Wednesday there were always store coupons in a newspaper insert, which she balled up and stuffed in the woodstove. (In summer, when the stove wasn't used, these newspaper balls overflowed the black iron belly so that, after the middle of July, the door never closed all the way. When heating season came around again in the fall, she'd scoop out most of the balled-up newspapers and leave them in a pile on the floor, put in some kindling and one or two of the dry hardwood billets my father stacked in the yard, and light a match.)

Every two weeks there was the eight-page *True Home and Country* newsletter in the mailbox. If she was in a good mood, my mother would read aloud from it at night, with my father sitting at the other end of the couch, eyes turned away, listening closely, sometimes pressing his lips into a frown if he found the news—what the government was doing to us, what a conspiracy of environmentalists or homosexual activists or Jewish financiers was doing—especially disturbing. *True Home and Country* had other articles I sometimes looked at: articles claiming nuclear power was a trick of the government to make people sick and control them; that Jews, especially, but Catholics and Muslims, too, had spies and scouts hidden in the population. They were searching for Christ, who would come in disguise this time. Perhaps he had already come and was hiding from these demonic groups. When they found Christ, who, the Bible told, had promised to come to America this time instead of Egypt, these scouts were going to take him to a secret location in the mountains of California, torture him, kill him, burn his body, and scatter the ashes in 144 different places on earth so he would never be able to return to save the good white people, the people he had come to protect in the first place, since the Egyptians were the only whites in all of Africa.

Mixed in with these feature pieces were other, shorter articles, giving practical suggestions about hunting, trapping, fishing, putting up vegetables and salting meat, books to read and never to read, ways of arguing with non-churchgoing people so you could convince them of the truth, and tips for chastising children according to what the newsletter referred to as the Ancient Way of the Lord. Dousing. Facing. Boying or girling. Hungering. And so on. It was through the *True Home and Country* newsletter that my parents had found Pastor Schect (who had relocated to West Ober from parts unknown eight years earlier), and these articles and the pastor were all the spiritual guidance they seemed to need. It felt to me, though, even then, that they needed this guidance, and needed the newsletter and the visits to the church in West Ober, in a desperate way, as if without the advice of such people, they would find themselves adrift in a world so complicated and terrifying it would, as my mother put it, "run you right off insane."

In terms of the most anticipated mail, though, *True Home and Country* stood in a distant second place behind my father's check. When the check came, my mother and I always made sure to put it on top of the small stack of mail one of us carried into the house. During the day, my father liked to be out in the forest, or splitting stove wood in the yard, or—if it was pouring rain—nursing a draft beer at Weedon's Bar, where he was allowed to run a tab. So it would almost always be my mother who first saw the mail I brought inside. She would be balanced up on the counter on her small hips, smoking and drinking; or she'd be standing over beans and creamed corn at the stove; or she'd be lying down in a "sorry mind," as she called her bad moods, on the worn sofa that had been there since Dad Paul's hunting days, with her face pressed into the corner of the cushions and an ashtray on the floor near her dangling arm. Whatever position or state of mind I found her in, I was supposed to immediately show her the mail. If she saw the envelope from the insurance company it would be as if you snapped on a flashlight and shone it on the features of her face. She'd sit up on the couch, or step away from the stove, or slide down off the counter. For a second, a twitch of a smile would show in the muscles of her cheeks, and a sense of relief would surround her, as if she had spent the past fourteen days and nights imagining various scenarios in which the money failed to arrive. She would never dare open the envelope, but would take and set it in the middle of the dining room table, with nothing around it, so my father would see it as soon as he stepped into the house. Then, if she hadn't already started cooking, and if there was time to send me to the 112 Store (where we were also allowed to buy on credit), she would prepare his favorite supper—hamburger and onion fried crisp, mixed with a can of tomato soup and poured over white rice. The presence of the envelope in the house would change the language of her body. Sometimes, if the meal was ready and my father wasn't yet home, she'd take a shower (my parents never used the timer and could stay in the shower as long as the hot water lasted) and change her shirt, and then anyone could see that she really had been pretty once, as people said. On the night of the check's arrival—I understood this as I grew older—my parents would drink a little and talk a little until I went to bed, and then they would have sex. I could hear the sounds of it from my room. The head of their bed would knock against the wall in a certain urgent rhythm, and my father would be saying, "Hurt, hurt, hurt, hurt, hurt!" loudly, while my mother made sounds that fell somewhere between whimpers of pain and small bullets of laughter. I'd lie in my bed, looking up at the dark ceiling, wondering how much of what kids in school said about it was true.

The other thing I could count on when the check arrived was that, at some point within a day or two, my parents would disappear. This had been going on for years and I was used to it. When I was younger— ten and twelve and fourteen—I'd been left alone many times, and had, except for one bit of trouble (I tried to cook an egg in oil and started a small fire and put it out with a dish towel), managed fairly well. But when I was about fifteen, something changed, I never understood what, exactly, and my aunt—who'd moved back closer to home after years of living in other places—would usually come stay with me. I was old enough to be alone by then, of course, but she said she wanted to spend time with me and so it wasn't a surprise to see her car there on those nights. My mother and father never told me when they were going, never left a note. This is something I have neglected to ever ask my aunt about, but I suppose my mother went to the pay phone at the 112 Store and called to say they were going, or they had some other kind of arrangement. A day or two after the check appeared, I'd come home from school—or, in summer, get out of bed—and find that my parents were gone, the truck gone, the house quiet, and Aunt Elaine making breakfast or dinner at the stove, or standing in the doorway to greet me when I walked home from the bus.

Aunt Elaine was older than my mother by seven years. Their lives

belonged to different universes. So different, in fact, that I often imagined they weren't really stepsisters, but that they'd formed some kind
of agreement to tell people they were. I sometimes even imagined that
my mother paid Aunt Elaine to pretend she was her sister, and that,
when I grew to be an adult, I might find someone I could hire to fill the
same role. In the time since she'd returned to the area, we visited Aunt
Elaine only once a year, for Thanksgiving dinner, and it was a torment
for my father to do even that. Beyond his occasional beer at Weedon's,
and a few sips of wine to celebrate the arrival of his check, he wasn't a
drinker, not compared to my mother, at least, but on Thanksgiving he
would start drinking whiskey from the early morning and be so drunk
by the time we left for Watsonboro that he'd be forced to let my mother
drive the pickup, something he rarely did. With its sunny rooms and
raked lawn, Aunt Elaine's house always seemed like a kind of heaven to
me, but I knew that it was, for my father, one of the promised torments
of hell. He would rather pull a fishhook out through his fingernail, he
said one time on the way home, than go to that Elaine's. He would
rather step in a sharp-tooth fox trap barefoot. "Oncet a year ain't much
even for visitin' to hell," my mother told him, but my father didn't even
look at her.

   Aunt Elaine was pretty and dark haired, like my mother, though
they had no blood relation and did not resemble each other. Elaine's
nose was wider, her hair a few shades lighter and touched with streaks
of gray. She had no husband or children, or even any particular friend,
as far as I could see. She worked as a nurse in the children's ward in the
hospital in Watsonboro, and lived in that city, in a small yellow house
with a porch. Forty minutes south and across the wide river into Vermont, Watsonboro was so alien to my mother and father and to me—
ethnic restaurants, bookstores, yoga studios—that it might as well have
been a place we needed a passport to go to, a place where a different
language was spoken.

   It was, I came to understand, the orderliness of Aunt Elaine's
life that tormented my father. The walls of her house were carefully

painted, books in bookcases on the walls, pans and pots hanging from hooks. The slate roof didn't leak, the front steps weren't soft with rot, the toilet always made a clean flush when you tugged down the handle. Aunt Elaine's hair was tied back with a bright clip, her eyes were clear, her fingernails trimmed; the dishes she put on the table when we visited were shining and unchipped. As if by magic, everything seemed to go well—the turkey was never overcooked, the wine wasn't spilled, the dessert came to the table on small plates with golden trim. Cast against this tidy background, the life we lived became a spectacle of shoddiness, and every year I had a stronger sense of the shame of that.

On the night when I walked home from the 112 Store after meeting the strange Mr. Ivers, I saw Aunt Elaine standing on the front steps of the house, and I felt suddenly brave and grown-up and hopeful. My aunt was strongly built, full hipped and full breasted, dressed that day in new sneakers, clean jeans, and a red and cream striped woolen sweater. Standing there, with the sagging, half-painted, badly patched house sinking and slanting behind her, Aunt Elaine looked like a new store-bought doll set down in front of a dollhouse that had been rescued from a trash can. "My Marjorie," she said, holding her arms wide and hugging me close. The top of her head came up to the point of my nose. "You look so beautiful, a beautiful young woman."

Inside, the table was set for the two of us, and I could smell chicken cooking. "Wash up," my aunt said. "Food's all ready." Like everything else that came out of Aunt Elaine's mouth, this was said in what I thought of as a "clean" voice, a voice some of my teachers used, a voice that gave me a feeling like the feeling you have when you've begun to sense the flu leaving your body. It wasn't the words and the grammar, but an underlying tone—something with no threat or worry in it. I washed my face and hands and brushed my hair and then came and sat close to my aunt at the corner of the table. There was steam coming up off the chicken breasts and mashed potatoes. From Watsonboro, Aunt Elaine had brought a loaf of the kind of bread you have to slice yourself, and there was a slice of it, brown and already buttered, on a small dish beside my plate, and a glass of milk, and peas with butter melting on them.

"Eat a few bites," Aunt Elaine said, "and then tell me about your day."

I knew we wouldn't be saying any blessing so I cut a small piece of chicken and put it into my mouth, but I couldn't swallow at first, couldn't get the food past what was in my throat, and couldn't look at her. The plate full of food was blurry. I blinked my eyes and concentrated on opening my throat, on chewing, and my aunt pretended to go to the stove and check on something she had in the oven. In a minute, I could swallow again. Juicy chicken, creamy potatoes, peas coated in butter, and the thick slice of bread, which I nibbled at to be polite but did not really like the taste of. It seemed to me that the silence around us had a different quality from the silences I was used to, as if it wasn't silence at all but something as sweet as birdsong in deep woods, the vireos whistling their down-swinging circles on a summer night.

"Eat slowly," Aunt Elaine said. "There's no rush. There's cookies for afterward but just take your time, honey. School was all right?"

"Good all."

"The kids aren't causing you any trouble?"

"Some of them can for times. I don't to make a pal with them."

"You and Cindy are still close?"

"Cindy has got to having a boyfriend now. Carl. She does a lot of the time with him but in lunch we see."

"Only lunch? You don't go out together? Bowling? Or for ice cream?"

"In the summer we have swimming on the quarry, but now I don't have a time for it because today I got to be given a job."

"Really? Tell me."

I told her about going to Warners', and the slip of paper, and the strange man with the funny name who was going to build a cathedral where St. Mark's had been, if he wasn't lying. My aunt watched me as I talked, her eyes running this way and that across my eyes and mouth and hair.

"Do your parents know?"

"They knew I was going asking."

"They'll be pleased."

"Sure."

"Well, I think it's wonderful. He sounds like a good man, too. Does he seem that way to you?"

"I was worried a little that he could might to be the kidnapping person. I think he's not a white man. The way he had talk with me on the phone, then the way he looked on me. I had some to be afraid, getting in his truck. But then when he went us on at the church and started having talk about what he was to do, it just was that he could be weird, not scary."

"It sounds good," my aunt said, but something in the way she said it made me suspicious. Just then, I remembered Zeke Warner saying he knew her, and I remembered Mr. Ivers telling me about the payment arrangement. "You know to him," I said. "Or was he making a lie about it?"

Aunt Elaine got up and went to the stove. She pulled open the oven door and bent down to look in, and it seemed that she was trying to keep from showing me the expression on her face. "He won't hurt you, I'm sure of that."

"He told he is for paying you, not me."

"He won't cheat you, honey. And you know I won't."

"He said to pay eight dollars in for the hour. No girl can to make it eight dollars. Not too many of grown-ups make."

"I wanted to talk to you about that," Aunt Elaine said, coming back to the table.

"Oh."

She smiled, but there was now clearly something crouching behind her face, not deceit exactly but some kind of disappointing secret about to be revealed. I knew eight dollars an hour had been an impossible amount and told myself I'd been right to hold my hope tight and not let it soar up.

"Are you finished? Did you save room for a cookie or two?"

"I'll to clear off the dishes and so."

"No, stay. Sit."

"He won't then give it for paying me? It was a trick?"

"He will. But I'm going to keep some of that money in an account for you. How much did he say you'd earn in a week?"

"One hundred."

"Okay. How about if I give you fifteen for yourself and another twenty that you can give your parents, and I'll put the rest in the account for you for later. Would that be all right? It could earn some interest that way."

"Fifteen for me? Dollars to a week?" I stopped and looked down at my plate. I could feel the hope soaring up through the middle of my chest and I wanted to wrestle with it and get it to lie flat there and not cause me trouble.

"You can say anything to me, honey. Always. Anything."

"For the, for my father, I could think . . . he isn't liking twenty dollars from the one hundred."

"Let me take care of that."

"You will, but for twenty from the one hundred, he doesn't like it sure. Or my mother much."

Aunt Elaine looked at me for a few seconds then went back to the stove. She took the tray out of the oven and set it on the stovetop to cool. One of the many things I loved about her was that, though I knew it sounded odd to her ear, she never tried to correct the way I spoke.

"Your mother had a spatula last time I was here."

"Broke it up. She uses now the big knife. Sidewise."

"What does she do when she makes an egg?"

"She boils."

The drawer Aunt Elaine opened and closed made a squealing

sound. "Does she hit you, honey?" she asked then, not looking at me, working the knife under the edges of the warm cookies and lifting them carefully onto a plate. I will remember that question as long as I live, because it wasn't something she had ever asked me before and because it was a moment when the truth—that ferocious animal—came nosing its way into my life. I shoved it back, naturally I did, but it was there, I could feel it. I could taste it.

"No," I said quickly.

"Does your father?"

"No."

"Really?" Aunt Elaine was still peeling cookies off the tray and sliding them onto the plate, piling them there in overlapping circles as if making a design, not looking at me, talking over her shoulder in a casual tone.

"Could I drink one other milk with of them?"

"As much as you want. I brought extra."

"Do you want?"

"I'm fine, thanks."

I poured the milk and put the container back in the refrigerator. Of their own will, my legs seemed to be pulling me toward my room. I stood at the refrigerator for a minute, sipping, keeping my back to my aunt.

"Honey?"

I turned and looked at her, a few drops of milk spilling onto my hand.

"You can tell me. Nothing will happen."

"Nothing bad they do."

"Really?"

I nodded and returned to the table. I had just taken one of the warm cookies into my hand when my aunt said, "What is 'facing' and 'boying'?"

I shrugged, avoided her eyes, concentrated on breaking the soft cookie in half.

"You don't know, honey? Really?"

"I think in the school I heard kids say about it. Thank you and this cookie and milk. And the food for I'm thanking you."

For a long few seconds I chewed and sipped, feeling my aunt's eyes on me but not meeting them. I was working hard to pretend to be a young, innocent girl in her eyes, to push the truth down hard into its hiding place and keep the anger from rising up. The rare good hour in that house had been turned toward the bad again, even by my aunt. I ate another cookie and still didn't look up, and after a time Aunt Elaine ate one, too. The only other question she asked was about *True Home and Country*. I said it was a newspaper my parents looked at sometimes, that was all I knew. Though it felt wrong and risky to do it, I found a recent copy near the sofa and brought it to her, but she only glanced at it and set it aside, and let the conversation die.

We washed and dried the dishes together. When everything was put away and clean, Aunt Elaine hugged me and said I was growing into a beautiful woman and I said I wanted to go to bed early because I was starting work the next day. I thanked her four or five times and let myself be hugged and kissed, and then, even though I could feel she wanted to go on with the earlier conversation, I went to my room and closed the door. My whole body was shaking. I climbed under the sheet and blanket with my clothes on and turned off the lamp and lay awake listening to the sounds in the woods, and I thought about the lies I had just told, and about what Aunt Elaine might read in the *True Home and Country*, about the mall and about steel-toed boots, and what might happen in the house if my parents came back early. It seemed to me that, in one day, some huge shift had taken place in my world—Aunt Elaine asking about things she'd never asked about before, the possibility of the job. It felt as though someone was lifting up the aluminum bucket and shining a light underneath it. I wanted that, of course. But at the same time it was like being in the start of an earthquake. Before that, whatever else happened, however bad things had been, you were at least sure the ground would stay still.

Six

On my first day of work, instead of getting on the bus, I walked from the high school to the place where St. Mark's church had once stood, about a mile and a half. It was a sunny day, I remember, but raw, which was typical of April where we lived. The wind gusted hard down the valley. The roads had been sanded all winter and specks of grit flew against my cheeks so that I had to squint. Past the bank I went, with my backpack, my secondhand school jeans and wool hat, and my nagging worry about not having work boots to wear. That morning I had thought about asking Aunt Elaine for the money, then realized I wouldn't have time to buy them anyway. Only one thing so far Mr. Ivers had asked me to do and I hadn't done it. I went past the Boxing Club, the Christian Book Store, past the Laundromat and the empty shell where Video Nation had been, and then past another storefront that had been unoccupied for as long as I could remember, the FOR LEASE sign in the window strung with cobwebs and missing a letter or two. All that way I felt as though I was holding a thought in my hands—no boots, no boots—and fingering the edges of it.

When I came near to the ruined church, I saw that Mr. Ivers had pulled his truck right up onto the weedy lawn and was throwing stones and pieces of concrete into the bed. The noises echoed down the sidewalk like gunshots in the woods. I took off my hat and squeezed it into my pocket because I thought it made me look young. I had a sudden urge to turn around and run, but my aunt had given me two dollars and two quarters to hold in my pocket for luck, and warned me there would be a feeling of nervousness before I actually got started. First-day-on-the-job jitters, she called it. She knew it well, she said, from all the different nursing jobs she'd had in the years when she was moving around. It was natural, like a first day at school, or a first date. (I didn't tell her I had never been on a date; boys had asked me, three or four different times—a movie, school dances—but I said no without even bothering to check with my parents.) Aunt Elaine had made oatmeal, and given me the money, and said my mother and father would be home at the end of the day, and that they'd be proud of me for finding the job, she was sure.

"You showed up!" Mr. Ivers said, almost the way a happy boy would say it. He looked at me almost the way a boy would look, too. Then he seemed to remember he was the boss, and a man, and he stood up straight, facing me, and immediately glanced down at my feet. "Are your boots in that big backpack?"

I couldn't seem to move my eyes away from him. I could see again how strong he was, just by the width of his shoulders and the thickness of his neck. He was wearing work boots and jeans and an old sweatshirt and he had brown leather work gloves on his hands. Seeing him there—throwing stones into his black truck, with no one bothering him, no police telling him to get off the lawn and stop stealing church property—made me understand that what he told me must have been true. He really had bought the church and really would be working there.

"I can't to have any money for boots now but I can at tomorrow maybe or another time."

He watched for a few seconds. "All right. Just don't drop anything on your toes or you'll be walking around in a cast for a month."

"I'm here for to work now."

"I'm glad. What do you like to be called?"

"My father and my mother are calling me on Majie."

"May-gee? Do you like that?"

I shook my head.

"Marjorie then?"

I wasn't sure what to say. I didn't like my name at all, I'd never liked it. "What do you want for you?" I asked him.

"My first name is Arturo. My father's name was Arthur and they named me after a writer they knew. But I don't like it. As a boy when I played sports I had some friends who called me Sands. My middle name is Sanderson. You call me Sands, okay? And I'll call you, what? Marge?"

"Laney," I said. It was a name I sometimes called myself in secret. "My second other name is for Elaine, like my aunt is."

"Good. Laney. There's a pair of gloves for you in the cab, probably a little big, but I guessed."

"I have hands and feet that go big. The boys put their hands against of mine and they say it, on school."

"I bet they do." He started to say something else and then stopped.

When I put the gloves on—they almost fit—and walked around to the back of the pickup and stood near him, I felt as though the nervousness in me was being spoken to silently by a nervousness in him. It wasn't what I usually felt around adults. In fact, I never remembered feeling it. When he talked to me, he pushed the thick glasses back up against his nose twice for every ten words, and he talked fast, sometimes looking at me and sometimes not.

"What we're doing to start off with here," he said, "is getting rid of the bad stuff. Clearing the site. Okay? Once we clear the site we can start building, which is hard work but it's also the fun part. But every job has a boring part, or some boring parts, and this is one of them. Take any small pieces of broken stone or concrete you can lift without straining, and whatever you do don't drop them on your toes. Put them in the truck and push them back in as far as you can. We want to get rid of as much of the junk as possible before we build. Save the big ones for me. Then set the good stones—see, like this, ones we can use—set the good ones aside in piles if you can lift them and try to sort them basically according to size. Large, medium, and small. That will make it easy later, okay?"

"I could, sure," I said, and I started picking up pieces of rubble and putting them in the truck as Sands had been doing. He watched me for a minute and smiled; I could see it out of the side of my vision. I reminded myself that the manager at Emily's Dough Nuts had been nice on the first day, too, and that Pastor Schect had seemed like a kind uncle when we'd first started going to the Quonset hut in West Ober.

Work is something I've always had a talent for. From a young age I did most of the cleaning around the house. (My mother didn't mind cooking, but washing toilets or sweeping the floor or dusting—those things were alien to her. It wasn't so much that she refused to do them, as that she had the ability—I don't know if she was born with this or developed it—not to see that they needed to be done.) I often helped my father with repair projects (which he did very poorly) and with cutting and stacking stove wood (at which, like many men in those parts, he was an expert). From my work at home and from my year and a half at Emily's, I knew how to listen to instruction, to keep my opinions to myself, to try to please the person who paid me.

It didn't take long for the work to take away the afternoon chill and for me to begin to understand, without asking, which pieces of stone Sands wanted to keep and which pieces he wanted me to load into the truck. While I concentrated on the broken strips and chunks of old mortar—setting them in the bed as he showed me, so that they rested tight against one another near the cab end—he wandered around the remains of the church putting the heavier stones into piles. In an hour and a half the pickup bed was full, and I called over to tell him that.

Set against the background of the small stone rectory—abandoned and not as badly damaged as the church—Sands looked like a strange figure. With his giant's arms and thin body, his scraggly ponytail, his dark skin and thick eyeglasses, the way he had of being large in the world, physically, and yet shrinking back behind a quietness, even when he spoke, it was as if he was carrying around another person inside himself. I was like that, too—carrying a real seventeen-year-old there underneath a foolish little girl—and so I could almost see that other person inside him. But I thought it would be wise not to let Sands know that I could see it.

"Dump run!" he called out boyishly, and he started across the piles of stones with high-stepping strides that made him look like a clown.

I had never liked the dump, even after the name was changed to "transfer station." I hadn't liked it, in part, because, on the few times my father let my mother drive, she would take me there in the pickup to discard those pieces of household trash she didn't throw into the woods, and then she'd go into a small wooden house, a shack, really, where people brought old clothes and hung them on plastic hangers or left them folded on shelves. From my first memories, just about all my clothes had been transfer-station hand-me-downs, some of them in good condition but none especially pretty or well fitting. Almost the only new things I owned had been given to me by Aunt Elaine, a series of birthday and Christmas gifts sent in the mail—the backpack; the knit sweater and scarf; a yellow, blue, and red striped long-sleeved jersey; the warm pajamas—and they were treasures to me, gems marking a thin path through a landscape of the shabby and plain.

On route to the transfer station, driving slowly with the full truck bed, Sands talked again about the work, and again I could sense that nervousness in him and it sucked away some of my own. He didn't smoke and didn't comment about the driving habits of the other people on the road. He had all his fingers. I looked at him only in quick glances, but I listened beyond the words. "Water damages a building, any building, even a stone one, and in this case fire and the explosion damaged it first and let the water in. But there's some solid material there—I wouldn't have bought it otherwise—and so the first step is to clear everything down to the foundation, and then to see if you can use some of the damaged stuff. You need to have a foundation that's level and plumb. Do you know what plumb is?"

I shook my head. There was an image of a piece of fruit in it.

"Plumb is when the sides of something go straight up from the earth. So the corners and sides of that foundation—we have to make sure they're plumb and level."

"Okay. How for to do it, though?"

"Good question. I'll show you when we get back. With a tool called a level, that has small tubes with liquid and air bubbles in them. Or sometimes, if you need to check over a long distance, with a transit —which I don't have—or a clear plastic hose with water in it, which I do. Water finds its level at each end of the tube. . . . Anyway, once we get to that point—where the foundation is in good shape—then we start laying the stone for the walls. Later, in order to get to the higher work at the tops of the walls and the roof, we'll build wooden staging to stand on. So you're going to learn carpentry skills, too. If you stay with it." He looked at me, turned onto the gravel road that led to the dump. "Have any questions so far? Don't be shy."

"I'm not for shy."

"Sure you are. Don't be."

"Maybe you're for shy," I said, out of a hurt place in me, a place that didn't want criticism or attention to flaws. I hadn't meant to say it and was surprised to hear the words come out. Two mistakes now, I thought, the boots and this.

He looked at me, turned in at the gate. "You're right. I was shy as a kid. Still a little bit sometimes."

"Why for?"

"Long story."

I focused on sitting up straight—it was something Pastor Schect insisted on—and trying to think before I spoke, but the man who seemed like a boy inside didn't appear to be angry with me about the boots or the questions, and, as sometimes happened with Cindy or a teacher in school, I felt that I could step out of the circle I kept myself in. I thought of it not as a circle exactly but as a wooden keg, like the kind you could still get pickles from at Boory's. I stood in the middle of the keg, a naked girl, holding it up around me, putting words out over the edge of it, timidly, and waiting to see what response they brought. "How can you to know where what goes?"

"What do you mean?"

"Where to put."

"The stones, you mean?"

I nodded, retreated, ducked part of the way back down inside the barrel.

"I have blueprints. Right after I bought this place I spent a few days drawing them up with a friend of mine who's an architect. You can't just think about the outside of something. You have to consider where everything is going to be inside, from bathroom to altar, if we were going to have an altar, which we're not."

"What kind of church would you make it then? For your house?"

"My house is going to be—is now—the rectory. Good name for it, too, because it's a wreck inside. I'll show you sometime. It's not close to being ready for a tour yet. I sleep there and try to fix it up a little every night. Someday soon it's going to be beautiful, just right. What we're making isn't a church, though, it's a cathedral."

"In what religious?"

"A bunch of them."

"How a bunch? Who comes?"

"I don't need anybody to come. I'm building it for my own plea-sure. Because I love old churches. Because I think it's important to make something that looks good—in a town like this, especially—out of something that doesn't. Because it feels right."

He went on and said other things, but I was stuck on the "for my own pleasure" part. It was clear to me then that Sands—it was still a struggle to think of him by that name—wasn't a man or a boy but something else, that he was odd and unusual, of a different species even than my teachers and Aunt Elaine, and I was working my thoughts, kneading them, turning them, trying to understand if there was any-thing threatening in the species or not. People are going to laugh at you, I wanted to say. You don't know the people in this town. They're going to put your picture on the front page in the newspaper and every person from Weedon's and Boory's and the doughnut shop and the haircutter is going to come and look and laugh. After a few seconds of this it occurred to me that, if he kept me on the job, I would be half of what they were laughing at.

Sands turned in through the transfer station gates. There, an overall-wearing supervisor made him pull out his demolition permit, which flapped in the wind as he held it. The man looked at me as if I'd stolen all the clothes from his exchange table and come back for more. After examining the permit for a long time he handed it back to Sands and waved us through and we unloaded the mortar and broken stones piece by piece onto a pile of dirt and gravel—it took us a while—then drove back toward town.

"Hungry?"

I shook my head, a lie without words. I don't think I had a par-ticularly large appetite in those years. I was finished growing. But sometimes at home there wasn't much food in the cupboards or the refrigerator, and sometimes my parents made me miss a meal or two, or go a whole day without eating, as a penance. Once you've been hungry like that, no matter how much you eat, part of you always re-members the hungry feeling.

"We stop for coffee for twenty minutes every afternoon. It's part of the deal. Boss buys."

"Nothing for me for it. Thank you, even though."

"Sure?" He was turning into the drive-through of the doughnut shop, a few blocks from where Emily's had once been.

I remembered what I used to eat at Emily's. "If they might had chocolate milk," I said, and immediately wished I hadn't spoken.

"And what to go with it?"

"Honey frosting on a doughnut." The words seemed to be flying up out of my belly and past my teeth. I looked out the side window and clamped my jaws together.

Instead of heading back to the work site, Sands drove north from the doughnut shop, out of town, and when he turned that way without saying anything, I felt as though my arms and legs went to ice. I was holding the small carton of chocolate milk in my lap. I had eaten only two bites of the doughnut.

"This is a different of a way," I said.

"I know it."

He was sipping coffee, driving with one hand, not looking at me. I wanted to ask where he was going but couldn't make myself. There were dirt roads off to the sides of the highway there, and they led deep into the woods where people hunted and trapped but no one lived. The honey-dipped doughnut rested on the top of my thigh on a napkin. I listened to the truck tires against the pavement and thought about what it would be like to jump out while we were going at this speed. Into my mind came a picture of the girl on the other side of the river, and then all the things my teachers had told us about how to protect ourselves. Never ride in a car with someone you don't know well, they had said. Never let yourself get into that situation.

But instead of turning onto one of the dirt roads, after another mile or so Sands pulled into the parking lot of the mall, a place my parents never went. I knew about it, naturally, had heard the kids talking about it, had driven past it, but had never been inside. Sands found a parking space and turned off the truck. "Finish eating, okay?"

I forced myself to chew the doughnut and sip the last of the milk. I wiped my sleeve quickly across my mouth and looked at him.

"We're buying your work boots," he said.

I watched him knock the glasses back up against the top of his nose; I looked at the color of his skin. I had the fleeting sense, again, that he reminded me of someone. I had the thought that I was going to get boots now and he would tell me we were going hiking in the woods, just like he'd told me about the snack. It was part of the job, he'd say. That was his trick. "I won't to have the money for," I said.

"I'm advancing you the money so you don't break your toes."

I looked at him.

"I'm paying for the boots, and then you can pay me back when you get your earnings. Little by little if you want. A dollar a week or something. Let's go."

I got out of the truck and followed Sands toward the mall entrance, hanging back a few steps. Twice, he looked over his shoulder to see where I was. Just inside the front doors I stopped and stood still. It was as if they had taken the center of our town, filled the empty windows with new things, washed and polished them, turned on music and bright lights, and moved it all here. Sands turned and waved for me to follow, impatiently it seemed. We walked down a gleaming corridor of glass, light, and plastic advertisements, with radios and earrings and summer sweaters on display in store windows to either side. People strolled along in groups of two and three, holding shopping bags and pushing strollers, and it seemed to me they were people who'd come there from another state, a different river valley. Only some of the teenagers, with their eye makeup, pierced noses, patched pants, and sideways glances, seemed like a species I knew.

Sands walked along. The music flowed over his shoulders and back against my ears. He turned into a store with boots and sneakers in the window and women's shoes with high heels and he led me all the way to the back, where there was a bench to sit on and shoe boxes on shelves. "What size are you?" he asked.

I looked at him and felt my lips quiver. "Middle of size," I said, and one side of his mouth curled up before he could stop it.

"Your feet, I mean. Do you know?"

I shook my head and moved my eyes away from his. At that moment a boy who couldn't have been long out of high school walked over to us. He was wearing a green shirt with a name tag pinned onto it, and the name tag read IAN. I felt his eyes on me for a few seconds, and then, when I didn't meet them, he turned to Sands and asked if he could help us.

"Steel-toed work boots," Sands said confidently. "For the young lady."

"What size?" the boy asked, looking at me again.

I met his eyes for only an instant. My chin sank slowly down. They were both looking at me now and I was noticing that the square of linoleum beneath my feet was chipped in one corner.

"She needs to be measured," Sands told the boy. "She's grown since her last pair."

The boy hurried away and returned with an odd flat piece of metal, silver and black with lines and numbers on it. "I need you to take off your shoes," he said, and in his voice I could plainly hear that he knew I had never been there before, knew I was foolish for not being able to say my size, knew how much smarter he was than I would ever be. He was looking at my worn jeans and sweatshirt, the dirt under my fingernails. It reminded me exactly of a time when I went to a plumbing supply store with my father, who was trying to fix our kitchen sink. The man behind the counter there had started asking my father questions about the part he needed, and my father didn't know what to say. With each question, my father seemed to shrink into himself more and more, and at the same time I could feel the cloud of anger swelling around him and reaching out toward the clerk. The clerk, a blond man with a goatee, became less patient with each question, and his first politeness gradually turned into a tone of voice that had a lining to it of something like scorn. He seemed to me, foolishly, not to be aware of the swelling cloud of anger at all. "You have to know the model number," he said after the string of questions, "or how am I supposed to go back into the stockroom, where there are five hundred boxes, and find the one you want?"

My father went still as stone. He had his cane in one hand—it was just a carved piece of oak—and his eyes drifted down to the floor, and for a few seconds I thought he was going to swing the cane and break the man's skull with it. At last, with the clerk pressing him, and other customers waiting, and me standing there watching, my father spun around on one boot and hurried out the door. On the sidewalk the parts store had set up a plastic statue, about three feet tall, of a man dressed in their store colors and holding a plastic wrench across the front of his body. The little man had a small round smile between his plump cheeks. Without, at first, having seemed to even notice it, my father swung his cane once, very hard, and snapped the head off the plastic statue so it fell over sideways and hung there by a shred. The blow made a noise like someone striking a drum. People turned to look. My father and I hurried to the truck before anyone could stop us, and all the way driving home it seemed to me that a bubble of laughter—something I almost never heard from him—was trying to force its way up from beneath the hairs of his beard. Neither of us ever said a word about it to my mother. So many years later the sink still leaked.

"You need to sit and take off your sneakers," Ian was saying.

I sat on the cushioned bench. I was halfway done unlacing the sneaker on my left foot when I remembered that my socks had holes in them, a small empty circle at each heel. It was too late to do anything about it. Ian was kneeling in front of me, waiting. Sands was watching. I hesitated for a second, two seconds, then yanked off the shoe and tried to push my foot back against the bottom of the bench so they couldn't see the hole. But Ian was reaching for my foot. He took hold of it, his fingers wrapping around the back, just where the hole was. He flinched. A little smile went across his face and he squeezed the muscles around his mouth to disguise it. "Ten, women's," he said to Sands. "We should check both feet, though. A lot of times people have different sizes of feet. Most of my customers do."

So I peeled off the sneaker on my right foot. Another hole in the sock. The metal measuring device was cool against the back of my foot but my cheeks were hot and my eyes squeezed half-closed. In a moment Ian was off to the stockroom. Out of the corner of my eye I could see Sands pretending to be examining the display boots, lifting one up, turning it over, flexing the sole in his hands. I thought then that I'd quit the work and tell him I didn't want the boots and just go home to my room. I would be boyed or doused, but at least those were things I was used to. I'd started to say something about not wanting the boots after all when Ian came back into view, opening the shoe box as he walked. A sheet of tissue paper showed there.

I let him put the first boot on and lace it up. I couldn't move. It made me think, at first, of Pastor Schect's work boots. "These are men's eights, we don't have steel-toed for women or girls. How does that feel?" he asked, and I searched his words for ridicule but didn't hear so much of it now.

I nodded.

"Wiggle your toes around some."

I moved my toes halfheartedly.

"I can't press in there to feel your big toe because of the steel," he was saying. "You have to tell me whether they're tight or pinching or anything. Let me put on the other one and you can walk around."

When the second boot was laced up, I was told to stand and walk. I took three steps and returned and nodded again.

"You're sure?" Sands asked me. "They'll loosen up some but if they're pinching you now you'll be uncomfortable all summer."

So he was going to let me work for the summer. I glanced at him quickly and nodded, then looked away. Ian was standing close, waiting for an answer, ready to show me another pair, to see my bad socks again, to tell his friends about it once we walked away. "Good of the size now," I said quietly to Sands.

"They're seventy-four fifty, but on sale this week for sixty ninety-nine," Ian said.

"Fine."

Sands was taking out his wallet. I was running the numbers through my mind, sure that there must have been a mistake. But when I glanced over I saw that Ian had a bill in his hand, and the bill had the numeral 100 in one corner. "Right back with the change," he said cheerfully.

I stood still there, staring at the wall.

When we left the store and were walking back down the corridor of shops and out into the windy cool day, I felt as though I had two blocks of wood attached to my feet, and I knew that most of my first week of work, all that pay, would go to Sands and not to my parents or my aunt or me, and I could still feel the blood in my cheeks and see the look on Ian's face when he'd felt the bare skin at the back of my heels. But the boots were absolutely beautiful to my eye, smooth light-brown leather and a cream sole, the loops of the laces falling to either side of my ankles like ribbons on a gift. I wondered, as we walked across the parking lot, how many people were turning to look.

For the rest of that windy afternoon, with the new boots stiff on my feet but so wonderful I couldn't stop looking at them, I loaded up the truck bed again while Sands went around the site, shifting stones into piles. From time to time I glanced at him without letting him see. When the truck was full I called to him, but before he got into the cab this time he stood and ran his eyes over the work site. I looked where he was looking and saw that the church, or what had once been the church, was still a disaster area, with weeds growing everywhere and only a small portion of the rubble sorted. Even so, I could see evidence of my own effort, and of his—a patch of clean ground and small piles of usable stones. My hands hurt. There were blisters on the backs of both heels and a pound of dust in my hair. The sun had fallen behind the hills by then and the day had gone from cool to cold, and I could still feel Ian's eyes on me. But I had such a proud feeling then, standing there in the new boots and looking over the work we'd done. It seemed to me that Sands was having the same feeling.

"Dump's closed now," he said. "I can take this load over tomorrow morning."

I didn't say anything.

"How are you getting home, Laney?"

"Everywhere I go walking."

"How far is it?"

"Past on the 112 Store but only not too much then."

"That's three or four miles from here. Your feet must be sore in the new boots."

I looked at him and then back at the site. I moved my toes inside the boots and decided I would change back into my sneakers before making the walk—not only because of the blisters but because I didn't want my parents to see that I had something so new and expensive. For a minute I thought of asking if I could leave the boots with him, but that would have led to more questions, so I didn't. And then I saw that questions from him would be better than from my mother and father, so I said, "Could I to leave them here? These boots?"

Sands nodded, watching me in a way I didn't like. I could feel his eyes on me as I changed into my old sneakers.

"How about if I drop you home?"

"I'm to walk there. I want it."

"How about if I drop you at the store then? I have to pick up a few things for supper anyway."

I said I thought that would be all right, but by the time he pulled the truck slowly across the sidewalk and onto Main Street, it was almost dark, and I was unused to being in a truck in the darkness, and the cold chill was running up the backs of my arms and shoulders again. I looked at the door lock to make sure it wasn't down.

Sands drove across the rattling metal bridge, going very slowly with the heavy load in back, and then slowly along Route 112, curling beside the smaller river. My hands and the muscles of my arms and back ached. The new boots sat side by side on the floor, against my left foot. Sands turned on the radio and I flinched, and hoped he didn't see. A very clean voice there was reporting the news, talking about countries I'd heard the name of in school but didn't know much about, using words I'd heard before but didn't really understand. *Acquiesce.*

Negligible. I loved the sound of those words, and of that voice. I felt as though I was listening to a broadcast from space. It made me so happy on the one hand, and on the other hand I knew Pastor Schect would give me the face if he found out about the radio.

"Nice job today," Sands said when he'd pulled into the store lot. "Soak in a hot bath and take a couple of aspirin and you won't be too sore tomorrow. I'll see you Friday after school. I'll keep the boots right here for you."

"Not for tomorrow?"

"Okay, if you want. Tomorrow's Wednesday so that would put us back on our regular schedule. I just thought you'd be sore."

"I wouldn't be."

"Okay. Good. See you tomorrow then."

I didn't remember to thank him until after I'd closed the door of the truck, and it was too late then. I made a small wave but he didn't see me. I thought he must have changed his mind about buying things at the 112 Store because he drove out onto the highway right away and headed back in the direction of the town. I walked to Waldrup Road, turned left there, and went home.

Seven

When my father and mother returned from one of their nights away they were never in the best of moods. I knew enough not to ask about where they had gone or what they'd done, but I couldn't keep myself from wondering. They went riding in the hills, I imagined, and then had a restaurant meal and checked into a motel and made the bed bang against the wall. They were happy not to have me around.

As always after one of these trips, my mother was too tired to cook. On the way home they had stopped somewhere and bought a pizza—cheese, onion, and pineapple, always the same. My mother ripped the top off the box and put the pizza in the middle of the table, tossed a stack of paper napkins next to it, set out three cans of Coke, and sat down. She lit a cigarette and laid it across her opened Coke can so the ash dropped over the side, and she dragged a slice of pizza across the table toward her, and took a bite, crust-end first as she always did. My father ate in silence, as he almost always did, chewing in slow circular flexes and running his eyes back and forth across the grease stains on the underside of the box's cover as if he was working through a difficult problem and the pattern of the stains might give him some clue. There were eight slices in the box. My parents pulled three each toward themselves and left me two. They chewed and swallowed and drank and didn't look at each other. I sensed, sometimes, a particular kind of shame or guilt between them when they returned from their overnight trips, though the possibility that they could feel guilty for having left me was an idea that made no sense.

When we were finished that night, I got up and put the box in the trash barrel near the front door, threw the napkins in after it, wet a dish towel, and carefully cleaned the drips of hardening cheese from the tabletop. My father's eyes followed my hands as I worked, peering at the curved lines of moisture the towel left on the wooden surface, sensing something, puzzling over something, looking for something. Without raising his eyes to my face he said, "What for the job, you Majie?"

"I started on today."

"What for doing?"

"Stonework."

My mother grunted. I understood by then that there were times when she did not like my father giving me any attention. It was one of the reasons I'd learned not to say much at the table, to eat and move as inconspicuously as possible and then disappear into my room. Those times when I felt a kindness from my father—for example, when I helped him stack wood in the yard and he talked to me about the different kinds of trees and what they were used for—my mother would often do something to pull his attention toward her. She'd yell a sarcastic remark out the front door. She'd come outside and try to make conversation with him when he obviously didn't want to talk to her. She'd empty the trash loudly and kick the tin cans and paper boxes a little farther into the trees behind the house. Once, without asking him, she had even taken the pickup and driven herself into town. That had sent my father into a fit of spitting and stomping, but it had succeeded in swinging his attention back to her and away from me. It seemed to me sometimes that my mother had a secret need to be the only female on earth.

"Smelling on stones?" she asked me in a mocking way. She took a long pull of her cigarette and slanted her eyes down the table almost as far as my father's fingers. "Feeling stones down between the legs?" She laughed a short laugh and glanced at my father. "What, rubbing on stones for a genie coming out? You gotten three wishes, you Majie?"

That finally raised a one-note, unsmiling grunt out of my father. He lifted his eyes and was admiring his wife, working his jaw muscles so the hairs on his beard jumped.

"Taking of old concrete at the dump," I said. "Putting the stones by a size."

"Where in?" my father wanted to know. He had a smear of pizza sauce on his beard, and his hair, color of rust and standing up in short, ragged points, looked as if it had been frozen as it was trying to escape.

"Into the town."

"Where part of?"

"Where was the church before. St. Mark's. The person has work to make another church at there now."

They both had their eyes on me.

"Keep lie-making," my mother said. "And someone goin' to boy you."

"I don't want of to be boyed. It's not a lie. You ask . . . you can come at town and even see. He told I can be with the job for one year I do good." I thought of telling her about the boots then changed my mind.

"And when's pay for you? Christmas?"

"Every on the month."

"Month," my mother said. "Month?" She pulled hard on her Prime and tunneled the smoke out the side of her mouth. Her eyes flicked once to my father. "What about every week, lie-making Majie."

"He's to paying a—" I stopped because my father had fixed his eyes on me with a certain bitterness I recognized. Things weren't the way he wanted them to be. Almost always, it seemed, things weren't the way he wanted them to be. The events of living were a constant disappointment to him. Sometimes I disappointed him, sometimes my mother did, sometimes it was the weather, or the lack of money, someone at Weedon's, another driver on the road, the governor, the president. Only Pastor Schect, it seemed, was exempt. I sensed this quick swing of mood in him from downcast to on guard to angry as if it was my own mind traveling that route. I knew he felt ashamed about not having a job, and I knew his feelings about Aunt Elaine, and I was trying to find a way to tell him the details of the payment arrangement without lying about it, or seeming to brag about it, and without mentioning my aunt's name. Something, some spider of bad feeling, scurried up from between my legs and along my spine—it was the feeling I always got when they talked about boying me. My father was watching. I decided to tell the truth. "He is for to paying Aunt Elaine on the every month and Aunt Elaine is for to paying some with you and—"

"Some?" my mother said. She had her eyes on my father, not on me. "That sounds a big mistake, that *some* word. Either that or somebody's gettin' boyed."

It didn't take much for her to lead my father where she wanted him to go, to aim his disappointment in whatever direction pleased her. He pondered this turn of the conversation for a few seconds, his lips working and the four fingers of his left hand tapping out a tune on some imaginary tabletop drum skin. I could hear the breath going into and out of his nostrils.

"Pastor Schect don't like on no other church workin'," he said.

"It's not as a real church. And there will to be good money for—"

"Lie-makin'," my mother muttered.

My father chewed his lips for a few seconds, scraped his eyes back and forth across my face, drummed his fingers in the broken rhythm, and said, "Tomorrow you to stay to home and we put a fix on the roof then, boy."

"But tomorrow is for a work day. I won't get some money."

"Boys don't to give their man a backtalk," my father said, and he stood up and went stomping out the door. Another few seconds and I heard him working in the darkness, splitting wood, which was, for him, the kind of relaxation that watching sports on TV or having a beer with friends would be for another man. I heard the maul hit—*bang*—and then there was a pause, another strike, *bang,* a pause, and then the sound of the billets (my father called them "bullets") being tossed into a pile. He was working in just the light from the window, but I knew he could have done the job with his eyes closed. I heard another strike.

My mother smoked in a satisfied way. "I'll bring home a big money paying for you," I said to her. "Know how much?"

She went on smoking and didn't look at me. She was listening to the sounds of the wood-splitting the way another woman might listen to a piano being played in an upstairs room by someone she loved. When I started to speak again, she raised the hand that held the cigarette. Her wedding ring was loose there between the knuckles, and I remember seeing scratches on the back of her hand and wondering if she and my father had fought when they were away. "I'll put your boy clothes out at the bed tomorrow," she said. "And don't tell me you dint have no warning on it neither, you Majie."

Eight

Whenever I was walking the roads, or—before my father smashed up my old bicycle in one of his fits—whenever I was taking my long solitary bike rides along Route 112, I would occasionally find myself carrying on a debate about which was the worse penance, boying or dousing. Dousing had the physical pain to it, but it didn't last long, and I had learned a way of being strong inside during it. Even in March or April, when the water in the stream had been ice not long before, I had trained myself to turn the cold on my skin into some other feeling and pretend I liked it. I wouldn't make a sound. Sometimes when my father released me with a tap on the shoulder I would walk, not run, to the house just to show him how strong I was, how unaffected by the punishment.

Boying had no pain to it, but usually it went on for a whole day. And it seemed to bring out a hidden evil in my mother and father that I never saw when they doused or hungered me. When he was holding me by the hair and marching me across the yard toward the stream, when he was leaning down and filling up the bucket, I often had the sense from my father that he didn't actually want to do what he was doing. That it was Pastor Schect's idea, or my mother's, not his. That he was only following instructions in the hope of not being punished himself in the afterlife. My mother showed an occasional spark of feeling about it, too. If it was an especially cold day, she might heat up a can of soup for me to eat when I came out of the shower, or let me have two or three sips from her coffee mug as soon as I stepped into the house.

But boying seemed to stimulate an evil humor inside them. It was almost like a game they played together, and it was a ritual they seemed to need to perform every few months in order to release something from their troubled hearts. When I was being boyed, I had the feeling that a whole nest of snakes was crawling inside me, slithering around, moving up toward the inside of my skull, where they would swarm and swirl and writhe. And on the day after being boyed, if I had school, I found it was difficult to look anyone in the eye, even my friend Cindy; even Aaron Patanauk, who had taken to talking with me more and more often, and not making fun of the way I spoke. He'd even given me a few compliments on the way my body looked. When the day of boying was over with, my mother would take the clothes I'd been wearing and put them in the pile she took to the Laundromat, "to wash off the Majie in them," she said, and I would go to bed in just my underwear, lying on my side staring at the dark wall. I'd push my hands down inside my underwear but not do anything with them there, just hold myself that way until I fell asleep.

In the morning after our pizza dinner, I woke up thinking about school and work and the new boots, and then I saw that my mother had set a pair of my father's briefs out on the end of my bed, and his work pants with pins inserted to hold the cuffs up on the legs, and a length of rope for a belt. She'd put one of his white T-shirts on the pile, a flannel shirt, socks, and an old, worn-out pair of boots he never used anymore and that were so big I knew I'd have to struggle all day not to fall over myself in them.

On boying days there would always be a job to do, a house repair project usually, something my father had been putting off for a long while and that I knew he'd have trouble completing once he started. It was almost as if he really did want a son there to help him. That day the job was roof repair. During the winter a leak had appeared in the living room ceiling, staining the old Sheetrock with coppery circles. When I was eating my oatmeal, my father came to the door wearing a tool belt with a hammer hanging down against his thigh, and nails—squat, wide-headed roofing nails—overflowing the pocket. "Fetch on the ladder, boy," he said.

On my way to the sink, walking sloppily in the too-big boots, I spooned the last of the oatmeal into my mouth. I rinsed out the bowl and hurried outside to the doorless shed where my father kept his traps and chain saw and cans of gasoline and oil. The summer before, he'd worked for a whole week to fashion a homemade ladder out of two saplings and arm-thick oak branches, all lashed together with elaborate knots and nailed for good measure. The ladder was leaning sideways against the shed. I carried it over to where he stood near the front steps and he took it from me and rested it against the edge of the roof.

I watched him, the rungs roped on unevenly and bending beneath his weight, the roofing nails dripping out of the pouch as he climbed. "Handen me up what tar paper, boy," he called when he reached the top of the ladder.

I went back to the shed and found the roll of black paper, tall as my waist and heavier than a basket of wet laundry. I hoisted it onto my shoulder and carried it over to the house, wondering why my father had climbed the ladder first and asked for the whole roll, instead of cutting a smaller piece and carrying that up.

"Broughten it here."

I balanced the tar paper on my shoulder with one hand and used the other to hold the rungs of the ladder. When I'd brought the roll up to him I stood with my hands on the top rung and watched as he worked. He took his hunting knife out of its sheath, nine inches long and sharp as a surgeon's scalpel. He opened the roll, flattened a section of the paper against the roof, and began working the tip of his knife into it, cutting a pattern that was more or less square. I could see he was pushing down too hard on the knife, running the sharp tip through the worn shingles on the roof and the half-bare papered sections, but I didn't say anything. My father made cuts for the other three sides of the square, all of them too deep, then pushed the roll aside so he'd be able to set the square of paper in place. But he pushed too hard; the roll went over the edge of the roof. It slammed down against the front steps, breaking off a piece of rotten wood, and rolled partway open.

"What is going!?" my mother yelled from the kitchen.

My father spat toward the roof's ridgeline, away from me. I could hear him muttering. He held the cut square of paper in his hands as a gust of wind blew, then he leaned both hands on it and pressed it down against the part of the roof he assumed to be leaking.

"Reach and hold for that side, boy, you boy," he said. Still with my feet on the ladder, I leaned over and placed my hands flat, several feet apart, along one edge of the square. In that position, I could feel my breasts hanging down against the T-shirt (my parents wouldn't let me wear a bra on boying days). Girl, girl, girl, I said in my own mind. Girl.

My father took two nails from the pocket and put them between his lips. Another gust of wind came, and when he went to take hold of his side of the paper the nails slipped out of his mouth and went bouncing down the slope of the roof and over the edge. "Go, boy," he said. "See sure they ain't put now where the tires will make flat for the truck."

I climbed down and searched for the nails until I found them. I picked up another half dozen as I went. I heard my father muttering, and when I looked up I saw the square of black paper floating softly down toward me. It landed beside me in the dirt.

"Boy!"

I brought the square of paper up the ladder, only to find that it had been torn fairly deeply into one side. I went back down and carried up the now dented roll again. My father made another square, uneven, larger, threw the roll violently over the edge of the roof, put one nail into his mouth, flattened the square onto the old shingles, took the nail out quickly, and banged it home with his hammer. He banged in two more nails while I held the loose edges, then he banged in several more in no particular pattern and took his knife and tried to trim the excess away. It wouldn't trim easily, so he tore at it with his red hands. "Boy, broughten a caulkin'," he said. "Truck. Shed."

I climbed down. In the truck I found a new tube of gray caulk, and in the shed the metal caulking gun used to apply it. I carried the supplies up the ladder, and after some moments of struggle, my father fixed the tube of caulking into the applicator, hacked off the plastic tip, held the whole thing in his hands as if he was squirting a fire hose, and made an attempt to spread a bead of caulk evenly around the edges of the new square of paper in order to seal it. But he'd cut off too much of the tip, and the caulk came flowing out in a thick burst, onto the tar paper and onto his pants. He couldn't curse—Pastor Schect would not allow it—but his teeth were grinding against each other, and just then, with her perfect timing, my mother opened the front door and called up, "Goin' good?"

"Okay," I answered quietly, but my mother let out one of her cigarette-smoke laughs as if she knew better.

My father was wiping the hand with the missing finger on the tar paper, smearing gobs of sticky gray caulk in wide swaths. His face, on the reddish side at the best of times, had gone the color of a ripe strawberry. "Rag," he spat out. "Towel, boy."

"Ma want put up for a towel?"

"Boy talkin' to me?" my mother replied. She stepped out, trying to catch a glimpse of my father, but the edge of the roof still hid him from her view.

"Some trouble on at the caulkin', Ma. Quick."

"It's for boys to get towels," she said, shifting her eyes toward the roof again and speaking loudly enough for her husband to hear.

"Ma!"

I could see that my father had sat back on his heels with his wrists on his knees and his hands hanging down, a posture of defeat. There were beads of sweat shining on his forehead. He breathed in once, twice, and then shouted out, "Devil!" and threw the tube and caulking applicator off the roof. I watched it fly awkwardly through the air, end over end, and make landfall a few feet from the shed. I could see the caulk on his work pants and on his hands, in the hair of his wrists. By the time I had hurried down the ladder in search of a rag, he'd left the roof and was climbing down, too, his hands leaving sticky gray reminders on the sapling rungs. Feet on the ground again, he lifted the ladder from the bottom as if it weighed two pounds and carried it over to the shed, brushing past me, knocking over cans inside, traps, wires, an old rusted rake with a broken handle, trying, with sticky hands, to fit the ladder where it would not fit, then remembering where he kept it and throwing it down outside.

His face, when he finally turned it to me, was almost purple. "Turpetine!" he screamed. "Go at 112, boy! Turpetine! Turpetine! Turpetine!"

I had blisters on the backs of my heels, and I thought for a moment about changing from my father's boots to sneakers, but it seemed wiser to get out of the yard as fast as I could, so I hurried off down the driveway and onto Waldrup Road, staying along the edges where the mud wasn't deep, moving as quickly as the boots and the blisters allowed. I felt like a clown in the clothes, of course, the rope belt, the man's shirt, the baggy pants. I felt as though I was hurrying along in a hot spotlight, and I was sure somebody from school would see me and tell the whole world. At the corner of Route 112, the right boot went sideways and fell off. I stopped and laced it up tighter. As I passed C&P Welding I couldn't keep myself from looking at the building, but there was no sign of Cary Patanauk there.

In the 112 Store, Mrs. Jensen sold me a can of paint thinner on credit ("Margie, are you helping your dad in those clothes? Nobody calls it turpentine anymore. Why, you're all out of breath!") and I carried it back as fast as I could and found my father sitting on the oak stump where he split wood, his chin on his chest, his hands resting palms-up on his knees, covered in sticky caulk. I unscrewed the can, only to find a thin metal seal over the opening. My father was lifting his heels up and tapping them on the dirt in an impatient rhythm. "Screwendrive!" he yelled. "Screwendrive!" I went to the shed, found a screwdriver, and poked it through the seal. He held his hands out in front of him and I poured some paint thinner on them and watched him rubbing his palms together furiously, then trying to get the caulk off with a rag. He didn't look at me. He put his hands out again, and I poured more paint thinner into them, and I could feel my mother watching us from the half-open window, getting ready to make one of her remarks. She seemed to me incapable of not making those remarks—little acid-tipped darts aimed at her husband's eyelids and lips—but, at the same time, she had an understanding that there was a line she shouldn't cross. On those times when she did cross the line, accidentally or otherwise, my father would respond, usually after some delay, with a show of craziness. It was like a lion roaring in the jungle, *Stop or I'll kill you!* Once, when I was very young, probably only about four, he burned down a larger and better-built shed that had occupied the place in the yard where the ramshackle shed now stood. An hour or so after their argument—I was too small to understand what they'd been fighting about—he went to the shed and methodically took out the shovels and chain saw and his traps, laid them in neat rows some distance away in the dirt, with me and my mother watching from inside the house. He spread gasoline along the base of the outside wall of the shed, set the can down with the rest of the tools, and tossed a match. I had the feeling my mother liked seeing him that way, that it excited her. It was one of my earliest memories, watching that shed burn, the scarlet flames licking up near the trees, my father standing ten yards away with his arms hanging down and his head tilted sideways. Another time he flattened two tires of his truck and left it sitting like that for a week. Another time—this was when Dad Paul went to jail and my mother said he deserved to for what he'd done—he punched his good hand through a pane of glass in the living room and it was a long time before he could stop the bleeding.

In the midst of the caulk and paint thinner cleanup, my mother opened the window and called over, "Messy job, huh?" My father didn't respond. His face didn't change. After another minute, he stood up. He ran the rag over the stump of his left index finger and wiped it uselessly across the caulk on his pants. When he threw it on the ground, I reached to pick it up, and he aimed a kick at me and caught me in the back of the left thigh. I fell over, surprised. Except for two whippings with braided willow branches, it was the only time he'd ever actually struck me. I picked up the rag and limped over and threw it into the woods where my mother tossed the trash. Then I put the roll of tar paper back in the shed, and the caulking gun, and I looked around for any more nails on the ground, making sure there was nothing left anywhere that might remind my father of the project.

We had one of our silent lunches, baked beans and bacon, my father wearing different pants and eating very slowly and my mother trying not to smile between bites. For the rest of the day my parents left me alone but wouldn't let me change out of the clothes, so I read a schoolbook in my room, then went out and sat on a stone by the stream because I've always liked the sound of running water. Missing a day of school didn't matter much to me, but I worried Sands would fire me for not coming to work, and I tried to trace back the line of events that had led to my penance. What could I have done differently? How could I change things in the future so this wouldn't happen again? Was there some way to impress Pastor Schect with the amount of money I'd be earning, maybe put a dollar of my own in the woven basket, so that he'd tell my parents good things about me? Or was the idea of working on another church such an enormous sin that no amount of punishment or sacrifice could erase it?

It was typical of what I'd do after a penance—that kind of desperate searching for answers—but it was useless, and part of me knew that. There was no particular logic to my parents' thinking. Something came into their minds. They held that something up against the background of what they'd been hearing in the Quonset hut in West Ober, and reading for years in *True Home and Country,* and then my mother would make a suggestion to my father, and eventually he'd agree. In their minds, in Pastor Schect's mind, a child being punished according to the Ancient Way of the Lord was an act that paid for the sins of everyone on earth, as if we were underage stand-ins for Christ on the cross.

In later years, long after these penances were finished, I told a therapist about them and she asked why I hadn't run away. "I did run once," I said. "To my aunt's. But after two days I went back home. My aunt tried everything she could to keep me from going back, but I lied and told her it had happened just that once, an argument, a small punishment." The therapist asked me why I had done that and I wanted to say, "Because I knew I was a sinner in the eyes of God. Because I wasn't at home in the peaceful world. Because I wanted my father to love me." But the real reason runs deeper than that, scurrying around behind the walls of the pain museum. Any person who goes back to being beaten knows about that. The real reason hides in a deeper place.

Nine

As always on the day after a boying, I woke up feeling disconnected from my body. I was happy to be able to dress for school in my own clothes, but, with my underwear especially, it almost felt as though I was putting the fabric over someone else's hips, shoulders, and breasts, and that was not a feeling I liked. I went into the kitchen and before I'd even poured myself a glass of lemonade or taken a square of the gingerbread my mother had made, I said, "Pa and you should to let me to work for this job. For the money they'll be, I—"

"Who's not letting you?" my mother said over her shoulder. She turned from her place at the table, ran her eyes over my pants and shirt and sneakers and nodded the way she did when she was satisfied with something.

I knew enough then to swallow the next words in my mouth. Just from seeing that she had made gingerbread I should have known my mother's mood was good—which almost always meant my father's mood had been good, also, before he went out to the forest. From the gingerbread, from the expression on her face, the corners of her eyes slightly turned up, her mouth relaxed . . . I understood that the winds had shifted during the night. It was important not to do or say anything to shift them back.

"Go work for all you want to," she said, then she returned to her coffee and her food.

I drank half the glass of water, wrapped two pieces of gingerbread in a paper napkin, lifted my backpack onto one shoulder, and stepped out the door. As I went along Waldrup Road eating my breakfast, I tried, for the thousandth time, to puzzle out the mystery of my parents' thoughts, to see if there might have been some trick there, behind my mother's encouragement. I had been boyed; that always flushed some of the anger out of them. But it was more complicated than that, more complicated even than what they might have done with each other in the bedroom at night, or how much money they still had in the jar on their bureau, or what they'd decided they'd get from me in the way of income. Their moods shifted the way a bat flew at twilight, not in a straight line, not according to any pattern anyone else could understand. That morning, unless there was a trick, the winds that blew across my parents' inner landscape had simply turned in a different direction. They would be happy now, for a day or two; my father would be contentedly splitting wood when I came home, and might carry his plate to the sink after dinner, or sit on the couch and listen to his wife read. My mother might touch me on the shoulder before I went to bed, or ask for a kiss.

I waited for the bus and thought about them. My father spent most of his time in our woods, twelve acres that were thick with old-growth pine, spruce, and the typical mix of northern New England hardwoods. Most days he'd go out in the morning, without a helmet or any kind of eye protection, usually without gloves, and fell a tree. (I remember, as a small small girl, being terrified at hearing the slow passage of the falling tree through the limbs of its neighbors, then the big *crash-boom* when it hit the ground.) He cut the tree into stove-length logs, piled the logs into a wheelbarrow, and ferried them back to the yard. Depending on the size of the tree, and the distance, this could take twenty loads or more and all of a day. When that job was done, he'd split the logs into billets and, sometimes with my help, stack them in one-cord piles, eight feet long and four feet tall. These piles, more than two dozen of them, sat at various angles around the yard like stacks of oversized coffins awaiting selection by the bereaved. Altogether, there was enough drying firewood near the house for three or four hard winters into the future, but my father kept felling trees, sawing them up in a roar of chips and fumes, hauling in his harvest of logs. I sometimes saw it as an act of love, as if he had a premonition that the Lord would take him from us at some point in the near future, and he wanted to make sure his family didn't freeze.

When he grew tired of putting up stove wood, or when the precariousness of our money situation came into clear focus for him, my father would set out his traps in the woods, sometimes on land that didn't belong to us. His late friend Mac Kins had taught him how to boil and paraffin the traps to keep the human scent off them. Setting them could be done only in winter, when the animals' coats were full and when, as my father said, "they bring off a good price." Beaver, fox, possum, coyote, otter, woodchuck, mink, fisher cat, weasel—even selling them to a less than fair buyer, these skins brought in significant cash, and, because of that, my father paid as little attention to the dates of the legal trapping season as he did to the NO TRESPASSING signs stapled up on trees at the border between our property and our neighbors'. "No one couldn't say on you what you do and don't do in the woods," he told me, more than once. "Dad Paul told."

He fished, too, but wasn't good at it. He used a bobbin and a worm in our stream, which had never been stocked and on which most other fishermen might have chosen to use flies and light tackle. On days when he was feeling less angry at people, he might take his cane, fishing pole, and a can of worms, go to the far side of town, and fish from the bridge that crossed the Connecticut. There he had better luck. Sometimes he'd bring home a walleye ("wally" he called them) or a large trout. My mother would cook it up, and we'd have a family feast, with a little talk, some wine for the adults and lemonade for me.

In poor weather—sleet or hard rain—he drove to Weedon's Bar, where he nursed a single draft beer for hours and made conversation with an acquaintance or two, people who shared his ideas about the government and the laws. He knew men who belonged to a local militia—the Granitemen, it was called—and he told me that on more than one occasion he'd been asked to join up. But he never did. It required a firearm, for one thing, and for another thing, it was too social an activity for him. Other people involved, meetings, training sessions, talk. Once, in one of his spurts of fatherly affection, he took me to Weedon's with him. We sat at a table, not the bar, and he let me sip from his glass, and listen in on his conversation, and though I was under the legal drinking age, the owner made no complaint about it. My father wasn't much for celebrating holidays or birthdays, but on the day before Christmas he'd go into the woods, cut down a balsam fir, and lean it in one corner of the house for a week. When I was younger, in the years before *True Home and Country,* he would occasionally make me a present. One birthday he carved a small bird out of a piece of maple and set it at my place at the table. He didn't like to be touched or embraced, so I thanked him three times and left it at that. I have the carved bird to this day.

My mother had come from a different background: a family that didn't know the woods, a house with books and women in it, a father who hadn't ended up in jail for crimes no one talked about. Unlike her husband, she could read well, and in certain moods she'd read aloud from the tabloids: stories about a mysterious epidemic of black babies being born in China, or a government conspiracy involving nuclear power, or the affairs of one celebrity or another. Someone famous was secretly homosexual. Someone else had a drug habit, or had given a baby away because it was black, or was actually a mass murderer. And so on. These accounts held the force of biblical truth for her and seemed to reinforce her sense of the chaotic nature of the world, as well as her good fortune in having married a man who liked living apart from it. Sometimes my mother would hum pieces of songs from her childhood, tunes with no real beginning or end, just a twirl of melody. She smoked as much as she could afford to, and drank a bottle of cheap wine when she was lonely, and she met her household responsibilities with some sense of discipline: buying and cooking the food and paying the bills with money orders from the post office. In certain moods, more common as I got older, she'd seem to float out of herself and walk around in a distracted way, mumbling, humming, whispering parts of sentences that made no sense. And she seemed to me to be excited by an odd power: saying and doing things that made her husband want to hit her—though, as far as I could tell, he never did that. In a kind of twisted foreplay, she'd lead him right to the edge of his patience, taunting him, ridiculing him, doing things (dropping cigarette ashes inside the truck when she smoked, boiling the eggs four minutes instead of five) she knew annoyed him, choosing the worst possible moment to remark on the shape of his face, his missing finger, the slant of his ears.

I was a watcher, and I knew all this from years of observation, but what my parents actually thought about most of the time remained a mystery to me. They had a huge fear inside them, Aunt Elaine told me once. They lived as if enemies surrounded them on all sides, and they were terrified of being humiliated—for not being able to pay the property taxes or a doctor's bill, by seeing a newspaper ad for a vacation they could never afford to take, by their clothes, their speech, the cough and stutter of our truck on the downtown streets. "Your father was brought up to be constantly afraid," Aunt Elaine told me. "His father—Dad Paul, you knew him before he was sent upstate, didn't you?—was a very odd man. He had your father with a woman twenty years older than he was and never lived with him until the woman died. He'd visit him at her house once a week, take him out in the yard and teach him to fight. People would drive by and see them wrestling in the dirt. When your father was just a teenager, Dad Paul would take him to visit prostitutes in Montreal. At his job, he'd pump gas and yell at the customers. You'd see him downtown, drunk, pounding on store windows. The whole town was terrified of him."

I'd been afraid of Dad Paul, too, and was still afraid of my father and mother at certain times. But I had decided during the night that no amount of fear—not of dousing or boying, or even of facing or hungering—was going to keep me from the church project. Running down inside me, very deep, was a stream of rebelliousness. For the most part, I worked hard to please my parents and to offend God as little as I could. But there were moments when I found myself talking back to my mother and sometimes even my father, when I'd do something I knew they wouldn't approve of—looking at a magazine in the school library, failing to say my prayers, sneaking a glance at a television set in a store window or at my aunt's house. I had my protective shell of funny talk and shyness, but underneath that lived a wilder me, a girl who would take punishment, and take it, and take it, but who would never let go of herself all the way, never completely surrender.

I heard the rumble of the school bus engine as it rounded the curve (Waldrup Road was so narrow and rutted and so icy in winter that Joanne the bus driver was not required to use it) and tried to make myself stop thinking about things that had no explanation. Joanne smiled at me when I climbed the steps, as if to signal that yes, spring had, in fact, arrived. On either side of the highway the hillsides were starting to go into bud. That dark, that cold, that ice, that snow piling up to the bottom of my bedroom window by mid-January, those gray skies—it took a few weeks of forsythia blossoms and free-running streams to make the people in our part of the world believe the fist of winter had really gone loose. Joanne was the first person to show a smile in springtime, the first spark of hope. I chewed my last bite of gingerbread and smiled back. The warm morning had brought out the wildness in some of my schoolmates. Walking down the aisle, I saw that my friend Cindy wasn't on the bus—sick again, or trouble at home again—and that the boys in the back rows were punching and wrestling with each other as if a small war had broken out there. "Hey," one of them called out, "Margie's teachin' Mr. Bronsante's English class today, ain't ya, Marge! I don't can't say why for!"

"She don't can't of say why for!"

"She can't don't! No at!"

I took my usual seat midway down the aisle on the right and made a study of the smaller river as we went along our route. Beyond the metal bridge the bus made a loop through what I thought of as the close-together houses and then turned back onto Main Street and rumbled past St. Mark's.

"Hey, it's Margie's office!" the same boy yelled.

"It's where at she works of now!"

"She don't can't say why for!"

The fact that they knew about my new job meant Cindy had already told someone, but that didn't matter much to me. Cindy wasn't the kind of person you gave secrets to for holding. And, in any case, I heard the voices at the back of the bus as if from a great distance. Little mice squeaking in the bushes. Just seeing the work site made me happy, just feeling the soreness in my hands and shoulders. I caught sight of Sands as we passed. He was sitting on the rectory steps in the morning sunlight, so still he seemed to be sleeping. I would work twice as hard that day, I told myself, to make up for the fact that I'd missed. If he asked about it, I'd tell him I'd felt sick, that there was no phone in the house, no way to call and tell him. I'd ask him not to fire me off.

It was a testing day at school. With the rest of my class I sat over the state booklet all morning, filling in squares with a number-two pencil. Geometry—which I liked and was good at. Vocabulary. Social studies. Reading comprehension. A fog of anxiety hung over the rows of seats—it meant staying back or not staying back for some of the others—but I had gotten fair grades that year and testing days were the best part of school for me: no answering questions aloud; no chance of a teacher making you stand up and give a presentation. At lunch, Aaron Patanauk sat diagonally across the long table from me, close enough to say something when the other kids had left. "That's a devil's church you're making now, everybody says it. You're a she-devil."

Aaron and his family, including his uncle Cary, had gone to Pastor Schect's church for a time and probably believed things like that, but I knew he was just teasing. "Boys don't of know," I said.

"Your boss is a boy, what I could hear."

"Not the kind as you."

"That's right," Aaron said happily. He took hold of his tray and stood up. "I'm white."

"And skinny."

"Not everywheres."

At the end of the day, with my books and papers stuffed into the pack, I walked from school into town, and when I reached St. Mark's, Sands was standing there, waiting. Instead of lying I said, "I'm sorry at not being for work. I won't again."

"You feeling okay?"

"Okay, sure."

"It's not too hard for you."

"Not ever."

"All right, I made a couple more dump runs yesterday, so in another few days we can start getting ready for the walls. Get your boots on."

"I'll be to paying you for them."

"I'm not worried."

"You're not going to fire me off?"

"Probably not. We'll see how you work today."

He smiled, so that I wondered if he could be joking. I changed what was on my feet and started filling the truck bed with the broken mortar and slate and small pieces of stone.

"Whoa," he said. "Whoa, Laney. You can't keep up that pace. Take it slow."

But I worked like a plow horse that afternoon, not stopping to rest until Sands forced me to, packing stones and scrap into the pickup as if my survival in this world depended on it.

Ten

And my life did depend on it, I see that now. The work saved me. Little by little, day by day, I started to know stone, to understand the fault lines along which a piece could be broken with a single hammer strike and the ways two stones could best be fit together in a wall. I learned how to make mortar by adding water to the powdery gray mix that came in eighty-pound bags (Sands had to lift those). I learned to be careful opening the bags with the shovel blade because the dust would burn your eyes, and to clean the shovel, hoe, and wheelbarrow immediately to keep the mortar from hardening there.

Sands showed me these things with a teacher's patience, and seemed kind enough, but he was a mystery, too. He talked only a little more than my parents. Concentrating on setting a stone in place, or on sawing and nailing pieces of wood to make the frame for the thick lower section of the walls, he seemed to me to be working out some problem in the center of himself, and I suspected it had nothing to do with what he called "the cathedral." I studied him the way I studied all the people in my life, noticing the changes of his mood, the times when the edge of his patience came into view, even small physical details like the sickle-shaped scar on the top of his right forearm and the small flourish he made with his hand whenever he set down a tool, as if he was brushing bad air away from it.

Sometimes when I arrived at the site in the afternoon I'd find him sitting on the rectory steps with his eyes closed, very still and quiet. It reminded me of the glimpse I'd had of him from the school bus that one morning. "Just praying, sort of," he said when I asked about it. "Just a little internal relaxation. My parents are both gone. Sometimes I send them a thank-you."

I wanted to ask him other questions about his life, but I made a promise to myself not to do that. I brought lunch in a paper bag—a peanut butter sandwich, usually—and he'd share his cookies or fruit for our snack, and sometimes, on Saturday especially, take me into town to Art and Pat's for soup or a sandwich. But even sitting beside me at the counter there, or on what had been the front steps of St. Mark's, he talked only a little, and mainly about the work. I began to understand that the project was more than a job for him, in something like the same way it was more than a job for me. But I was too shy then, too afraid of making a mistake, to ask him about that.

There was hardly any anger in him, and after a time I started to come slowly around to believing that maybe he was a good man, or at least, as Aunt Elaine promised, that he wouldn't hurt or cheat me. I went to sleep thinking about the work, and woke up thinking about it, and suffered through Tuesdays, Thursdays, and Sundays, half-alive, just doing what I had to do.

It wasn't long before word spread through the town that something other than a regular church was being built where St. Mark's had stood. I worried Pastor Schect would hear the news and try to make me quit, and every Sunday I rode to the service with a gnawing fear inside me. But for some reason that didn't happen. Pastor Schect didn't live in our town, and it's possible he didn't hear about Sands's project, or, if he did, he wasn't made aware that one member of his congregation was working there. I doubt my parents would have told him. In school, the reaction was mixed. Some of the girls assured me it was a devil's chapel or the wrong kind of work for a girl. Some of the boys thought it was cool, a good skill to learn, and they asked if Sands was hiring. Once, someone drove past and yelled "Jews!" out the window of a pickup truck.

Sands didn't seem to care what people were saying. If passersby stopped on the sidewalk and watched us, he'd say hello or wave a hand and go on working. When a reporter from the newspaper came to do an interview, he stepped aside and patiently answered her questions for fifteen minutes—I watched the way he stood at a slight angle to her, as if too shy to make eye contact—then he made me pose for a photograph, standing beside him. (I saw myself in the local paper at the 112 Store but didn't buy a copy, and didn't mention it to my parents.) When a delivery truck from Warners' brought more bags of mortar mix, and the driver said, "You're another nut like all the rest of the nuts around here, aren't ya?" Sands smiled and gave him a five-dollar tip, and every time the man passed by the site after that he'd sound his horn. I know now that, in films and on TV, small-town life is often made to seem like a kind of lesser version of real grown-up living, the people simple, eccentric, and unsophisticated, ignorant of the larger world. It's not really that way. But it is true that news spreads fast and that local events carry more weight than they might in a big city. In that town, in those days, an outsider who had a ponytail and a girl helper and who was building some kind of religious structure on the commercial strip— that was a story to put in second place, behind the tragedy of the disappearing girls.

At the start, when we had just been clearing rubble and moving piles of stones, my arm and back muscles were sore every day when I woke up. Even with the gloves, there were blisters and then calluses on my hands, and I didn't like that. But by the time we'd moved on to the next stage of work—repairing the foundation wall and the floor where the explosion had been—the soreness had mostly disappeared.

I helped Sands lay down a chalk-line perimeter of the cathedral, a "footprint," he called it, which was smaller than the footprint of the church, and more intricate. Then wood arrived on a lumberyard truck and I helped him make the frames that would hold the concrete in place when we repaired the foundation. Every day when I showed up for work, he had a new tool to give me, sometimes still in its plastic casing: a trowel, a carpenter's belt, a hammer, a measuring tape, a square, a small stone chisel and then a larger one. He built two sawhorses and let me use the circular saw to cut lumber—watching me carefully at first to make sure I wouldn't slice off a finger or a hand, and then leaving me on my own.

It wasn't long before two of the walls came up as high as my knees, and in my mind I could begin to connect the work Sands and I did every day to the drawings he showed me—the twelve-foot-tall stone walls and arched windows, the various roof lines intersecting at neat angles.

At times—usually just when things seemed to be going well between us, when the work was progressing, when I'd learned something new, when I felt close to him—Sands would put a sour drop into my mood by trying to correct my speech. "Say, 'Can I use the saw again?' Laney, not 'Can I saw for another?' Okay?"

"Sure," I said.

"Say, 'Is it time to put the tools away?' Not 'Can we finish on the tools?' All right?"

"Sure," I said. "Thanks." But instead of changing, I relied, as much as possible, on a strategy of one-word sentences.

The cathedral filled my life. I ate better, thanks to his snacks and our trips to town. My arms grew stronger. In school, partly because of the picture in the newspaper, I'd become something of a minor celebrity, a curiosity in a positive way for once. There was still mockery and meanness, but not as much. I learned how to make a ninety-degree cut, to nail two boards snugly together, to anticipate what Sands was going to do and set a sawhorse in place, or move the extension cord, or carry the saw over to him, or set up the wheelbarrow for mixing mortar. If he was looking for a certain-size stone, I hurried off to find it. When he asked for sixteen-penny staging nails, I knew what they were and where to get them. When he needed the saw plugged in or the sawhorses set a certain distance apart, I did that. "It comes natural to you," he said once when he was in a talkative mood. "You're a natural worker." And every time he said something like that I felt as though I was wrapping the words in paper and setting them in a neat stack inside myself, gold coins in a vault.

After two weeks of work, Sands gave me an advance—twenty dollars—and told me that if I didn't use the money to buy some nice clothes for myself, he'd fire me.

"I now should to pay you off for the boots for part."

"No, you shouldn't. You didn't hear me. Buy yourself some clothes. And don't give it to your parents, their share is coming."

So I used the money to buy a skirt and a pretty blue shirt at the secondhand store in town, got up early to put them on, and changed out of them after school in the rectory bathroom and carried them home in my backpack after work so my parents wouldn't see. For those weeks at least, their mood stayed good, or at least neutral. There was no more boying, no dousing, no conversations about my job. I wondered if Aunt Elaine had spoken to them, or if they'd just had a talk with each other and come to the conclusion that some money once a month was better than no money at all.

But then my mother—who would periodically go through my drawers and closet—found the skirt and the shirt and started to wonder what other secrets I was keeping from her, and my parents' mood made a bad shift. By then, the money from my father's check was running out; my mother mentioned that once, then a second time. I watched my father when he came into the house from his day in the woods, noticed that his eyes went immediately to the center of the table, looking to see if I'd been paid and had set the green bills there for him to count. I'd told my mother I'd be paid after working four weeks, and I could feel them watching me, counting days. In hindsight I can see that my mother wanted the money from my work but didn't want what went with it: the fact that bringing home a regular income would give me a new status in the family, make me more important in my father's eyes. She'd always had a taste for ugly remarks, but at that point she started to use her razor tongue more often. "Majie the church builder comes home now from work, hi, Majie." And "That's a devil's church you're building, you Majie. Everybody says so, girl you. Wait till when Pastor Schect hears." But there was a way in which her remarks could no longer dig deep into me. They couldn't reach as far as the neatly wrapped compliments Sands had given me. She sensed that, too, and turned up the volume: "Ugly Majie with her little skirt to show fat legs. What boy wants a stone lifter girl, ugly Majie?"

"Aaron has a like for me. At school."

"Aaron Patanauk? Yah, he has a like. Real like. Like for what's between your legs. Even ugly Majie has one of them."

My father changed, too, but in a different direction. Twice, on afternoons when I wasn't working, he let me accompany him into the woods. He showed me places where he'd set the traps when winter came and showed off how much he knew about the trees—that a certain kind of edible mushroom grew near oak trees but never near ash or maple; that some people made a drink out of the sap of the white birch; that if you ever needed to make a fire in winter, or in rain, there was usually dry deadwood on the lower part of a spruce or hemlock. Popple burned cool but was good for cleaning off the inside of the stovepipe. Hickory gave the best heat. Beech you had to cover and dry for two years before you burned it. On these outings there was something close to kindness in him. I knew that his own father had taught him similar things, and I knew how much he'd adored Dad Paul, and I had the feeling, maybe only because I wanted to, that he was trying to reach out some warm hand to me through a curtain of hard memories.

Though I worried about it constantly, I didn't raise the subject of my pay with Sands. Long before I ever met him I'd made a rule for myself never to tell outsiders anything about my family, and though

I accepted his offer of a ride after work, I never let him drive me beyond the 112 Store and tried not to give him any indication of what the money would mean to us.

Two more weeks passed—eleven working days in all. Two large walls and a small one stood as tall as the middle of my thigh by then, and I was beginning to have a better sense of the shape of the building and of Sands's personality.

One day, when I had been working with him nearly a month and we were taking our afternoon break, he said, "You don't have to kill yourself, you know." I thought, for just one moment, that he meant it literally. The fathers of two schoolmates had killed themselves within a week of each other when I'd been in fifth grade. On Labor Day weekend the year before, a boy in ninth grade had jumped to his death from the big bridge. Showing off, some people said, but I knew him in school and didn't think so. On particularly bad days, I had thought about it. I assumed everyone had thought about it at one time or another.

When spring finally came for us, it came quickly. The last small piles of grainy snow were suddenly gone, the maple syrup lines and buckets disappeared. At lunchtime, the sun was almost hot. One day, Sands and I were sitting on the piece of marble that had been St. Mark's front step. He'd brought me a blueberry muffin, and I was drinking a warm Coke. While we were eating, an old man and an old woman, walking arm in arm, stopped on the sidewalk, facing us. The man nodded. Sands nodded back, and then the couple walked a few steps closer.

"What is it going to be once you're finished?" the woman asked. In the mild air she was wearing a wool coat.

"A cathedral," I told her, because I loved to hear myself say the word.

"What kind?"

I looked at Sands. He wasn't a particularly neat eater, I had noticed, and he was brushing crumbs off the front of his T-shirt. "Church of the Loving God," he said, looking up at them through his thick spectacles.

It was the first time I'd heard those words. I studied his mouth, trying to see if he'd meant it as a joke.

The old man and the old woman made identical faces, mouths down, eyes squinting. "Catholic?" the man said suspiciously.

"Denomination of love," Sands told him.

The man narrowed his eyes still further. "Some cult?"

"It's just a private cathedral, a place to come and sit. I might make it available to the public some hours if people want."

"Who would want it?" the man asked.

Sands shrugged his big shoulders and gave a two-second smile. "Old retired stoneworkers," he said. "Farmers, carpenters, insurance salesmen, nurses."

"A place for the aged?" the woman asked. "A senior center?"

"Seniors, juniors, anyone who wants to."

"If you leave it unlocked, they'll come and steal the chalice for drug money," the man warned Sands. They stood there another minute, examining the partly built walls and the damaged rectory, running their eyes over the skin of Sands's face, his ponytail, his girl helper. Then they nodded in tandem, turned, and shuffled on.

"Is that what you're making it on?" I asked when they'd walked away.

"I'm surprised you haven't asked before."

"I'm a mind for my own business, is what."

"And it's not your business to ask that? After all the sweat you've put in?"

It came into my mind to make a joke—Sands seemed always so serious—and I battled inside myself for a few seconds then said, "Sweat and a little of blood," but he didn't laugh.

"Even more so, then. You weren't curious?"

"Curious killed nine cats."

"You really believe that, Laney?"

"No," I said, because I thought it was what he wanted me to say. It was hard to make a joke with him. And it was clear I'd be wiser to just keep quiet about things. It felt like I had wandered off the safe route and sprung a trap on myself and now my leg was caught. Sands was watching me, the tip of his nose and his lips moving just the smallest bit, the way a cat does when it's sniffing. I worried that something I might say would lead him to fire me, and if I were fired then it would be like a furnace exploding underneath the little house of satisfaction I'd built over the past few weeks. So I just looked back at him and said nothing.

"How many places do you know where you can go and sit and be quiet?" he asked. "Let your mind be quiet?"

"My room for late if no one wants being up then. The stream in the woods. Those of two places."

"How many churches do you know where you can do that?"

"They locked every of them. The man said for why."

"None, right. Sometimes you have to formalize things, to have a practice, in a certain kind of space. To have a public structure that stands for something other than making money."

I looked at him. He had a crumb of blueberry muffin caught in the corner of his lips.

"You have to take a little time to appreciate being alive and breathing instead of wondering what you have to do next all the time. You have to stop and do nothing for a little while every day."

I thought then that he must be slightly crazy. There was something in his eyes and voice when he said those things, some note of urgency or pain. It might be, I thought, that he *was* crazy, in the religious way, like the people at Pastor Schect's, and he wanted to convert me to some new religion. It would be a waste of time, I almost told him. They've already made me have one religion. They've already converted me.

He pushed the glasses back up against his nose and waited for me to speak.

"All right," I said. "Now we have at to work again by now, don't we?"

"No, we don't."

He seemed suddenly angry. It was very strange. All the times I'd expected him to be angry, he hadn't been. When I broke a shovel handle by accidentally dropping a stone on it, trying to lift more than I was able to; in the beginning, when I hadn't known to wash out the wheelbarrow right away, and the mortar dried in it, and we'd lost an hour chipping it off. Neither those things nor a dozen other small mistakes I'd made—none of it had brought out this tone of voice in him.

"No," he said again, in the same forceful way. "At this point you should understand what it is you are making."

"All right," I said. "I do."

"I don't think so."

I had words coming up fast and couldn't catch them in time. "You just don't want for paying on me, that's all. Now you're in mad, because you don't want for paying on me. I'm doing at the work as hard for I can, and——"

"I'll pay you. Of course I'm going to pay you. Your aunt already has the money as a matter of fact. You've been working like a team of oxen, you learn faster than anyone I've ever seen, why wouldn't I pay you? What are you talking about?"

"Why else being so mad then?"

"Who's mad?"

"You. And to convert me."

After a second or two of watching me, Sands reached out and put his hand on top of my right arm. It was, after the hello and good-bye handshakes in the 112 Store parking lot, only the third time he'd touched me. He kept his hand there for a moment, then squeezed gently and removed it. "I'm not mad," he said in a different voice. "And I'm not into converting, you or anyone. I have nothing to convert you to." He made what I thought of as a bashful sound, almost a laugh, but not really. "I'm sorry."

I think it was the first time in my life that an adult apologized to me, and coming as it did on top of the worry about not being paid, and

Sands's unexpected anger, it brought up a quick spurt of tears. I blinked them away.

"I'm sorry," Sands said a second time. "I just wanted you to see something. I went too fast. I do that all the time. I'm not great at talking to people. I have all these thoughts bunching up inside my head and then they come out like a dam bursting or something. I'm sorry. You're a great worker. You just go around every minute like you have to work twice as hard and twice as well as any normal person—"

"You'll fire me off the job if I wouldn't. I don't want being fired off."

"I'd be crazy to fire you."

"I like on this job."

"I'm glad. But . . . who's this now?"

As if in a scene from a bad dream, I looked up and saw my father standing on the sidewalk, just where the old man and woman had been a few minutes earlier.

He was wearing the floppy leather fedora, color of a potato skin, that he put on for special occasions: the funeral of his one real friend, Mac Kins; Easter service at Pastor Schect's; and on the first day of school every September, when, even into my high school years, he drove me in his truck instead of letting me take the school bus, and got out and watched me go up the front walk, as if there might be evil men lurking in the bushes who wanted to kidnap me and kill me or sell me into slavery. He hadn't shaved around the edges of his beard in a day or two and the reddish stubble looked like a blood shadow on his throat. His eyes seemed even farther back in his head than usual, focused on something else there, and I thought, for a moment—I don't know why such things came to my mind—that he'd come to kill Sands, or me, or both of us. I sensed instantly that something had changed in him, and I'm almost certain now that my mother had been working on him, talking to him about me, my job, the skirt and blouse, the lack of any income from what I said I was doing.

It was a warm day, but my father had a flannel shirt on, red and black checked, and he'd rolled up the sleeves so the muscles of his forearms showed like cables under the skin. He had his good overalls on, and his work boots, stained with chain-saw oil. In those clothes, and standing there with one shoulder lower than the other and his eyes peering out from another world, and the hat brim pulled down, he reminded me exactly of Dad Paul. I saw that he had gone out and bought chewing tobacco, like Dad Paul, and pressed it back into his cheek. It had been three years since I'd seen my grandfather, but the memory of him was etched on my inner eye. His hands were always moving, and yet when he looked at you this way, the air around him was like the hum of death, an emptiness, a stillness that seemed to echo a violent scream. When he'd been a free man, Dad Paul hardly ever spoke to me, though I believed that if I'd been a boy he would have taken me into the woods and taught me the things he'd taught my father, and taught me to fight and whistle between my fingers, and how to talk to girls. He had—I would learn later—been discharged from the army for repeated violent behavior, been fond of going to see the street whores in Montreal when he was young and then picking up men when he was older—a great shame among people like us. He'd fathered a child with a woman almost twice his age, a coworker at the mill. He chewed tobacco, often spitting it in the yard so that my mother yelled at him about it one time and afterward my father smashed dishes in the kitchen sink, then went away for three days and we wondered if he was ever coming home. There were times when it seemed like Dad Paul was half-tree or half-animal, just a pillar of urges and needs dressed up in human disguise.

Dad Paul would visit unannounced, at strange times. I'd wake before anyone else, in the morning darkness, and find him sitting with his slightly rounded shoulders at the kitchen table, waiting silently for someone to make him coffee. When there was a bad snowstorm he'd often venture out on the roads in his old powder-blue Dodge pickup, cement blocks in the bed for better traction, and come fast up our driveway with snow splashing out from under his tires, and he'd work in silence, shoveling furiously while the snow was still falling. He'd leave after he'd exhausted himself, and soon the wind would cover over his work and my mother would laugh about that. In warm weather he'd come and split wood, shirt off, his chest coated in a fine fur of white hair, muscles running beneath the skin. "Dad Paul has a like of to work," my father often said. "A true like."

To me, on that May afternoon, the signs were all bad—the hat, the tobacco, the way I was thinking of Dad Paul, the look in my father's eyes, the feeling I had that his mood had turned suddenly vicious. All bad. He shifted the lump of tobacco around in his cheek, glanced at me, then fixed his eyes on Sands and spit on the sidewalk.

"My dad," I said, the words slipping out of me in a patch of sound that was as weak as a dying flame whispering in a woodstove. "That man is my dad."

Sands stood up. My father, who was not without a sense of manners, took off his hat and stepped closer. "This here's Majie, my the girl," he said.

Next to my father Sands looked like a giant. He wiped his right hand on his pants and held it out, and though I knew my father hated to, he shook hands.

"Good to meet you," Sands said, pushing the glasses back against his eyebrows. "Your daughter is a good worker, a good girl."

My father turned his head to the side and spit again, then lifted his eyes to Sands's. "Came for that she gots paid."

"Really?" Sands said, and I wanted to go hide someplace then because what I heard in his voice was a note with no fear in it. A drop of sarcasm, a little curiosity, but not the smallest hint of fear. "I thought maybe you came to admire the work she's been doing."

I saw a twitch in the muscle near my father's left eye. I wanted to say something to make Sands understand.

"Don't take kind to who don't pay."

"What makes you think I haven't paid her?"

My father turned to me. "You, Majie. You had on it?"

I shook my head, barely able to. My father spit again. His eyes dropped to the hat, which he was holding in his two hands, then he raised them to Sands's face and I saw something in them that I had never seen before, even in his worst moods: I saw clearly then that he could kill a person. It was written there as if in letters. I remembered him taking me once to check his traps in late winter and coming upon a squirrel caught in one of them, still alive. "Don't to look away on it," he ordered me when I made a noise and turned my eyes. He found a branch, broke it in two over his knee, put the pieces to either side of the squirrel's neck, and snapped the bone there as casually as if he were taking the plastic cap off a milk bottle. I watched him looking at Sands and I thought of that.

"I paid her aunt," Sands said. "This morning. That was the agreement."

"Not 'ith me."

"No, not with you. But then, you're not working for me so I don't give the money to you and I don't make agreements with you. Would you want to see the work she's done, or wouldn't you?"

"Enh," my father said. It was a syllable that meant no, and, as always, it was accompanied by a quick sideways and downward jerk of his head. Sands leaned toward him an inch. The difference between them was the difference between a beech tree, its bark smooth and its branches horizontal to the earth and strong enough to hold ten people, and an old black cherry tree with scaly dark bark and a crooked trunk and the branches weak and way up out of sight. Like a man lost at sea and rationing his food, my father kept a small daily supply of words. It seemed to me he had used them up and that he would shift one of two ways then, either to some action or deeper into himself. He stood there for what seemed a long time, his eyes just to the left of Sands's face, his fingers pinching the hat brim. And then he swung his eyes slowly to me, like a frog following a fly. "Douse ya," he said, so quiet I wondered if Sands had heard, and he turned his back and started walking. I watched his legs go, his left shoulder tilted down, and I wondered where he'd parked his truck, and why he hadn't driven there, and I pictured what he was going to do to me when I got home. After his recent kindness, it felt like he had slapped me, or kicked me again, and a big sadness welled up under the skin of my face.

Sands watched my father until he'd turned the corner and was out of sight, and then he slapped his hands together a few times the way he usually did before he went back to work. There was more force to it than I remembered seeing before.

We nailed up the staging on one side of what would be the south wall, eight feet high and braced in all directions so we could lean a ladder against it and lay different-size stones on it and it would hold steady. We needed the rest of the afternoon to do that. While we worked, Sands did not speak to or look at me, and I was sure then that I'd be fired. A boss didn't need crazy people coming to the work site demanding money. As sometimes happened in those years, my thoughts started on a downhill ride, one bad thing after the next: I'd be fired, I'd be doused, my father didn't love me after all, I'd never find work like this again. And so on. It required all my energy to keep working underneath that hard waterfall of bad imagining.

Shortly before five o'clock, Sands said, "That's enough for today," the signal for us to start putting away tools. With the work site right there on the main street, and with things the way they were in the town, he knew as well as I did that we couldn't leave anything out overnight, not even a hose or a dented wheelbarrow. There was an entrance into the rectory basement, no window, padlocked, and we brought the wheelbarrow and saws and other tools in there, set them on the damp floor, and pulled the string on the lightbulb, then closed and padlocked the door. I kept waiting for him to tell me I was fired, but he was silent and seemed distracted.

At the end of the afternoon Sands always stood for a few minutes, looking over the work we'd done. Ordinarily, I loved that part of the day. I took up a position a few yards away from him, behind and at an angle, so I could look at the work, and also at him. That day, though, I could feel the bad thoughts crawling around inside me like carpenter ants in a rotted piece of wood, chewing, destroying, scurrying here and there. Sands didn't look at me and wouldn't turn around. I waited. After he'd run his eyes over the low walls and the new staging, he finally turned to face me, but instead of firing me, he said, "I'm driving to Boston on Sunday, just for the day. Have you ever been?"

I could not get a word to come out of my mouth. A little flame of hope had been lit.

"Have you?"

Boston, Pastor Schect had told us, was a place filled with colored people and prostitutes, men who did not obey God, who spat upon his face and did the devil's work of deceiving him. I managed to shake my head.

"Would you want to come along?"

I felt the word *yes*, like a satanic breath, skipping from side to side at the back of my mouth. I swallowed hard. "We have church for Sundays."

"What about after church?"

"We have food going out for at Mimi's, times."

"What about after that? We can drive there in two and a half hours. I'd get you home by nine at night."

I imagined myself walking in the door of our house at nine o'clock at night.

"Why do you ask me on that?" I said, because I was especially curious about him then. I had seen that he wasn't afraid of my father, and that didn't make sense. Everyone was afraid of my father, everyone except Dad Paul, and, at certain moments, my mother. It made me wonder if Sands might be even more capable of hurting a person than my father was, and it resurrected the idea—which I'd covered over in my thoughts again and again—that he was playing some elaborate trick on me. Whoever was killing the girls did it at the rate of only about one every six months, which meant that he took his time setting up his next victim. It probably also meant that he was someone who didn't seem like a killer, someone very careful and slow and sneaky, the kind of person you could walk past in the grocery store and never worry about.

"Why? Because I'm going to look at a museum. Then out for a meal at an Italian restaurant I like. Nothing would cost you anything. Nothing else would happen."

"If I can't, will you fire me off?"

He just looked at me a moment, his strong arms hanging at his sides, and I saw something else in his face, something close to defeat. He was, I thought, a little bit like the boys in school. They seemed to want something from me they could never come out and just ask for straight. "You're afraid of me still," he said. "After all this time. Either that or you just don't like me."

"Afraid for nothing," I said, but it was a lie and I thought he could probably hear that in my voice.

"But you won't go."

"Can't to."

"Why?"

I shrugged and watched him, waiting for him to fire me. I would run then, I told myself. I wouldn't go back home even for one night.

But he only made a sad smile, just a flash of it, and looked away. "I'll drive you to the store. Your aunt will get the money to you before you come to work again next week, don't worry."

"Friday is a day for work again."

"Right. Friday and Saturday. You'll get it before next Monday."

"And I can to work Friday?"

"You better show up and you better work hard."

It wasn't until we were in the truck that I realized he might have been trying to make one of his halfway-jokes.

In the 112 Store parking lot, with my backpack on my lap and my fingers on the door handle, I said, "Thank you," as I always did. And then I added, "For on the ride and the job too."

"When school gets out you can work more hours if you want. More money, too."

"Thank you," I said a second time, but by then I wasn't sure of my voice anymore. I wanted to say something about my father, to explain him to Sands—the way he looked, the way he talked, the way he acted—to apologize for him and for not being able to go to Boston, but the words just wouldn't come out of my throat.

"And I'll ask you again about Boston. Another time. You'd be welcome to bring along a friend . . . if she's skinny enough to fit on the seat here."

"Okay," I said. I opened the door.

"That was a little joke, but I meant it about the friend."

"All right then."

"What's *dowsha*?" he said when I was standing on the gravel with the door still open.

I squinted my eyes as if he'd said something I hadn't quite heard. The gesture felt to me exactly like telling the lie had felt. It caused a particular kind of sourness to run up into my mouth.

"What your father said to you at the end. 'Dowsha.' What did it mean?"

"I didn't listen on it," I said, and I thanked him again, quickly, before he could say anything else about it or change his mind about my job. I closed the door and walked away.

Eleven

At that time of year, the middle of May, the blackflies fill the air, as Aunt Elaine says, like pepper grains sprayed out of a fire hose. They like the damp, and the cool, and places where the water runs, and they swarm around people's faces as if they've been waiting all winter for the taste of human flesh. Mosquitoes you can hear and kill fairly easily, but blackflies are small, quiet, and quick. The best you can do is swing your arms around or hope for a breeze to push them off. Sometimes they get into your mouth and you swallow one. "The price we pay for living in a great place like this," I often heard people say about the blackflies. They said it, too, about the long winters, the twenty-below-zero nights, about frost heaves on the road, and mud season, and power outages caused by falling trees in ice storms, about the flocks of tourists who come in early October to see the leaves change and clog the roads. There were, I sometimes thought, a lot of high prices to pay for living there.

That afternoon, while I was walking away from the 112 Store along the highway, the blackflies were especially bad. There were times when a driver passing a pedestrian waving arms around her face in May would stop and offer a ride. It is fairly typical of that part of the world, where, even now, strangers often stop to help a stranded driver push a car out of a snowbank, and where, when I was a girl and before the abductions, you'd still occasionally see someone hitchhiking without being afraid. But I never accepted those offers. Even before the girls were taken I had been afraid to do that.

That day no one stopped. With the blackflies swarming around me, I hurried past Warners', and Patanauk's, and the two houses, then made the left onto Waldrup Road and slowed down. I didn't know what effect my father's trip to the work site would have on the mood of the household, but I knew it wouldn't be good. Sometimes he said he'd douse me and then he seemed to forget or have a change of heart. Sometimes, after an embarrassment or an argument or a bad moment with my mother, he'd fall silent for a day or two, and I could feel the anger and the humiliating memory growing inside him. And then he would act. You never knew. My parents were like gasoline spread around a room—there was the sharp smell of danger, the threat that something might erupt, but it could just as easily evaporate as explode.

Lately, my mother had started throwing up in the bathroom—from all the years of drinking wine, I suspected. It hadn't made her any easier to live with. On top of that, my father's mood usually turned sour in spring, when the soft earth and bugs made it more difficult to work the woods, and the uplifted spirits of everyone else formed a sunny background to his belief that life was made up of nothing but disappointment and insult.

I was sure of this: Anything having to do with money carried the potential for trouble. So I wasn't surprised to step into what felt like an ominous quiet in the house. I could smell food being cooked and knew instantly what it was: beans and baked potatoes. That meant we'd come to the point in the month where there wasn't enough money for meat. My father's store of homemade venison sausage had run out. The money from the check had almost run out. This was the worry that had driven him to come to the site; I understood that now. I knew he'd spent money on chewing tobacco that should have been spent on something else, perhaps a pound of bacon or hamburger, but that he hadn't wanted to face Sands without that prop, without his good hat; hadn't wanted to drive his loud, rusted-out, ten-year-old truck to the site and ask somebody he didn't even know to pay his daughter an amount he wasn't even sure of. It had been a big event for him—dressing up, going to a store, leaving his cane in the truck, and forcing himself to walk through town to where his daughter was employed, while he wasn't and hadn't been for years. The few minutes with Sands—so big and young and unintimidated—had been an enormous humiliation for him, and it had been smoldering in his mind all the hours since. I knew that without looking directly at him where he sat, his chair angled away from the table, the hat and tobacco gone, his eyes cast down and to the side and fixed there, while his fingers jiggled on his legs.

I helped my mother by putting out the bowls and spoons and then serving the food into them. My father didn't turn his chair to face us as he ate and made no eye contact. No meat, no meat, no meat—that was the chorus running through his thoughts, I was sure of it. That and the idea of Aunt Elaine with cash money in her hand while his family ate beans and baked potatoes. I kept my eyes down. I listened to the sound of fork tines scraping the potato skins for the last bits of white; I heard peeper frogs whistling in the stream outside. It took us only minutes to finish the meal. I brought the bowls to the sink and washed them, turning them upside down on a dish towel to dry. My father went out to his woodpile. My mother told me to light in a Prime, then sat tightly squeezed into a corner of the ratty sofa, surrounded by smoke.

I retreated to my room and lay down on my stomach so that the pillow pressed against the place where I felt hungry. Outside my window, the peepers' song moved up and down in a slow, whistling rhythm and I could hear the *bang . . . bang* of my father's maul, regular as a clock. I imagined going to Boston in Sands's truck and eating with him in a restaurant there. I thought he probably wasn't playing any kind of a trick on me, but even if he was, it almost didn't matter.

Twelve

It seemed strange to me that we went to the service that Sunday, because usually when my parents had come to the end of their money for the month they stayed home. Even if we skipped the luxury of the breakfast buffet at Mimi's—which we surely would—there was the two dollars for the collection basket and the cost of gas to consider. But when I'd been awake only a few minutes, my mother put her head in past the doorjamb and told me to dress for church, so I did. We made the forty-minute drive in a light, steady rain, the smoky inside of the cab as gray as the overcast sky. In the Quonset hut there were only about half as many people as on a typical Sunday, and I suspected some of the other families had run out of money, too. On Pastor Schect's face I thought I could see ripples of anger bubbling his skin from the inside, pressing against his eyes, as if the rows of empty chairs were taunting him.

As he often did, Pastor Schect began the service by walking back and forth in front of us, head lowered, arms hanging limp at his shoulders, his voice little more than a mumble that seemed to evaporate into the air before it reached the arched metal ceiling. But after a time—and this, too, was typical—as if he had needed only to warm up his vocal cords, Pastor lifted his eyes and strengthened his voice, and stood still facing us. He raked his wounded gaze across the empty chairs and the handful of attentive faces. "Jesus Christ the Lord of Lords, what did he do when there were sinners amongst the youths nearby him? *What did he do?!*" Pastor Schect shouted those last words, the veins in his neck and forehead bulging and his dyed hair making small jumps on his head. A little boy in front laughed at the sight. Pastor Schect looked straight at the boy and shouted, "He stoneth them, say!" so forcefully that the boy burst into tears and wrapped both arms around his mother's leg. Pastor Schect went over and stood behind the homemade pulpit. He slapped the palm of his hand down on it, and the *bang!* echoed around the church. "Stonethed them! Let he cast the first stone! Let he!" Pastor jabbed himself in the chest with a straight index finger. "It would be better for the children, say, if they had a mill hung around their necks and were dropped in the river, it tells in the Bible. Isn't it?"

Men and women nodded solemnly, but I noticed that a certain kind of stillness had fallen across my parents. They weren't moving at all; they seemed not to be breathing. The silence came off them like the charred smell after a house fire, and I puzzled over it, almost to the point of not paying attention to Pastor Schect's words. Something was different. Something wasn't right.

"So we come forth in saving penance," he was saying. "When you have a headache, you are saving penance, say! When you cut yourself with a knife. When you bang yourself and hurt, the pain is for a penance. Bad backs are for a penance, say. Bad backs! All the cancers are our penances being saved, say!"

He stopped. He lifted his face to the ceiling, pushed out his lips, and his eyes seemed to go as empty as the dozens of empty chairs. His voice dropped so that he was almost humming the words. "But sometimes that God-given penance isn't enough, say. Not enough. Sometimes the Lord of Gods wants more out of us. Suffer the little children, said Jesus Christ the Lord of Lords. Suffer the little children to our penance!"

He closed his eyes as if in ecstasy, and at that moment I understood where everything was leading, why my parents had come to the service despite the money situation, why they were so still, what Pastor Schect was talking them toward. One drop of urine went into my underwear. I squeezed my legs together. I made my hands tight into fists and fought down an urge to sprint for the door.

It was three or four more seconds before Pastor Schect went up on his toes and shouted, "Which parents among them, say, have a penance child today? A sacrifice! A child who must be *faced*!?"

I noticed that my father's arm moved a few inches, then flapped back down at his side. I felt a sweep of relief for all of one second before I realized my mother was raising her arm, so slowly that I wanted to reach out and take hold of it. I watched Pastor Schect's eyes turn and fix on my mother's hand, her fingers pressed tightly together, the elbow straight, the back of the hand slanted toward her as if she was a smart pupil who knew the answer. I squeezed my legs and hands to keep myself from running.

"Come ye then, say," Pastor Schect yelled in a victorious voice. There wouldn't be much money in the woven basket on that day, but there would be a facing. A facing would help his reputation spread. Soon the multitudes of grateful parents would come, having found, at last, a God-sent man who could help them tame their children. That was Pastor Schect's entire strategy, a strategy that came from the fact that, deep down inside him, he could not bear to see a child who was beyond his control. I understand that now. I have thought about it a thousand times during all these years. I've felt the same feelings in myself at bad moments with my own children, maybe all parents feel it—do what I want you to do, don't disobey, don't disregard me—but in him it was children in general, all children, and the feeling was intense beyond describing. He was smart enough to have an intuition that other adults felt the same, and he had staked out his corner of the spiritual territory as the pastor who could fix all those terrible kids, who understood what trouble they caused, what feelings of frustration they raised. He had an answer for that.

From a shelf inside the pulpit he took a plain paper shopping bag and held it over his head. I felt my mother's hand on the back of my neck, the fingers hot. I had a sense—I didn't know where it came from—that my father might shout out "No," just then, might take his wife's hand, remove it from my neck, and tell Pastor Schect that she'd made a mistake, they didn't have such a child, not this week. No. But in all the years we'd been going there for services, no one had ever challenged Pastor Schect, no adult and no child, and in another moment I felt my father's hands on my shoulders, turning me, and I kept my eyes on my mother's denim shirt as we walked out of the aisle and up to the front of the church. I forced myself not to urinate, not to move my eyes from the blue and white threads of the cloth covering my mother's thin back, not to run.

"Name!" Pastor Schect yelled when we were standing in front of him. He had his back to the congregation now and I could see them studying me, wondering what my terrible sin had been.

"Majie Richards," my mother said, almost proudly.

"Sin?"

"Disobey," my father said, but I heard a tremble in his voice, something to match the muscles in my legs. For one last second I hoped he might rescue me.

Pastor Schect shook the brown grocery bag once, violently, so it opened with a snapping sound. He lifted it up high again to allow the congregation a better view. And then, with a ceremonial flourish, he brought the bag down over my head so the open edges of it rested against my collarbones and the back of my neck. There was a small hole near my mouth, but even taking in short, fast breaths, I couldn't quite get enough air through it. I felt my mother's fingers holding the bag in place, and I knew Pastor Schect must have waved his hand then, because I heard a scraping of chair legs against the concrete floor, and clanking metallic noises as the chairs were pushed back and knocked against each other. I heard footsteps, a little girl starting to cry. A few drops of pee went into my underwear. "If ever you get faced," Aaron had told me once, "just keep your eyes and your mouth real tight closed and pull down your chin so somebody by accident or on purpose don't hit your apple." So I did that. I listened to the sounds of the shoes and boots on the cement floor. The girl was still crying. Someone stopped in front of me. I felt my parents' hands go tight on my arms and then heard a woman's voice, "Go, sin no more." The woman jammed two rigid fingers hard into the bag and hit me just beneath my right eye. I made a small noise; I couldn't help myself.

"Go, sin no more," a man said next. He poked me hard, too, right in the eyelid, and I cried out and tried to lift my arms but they were held down against my sides.

"Silence, sinner," Pastor Schect ordered.

One after the next—probably fifteen adults on that day—people came up and poked two straight fingers into the paper covering my face. There were some who didn't hit with much force or who purposely aimed for my forehead, where it would hurt least. But my lips were hit several times, my right eye, my cheeks, the tip of my nose. Someone hit me in the throat, and I coughed, squeezed my hands so tight that the nails, even worn down by the stonework, cut into my callused palms. The last person, a woman muttering words I didn't understand, hit me straight in the mouth and I felt the tip of one fingernail go between my lips and hard against my teeth. I tasted blood. I couldn't stop crying then, couldn't stop my legs from shaking.

Pastor Schect made me wait inside the darkness of the bag, let me wonder if there were more people in line or if he would call them all up for a second turn. I felt my father squeeze my right wrist, three quick squeezes, a signal that it was over, and then Pastor shouted out, "Go, Majie Ree-shard, sin no more, say!" And the people answered him in unison. *"Go, sin no more!"* And I felt the bag—it was torn and bloodstained by then—lifted up over my head. The light hurt the one eye I could keep open. I gulped in big breaths of air. I couldn't look at anyone. Pastor touched me on top of the head in a blessing, and then I was aware of nothing else until I was outside the church with my mother and father, and I could see my father's truck, a blurred red shape in the rain. My lips and nose were bleeding, but not very badly. I couldn't see out of my right eye and felt the throbbing pain in a dozen different places. But I didn't cry and I didn't speak and I didn't turn my good eye to look at them.

"There's not no money for Mimi's today but at Pastor's he's having people on to coffee and so."

It seemed to me that my mother expected an answer from me, but I wouldn't give it.

"No," my father said, after a few seconds. "To home." We got in the truck and pulled out of the lot so fast the tires spit stones.

The rain stopped. The pain in my face grew stronger, and the smoke from my mother's cigarette made me close both eyes. I didn't let my body touch any part of my parents' bodies. Every time the truck went over a bump in the road the pain ricocheted around the bones of my face, but I kept my mind fixed on the cathedral, the work that waited for me there. I went deep inside myself to a place where the pain seemed distant, and the memory of the humiliation only circled and circled without touching down. I went deep and tried to speak a prayer to God to ask forgiveness for everything I had done wrong in my life. But God's face didn't appear to me then, and the words wouldn't come.

At last, the truck turned onto Waldrup Road and bounced along there, making the pain shoot through my lips and eyes and the skin of my bruised cheeks. I opened my eye just as my father was turning into the driveway, and what I saw, as if in a vision, was Aunt Elaine's car parked in front of our house. My aunt was standing on the front step. I heard my father mutter, and I wondered if he'd turn the truck around and drive away. But he pulled into the yard and snapped the key to off. For one moment we were still and quiet in the cab, the three of us, and I wondered how I would explain myself to my aunt. But then something shifted inside me—I will never understand why it happened then. Maybe the facing was the work of God, after all, a blessing in thick disguise, baptism into a new life. Maybe in a strange, sick way, that's what it was. I followed my mother out the passenger side, but then she hesitated there and I pushed past her toward the front of the house. I felt my parents lagging behind. I forced myself to keep moving forward, stepping through a dense fog of fear and old habit. Aunt Elaine was staring at me. When I reached the steps, she held me away from her at arm's length, running her eyes over my face, then she wrapped her arms around me and hugged me very tight.

Thirteen

For as long as I could remember, I had heard my mother refer to Aunt Elaine as "my sister," though, in fact, they were stepsisters. My mother was the child of a man her own mother never spoke about. She'd been eighteen months old when her mother moved in with Aunt Elaine's father. The stepsisters were as different from each other as two people could possibly be. When my mother was paying for food at the market, or cooking something at the stove, or sitting poor-postured in the passenger seat of the pickup, it often seemed to me she was only half-present, that her real self, her spirit, lay hidden behind the disguise of her face and slim body. In certain kinds of light, I saw her as a skeleton or a ghost, the clothes and skin and flesh and hair just things that had been pasted on and could fall away with one shake. Even her eyes seemed to turn inward, most of her attention focused backward and down, as if she was looking for herself in there, or looking for a way out of the person she had become.

Aunt Elaine, on the other hand, was like the black bears that passed through our yard in May and June when there wasn't yet enough food for them in the deep woods. Not that she was particularly overweight. It was more a way she had of appearing to control the air around her, just the way the bears seemed to, a complete not-caring about what others thought, a large-scale unselfconsciousness.

When she stood on the front step of our house that day—the day I was faced—there was the sense that you wouldn't be walking past her without something happening. There was a bear on the front step and it had no natural predators. It wasn't so much that she was about to attack you—black bears rarely hurt people—it was just that you somehow couldn't ignore her, and you knew that, and the bear knew it, too.

"What in God's breath happened?" she asked when she had me at arm's length again. But I knew she was sending the question back toward my parents and not at me.

"She tried running out church," my mother said. "Tripped. Gravel. Splat at her face. Big-chest girls like her shouldn't to run."

Aunt Elaine kept moving her nurse's eyes over the marks on me, moving her gaze across my cheeks, my closed eye, the blood on my lips. She was a few inches taller, but only because she was on the first step and I was standing on the dirt. "Is that true, Marjorie?"

I heard my father slam the truck door. My mother was so close I could smell the cigarette smoke on her clothes. "No," I said.

"Majie!" my mother hissed. "No lying, you Majie!"

"Is it true that you fell?"

"No," I said a second time. That word seemed to rise out of me like a bird that had escaped its cage. Ten, fifteen, seventeen years it had been held there behind thin metal lies and now it was out in the air. I said, "I got faced is true." And, really, a new life began for me at that moment.

"What is 'faced'?"

"Faced is tripped on the gravel in your face because you runned," my mother said.

I heard my father spit.

"What is 'faced,' Marjorie? Tell me."

"Faced." I was able to speak that one syllable before my mouth snapped closed and the words that were lined up behind my teeth all died. My good eye went sideways. I was no longer seeing my aunt, but the four shagbark hickory trees that stood next to each other near the stream. They looked, with their fraying dark skin, as if they had been whipped every week of their lives.

Aunt Elaine took my chin gently in her fingers and turned my head back to her. She seemed to ask the question again with her eyes, and I felt the words again, pushing at the inside of my sore lips. The air around my head swirled with pain memories: dousing, hungering, boying. I almost wanted to reach up and swat them away, but then Aunt Elaine gave me the gentlest of shakes and the words broke free. "Faced is how somebody takes a paper bag over you in at the front of church and people come up. The people two-finger you into the bag, hard."

"It in receiving a penance," my father spat out behind me.

"Penance?" Aunt Elaine didn't speak the word, she growled it. To me the sound seemed as hard as a frying pan. "Penance!"

"Right with our religious. No one knows you to understand it so."

I could see Aunt Elaine only as a blur in front of me. There was something like electricity coming off her body. I half expected the brown and gray hair to go standing up away from her scalp. "I'm going to tell you now about understand," she said, in a voice that wobbled with fury. "We're going in the house and we're going to sit at the table, all of us, and I'm going to tell you about *understand*."

I had never in my life heard a person speak that way to my father.

Aunt Elaine held the door open with her arm. There was something like a command in the way she did it. I went inside and stood next to the table because there weren't enough chairs for all of us. My mother came in, my father. Aunt Elaine let the screen door slap and followed my parents inside. She seemed, at that moment, three times as big as I remembered her. "Sit," she ordered. "Marjorie. All of you. Sit."

For a second, I was sure my mother and father wouldn't do it. My mother had a cigarette in her hand, and I expected to be told to light it in. My father slid one foot along the floor planks; he rubbed the stump of his index finger with his thumb.

"Don't smoke," Aunt Elaine said. "And don't dawdle."

Amazingly, my parents sat, though my father kept himself half turned away.

Aunt Elaine came around behind me and put her hands on the back of my chair. "For this kind of thing," she said in the frying-pan voice, "people go to jail. Do you know about that law, Curtis? Do you know about it, Emmy?"

Out of the side of my working eye, I saw my mother and father look away from me, as if I was a dirty thing, dangerous to them in the way an infectious disease might be. I did not ever remember hearing my parents' names spoken in that room. The names seemed to knock against the walls and the glass in the windows and then come echoing back over the table like the sound of frozen tree branches cracking on a winter night.

"Do you?"

"Not if the pastor what tells you to," my father said through his teeth. I looked at him. He was squinting his eyes, slanting them down to the floor.

"You believe that, don't you?" Aunt Elaine told him. "You're that much disconnected from reality that you believe it."

"Gone from out my house," my father said.

"Is that what you want, Curtis? Really? Because if I go from this house now, I don't ever come back, and not only don't I come back, but no money comes back with me, not Marjorie's money, and not any more of my own. No money, no food, no clothes, no gasoline for the saw, no repairs for the truck. No lawyer when you need it, no bail, no insurance. Not anything. Is that what you want?"

My parents didn't speak. For me, it was the same as when my father took the plastic off the outside of the windows in spring. One sheet, then another, one opening-up after the next. Light in the house.

"I have eighty dollars for you," Aunt Elaine said, turning to my mother and then my father as she said it, her voice stronger in one ear and then the other. "Twenty dollars a week, which is your share of the money from what Marjorie earned for working a straight month."

"Majie," my mother corrected her.

"I am calling her by her name. Eighty dollars a month is nine hundred sixty dollars a year. I came to give you the eighty dollars because she has finished working one month. And I brought food—fried chicken in a box, apples, and bread—the way I always do. I'm going to give you the eighty dollars, and I'm going to tell you what is going to happen. Marjorie will not be hit again. Ever. Not by the preacher, and not by you. Not ever. I am going to give her money every week for buying clothes and things she needs, and you are not going to take it away from her for your own spending. When I get home, I am going to call the police and report what goes on at the church, without mentioning her name or your names. If you want to fight that, good, fine, you go talk to the police about it, but I am going to close down the church. In two weeks I'm coming again with twenty dollars more, and I am going to take Marjorie out and have lunch with her, and look at her, and talk to her, and if I see the smallest mark on her from you, or hear the smallest little bad story about what you've been doing to her, then you are going back upstate, Curtis, to be with your dad. And, Emmy, you are going right with him to the woman's side." Aunt Elaine stopped for a breath. I could feel the back of the chair shaking but I didn't know whether my aunt or I was causing it to shake. "Now," Aunt Elaine said, moving her hands onto my shoulders. "If you have something to say back to me, you say it. It's your house, Curtis, you're right, and your and Emmy's daughter here. But things get taken away from people who don't care for them. Even dogs get taken now, when they're badly treated. Dogs, never mind young women. You want to say something to me, you say it."

My mother tapped the mouth end of the unlit cigarette on the scratched-up wood between her hands. She looked down the length of the table at her husband, and then, just for an instant, at me. "Because God didn't given you a girl for your own," she said.

"Meaning what?"

"You want charge of ours."

"That's what you think?"

My mother nodded, once.

"God bosses," my father said, but I could hear a kind of crack in the words, a line in stone where it was weak, where you could break it by hitting it sharp with the hammer in a certain place. He was worried about the money. About how he would live without help from Aunt Elaine. Almost one thousand dollars a year, plus what Aunt Elaine gave them from her own pocket—that was too much money to let go of easily. "God bosses," he repeated, his voice quiet and unsteady. "God needs a given penance."

"God gave you a child and you let someone do this to her," Aunt Elaine said. "Look at her face, Curtis. Look at it, I'm saying. I should by all rights take her to the emergency room and report this to the police. I have a mind to do that. Look!"

My father's eyes slid over to my face for one second and jumped away.

"God knows who gets a child," my mother said. "God's law makes it so."

"Should I talk to Chief Allans about God's law?"

At the third mention of the police, I felt the air crack around my ears.

"Should I?"

"Enh," my father said, one syllable of surrender. He moved his chin to the side and down.

I felt my aunt's hands shaking on my shoulders, then felt them move away. I saw money being counted out onto the table. Eight tens, fresh from the bank, gray-green and perfectly unwrinkled. I watched my father try to keep his eyes away from the bills, but he couldn't do it. On his left leg his hand was moving in quick jumps.

The money sat on the table like a noise. "Marjorie, come outside," Aunt Elaine said when she was finished. I thought, at first, that I wouldn't go, that it would be too much to step back into the house and face my parents after Aunt Elaine had left, that I ought to make some gesture of loyalty to them, for the sake of my own survival. But I stood up, feeling cold air on the back of my neck. By the time I was standing in the dirt next to one of the woodpiles, looking at my aunt, my breath was coming as fast as if I had run all the way from the 112 Store.

"Hold out your hand," my aunt said. She put some more bills there, then folded my fingers up around them. She reached up and touched my face gently and I pulled back. "Honey, look at me. Do you want to come and live with me? Right now?"

I shook my head.

"Are you absolutely sure? I'll take you in a second if you say yes. I have room. Are you sure you want to stay living here?"

I nodded.

My aunt waited, her head tilted up at me, her eyes going back and forth across my face. "If anything else like this happens. Just one time. Anything, you tell Sands and he'll tell me, or you get to a phone and call me and I'll come for you. Do you understand? No matter what time of the day or night."

"Sure."

"You're not going to that church ever again."

"I don't want of."

"You won't. If your parents try to make you, you go to the store and call and I'll come get you."

I wanted to tell her then what had happened the one time I'd run away and gone to her house, but there had been enough trouble for one day, and there was more trouble coming to me, I knew. I wanted to leave with my aunt, but I just could not make myself do that. Every leaf on every tree, every word, everything seemed to have a coating of fear hanging from it, as if the temperature had dropped thirty degrees and there had been an ice storm while we'd been inside. I was frozen almost into a solid block.

"I'm going now. You're working on Monday, tomorrow, right? If you're not at work, I'm coming here. I'm going now and I'm going to call about the preacher. What is his name?"

"Pastor Schect," I said quietly.

"Where is the church?"

"Into Vermont. West Ober."

"You're sure?"

"Sure."

"Did this happen to you ever before?"

I shook my head.

"Does it happen to other people?"

I shook my head again, and then changed my mind. "Twicet I saw."

"Does it hurt very much now?"

I shook my head. "Don't to say to the police about of my parents."

"I think I just will."

"Don't to, kindly. My father then will be time upstate. And my mother will to have me alone."

My aunt got tears in her eyes then. For a few seconds there wasn't much of the black bear in her, and I remember, just for that little time, that I felt like the stronger one of the two of us. Older even. I knew how the world worked and she didn't. I could stand there and not cry and she couldn't. Being tough was what people like us had to be proud of—boys and girls, both—instead of a good house or a good job or money, or other things. It has taken me all these years to see that, and to halfway let it go.

"You put a cool washcloth on your eye now. And if you can't see out of it tomorrow, you call me, understand?"

"I will."

"And one more thing. Listen to me. The next time Sands asks if you want to go to Boston with him, you go, understand? No matter what it seems like, or what your parents are going to say about it, you just go. Even if you're afraid, you go."

I promised I would, but I was surprised she knew he'd asked me. Still with water in her eyes, Aunt Elaine touched me on the shoulder with one hand, then got into her car and backed it up so it was facing out the driveway. She looked over at me one last time, as if she'd heard something, and at that moment I wanted to yell out to her to stop, to wait. But the fear of what my parents would do caught me in its cold fingers again, and the pride in being tough caught me, and in another second there was a small puff of dust behind the car and it was going up Waldrup Road, out of sight. I watched the dirt settle, and then I couldn't think of anything else to do so I pushed the money down into my pocket and turned and walked into the house. My father wasn't at the table. My mother was standing at the counter in a cloud of cigarette smoke, holding a leg of fried chicken with one hand. I was hungry but I knew I wouldn't eat. As I went toward my room I heard my mother say, "Who's gonto take a whippin' now, you Majie? Now who's gonto?"

Fourteen

There had been one other time in my life—
much earlier—when someone had tried to
help me the way Aunt Elaine tried that day. I learned about it only as
an adult, on my private project, my research into the past. On my second or third trip back, I stopped in the cathedral for an hour of private
prayer, and during that prayer I thought of looking up Mrs. Jensen,
the woman who'd owned the 112 Store. She was in late middle age by
then, and had sold the store, but she still lived in the town and I found
her without any trouble and we sat in her living room and had a cup of
tea. During that conversation she happened to mention a man named
Ronald Merwin, who, she said, had been the person responsible for
my going to school. I'd never heard the name before that day and had
never thought about why, after years of keeping me at home, my parents suddenly decided I could go to school.

Merwin was an established painter with an apartment in New York
City (I found him there, in his seventies and still painting). In search of
a quiet country retreat, he'd purchased a cabin on twenty acres off Waldrup Road, and he lived there most of several summers, working on his
abstract canvases, putting new siding and a new roof on the cabin, and
taking long solitary walks up and down the eight miles of dirt road. If
he followed the road northeast, it came to a dead end at the boundary

of the state forest, and sometimes he hiked on the trails there. Walking in the other direction took him past our house and to Route 112.

Merwin was a quiet, middle-aged man, divorced, childless, immersed in his art, and fond of solitude. If he passed anyone on his walks he'd say good morning or good afternoon, or he'd raise a hand in a polite wave, or, rarely, stop for a few minutes' conversation. When I found him in New York, he told me that, more than once on those walks, he'd seen me out in the yard helping my father or playing at the stream. He waved to me but he said I only looked at him with an expression he couldn't read. He waved or nodded to my mother and father, also, but, unlike the other country people he encountered, they didn't acknowledge him, sometimes even turned away so he couldn't see their faces. He said I was a pretty child—long legs, light brown hair—and he remembered me and even occasionally put a partial image of me into his paintings.

During the summer when I was nine, Merwin happened to run into me in the 112 Store, where I'd gone with my mother. I don't remember that encounter, but Mrs. Jensen did. Merwin noticed—he had a painter's eye, he said, as a way of softening the observation, I think—that I was poorly dressed, even a bit dirty it seemed, and that when I spoke to my mother it was in a dialect of the English language he'd never before heard. My way of talking piqued his interest. Out of innocent curiosity, he began to walk more often toward Route 112, and to look for me and my parents as he passed. On one of those trips he saw something strange: me dressed as a boy, in huge work boots, huge overalls, and a cap, being ordered about the yard by my father in a series of short commands. We had some project going—rebuilding a shed, it seemed—and even from a momentary glance Merwin could see that my father was inept. Merwin was a decent carpenter and would have stopped and offered assistance, he said, except that when my father saw him, he hustled me inside.

This only made him more curious. A week or so later, he saw me in the store again: My mother was pushing me roughly out the door. He asked Mrs. Jensen about our family. Mrs. Jensen said we were an odd trio, that the pretty light-haired girl might even be mildly retarded, she couldn't tell. As far as she knew, the girl never went to school.

"She has a strange way of talking, doesn't she?" he said.

And Mrs. Jensen said, "Yes," and kept her eyes on him for a moment, as if his interest seemed unhealthy to her, the probing eye of the uppity outsider, or as if in commenting on my speech he was casting a critical net over all the people who lived in those parts.

Curious as he was, Merwin might have chalked up everything to the eccentricities of rural existence, except that late one afternoon, just as the light was fading, he was driving past the house and happened to see me standing with my back to the stream. My father was emptying a bucket of water over my head. For a moment, he said, he thought it was the country equivalent of letting kids play in the spray of a fire hydrant. But the day was cool and rainy, and, from that distance, he thought he detected an expression of pain on my face. Just as he was about to pass, he saw me sprint away from the man—my father—who stood there, with the bucket held low in one hand, watching me go.

Merwin debated with himself that night, and the next day he made a call to the state social services agency. The call prompted an investigation. A caseworker came to the house—I have a memory of this woman speaking to us at the table. Many questions were asked of me and my parents, we all told careful lies, and in the end it was determined that I was not a victim of any serious abuse. However, my parents were informed they had to send me to school beginning that September. Not long after that, Ronald Merwin put his cabin and land up for sale and retreated to the city—no one knew exactly why; people thought he'd been happy there. But Merwin told me that my father had gone to his cabin one afternoon shortly after I started school and run his chain saw through the railing on his deck and the casing of his front door—with Merwin watching, horrified—and told him not to call the police, and not to come back the following summer, or, next time, my father said, he was going to "send the saw through halfway on your arms."

"I suppose it was cowardly of me," Merwin told me, sitting in his Chelsea apartment with a glass of beer in front of him and the sunlight showing a white forest of hair sprouting from both ears, "not to call the police and charge your father with assault or damaging property or something of that sort. I suppose I should have stayed and fought. But I had gone there for a peaceful escape, a place to work quietly, and there wasn't much peace for me there after that. . . . I'm glad, at least, that it all resulted in your going to school. I'm glad you made the effort to find me. I'm sorry."

In my first hours of my first day at school, the teacher realized I couldn't even identify all the letters of the alphabet. I knew some numbers but couldn't do even the simplest math problems. They asked questions about my family. I made up simple lies, said my parents were shy people, good to me, said they wanted me to learn but had been afraid to send me on the bus to school. The teachers did some tests, and the tests showed I had a capable mind. I was put in a special class. By the end of the first year I'd learned to read and write and solve basic addition and subtraction problems. And I'd made a friend, a girl named Cindy Rogers.

After that, year by year, with the help of several caring teachers, I closed the gap between myself and the other kids my age. By the end of my second year—I was ten years old—I could read simple chapter books. I stayed in the special class because the teachers were concerned that I'd be socially and academically out of place in fourth grade. Cindy and I were inseparable.

By the time we reached high school age, Cindy was still in special classes for part of the day but I had climbed to within a grade of the other boys and girls my age. I was in the bottom section in all areas of study, and nothing the teachers tried could shake me free of my way of speaking. But I could read capably, I could understand what I read, and whenever I handed in a written assignment it was in something close to standard English. There were more interviews and evaluations. There were arguments among the teachers and administrators as to how hard they should push me toward proper speech. Some of my classmates made fun of me—it was really not much worse than what they did to a few of the other boys and girls—and some didn't, but through it all I was happy to walk to the bus stop in the morning, happy to have a friend, happy to be around adults who were interested in learning and treated me well. There was always a strain between the way people wanted me to talk at school and the way my parents expected me to talk at home. From the start, my mother and father watched carefully to see if going to school would change me. When, in the beginning, I came home with books under my arm and said things like "I brought them home to read" instead of "I broughten them to home for a read," they willow-whipped me, six strokes. That was enough for me: It was not a hard choice between having a few kids make fun of you and having the skin at the back of your legs ripped raw with a braid of three thin willow branches. Not a hard choice at all.

When the teenage years arrived, though I was poorly dressed and poorly groomed, a few boys started to show an interest. One boy was a bit kinder than the others. His name was Aaron Patanauk—nephew to the welder—and if none of his friends was close by he would sometimes make a little conversation with me. Aaron and his family and his uncle had been regulars at Pastor Schect's church for a while, and then stopped going. He was the first person I ever saw faced. I'd even walked to the front of the church with my parents and watched as they poked their fingers into the bag; I still remember the noises he made, whimpers and quick shrieks. He was a big gangly boy whose arms and legs moved like puppets' limbs, hinged at the joint.

Aaron was sixteen and a half in ninth grade. During the summers when I was fourteen and fifteen, I had sometimes been allowed to ride my bicycle to Cindy's house, which was just off Route 112 in the opposite direction from town. Aaron lived nearby, and sometimes when he saw me there he drove over in the truck his uncle had given him and asked if I wanted to take a ride. I always declined. Cindy and I called it the Ugly Truck because the driver and passenger doors were gray and the rest of the truck a rose red, and the whole thing was dented and patched in a dozen places, the front seat torn, the tires almost bald. The next summer when Cindy and I went walking to the pond behind her house, Aaron followed along on foot. Sometimes Cindy left us alone, and Aaron and I talked a bit, and twice I let him kiss me, and once put his hands up inside my shirt. Somehow my father learned about it—I never understood how; Aaron must have told someone, who told someone else, and word had eventually circled around to my father or mother—and in a fit of anger he smashed my bicycle to pieces against one of his wood piles and forbade me from ever going to Cindy's house again. The next year Aaron had some trouble and went away to a place we called Robertson's Farm, which was a kind of minor-league jail for teenage country boys. He said he'd sent me some letters from Robertson's, but I never received them.

In any case, when I came to school on the day after my facing, I rode with Cindy on the bus, as always. She asked only one quick question about what had happened. I answered with one quick lie. She had odd parents, too, and after the bicycle-smashing incident we'd fallen into an unspoken agreement not to talk about what went on in our families. My right eye was closed and purple, and there were small round bruises, like dark pennies, on my cheeks and throat and around my eyes. My top lip was still swollen. Things are different these days, of course. Teachers are more aware of abuse in the home, more willing to involve the police. But twenty years ago, at least where we lived, they would sometimes choose to ignore the signs of children being hurt. I was happy enough to be ignored; I preferred it, in fact. When Mrs. Land, my third-period teacher, asked about the injuries, I told her what I'd told Cindy—that I'd been in the woods near the end of the day and had run straight into a tree with a lot of low branches. It was an obvious lie; the other girls and boys laughed. After class Mrs. Land sent me to see the assistant principal, Mrs. Eckstrom.

I'd been to Mrs. Eckstrom's office twice before, both times for conversations about my speech problems. I didn't like the woman, didn't like the solid-color dresses she wore that always came exactly to the middle of her kneecap, didn't like the sound of her heavy-heeled shoes in the corridor, didn't like the way she made me wait outside her office where passing students could see and then ordered me inside and made me sit facing her across a desk with nothing on it but a sheet or two of paper and two perfectly lined-up pens.

"What's this now?" Mrs. Eckstrom demanded. Her eyebrows made dark lines across the top part of her face. "Some kind of fight?"

"Nothing kind of," I said.

" 'Nothing kind of '? What language would that be? The language of the woods? If you are a student here you will speak properly."

"Yes," I said.

"What happened?"

"I had a fall."

"On school property?"

"No."

"Do you need to see the nurse?"

I shook my head. The palms of my hands were wet so I tucked them under the tops of my thighs.

"What then?"

"I'm trying for . . . I'm trying to talk different now. Mrs. Land said to tell."

"To tell *you*."

"No." I pointed at Mrs. Eckstrom across the desk. "To tell for you."

Mrs. Eckstrom fixed her eyes on me, her gaze flicking to the bruises and closed eye. One blink. A widening of the nostrils. "The apple doesn't fall far from the tree. Do you know that expression?"

"Yes."

"Do you know what your grandfather went to jail for?"

"No."

"You truly don't?"

"No."

"Well let me give you three pieces of advice then. First, stop drinking. Second, learn to speak correctly. Third, if the day ever comes that you have children of your own, male children especially, and if your grandfather is back in circulation by then, keep them away from him. Understood?"

"Yes."

"Go."

At lunch, Aaron sat directly across the table from me in the cafeteria. His boxy head was tilted to one side and he waited until no one else was around and then said, "Looks like you got faced."

"Aren't you a smart to of notice."

Aaron smiled. "Hurts, don't it? But only a few days. Then they usually don't never face anybody twicet."

"I think Pastor Schect is going to call some trouble on for himself when he keeps to facing kids."

"Your dad gonna fix him?"

"Somebody would."

"People worry about your dad, you know. Word is he kilt a man when he was younger an me."

"Who lied that?"

"My uncle. Only it ain't a lie. Maybe he kilt other people, too."

"He never kilt," I said, but inside myself I had the same feeling that had come over me when Mrs. Eckstrom mentioned Dad Paul. It was as if the walls of my mind were crashing out sideways, creating a new, larger room, and the new room had bureaus and closets in it, and the shelves and drawers contained secrets coiled like snakes.

"He never about hits me," I said, which was not exactly the full truth, but I was used to saying it to the teachers and was able to repeat it to Aaron with some conviction.

"It was a long time ago, but my uncle says it happened."

"Your uncle hasn't a lie maker ever either, right?"

"Girl chaser not a lie maker," Aaron said. Another smile. His top front teeth folded one over the other. "The talk-funny girl," he said, but almost kindly. "Everybody's still goin' on about the big church you're building in town. It looks nice."

"I make some money on it."

"Sure. You're lucky. Could I drive you home someday after you're done working?"

"So you can put your hands up at my shirt, that's why."

"Aren't you smart to guess," he said, and he smiled and stood up, with the hinges flexing in his legs, and he went across the cafeteria like a puppet worked by strings from above, lifting his knees and swinging his shoulders, leaning his boxy head to one side.

When I went to work that day, I could tell Sands was looking at the marks on my face, and I was glad he didn't mention them. But the facing and having to lie about it had stirred a small circle of anger in me. Something had started to shift and change. The few minutes with Mrs. Eckstrom had made me think, again, about the way I talked, made me think about Dad Paul and my father. The half hour with Aunt Elaine had upset me at a depth of emotion where I wasn't used to spending time. Many years earlier, I had set a heavy blanket over the feelings in that deep place, but now I felt them—just started to feel them— moving their arms and legs and pushing up toward the light. I tried hard to keep from thinking about what my parents would do, what kind of punishment was boiling now in the stew of humiliation in my father's mind. After years of practice, I was very good at concentrating on the present moment—schoolwork, housework, and now stonework—and putting off the inevitable hour of penance until it actually arrived. But something was starting to change.

That week, because the days were growing longer, Sands asked if I could work an extra half hour each afternoon—he'd pay me more, of course, he said, or that extra half hour could go to pay off the boots. I agreed without having to think about it. The cathedral was starting to have a shape. In the section we were building (which, Sands said, was going to be only about a third of the eventual size, but he wanted to have one part of the building roofed in before the snow came), the walls were as high as my chest. I could see the outline of the front door, and the lower part of the two windows in the front wall, and three each, evenly spaced, along the sides. At the base of those windows, we had to lay down what Sands called "sill ribbons," long pieces of red sandstone that contrasted in a way I loved with the grays and browns of the rest of the stones. The sills were too heavy for him to lift up that high on his own, and I couldn't lift them at all, so we built a system of moveable wooden steps, four feet wide, to help us get the sill ribbons in place. Sands lifted one end up onto the first step. I held it there by leaning all my weight against it to be sure it didn't slip. He went over to the other end of it, said, "Ready?" and then lifted while I held my side.

Little by little, with time allowed for Sands to rest, we moved the sill up onto the top step of the makeshift stairway. I prepared a small batch of mortar, my face so sore in the gritty wind I was nearly crying into the mixture, and Sands showed me how to trowel it evenly onto the layer of stones where the sill would rest. When that was done, it wasn't hard to move the sandstone across and onto the mortar. Sands checked it with his level, tapped it a bit this way or that with the heel of the trowel handle, then we stood back and admired the work.

"Do you see how it's slanted on top, down away from the inside of the building?"

"Sure," I said. "So the water can run away out, if while it rains."

Sands looked at me the way he sometimes did, a way that partly pleased me and partly made me uncomfortable. I thought it might be the way an older brother would look at me, if I'd had one. "You're smarter than you act," he said.

"Same on you," I said, but again he missed the joke, and again I told myself to keep my comments within certain boundaries, not to forget that he was my boss and could take the job away at any time. There wasn't another adult on earth I felt I could joke with, not even Aunt Elaine, but something in Sands brought out a different part of me.

"Why, though?" he said, still looking.

I kept my eyes on the windowsill and shrugged. "If you have a like for school, you don't show, that's all."

Sands watched me for another few seconds. "Why not?"

"You're not of as smart as you look, for asking that."

He laughed but didn't look away. "Your father talks like you do."

"Same as."

"And your mother, too?"

"Not so as much but sure."

"Did they send you to school when you were first of the age to go?"

"I'm of my same grade except one now."

"Right, but did they send you?"

"They taughted me home until I was nine. I learned cooking, all the trees' names, things for fishing, to cutting wood."

"Those are good skills to know."

"Reading now I like. In my room a lot of times I do it if I have on a book from the library at school." He seemed to be watching me in a different way, peering down inside me, and the whole conversation was making me feel I had tiptoed out onto a high wire over the Connecticut River. I didn't know if it was wiser to go forward to the far bank or retreat. "Now we can might lift the other one," I said.

But Sands wouldn't let the subject drop. "Do the teachers bother you about it? The way you talk, I mean?"

"Just today one had bother for it."

"But that doesn't matter to you?"

"No," I said, not looking at him. "I can to work fair without it."

"The reading helps you?"

"A lot it does help."

"I could give you some books if you want."

"Thanks. But at home I have already."

He watched me a minute, and I could feel he was getting ready to ask what had happened to my face, so I walked off toward the next sill ribbon without saying anything.

After work that day and on Wednesday (the bruises were faded to a dull yellow by then and my right eye was nearly open) Sands drove me to the 112 Store as always. I liked it that there was no cigarette smoke in the cab and that he sometimes played music or listened to the news on the radio. My hands and arms were tired from the work, but no longer sore, and a strange new kind of pleasure filled me up on those rides, something left over from the few minutes we spent at the end of the day, looking at what we'd accomplished. I kept waiting, half-afraid, half-hopeful, for Sands to ask me a second time to go to Boston. "It's coming along beautifully now," he said, which wasn't the way anyone else I knew talked.

I thought of making a joke about it, telling him that *he* was the one who talked funny, that he might be a man after all but didn't sound like it, but as the words were coming up I diverted them and tried something safer. "A lot of people now put their eyes on going by. One of them came with his camera and took. You were at for work near the back part."

"Just wait until the windows go in. I have a guy in Hensonville making them. Stained glass. One day we'll take a ride over there and you'll meet him."

I'd heard of Hensonville. It was a hill town across the big river where the most recent disappearance had taken place, the girl on her bicycle. I felt the familiar tickle of fear run up along my back but made myself ignore it. "Who can be in at the window then? Jesus?"

"No," Sands said, but, though I waited, he didn't offer anything more about it, and I didn't ask again.

He turned in to the store parking lot and kept his truck engine running. I took some extra time zipping up my backpack and wrestling it onto my lap, thinking he might ask about Boston again if I waited long enough. But he didn't. I thanked him, as I did every day, then got out and started off along the highway toward Waldrup Road and home.

On Friday my bruises were nearly gone. At school, Aaron Patanauk asked again if he could come to the church and drive me home after I finished work. I said that he could. I look back at that and I don't know why I agreed. I didn't like him much, and I knew, on some level at least, why he was interested in me. But in my life that kind of interest was almost nonexistent, and I had a teenage girl's normal curiosity and desire. There was more to it, though, and while it might seem overly simple, I know it's true: A small part of me resisted Sands and Aunt Elaine because they were telling me, in different ways, that I was good or attractive or intelligent. I had never felt like a good or attractive or intelligent person, and so I think now that I was drawn to someone like Aaron because he confirmed my own opinion of myself. He saw me as something to be manipulated, to be used, perhaps even to be hurt. A large part of me saw myself that way, too.

Aaron arrived early but parked at a little distance and stayed slumped down behind the wheel of his ugly truck, listening to the radio, waiting.

"A friend come today now and is for taking me home," I told Sands when we'd finished for the day and put the tools away in the rectory basement. I pointed at the pickup.

Sands glanced at the truck and I tried to read his face. "Nine o'clock tomorrow then," was all he said.

"I will to."

Just beyond the 112 Store on the right there is a dirt road that angles up into the hills and still has no houses on it. Old Quarry Road it's called. Aaron turned his truck there. He drove up a ways then turned left onto a logging road, pulled into the trees, and killed the motor. "You can be a few minutes late getting home, right?" he said. They were the first words he'd spoken. I felt it wasn't really a question so I didn't answer.

My backpack was on the seat between us. Aaron pushed it forward near the shift, then reached across with one of his puppet's arms and pulled me closer. He kissed me, once, fast, and then his hand crawled up under my sweatshirt and felt around there in a way that was a bit rough but not unpleasant. I was worried I smelled from the day of work. He took my hand and put it in his lap.

"Unzip me," he said, and after a minute I did that. "Put your mouth there now," he said, and I did that, too, because there was something strange and new about doing it, like going to Boston in my mind.

That night in my room I thought about it and slid my hands down into my underwear. That was something I'd done many times before, a dependable pleasure in my life, but now it was almost as if there was another person with me, and I pretended the other person was happy after it was over, and that he even said a few words on the ride back to the corner of the road.

Fifteen

On Saturday mornings my parents slept late. I had cleaning chores to do first thing, and lunch to prepare for myself, but I finished my work and was out the door while they were still in bed. I carried a paper bag with a can of Coke and a peanut butter and raisin sandwich in it, and I walked to the end of Waldrup Road and then all the way west on Route 112 as far as the town. Altogether, that walk took an hour and ten minutes. After crossing the metal bridge, I turned left at the end of Route 112 and went along Main Street, past the food smells coming from Art and Pat's, where adults and children sat at tables near the big windows eating from plates—eggs and waffles and toast and pancakes and sausages—and then past the pharmacy and the Boxing Club and the bank, and then a block of offices in redbrick buildings—insurance, real estate, a vacant storefront—and then there was another block of brick row houses where the factory workers had lived when the factories were busy, and then, at last, the ruins of St. Mark's.

As I came closer to the work site I could see that Sands was standing next to his truck. For some reason, he'd parked it on the street, rather than pulling it up into the grassy lot the way he usually did. I noticed immediately that he hadn't taken out the wheelbarrows, extension cords, and hand tools we would need for that day's work. He was looking at me, waiting for me, and I wondered if I'd gotten the time wrong and was late.

"Good morning," he said when I was still thirty feet away. As I had done from earliest childhood, whenever someone spoke to me I listened for messages hidden in the words. It seemed to me that Sands was even more nervous than usual that morning, and I felt a terrible thought come pushing against me like a freezing wind in February: He had run out of money for the project, or I'd done something to displease him (maybe it was asking if Jesus would be in the windows being made by the man in Hensonville), and now he was going to say the work was finished for us, or for me, and try to be nice about it, and leave me with a spring and summer of staying home with my mother and father, stacking wood, cooking, cleaning, receiving penances, riding around with Aaron in his truck and trying to keep anyone from finding out what kinds of things I did with him there.

"No work today," Sands said. I was still some distance from him. He wasn't wearing work clothes.

He was such a big, strong man, and yet when it came to saying things he didn't want to say, he seemed to shrink down inside his body and become small and shy and young. It was that shrinking that gave me courage to speak to him in a way I never spoke to anyone else, but that wasn't the feeling I had that morning. He pushed the glasses back against his nose, he moved his feet—shoes there instead of boots—he stopped leaning against the truck and stood up straight, facing me.

I hadn't even said hello. The paper bag with the sandwich and Coke in it made me feel as foolish as if I'd taken my sweatshirt, T-shirt, and bra off right there on the sidewalk. Now the kids at school would know I'd been fired, or that the fancy church project had ended up being a failure, and my parents would know there was no more money coming in, and I'd have to go by the church and see Sands working alone, or with someone else, or just see the walls standing there half-built, like a naked person sitting in the middle of the street calling my name.

I moved the paper bag so I was holding it behind me with both hands. Sands looked into my face. He leaned one shoe against the other as if he was scratching his ankle.

"I'm going to Boston for the day."

I waited.

"I'll make sure you get back at the same time we would have finished . . . or maybe just half an hour later. And I'll pay you the same for the time . . . as if you had worked . . . because it's partly kind of related to work, what I'm going to do there."

I hadn't moved and couldn't seem to speak.

"Will you come?"

Before I answered I looked at the building Sands called a cathedral. Nobody else would ever call it that. It was a chapel. Maybe when he finished the other sections it might look like a church, but even I knew it could never truly be called a cathedral. The piece of it we were building at that point was only a little larger than a small-sized house. The light from the morning sun fell on it at a flat angle, and it seemed to me almost as if the stones had eyes in them, and the eyes were looking back at me. I had come to believe there were spirits inside the stones, just the way there was a spirit inside a person or a tree, and it felt to me that I would be accused of abandoning those spirits if I didn't keep to my regular schedule. The day before, Sands and I had worked very well together. We'd built the north wall up another two courses so I could see the shape of the three windows that would be there. Today was Saturday, a long workday, and Sands had told me we might be able to get the front wall up as high as the arch at the top of the door, and I wanted to do that. I would feel bad not doing it. I ran my eyes around the work site—in my imagination it was like someone who'd been beaten and broken up and burned and then chopped up in pieces and thrown into piles, and Sands and I were putting that person, that damaged spirit, back together again, making something beautiful out of the ruin, making a place in that town where people could sit and be at peace and not have to spend any money and not be praying to a God who wanted to hurt them. I supposed it was a superstition, and that Sands would laugh at me if he found out, but I'd formed a belief that if I didn't care for the cathedral with all my heart and didn't work on it with all my strength, then it wouldn't care for me, wouldn't give me the year, or even two years, of work I'd been dreaming about since the first time I'd stood there with Sands and heard him talk about my apprenticeship.

"Can't I not to work on here while you go off?"

"There will be plenty of good weather now, Laney. The stones won't go anywhere." He pushed at his glasses.

At that moment I was bumped by a memory of the way Aunt Elaine had spoken to my parents on the Sunday I'd been faced. It was something I wouldn't have thought possible, ever. Completely impossible that they would sit and listen to someone lecture them that way. I knew that my mother, probably, and my father, especially, had been hearing those words again and again since it had happened. I knew something bad was coming toward me from them, and I wondered if they were going to try to take me to Pastor Schect's the next day, and if there was a special punishment being made ready.

"Laney?"

I turned my eyes to Sands and in the few seconds before I knew I had to speak I examined his face and saw the muscles of his shoulders and his strong neck, the short ragged ponytail, and I wondered if he had any idea at all what might happen to me if I went to Boston with him and got caught. Did he know about things like that? Would he try to help me if that happened?

As always Sands insisted I wear a seat belt. I pulled the belt across my middle and tried to push it into the clip, but my hands weren't moving exactly right. Except for my sneakers, I was wearing work clothes—old jeans, a T-shirt, and a sweatshirt. How could I go to a place like Boston in clothes like that? The seat belt clicked. It was there, I decided, to keep my insides from flying out and bouncing against the windshield. I looked through the passenger-side window, away from him. He didn't have the radio on. He had smiled when I said I'd go to Boston.

Sands drove across the Honey River on the smaller bridge and went along Route 112, due east, away from town, just as if he was driving me home. Before we reached Warners' and the store and Patanauk's and Waldrup Road, we came to Weedon's Bar on the right-hand side, and I saw my father's truck in the gravel lot there—red, dented, rusted, the drooping tailpipe held up with coat-hanger wire. Never once had I known my father to go to Weedon's that early in the morning on a sunny day. I realized then that he might drive into town afterward—something else he never did—and that he'd see no one was working at the cathedral, and I'd have to lie to him, say that Sands and I had gone to Rochester for sill ribbons, or to Ober for iron headers, or to Hensonville to meet the window-making man, or to Second Construction in Balfour to look at slate tiles for the roof. My father would know I was lying: He could smell things like that the way a fox can smell human scent on a trap.

But I let the truck take me. All the way east on 112 we went, past the end of Waldrup Road, past a long stretch of woods and then the closed-up and shuttered Bakery Wholesale where I'd gone with my parents years before, every Thursday, to buy day-old bread and cup-cakes. Past the road to Cindy's house. In the lowlands, still part of the floor of the valley where the river ran, the air was warmer and the trees were into leaf. To one side and the other the woods lit themselves up in the sunlight. But as the road lifted into higher terrain I saw that there were still some dark branches, the ash and oak—they came into leaf last in spring and lost their leaves last in fall—with only buds on them. The buds and the first leaves in spring were always a lighter green than the leaves would turn out to be later in summer. I thought of it as a new green, and the summer color as real green, and the early fall color as old green, and I could almost have told the month by the way the woods looked. I wondered if Sands saw those kinds of things, if he knew the trees—their names, the quirks of their bark and branches, the things each species was good for and not good for: ash for tool handles, fir for outdoor steps, maple for firewood and sugaring, oak for flooring—and where he went in his life when he wasn't working or traveling to Boston, and how he knew Aunt Elaine, and how he knew the men in Warners', and why he seemed so badly to want to take a girl he barely knew to Boston and pay her for working at the same time.

But I kept myself quiet, and he was quiet, too, watching the road. In a little under an hour we reached an interstate I'd never seen before. I remembered my father's fear of the big raised highway, his belief that state troopers were lying in wait just for him. I thought about what Aaron had said, and though I was fairly sure my father had never killed anyone, still, whenever someone said something like that it made a kind of spot on your mind. And when a person did the kinds of things I had done with Aaron, those things made spots on your mind, too.

Sands steered the truck up onto the interstate, putting on his turn signal, something else my father didn't believe in doing. In another minute we seemed to be flying along the clean black tar. The truck swooped down through the hills as though it was skimming on a black river that tilted first one way then the other. The steady drone of the tires was comforting, a kind of music to occupy the mind. There were more tractor-trailer trucks in the first mile than I saw in town in a month. More cars, some with license plates from Canada, Florida, Ohio, Missouri. There was a green sign almost half the height of the cathedral walls and it said BOSTON 104.

"We're going to a museum," Sands said, after a long silence. "Have you ever been?"

"Oncet," I said. "To Darmuth the college. They have one of it there, and in fourth grade, we were all everyone going. My parents let me on to go then for the one time."

I didn't tell him that my mother had allowed me to go because she was drinking when she signed the permission slip and did it as a kind of joke. I didn't say that when my father found out I'd been to see a museum, and been to see a college, he conferred with Pastor Schect about it and they decided I needed to receive a special penance, and that was the first time I'd been hungered.

"Have you seen other colleges?"

"I never."

"How many times have you been to Boston?"

"No times."

"Montreal?"

I shook my head.

"Maine?"

"No places," I said. "We go, we used to go up West Ober at church there. We go at Watsonboro when for Thanksgiving with Aunt Elaine in her house. We go acrost on the river too in Westminster for when my dad needs a fix for his truck because a man knows that work there and goes to church at where we do."

"You mostly stay around home then."

"Most."

"Are you curious about Boston?"

"Afraid."

"Of the city?"

"Sure. All those animals they have at there. Bears. Moose. Cougar."

He didn't laugh. Again. If I could have controlled the urge in me I would have stopped trying to make jokes with him. I never made a joke at school. At home, there wasn't much in the way of lightheartedness. With Sands, with his serious face, his thick glasses, his big muscles, his shy way, his mysterious intentions . . . I made jokes.

"Tell me, really," he said.

The trees I saw out the side window were similar to those I saw at home, though there were more pine, spruce, and hemlock at that altitude, with white birch mixed in. There were some MOOSE CROSSING signs, and high-tension wires, too. Now and again I saw a house on a hillside, a lawn cut out of the woods around it, cars or a truck in the driveway. Once, a swimming pool. I swiveled my head to watch as it fell behind. Sometimes as we drove I could see towns from above, and I could tell the way they'd been built around factories and churches, the flat gray roofs and pointed steeples, the roads coming together. Pastor Schect didn't allow movies or TV; he was very strict about those things and mentioned them often in his sermons. But I'd seen television several times at Cindy's house before my parents had forbidden me to go there, and sometimes at school there would be a movie. At Aunt Elaine's, when my aunt and mother were in the kitchen preparing the Thanksgiving meal and my father was pacing the backyard spitting tobacco and muttering, I sometimes turned on the TV and watched for a little while with the voices muted. It was one of my small rebellions. In the 112 Store, in the pharmacy downtown, and in the library at school, I'd looked at magazines and seen New York and other places, photographs from other countries. I saw girls my own age dressed in fancy clothes, sitting together in a restaurant, laughing, and I read the letters they wrote about skin problems, boyfriends, making out, and trouble with their parents, who wanted them home at a certain hour after a date. I studied those pictures and letters for many minutes at a time, committing them to memory, building around them whole imaginary worlds. And at moments I felt myself drawn toward those worlds like the big pale luna moths at my window screen on a July night.

"I don't for why know I'm afraid," I said to Sands. "Because of there could be the black people maybe. Other kinds of, too."

"I'm half-black."

I was only partly surprised. Probably more surprised at the easy way he said it than the fact itself. Aaron had said something about it, and on some level, I'd known from the moment I'd first seen Sands that he wasn't exactly a white man. Dark-skinned men and women were exotic to us, tourists with New York license plates, pictures in a textbook or a magazine, one or two families here and there. "Your mother or of your father was, which person?"

"My father."

"You see them at town on days," I said. "Going back at New York from after skiing the mountain, or driving for the leaves color. They eat, they get gas to the cars. For a while there was one black girl at ninth grade where I go at school . . . The kids wouldn't make laughing at you and that?"

"Not so much where I lived, no."

I wanted to ask him then where he had lived, what kind of place it was where you could be half-black and not laughed at, not chased out of the school, not hit or spit on or have your dress ripped open from behind, but I was still hearing the matter-of-fact tone of his voice when he told me. We went some miles without either of us speaking, and I slid my eyes sideways to examine, for the hundredth time, his skin and hair and mouth.

"Do you know . . . ," Sands said, and then he hesitated, glanced at me across the seat, turned a dial on the dashboard to bring a bit of air into the cab. I was sure he was going to go on and tell me more about black people, until he said, "About sex and all that?"

That question changed the mood inside me. It made me feel young. Made me suspect him again after I thought I'd completely gotten past that. Trying not to let him see, I moved over another inch closer to the door. People said the girl who'd been kidnapped and killed across the river—maybe all the girls—had been abducted by a black man. I'd heard that at school. It had made another spot on my mind. My thoughts about Sands shifted completely, as if a bank of clouds had glided in suddenly across what had been, only seconds before, a clear blue sky. A certain voice was activated in my inner ear and the voice said that this was exactly the way a person who kidnapped someone would act: talking to you in order to get you into his truck, preparing it for weeks, step by step, letting you say no first and then getting you to trust him and then asking again. Tricks like that took time, which was why the girls had been disappearing at the rate of one only every five or six months. The man would trick you into his truck like that, and then he'd start talking about sex. It seemed to me that I'd read about this in one of the magazines.

"I know for what means a rape is."

Sands sent me a puzzled look, pinching up his face almost the same way he did when he banged his finger between two stones. A terrible quiet rose up between us then. He made the truck go faster.

"I know for it hurts," I went on, because, even raised on silence as I had been, I couldn't bear a silence like that one. "I'm not so young."

Again Sands squeezed his face. I saw three lines of wrinkles to the side of his eye, and for once he looked older than the boys I knew. After another few seconds he said, "You sound like you think I asked that because I want to have sex with you."

"Don't it?"

"You sound like you think I'm going to hurt you."

"You made speeded the truck up."

He laughed then, in just the way a kidnapper would laugh, a man who had fooled you into trusting him, and then took you away and raped you and killed you and threw you dead in the weeds at the side of a logging road for a hunter to find the next year. I know it was illogical and foolish of me to be thinking like that—Sands was ten times more deserving of trust than, for example, Aaron Patanauk. But Aaron was my own kind. White. Shy. Small-town. Bad, yes, but the kind of bad I knew. For all his kindness, Sands's way of being in the world was an alien creature to me.

"I just asked because I wanted to be sure you knew, so that nothing happened to you, so that you didn't have bad information about it, that's all."

"I'm not for a little young of a girl. I'm not for slow in at school."

"I know you're not. If you want me to stop talking about it, I will."

I said nothing. I watched the skin near his eyes and then the tendons of his wrist as he squeezed the steering wheel.

"I was molested as a boy. Do you know what that is?"

"Everyone person knows it."

"A man—he was a minister—did sexual things to me when I was ten and eleven. I was asking because I wouldn't ever want things like that to happen to you, that's all."

"Nothing of that didn't happen on me. And wouldn't of neither because my father would to kill the person if he ever."

"I don't think it will happen. If it does, you should always tell someone. Tell your aunt, or me, or a teacher. Anyone you really trust."

I thought about that for a moment, searching my list of adult acquaintances for one of them I could imagine talking to about such a thing. I said, "Nothing of that happened."

"You said that. Okay."

"And I'm not any of ten years old, in the case if you didn't see."

Sands squeezed the wheel and couldn't look at me. "You're a beautiful young woman. Anyone with half a brain would see that. That's why I asked you. There are men who might want to hurt you, or take advantage, that's all."

We drove along in a rippling silence. My thoughts skipped back to what I'd been doing with Aaron in the truck on Old Quarry Road. In school, Aaron had said to me something very similar to what Sands had just said—that I was beautiful—and I'd recognized it both times as a lie, a tactic, exactly the opposite of what I'd been hearing from my mother, over and over again, for as long as I could remember. "How do you are friends with Aunt Elaine?" I said. The words had been living on the underside of my tongue for a long time. I sent them out into the air as a way of not talking about what we had been talking about.

Sands didn't answer. It was clear to me then, from his silence, that what he wanted to talk about was sex, about the way I looked, about what men could do to me. It was, I suspected, the reason he'd offered me the job in the first place, the reason Mr. Warner had said he wanted to "train" somebody. I knew a little bit about that kind of training. Hurt, hurt, hurt.

But after another stretch of awkwardness Sands said, "She's my mother," and for me then it was as if the truck door flew open and the pavement of the interstate was flashing by a few inches from my face. In another instant I would fall out.

"That's a weird of a joke," I tried.

"Isn't a joke."

"I was to my aunt Elaine's house for three times. You weren't ever there, and not any other kids neither weren't, or any pictures of kids, or any husband or a boyfriend."

"She gave me up to be adopted when I was a few hours old."

I listened without looking at him, concentrating on the words.

"She had an affair in the summer after her first year of college and got pregnant. The man was black. Jamaican. Her parents were furious about it, her father especially. Partly because of her being pregnant, and mainly because of who had gotten her pregnant. Her father helped her hide the pregnancy by sending her away, and he made her promise she would give the child up—give me up—when I was born. Even your mother doesn't know. Nobody knew."

"She gave you off?"

He pushed his lips out and made five or six small movements with his chin, half nods.

"That's worse for than . . ."

"Than what?"

"Than of anything."

"Think so?"

"Sure so. At least for a person is supposed to be having a mother or and a father."

"I had parents. I had good parents. They were an older couple, in their early fifties when they took me. Both black. They'd never been able to have children of their own and always wanted to, and they didn't mind a baby who was half-white. He was a college professor, at Penn. She had a little florist shop in Center City until they decided to adopt, and then she sold it so she could stay home with me. They were as good parents as anybody could ask for. They're both dead now. They were pretty well off. The money I got from selling their home— the house I grew up in—and what they left me, that's what I used to buy the church. And what I live on."

"And for to paying me," I said.

"That's right."

"But you had somebody touch you on the wrong."

"My parents didn't know about it."

"Because of you never had told."

"That's right. I was afraid to tell them. Ashamed. They were religious people. To them, a pastor was like God's friend sent down to save us."

"Aunt Elaine didn't all that time know where you went, from one day?"

"We both went looking for each other and we finally found each other not too long ago. We met in New York City the first time—I'll take you there, too, if you want, it's my favorite place—and then, a few weeks later, I drove up from Philadelphia to see where she lived. Watsonboro. She took me for a ride up to the town where we work, where the cathedral project is, and then out on the road where I drop you off every night. I think she was going to introduce me to you and your family but changed her mind at the last minute and we ended up just going into Warners' and talking with her friend there. Zeke. You know him. I think she dated him for a while or something. I saw the town, and what was left of the church, and I had been working with stone for a long time—with a stonemason during the summers when I was in high school and college, and then on my own—and I'd always wanted to build something special. Something that would last. I'd just inherited the money, less than a year earlier. I'd been thinking of getting out of the city. And when I saw the church it all came together. I asked Zeke Warner and he said he had a feeling I could buy it for not very much money, and then I had the idea to build my cathedral. He called Elaine when you came in looking for a job, and she told me."

I filed this bit of information away, tried not to show any reaction. But I understood that I had been part of a complicated plan, a kind of trick, and while some of me was happy about the result, I'd never liked to have things hidden from me, and I wondered about what other secrets my aunt and Sands were keeping. I said, "To build a cathedral is an idea that for a weird person would get."

"I'm a weird person. You ought to have figured that out by now."

"I did figure," I told him. "I just think of how much weird, is all. Weird which of a way."

Sands smiled and I watched his mouth and thought that if he was a kidnapper, he was good at making up stories that made him seem like he wasn't.

"Weird which of a way besides in the way a pastor did bad things on you and so now you think to build up a church."

"There are different kinds of churches."

"There's something I know it."

Sands let the truck slow back down to the speed we'd been going before the conversation took its strange turn. I glanced across at him, and then at the road, and then back. "You have for something else to want saying," I said.

"That's right," he said, but for another mile he didn't speak. When I stopped watching him and turned my eyes forward again, he said, "I'm supposed to ask if you want to testify against the preacher who did that to your face."

"He wasn't who did on it."

"Somebody did it, though."

"Other people did on it. At in the church. I wasn't the only one who ever had it neither."

"Do you want to testify?"

"In the law, you mean?"

"In court."

"Do you want to of push a stone in your mouth and choke and die and go in hell?" I said.

"That's a nice way to put it."

"Because it's just as the same."

"Your aunt called the police about it. The police are going to try to get your mother or father to testify."

"They should have a good luck about that."

Sands stopped talking then, leaving me in a swarm of thoughts, with something, a bad new feeling, creeping up the bones of my arms like cold water. I was thinking about Aunt Elaine and secrets, and I was trying to form a picture of policemen coming to our house and asking to speak to my father or mother, but the picture kept dissolving into an image of me in the Quonset hut in West Ober, and Pastor Schect standing at the pulpit with a paper bag in his hand. Although I did not know exactly what they might be, I understood that there were penances worse than facing, boying, and hungering, and those things seemed suspended in my near future, inevitable as the coming of another week.

As we drew close to the city, I was able, by staring hard out the window, to put those thoughts to one side. Boston was a world of concrete and asphalt, of roads running together, huge buildings pushing at the sky, and what seemed to me like millions of cars . . . and then, as we turned off the highway onto smaller streets, so many people on the sidewalks that I couldn't sort them out one from the next, couldn't think of them as individuals. I was leaning forward against the seat belt.

Sands turned into a parking lot and pulled up beside a wooden shed that reminded me of the bus shelter at the corner of Waldrup Road. A man with the blackest face I'd ever seen took money from Sands for the parking and directed us to an empty space at the far corner of the lot. From there it was a two-minute walk to the museum. Sands seemed to have fallen again into one of his somber moods. He said nothing. He walked half a step in front of me, and I worried, looking around at the buildings and cars, listening to the street noises, the honking horns and echoing sirens, that he'd get too far ahead and lose me there. Aunt Elaine was his mother, he said. Aunt Elaine was his mother. He was her son. A half-black man. Molested. My father's truck had been at Weedon's.

The museum turned out to be a building nearly as large as my school, all huge stone blocks, with fifteen or twenty stone steps, wide and smooth, leading up to a double front door with a frame of dark wood. To either side of the door stood windows with glass so clean it looked like silvery paper. As I started up the steps, with Sands a few feet to my right and ahead, I all of a sudden became aware of what I was wearing: not-new jeans, a plain green T-shirt covered by a ragged sweatshirt my mother had found at Salvation Army. It was the color of peas and had AIR FORCE ACADEMY stenciled in worn gold letters across the front. I stopped. Sands went another few steps then turned and looked back. I took the cloth of the sweatshirt in my fingers and held it out away from my body like an apology.

"Doesn't matter," he said in a voice that other people coming up the steps could hear. I hesitated. He waved at me impatiently, almost angrily. I closed my eyes and opened them, and then decided to focus on the stone beneath my feet, to think about the people who'd placed it there and smoothed the mortar between the joints, to pretend they were speaking to me in encouraging tones, in the language of work, urging me forward.

Through the door I went, half a step behind him. In the dim light of the entranceway, I stopped again to let my eyes focus. There was a long desk or table set sideways to us, and Sands was gesturing for me to come up beside him, and then handing over more money to a woman sitting on a stool and wearing a puffy-shouldered white blouse and circular gold earrings. The woman looked at my sweatshirt and then into my face, but only for a second. I swiveled my head and tried to get a sense of the other people there. Even the little girls and boys were so much better dressed and groomed than I was. The other kids about my age looked like they belonged in a magazine and seemed more comfortable there—in that light, in that cool stone smell, beside the potted plants taller than a man—than I felt in my own house. The mothers and fathers were what I thought of as city people, though I couldn't have said exactly why. They seemed like they'd all taken showers a few minutes before stepping through the door, and the words they spoke had a quiet, happy tone to them that sounded like the voices of the reporters on Sands's truck radio, telling the news. It looked like someone had made their clothes just for them: It was the way the women's dresses hung so perfectly on the corners of their shoulders, the way the men's shirts had collars so neat and straight against their necks. Their pants had tight cuffs at the bottom. Everyone looked like a teacher on the first day of school, like they were going to church, like they'd eaten their favorite food for breakfast and every part of their life was filled up like a tire with exactly the right amount of air in it, something that would hum against the pavement with a confident note.

Beyond the front desk I noticed again how cool it was, and how quiet. The floors were dark speckled tile, shining like stars. Everyone walked at a relaxed pace, as if thinking deeply. Sands and I went down a short hallway and then turned into a windowless room with a high ceiling. On the walls of the room hung paintings as large as the door of a car. Men and women stood still in front of the paintings, or went past them very slowly, sometimes saying a word to the person they were with or leaning in to read what was typed on the small piece of cardboard next to the bottom of the painting. Everything—the floor, the walls, the frames of the paintings, even the letters on the pieces of cardboard, everything was absolutely immaculate.

The bright canvases showed apples on a table, and vases of flowers, and farmhouses set on green fields as if floating there. I felt that I already knew those things, beautiful enough but ordinary, and so once I'd run my eyes over a painting I tried to look at the other people in the room without letting Sands see I was doing that. I made a special study of two girls close to my own age, whose mother and father would periodically lean toward them and say things in quiet tones. They seemed to be sisters, or friends. Sometimes one of the parents would touch them on the shoulder.

After we had made a circuit of the room, I told Sands I wanted to go around again, and I could see from the skin near his eyes that it made him happy. I didn't say it was only partly to have another look at the paintings and mostly to study the way the people acted, the way they floated their eyes over the canvases as if the paint was whispering to them in a language they all understood.

"Do you like them?" Sands asked when we were most of the way around the second time.

"Can we go a more time again?"

"Another time?"

"Yes."

"There's a different room I want you to see."

I nodded as if I had known all along that there was more than one room to the museum, but as we left the first room I turned and looked over my shoulder. I didn't want to leave the colors and the cleanliness, the shirts and dresses and pants and faces. White faces and black faces and brown faces and what I thought of then as Chinese faces, all of them so calm. I didn't want to leave behind the feeling that no one in the high-ceiling room was ever going to use his hand or her words to hurt any other person.

"This is why I really wanted to come here," Sands said as we crossed the hall that felt to me like a cool shadow and entered another high-ceiling room, larger than the first. I could see that there were works of art in frames in this room, too, but they had no color to them. A quick disappointment passed over me. But then some of the people in front of me moved on, and I stepped close enough to see that the framed pictures on the walls were drawings, not paintings. The drawings were of cathedrals, and made in pencil, and so perfectly neat and orderly that I wanted to climb inside them.

I stopped in front of the first framed drawing, close beside Sands, and I didn't move. The cathedral in the drawing was made with stones not unlike the stones we were using, various sizes, a bit rounded at the corners, the faces chiseled and uneven. It was a much larger building than even St. Mark's had been, with a steep slanted roof three times as long from bottom to top as our driveway from mailbox to front door. There were at least a dozen arched windows and a large circular one above the main entrance. I didn't want to blink. After a time, Sands moved on, but I stayed and stepped in closer. He'd told me not to touch the paintings, and I saw that no one else was touching the drawings, but I had an almost irresistible urge to reach out and run my fingers over them. It was as if the people who had set those stones in place were connected to me, mind to mind. And there was some kind of sadness to it, also, because the cathedral in the drawing was finished. There was no longer work for anyone, no activity showing in the smooth land-scape around it. Still, I wanted to go inside it and sit, and look at the light coming through the windows, and understand the way the ceiling was supported, the doors cut, why the arches didn't collapse under the weight above them. From the moment I'd started to lay the first course of stones at Sands's side, some part of me had awakened, as if the laws of architecture and masonry had been sleeping in the depths of my brain. I'd watched him set the first stones, and this new sense of line, weight, and order gave birth to a happy creature inside me. As I stared at the drawings, that creature stood up and began to sing.

I understood then why Sands would want to make a cathedral, be-cause there was nothing in the structure in front of me that seemed connected to what had happened to him, or to what went on in the makeshift church in West Ober. Nothing. The stones created a space, and the space contained some feeling that life might turn itself around and be lit up with hope. For the first time it seemed true to me beyond any doubt that Pastor Schect had been wrong all those Sundays, that he had misunderstood and was causing my parents and the others to mis-understand. He had painted the wrong kind of God inside our heads. According to my old beliefs, that thought was a sin, surely. At the same time, it was as if I was standing in a shower, and the warm water was cleaning out something toxic inside my mind, washing it into the drain. Again, I had an urge to touch the drawing, and my hand lifted a little ways from my side. Sands turned and looked at me and I lowered it quickly. I wanted to touch him then—which was an unfamiliar feeling for me—touch his big arms and thin body, as a way of thanking him, or asking him to forgive me for thinking he might want to hurt me. No kidnapper would bring you to a place like this.

All along the walls hung drawings of cathedrals and churches and chapels, exteriors and interiors, some in frames taller than either of us, some in frames smaller than the smallest stones we laid. I stopped for a long while at each one and each time had the feeling that my mind was being washed clean. I could sense people around me but I didn't look at them. Small spurts of bad feeling rose up into the cleanliness— thoughts of Pastor Schect, the police interviewing my parents, boy- ing, dousing, the stained fabric on the seat of Aaron's truck. Then the incredible idea that Aunt Elaine might actually be Sands's mother. I wanted to let all of it be washed away. I wanted, with my new, pure mind, to go to the stream where my father doused me, and put in a small boat there and ride that boat down along the rocky stream as far as the river that went along beside Route 112, and then turn and travel that river as it grew wider, pass beneath the bridges near town, and then under the larger metal bridge my father sometimes fished from, and then splash down on the Honey River, past the mills and into the big river, the Connecticut, and drift away across the ocean to the places where other kinds of people made buildings like this and drew pictures of them.

I went around four times. By the end, Sands was sitting on an arm- less wooden bench in the center of the room and studying me as atten- tively as I was studying the drawings.

There were even more rooms, it turned out, but Sands said we'd save those for another visit; the exhibits there had nothing to do with stonework and contained vases and statues and sculptures he didn't think I would like as much.

When we were outside again—the light pressed into my eyes and

the buildings there seemed only halfway real—Sands kept turning to
look at me. "I forgot something, be right out," he said, and leaving
me at the truck, he went back toward the museum. After a few minutes of waiting for him, I felt the world around me coming back into
focus, but it wasn't the same as it had been, and I wasn't the same. On
a peculiar impulse, as if possessed by a different Marjorie Elaine Richards, I walked over toward the shed where the attendant was staring at
a miniature TV, and I stood a few yards away from it, watching the images jump and shift. The man looked over his shoulder and flapped his
hand for me to come closer. I was surprisingly unafraid. His skin was as
black as a piece of coal beside the railroad tracks, but I noticed that the
palms of his hands were pink. He turned his back on the TV to make a
slow examination of my face, my hair, my clothes. "How was that museum?" he asked, in what seemed a genuinely friendly way.

"Good."

"Which part was the best?"

"Those the cathedrals," I said. He kept his brown eyes fixed on me,
as if waiting for me to say more. "My friend and me do a work with
stone. We're making of one."

Unlike most people I spoke to for the first time, the attendant
seemed to have little trouble understanding me. He didn't squint or
shake his head. He didn't correct me.

"Whereabouts?"

When I told him the name of the town, he slanted his head to one
side as if he didn't know it. "Let me see those hands," he said. "Tell if
you're fibbing."

"I don't to fib." I took two steps closer and held out my hands,
palms up, and the man took them in his long fingers and studied the calluses and scratched skin. After a minute he squeezed the hands gently
and let go. "God bless you then," he said. "Make a good one."

"We could."

"I bet you could. Make one as beautiful as you are."

I felt my face grow warm, but I resisted the urge to look at my feet, the way I might have done in school. "You go in of the museum?" I asked him.

"Sometimes I do."

I nodded, watching him, aware of the flickering screen behind him, the darkness of his skin, and then of Sands's familiar footsteps.

"Thank you," I said to the man.

"What for, young lady?"

I turned away from him without answering and went to the truck.

We ate in a restaurant where the tables had cloths on them, and cloth napkins, and the waitress tried very hard not to look at my sweatshirt and boots. It didn't matter to me so much then. I was used to it, for one thing, and, for another, my mind kept looping back to the drawings in the museum. Every time that happened I felt the peculiar cleanness inside me again, as if all the world's evil had been conquered by sheets of off-white paper in neat frames. I knew the bad things were still there, but if I concentrated on the drawings, it seemed, for a little while at least, that the power had been sucked out of them. Sands didn't say much at first. He seemed comfortable in the restaurant. He didn't look around to see how the other people were dressed and how they were sitting and eating. After asking me if I liked spaghetti with tomato sauce, he ordered for both of us and then sat staring out the window at the street, as if his mind was also being pulled back to the museum. I wondered if we could go back for another little while, and if I should ask him, but I was starting to worry about the time by then, and when I would get home, and what I'd say if my parents asked where I'd been.

"You look a little like to Aunt Elaine," I told him.

"Makes sense."

"We would be cousins for each other now," I said. The thought—strange and amusing—had just occurred to me.

But Sands quickly shook his head. "No. Not by blood," he said, as if the idea bothered him. "Your mother and Elaine aren't real sisters. Your mother was already a year or two years old when she moved in with Elaine's dad."

I went quiet again, worried I'd said something wrong. When we were finished eating and Sands was drinking a second cup of coffee, and I was sipping slowly from my glass of Coke, he handed something across the table in a paper bag. "A small present," he said.

I held it in two hands. I could feel that a woman at the closest table had turned to look at us. The object in the paper bag was heavy, and I set it down on the table where my plate had been and I couldn't raise my eyes.

"You can take it out of the bag, you know, Laney."

"I know of it."

The top edges of the paper bag had been rolled together. I unrolled them, reached inside, and took out a large book, absolutely new and undamaged. On the hard, shiny cover was a photograph of an enormous church, and, inside, the pages were as clean and shiny as ice on a pond, with photographs and drawings of the same churches we'd seen in the museum, and some others that hadn't been there. When I had looked at a few of the pages, I tucked my chin down against the top of my chest so Sands couldn't see my eyes.

"I had a feeling you liked the drawings we saw," he said after a few seconds, and I heard the note of shyness there again, the unsureness that seemed to hover around him whenever he wasn't actually working with his hands.

It let me raise my eyes, at least, though I couldn't speak.

"This book has some of the great cathedrals of Europe in it, and a little bit about all of them, about the people who designed and built them, the construction techniques, all that."

I was glad the waitress chose that moment to come and bring the check. Sands took money from his pocket, counted it, set it on the check, and looked at me again. "Like it?"

I nodded, and saw from his face that it hadn't been enough of an answer. "Thank you," I managed to say, but that wasn't enough either. In his eyes I thought I saw something that hadn't been there before, as if he was interested in me the way one or two boys at school sometimes showed an interest. It lasted only the smallest second, and I wasn't really sure it had even actually been there. He was standing up, so I stood up, too, still trying to find something to say that would be equal to what he had done. He'd gotten the kindness into him that Aunt Elaine had, I told myself. She'd given it down to him. The apple fell near to the tree.

I had the book clutched in one hand and the paper bag in the other. We went out the door and along the sidewalk and back to where Sands had parked his truck, and all the way I was trying to think of the words I could speak into that look on his face. When we were sitting in the truck again, when we had our seat belts on, when he was watching in the side mirror and backing up and then getting ready to pull out into traffic, I said, "Thank you for of five hundred times," and a flicker of a smile went across his face, and I didn't take it as a sign that he was laughing at me.

Sixteen

Sands maneuvered the truck out of the tangle of Boston traffic and onto the interstate, and neither of us said a word as he drove north into the hills. By the time we left the big highway and turned onto the far eastern end of Route 112, still more than three-quarters of an hour from my house, I had paged through the book twice, slowly, and read a little about the designs I liked best. A hundred questions had risen up in my thoughts but it was hard to make myself say anything to Sands just then. I was thinking about the expression I might have seen on his face in the restaurant, about the feeling it made in my body, and about the museum, and about Boston, and about his pastor, and about Aunt Elaine, and about how I was going to keep my mother and father from seeing the book and finding out where I'd been. On top of all that, as we drove, it began to seem to me that there was something troubling in Sands's silence. It made me think he was angry at me, or disappointed, and I didn't understand what I'd done.

"I'll drive you home if you want," he said, and I clearly heard a sour note in his voice.

"No. I like of to walking that road."

I saw a wrinkle of what appeared to be hurt around his mouth. When we'd gone about halfway from the interstate exit to the corner of Waldrup Road, he said, "I want," and then paused a minute, and went on, "I want you to talk with me the way other people talk." He turned his face to me across the seat for a second, then back at the road.

"Why for what?"

He moved his shoulders up and down. The shyness was on him again, and something else. "Because I know you can. Because I know how smart you are, and talking the way you talk makes you sound like you're very young, or . . . slow . . . that's all."

"Why could it matter for at you?"

"I'm just asking you to. I'm not telling you. I'm not saying it will have any effect on working with me. I'm just asking."

"That's why you made me going at Boston?"

Sands pushed his foot down hard on the brake and skidded the truck onto the gravel shoulder. The beads on his rearview mirror swung back and forth. He let out a big breath then snapped the key to off and faced me. I could see clearly then, in spite of all his praying and peace talk, that there was a part of him that could hurt a person. I could see it in the way the breath went into and out of his chest, so much like the way my parents breathed when they were upset, but with something else on top of it.

"Look," he said, not loud but with a lot of force. "Will you let someone be kind to you without always suspecting them of having a bad motivation?"

I just stared at the scar on top of his forearm. "Sure," I said. The word wobbled in the air as if it had three syllables.

"Everything from giving you the work to driving you home to taking you to Boston you interpret as some kind of strategy to hurt you."

"Girls have getting hurt," I said, "around in here."

"I know that. I have a college friend here, she's in the state police, she's working on those cases. I know about them. Everybody does."

"She's a she? And on for the state?"

"Yes. She's part of the team that's investigating them."

"She's . . . you're liking her for a girlfriend?"

"No."

"You don't at work yell on me."

"I'm not yelling at you."

"For the sounds you are."

"I'm frustrated, that's all. You have a wall around you. I'm saying you could open a door in the wall and let me at least look in. I'm not going to—"

Sands stopped abruptly and I moved my fingers closer to the seat belt clip, hoping he didn't see. The eyeglasses were shaking on the bridge of his nose.

"You think I'm going to hurt you, don't you?"

"Not anymore for a while until just now I didn't."

"You even think I could be the man who's abducting young women, and everything about me is a trick to get you to trust me."

"In school they told he was to do it that way."

"In school they said he does it that way."

I nodded.

"Say it the right way."

I quietly pushed the button on the seat belt so that it came free.

"And what, Laney? You're going to walk home from here because I asked you to speak right?"

"I could of."

"I know you could. I just can't really believe you think I could hurt you. Or anyone else. That I'm like that."

"Until now I wouldn't have anymore. . . . And you're part of black."

"Meaning what?"

"At in school they said about the man was black who did."

"Who said?"

"Other of kids."

"My friend doesn't think so. She said it's somebody who lives here, who knows the way people act here, knows who they trust. Which places and roads are quiet at which times of the day. And no black people live here. Almost none."

"That part you're right."

"You really think I'd hurt you?"

"Yelling like this is. Mad like this is so."

"You don't ever get mad? You don't ever yell at anyone?"

I shook my head.

"Really?"

I shook my head again.

"I'm sorry then." Sands closed his eyes and opened them. "I'm just frustrated. I can tell you're smart by the way you work, by the way you looked at the drawings and the book. And when you talk to me like that, it's a kind of pushing away."

"Yelling is a kind of."

"All right. I'm sorry. Put your seat belt back on, I'll drive you home, or to the store. I'm sorry."

He waited a minute, looking straight ahead, and then he pulled the truck back onto the highway. At the corner of Waldrup Road, just when I worried he'd turn right, into the rutted dirt, and try to take me home, Sands pulled the truck onto the shoulder again and turned off the engine. "Look, I'm sorry," he said for the fourth or fifth time. "I spoiled a good day. I apologize. I'm like that sometimes. The anger comes up in me for no good reason."

"Doesn't matter," I said.

"It matters, sure it matters. You got treated a hundred times worse than me and you're not yelling at anyone."

"I'm forgot it," I said. "The getting of mad."

"Good. I wish I could. It will haunt me all the way home, and then I'll remember it for weeks. I'm sorry."

I started to tell him I would try to speak differently if it pleased him, but it would have been a lie, and I knew it. He was watching me in the new way. I thought, for one second, that he was going to lean across the seat of the cab and try to kiss me, and I wanted him to do that but I couldn't say so. After a few seconds I said, "Thank you," the way I always did, and then, getting out, "Can I still take for the book with me?"

"Of course you can take it. It's a gift, I told you. And I'm paying you for the day, I told you that, too. I'll see you on Monday, same as always. And I'm sorry I got upset."

"Okay and all," I said. I closed the truck door and started walking. I went a hundred steps down Waldrup Road before I heard his truck drive off.

Seventeen

I walked down the road holding the book in the paper bag against my right hip, so that if anyone was standing in our yard they wouldn't see it. Even before I turned into the driveway I could hear my father shouting inside the house, and though I couldn't make out the words, I knew from the high-pitched tone that it was no kind of ordinary trouble. Between me and the house stood one of the twenty or so stacks of cordwood that cluttered the yard. It was as high as my shoulders and as long as two cars together. I folded the end of the paper bag around the book, then set it down against the bottom of the stack of wood, on the road side, so no one could see it from the house.

Before I had taken three more steps I saw my mother hurry out of the house, leaving the door and the screen open. My father's voice came bouncing across the front steps after her. It seemed to go high in the air around the yard, the words like red balloons with spikes on them. "Make on a living for it!" was one of the things I heard.

My mother came across the dirt with her shoulders rounded and her cigarette held down against the side of her old jeans, a woman turning her back on a smoky fire. "What you hiding there, you Majie?" she said, but without much interest.

"A nothing."

My mother put the cigarette to her mouth and took a long drag, looking at me through the smoke. "Worked?"

I nodded.

"You're all clean of."

"Why's Pa mad?"

"Why you all clean of?"

"We worked on with the wood a little for it, then to see a man at the windows. Why is he?"

"Drunk. From Weedon's."

"For why?"

My mother put the cigarette to her lips and sucked on it, then blew a long gray stream of smoke out through her nostrils, all without moving her eyes from me. "I'm p.g.'s why. Baby land. Almost forty-year-old woman wasn't careful, gets p.g. Husband smashes a chair against the kitchen and makes sticks for a drum like a boy."

"You're not, can you?"

"Little thing about not bleeding for four months tells ya. Puking out your guts every morning tells."

"Not for really?"

"Money! The money! The money!" my father was screaming inside.

My mother hooked one thumb back over her shoulder and smoked with the other hand, half closing her eyes as she inhaled. This time she blew the smoke up with her lower lip protruding. "Show you a trick," she said. "For your good luck." She walked to the woodpile—my book was hidden on the far side—and took two billets off the top of it. For some reason I remember that they were white birch, the bark papery and curling away from the wood. You didn't need kindling with white birch, even when it was cold. You could just put it in the stove, touch a match to the bark, and watch it burn. My mother dropped the two pieces on the dirt in front of her then pushed them a few feet apart with the toe of her sneaker. "So's you know," she said. She touched the one billet with her toe and said, "Bleed number one." Then touched the other billet and said, "Bleed number two, after one month. See, you Majie?"

"Yes," I said.

My mother squatted and set the last inch of her burning cigarette on the ground in the middle and left it there, longwise, the hot end pointing at one piece of firewood and the mouth end at the other. Smoke rose from it in a gray twirl. Inside the house, my father was screaming and drumming with the chair legs. My mother looked up at me, and I could see something like a splash of youth on her features, a momentary affection for me, all mixed in with a tough-girl attitude that did not have the slightest trace of fear or worry or self-pity in it. "This here"—she pointed to the cigarette—"is the time when the man-seed grows on good ground in you. Right here." She stood up and twisted her foot on the cigarette until it went out. "I forgot that oncet, and now lookit."

We could hear my father banging sticks on the floor in a crazy rhythm, and then a piece of the back of a chair came flying out the open door and skidded on the dirt near the front step. My mother and I looked at it there, and I thought for a moment she would laugh. "Like this is just what he did, your smart pa, when I told him I was p.g. with you. Almost just the same, except in the place we lived over there in town."

I felt the remark like a kick in the stomach. I swallowed and tried not to show anything. After a few seconds I said, "When is the baby to supposed to be?"

"Before snow. So now you quit school and stay home to help me on it."

"I don't want to for quit school."

"I don't want to for having another little shit in the house."

"What could you do?"

My mother swiveled her head at the question and sent her eyes into me like two screwdrivers. "Do?" She reached into her shirt pocket for the package of Primes. "Get fat. Scream. Bleed. Carry home somethin' what eats and shits. Do? I had a baby to die on me oncet, he tell you that?"

I shook my head.

"Aunt Elaine, she tell?"

"Didn't never."

"Carried it half the long time and he died because of my sins. Paid that penance. Now I owe another one to God."

Late that night I went out and got the book and hid it in the back of my closet.

Eighteen

On the following Saturday, a week after the museum visit, Aunt Elaine came to see the cathedral for what I think was the first time. She hugged me, checking my face for fresh marks while pretending not to, then she walked around the work site, running her fingers over the stones that had been cemented in place, and the wooden staging, and listening to Sands tell her how we were going to finish this first section, so we'd have inside work when the cold weather came. How we were going to put the windows and doors in, make the arches, put the roof on. How, next summer, we'd begin another section, connected to the first.

I pretended to work but I watched my aunt closely. I noticed that she didn't ever touch Sands, though she often stood close to him. At moments, it seemed to me they were almost like friends, but that something else was involved, too, and that Sands was talking much more than he usually talked—about the different kinds of stone, the type of wood the beams had to be made from and where he'd get them, the angle of the roof, the weight of the snow, the building inspector's latest visit—all of it in a way that made it seem there were other things he wasn't talking about but wanted to.

Aunt Elaine glued her eyes onto his face as he talked. She asked questions. She said, over and over again, how wonderful the building was going to be, how spiritual. I'm sorry, I'm sorry, I'm sorry, is what I saw in the forward tilt of her body and heard in her voice. I loved you. I'm sorry for what I did.

I thought it wasn't the worst thing you could hear in the voice of your mother.

I was glad, when Aunt Elaine was driving me into town for lunch—just the two of us—that she acted in a way I thought of as "plain" with me and spoke straight without having hidden things in her mind. Instead of going to an actual restaurant, we went to Boory's store, which was at the northern edge of the downtown. As it does even still, Boory's offered shelves of canned soups and baked beans, beef stew, boxes of macaroni, cream of wheat, salt, cornmeal. There was an old penny-candy counter made of glass in a frame of dark walnut, where the candy bars cost fifty cents apiece in those days. In the middle of the store stood three old-fashioned Formica-topped tables surrounded by unmatched chairs, and the young woman behind the counter—who had a tattoo of a crucifix on one bare shoulder and a tattoo of a skull on the other—served customers from a small chalked menu of sandwiches and soup. For dessert there were cookies and homemade muffins.

We sat at the table farthest from the cash register. Aunt Elaine was wearing a blue T-shirt with gold stripes across it, and her hair came down in waves from the top of her head, falling on her shoulders in a splash of brown and gray. She suggested I try something different—the bacon, lettuce, and tomato sandwich—with my lemonade. She had the split pea soup and coffee.

"Ma's p.g.," I said, after the second bite. I had told no one. The news had been bubbling inside me all week at school and at work and running like a constant loud noise beneath every minute I was in our house.

Aunt Elaine stopped eating and put down her spoon.

"She told it for me when I came back after Boston with Sands. Pa was for breaking up one on the chairs for the eating table. He had to go over at the dump for another one. Now he goes a lot outside like always and he doesn't to talk."

"She told you herself?"

I nodded.

"Due when?"

"At October or November, I think. She told she was to give it the name Jesus, but maybe I think she was saying it at a joke. She said for me that I quit school to help for the taking care of."

"Quit school?"

I swallowed, watched her face. You didn't have to look very carefully to see a reflection of Sands's face there.

"You don't want to quit school, do you?"

"I can do in school for pretty good. One teacher told I would be near the best of everybody but for if early on I went like I should."

"Or if early on I had done something for you," Aunt Elaine said.

"You weren't to living near here anywhere then."

Aunt Elaine touched the spoon to her soup and made a circle with it there. "Your father's upset?"

"Sure. For the money about it . . . And probably the work about it, some."

Two customers—a man and a woman in bicycle shorts and T-shirts—came into the store and spoke to the clerk behind the counter, and paid for something she gave them. When they left and no other customers came in, I had the strange and wonderful feeling that any words at all could be sent across the table that separated me from my aunt. I didn't know what caused that feeling—my mother's news, or something in the plain way Aunt Elaine was speaking to me, or what I'd seen in Boston, or what Sands had said in the truck on the way home. For whatever reason, the dam of sticks and mud I'd built inside myself had been creaking and splitting all that week, and now, suddenly, some more snow had melted and it burst apart. "Sands told me something," I began.

Aunt Elaine watched me.

"You're his true mother."

She waited almost no time at all before answering me. "That's right."

"With of a man who is black."

"With a man I loved."

"He left you alone to having a baby."

"I left him is truer than he left me. And then he died."

I looked into my aunt's face, then away. I ran my eyes around the wood floor, the narrow pine boards shrunken away from each other by fifty winters of woodstove heat, the varnish long ago worn off except in the corners of the room where no one set foot. The thought came to me that it might have been true that my father had killed a man— certainly he'd seemed capable of that the other day, with his screams and crazy drumming—and that possibly it had been the man who'd gotten Aunt Elaine pregnant. If Aunt Elaine had been in college, my father would have been about the right age . . . if there was a right age for killing someone.

"What was my mother of a girl?" I said, instead of asking.

"Fairly good in school. Fairly well behaved in the early years. Pretty."

"You can see it on her still."

"Yes, you can. Before her mother married my father there had been some trouble in her family. Neither of them would ever speak of it, but my father mentioned something once in a vague way. Your mother's biological father had beaten her mother, I think. Badly. Regularly. We weren't close enough for me to ask about it. I was so much older for one thing and she was very young when they came to live with us. And for another, whenever I tried to ask her about her life she'd make a joke and walk away or change the subject. She was never an easy person to talk to."

"Not still."

"When I tried to do things for her, take her places, buy her things, she resisted. She preferred her friends at school, and that hurt me, and so, after a while, I pulled back. She never knew about my pregnancy. My parents sent me away before anyone could see."

Aunt Elaine paused to take a sip of her coffee and I noticed her breathing had changed.

"Do you know everything you have to know about how women get pregnant?" she asked.

"Why is everybody asking on me now?"

"Do you, honey?"

"I know for it hurts. What you do for boys to be happy. I know."

I was surprised then to see a silver film of tears come up in my aunt's eyes. She didn't bother to wipe them, but for a minute she couldn't speak.

"Why would you to give Sands away at another person?"

"My father forced me to. Or almost forced me."

"How?"

"He told me I had to, if I wanted to stay in college, if I wanted him to continue to be my father."

"Maybe they had something for a penance for you if you didn't. To punish you."

"I don't know that."

"Sure they could."

"I don't know. I just did what he told me. I think, deep down inside, there was a part of me that wanted freedom, that was selfish, so I don't blame them completely. It was my decision."

"But couldn't of the man helped you?"

"He had worked for several summers at an apple orchard—do you know where Walpole is?—cultivating and pruning the trees. I got a job there one summer. I sold apples and vegetables and pies at the stand on the road. We had a wonderful connection from the start. We talked and took walks after work. We went swimming, we kissed, we made love, I got pregnant right away. He was Jamaican, five and a half years older, and he was going to have to go back to Jamaica when the fall harvest was finished. Unless I married him. I had finished one year of college. I wanted to be a nurse, to break away from the life we had at home, which was stifling to me. At the same time, I wanted to keep the baby, at least part of me wanted that. And the man said he wanted to keep it. But my parents—it was my father, mainly; my stepmother, your mother's mother, was a very passive woman—told me it would ruin the rest of my life. He said I had to decide quickly, or he'd stop paying for college. He said I'd end up like some of the poor families we knew, where the girls got pregnant in high school and lived the poorest kinds of lives in dreary apartments near the mills. He said I'd never be allowed to live peacefully in this area with a black husband. But I had a stubborn part of me, and I was in love. I decided I would keep the baby and go to Jamaica and marry my boyfriend. His name was Edmund. At the end of the apple season—I was only two months pregnant then— when he was going to have to go home soon and I was going to have to go away so nobody would know about the baby and I could say I was at school, I arranged to meet him at the bus station. We were going to Boston first. He'd saved up money and we were going to fly to Jamaica and start a life there. I packed one bag of my things without my parents seeing. Your mother was young then, eleven or twelve. She had her own room. She didn't know anything about it. I sneaked out of the house that night and I had my bag of clothes and a few things, and I went out the back door very late, and I made it as far as the sidewalk in front of the house . . . and there was my father, standing there, holding a glass of whiskey at his hip, smoking, watching for me. He must have been waiting for hours.

"I couldn't run from him, so I walked up and stood next to him, and I didn't even set the bag of clothes on the ground I was so deter-mined to go. For a little time he just smoked and drank and stared out at the dark street. I told him I was going. He said I could go if I had made up my mind to go, but that I could never come home if I went, that he would no longer be my father.

"My mother had died when I was very young, and so for him to say these things to me was . . ."

"Would be like to having nobody."

"Something like that . . . I listened to him, and then I said that I loved him and I would miss him, but I was going. He turned away from me then, just turned his back and went into the house and as long as I live I'll remember seeing him go like that, up the walk and up the steps and through the front door without looking back. I stood there. I waited—a few minutes too long, as it turned out—then I decided and I started walking into town, to the bus station, and I was late, and hurrying, and then I was running, and when I got there the bus had just gone. I could hear the engine for a few seconds. A woman was standing near the door. I asked her if she'd seen a black man waiting and then getting on the bus, and she said no, she hadn't, so I assumed Edmund had not really wanted to have me leave with him and I didn't try to follow him. There were no more buses that night anyway. I would have had to hitchhike in the dark."

"Crazy you would to do that."

"Yes. The sad thing was, though, that the woman I asked was lying, or crazy, or both. Or she just hadn't seen him. Edmund had been there, it turned out, had been waiting for me, had decided I wasn't coming, and so he'd gotten on the last bus and left. He sent me one letter, which I still have. I'll show it to you if you'd like. I take it out and read it every few years. He was the first man I made love with."

Aunt Elaine paused and lifted her coffee cup to her lips, but I could see she wasn't drinking from it. She set it back down and after a minute she went on. "I stayed awake in my bedroom all that night, thinking he hadn't ever planned to go with me, hadn't come to the bus station. Even so, in the morning, I called the orchard and asked if they knew a way I could get in touch with him. They didn't know anything. The person who managed the orchard said all the Jamaican workers had left. She said she didn't know Edmund from any of the rest of them. So I sat there for a long while, trying to decide what to do. It seemed like I'd end up having the baby by myself and living . . . I didn't know where, there were no shelters then. After a long time I stood up and

went to find my father and I told him I would go away, and give the
baby away when it came. I could see how much it pleased him, and I
wanted to please him so desperately. He spoke to me again, treated me
like his daughter again. After another few weeks I went to relatives of
his in Wisconsin. Eau Claire. I stayed with them until the birth. My
father and stepmother told your mother I was away at school taking a
special course. I held the baby for a while, then gave him into the arms
of the nurse. . . . Every time after that, every day of my life, I thought
about him. I wrote Edmund, telling him what had happened, and he
wrote back that one letter I told you about. He wrote that he'd been
at the bus station and thought I didn't want to raise the child with him
and that was why I hadn't come. He was upset about the baby, but he
said we'd have other children, and we'd find the boy I'd given away,
and that I should come to Jamaica as soon as I could. I was going back
to college. I wrote him and told him I'd come as soon as I finished the
work for that term. And then I got a letter back, from his sister, saying
he'd been killed."

"By how?"

"A bus accident, strangely enough. So after that I got my nurse's
degree, and after that I moved all over the country trying to run away
from what I'd done—Idaho, California, Hawaii. All those years when
your mother was growing up, and then getting married, and having
you, I was gone. I barely knew her. When I did finally come back she
was changed into the person she is now, and you were in the world,
and she did everything she could to keep me away from you. That's
another story I'll tell you someday."

"And Sands found you on later?"

She nodded and brushed the back of one wrist across her eyes. "I
knew when he was eighteen he could come looking for me, and I kept
track of the time and I waited for that phone call, or that letter. Every
day I waited for that young man, my son, to come and knock on my
front door. Every day for years. Every time I saw a baby, and then a
young boy, and then an adolescent boy, I felt like I'd given away my

soul, doing what I did, that I'd been responsible for Edmund's death, that I'd killed someone, or something beautiful in the world. I devoted myself to nursing. I helped people—"

"Like for a penance."

"I was running away the whole time. I had a relationship in Hawaii, no children, and when it ended, I decided to come back here. There was a job in Watsonboro that was right for me. My father had been diagnosed with cirrhosis and given about six months to live. So I came back. I took care of my father while he was dying but we never spoke about my pregnancy. Your mother was like a stranger to me, extremely cold. It was only because I wanted to see you so much that I even had anything to do with her. And then I started to feel guilty about that, too—I had money, I had a decent life, I'd done something I couldn't forgive myself for, and even though she had so much less than I did she'd decided to raise her child and not give it away. She had always stood up to my father—her stepfather—in a way I hadn't been able to."

One tear broke from my aunt's eye and ran down her cheek but she didn't put a hand to it.

"But you never did to kill anyone," I said.

"No, but that's what it felt like. I knew what day my son would turn eighteen, of course. And when he didn't come looking for me, that day, or that year, or the next year, I finally couldn't stand it anymore and I started to look for him. There are various ways now. Your mother didn't know about all this. I tried and tried but I couldn't find . . . I spent all the savings I had, trying to find him. It turned out that he'd been trying, too, and eventually he found me."

"You gave for my parents money, too."

"Give."

"And they for that listen on you a little."

"Did you tell them about Sands being my child?"

"No."

"I'll tell them now. Have they taken you to that church again?"

"Not at last Sunday. But tomorrow maybe they could. You called with the police, my mother told. On Pastor Schect."

"I did," Aunt Elaine said. "They knew about him. They were already suspicious." She looked down at her soup; I looked at the cans of food on the shelves.

"Marjorie," I heard her say. "Honey. Do you want to come and live with me?"

I turned my eyes back to her. I heard people come into the store. I could feel her waiting for an answer, watching me, but I avoided speaking for as long as I could. "Why for?" I said at last.

"Why? I should have taken you away years ago."

"You for missed out with no baby is why?"

She swallowed. A wave of hurt went across her face. "Do you think it's normal, being raised the way you've been raised?"

"I'm a normal."

"I'm not talking about you. You have the sweetest heart of anyone I know. You're a miracle girl. Do you know how beautiful you are? How intelligent? You're stunning. But I'm talking about what's been done to you. Do you think being poked in the eye and mouth at church, by adults, is normal?"

"My boyfriend had at the same to him."

"You have a boyfriend?"

"Pretty much. Aaron."

"Does he treat you well?"

"Pretty much."

"Are you having sex with him?"

I looked away.

"Honey, I'm not meaning to pry. Has your mother told you about protection? About not getting pregnant, and not getting a disease and so on?"

I shifted in my chair and looked at the top of Aunt Elaine's uneaten soup, on which a film was forming. It did not seem to me the right kind of thing to be talking about in Boory's, with people coming in and going out, and walking right past the table, and with the girl with the crucifix tattoo standing behind the counter watching us, trying to hear.

"Honey." Aunt Elaine reached out and put her hand on my wrist. "You're not pregnant, too, are you?"

I shook my head.

"We haven't not hurt yet. I haven't done, I mean. You and Sands think I'm a young girl, the stupid girl."

"I don't think that."

"You weren't in protected."

"I know I wasn't. But for me and Sands's father there was tenderness, there was love. That's what I would want—"

"But he died and you never after had one husband."

"I know that. Why are you angry at me? Because I didn't help you all these years? I wanted to. You pushed me away just like your mother did. You came to my house that one time when things were bad—it must have been two years ago—you spent two nights and we got along so well and then you never came back, or called, or wrote. I sent you three letters you never answered."

"That time for I came to your house on of my own? And found a place where I called you on my own?"

"Yes."

"They had a whipped me very bad for that. Very bad. Three days I couldn't to walk. If I told you on that then, if I went and run to come to you again . . ." I took hold of my lemonade glass as a way of removing my hand from Aunt Elaine's. I had the thought then, just for one crazy second, that I would stand up and pull my jeans down right there in the middle of Boory's and show her the scars. Tears came up in my eyes and I looked away, then swatted at them with my forearm and looked back.

"Your parents whipped you? Or the preacher?"

"The first of."

"Where?"

"The back top on my legs. And no letters you sent I never saw them at the mailbox neither."

Aunt Elaine reached for my hand then, but I took it from the Formica and put it under the table on the top of my thigh.

"If I promised you that no one could hurt you again, would you come and live with me? If I went to the police?"

I only looked at her. After a few seconds I said, "Did my father to kill somebody ever?"

"Your father wouldn't hurt you anymore, I can promise you that. But you have to come away."

"Did ever he?"

"No."

"Didn't he been time upstate?"

"Yes. He was in jail for something he did before you were born. Eighteen months."

"Did for what?"

"It was a fight. Your grandfather Paul was famous for fighting and he brought your father up to believe that was the most important skill for a man to have in life. Your father started it, I think, though the man had done or said something he didn't like. The man was badly hurt and came close to dying, but he lived, and your father went to jail. When he came out he was different from the way he had been when he went in, or not really different but . . . what was inside him had been turned up louder. Then, in a little while, he married your mother. They had been seeing each other before he was sent away. No one in my family wanted your mother to marry him. My father was especially upset about it, but she wasn't really his daughter and she wouldn't listen in any case and she was old enough, legally."

"Aaron said he killed on that man, my father did."

"Finish eating, honey. We'll talk more outside. Finish up."

I looked at the sandwich and lemonade but couldn't eat. Aunt Elaine paid. We went outside and sat in her car in front of Boory's.

For a few minutes we sat there without speaking, looking through the windshield at the town's main street: brick-faced buildings and pickup trucks; a wide, northern New England commercial strip, all grays and reds with flecks of green from trees the town had planted the summer before. My eyes had dried by then. I wanted to keep talking about my father and mother, and I didn't want to.

"I can go to court for a restraining order," Aunt Elaine said, "and I think, I'm almost sure, I can make it so you can come and live with me, and your father and mother and the preacher can't come and hurt you in any way."

Almost sure, I remember thinking. Almost.

"Would you want to do that?"

"Then I couldn't have work with Sands. It's too far to you. My mother had nobody to help on the baby. My father had not enough money."

"I can give them some money still. You could get a license and drive to work. It's not that far, really."

"It's Watsonboro."

"You just come up the highway."

"In which of a truck?"

"Or . . . what if you lived in the church building with Sands? There's several bedrooms there and he said he's fixing them up. You could keep working, go to school still."

It seemed to me then that my aunt was having a spell of craziness of the sort my mother sometimes had, where the things she said had no link to reality. There were times late at night when my mother would come into my room and sit on the edge of the bed until I woke up and she'd be talking like my father but without making sense: "When they get of a age is a time for going, that's all. Your father knows. Pastor Schect. God sends a voice into a town and calls, and you answer for it to them. See?" And I'd pretend to understand her, and secretly sniff the air to see if she'd been drinking, and most of the time she hadn't been. If my aunt wasn't having a crazy spell like that, then she was talking about what I called "a dreamish life," the way Sands sometimes did. A dreamish life in which the police could determine what went on inside your family. A life in which I could live alone in a house with a man and nothing would happen, and no one in the town would assume it did.

I shook my head.

"You have a life of your own, honey. You have to finish school and then you can have a good life. You're seventeen. The baby is your mother and father's responsibility. And the money for it should be their responsibility, too, not yours."

"They don't have much for it though, and how would it be for it? Another like me, or worse?"

"You like working with Sands, don't you?"

"Sure."

"He says you're an excellent worker. He used those words exactly."

I couldn't think of any reply. I was imagining a baby girl in the house, my mother refusing to change its diapers, feeding it only when she was in the mood. I was thinking the child would surely die if she didn't have an older sister there to care for her.

My aunt reached across and put one hand on my knee, which made me jump, but I didn't move away. "Look at me, honey."

I turned my face.

"I love you," my aunt said.

I couldn't remember anyone ever having said that to me, not my mother or father and not any boy. All I could think to say was "All right."

"I'm going to make things better now. I promise you that."

"Things go along good just as now."

Another wash of water came up into Aunt Elaine's eyes. I looked away. It was a crying day for the two of us. Through the windshield I saw Aaron's ugly truck go past, but Aaron didn't see me, or if he saw me he didn't wave.

"Look at me please, honey. Things aren't fine, and they aren't normal, and there isn't a God anywhere who wants this to happen to you."

"Why could he of let it, then?"

"I don't know the answer to that question. But I know it is going to stop."

I looked at my aunt's face then. It was a good face, and kind, but the face of a person—this seemed obvious to me—who did not know much about the way the world worked. Not nearly as much as she thought she knew.

Nineteen

The next day, my mother and father didn't go to church. With the exception of once when my father had hurt himself in a bad fall in the woods, and those weeks when we were completely out of money, it was the first time since I was very small that I could remember staying home on a Sunday morning. Snowstorms, ice storms, the flu and sore throats, lack of decent clothes—almost nothing stopped us from making the trip to West Ober to pray with Pastor Schect. I was fairly certain why my parents weren't going: The police must have come when I was away and asked them what had been happening at the church. But I wasn't about to raise the subject.

For breakfast I made myself two slices of toast with peanut butter and honey, and drank two glasses of water to fill my stomach. (With my new earnings I had wanted to buy food for the house, but my father flew into a rage when I mentioned it—which was confusing to me: Hadn't he been the one who wanted me to work and contribute money? Wasn't he happy to have the extra income? So, instead of using some of it to buy food, I kept all my share of the money for myself, in an old pair of underwear in the back left corner of my closet, squeezed under a loose edge of Sheetrock next to the cathedral book.) My mother sat on her end of the couch, not offering to cook, not reading anything, not drinking, not even raising her eyes when I sat at the table. My father had gone out early into the woods, come back to get his keys (still holding his chain saw in one hand, as if it had become like another arm to him and he was unaware of it), and then driven away without speaking to either of us. I wondered if he'd gone to Weedon's, or to find and hurt Aunt Elaine, or if he'd decided, in spite of the police investigation, to go to the service on his own.

When I finished eating I went into my room, took the book Sands had given me out of its hiding place, and sat on my bed with it opened across my knees. I put the pillow beside it so I could cover the book quickly if my mother came in, and I turned the pages slowly, studying every aspect of the church buildings, every corner and arch, every stone and piece of stained glass and bell tower. Each time before I turned to a new image, I'd say a short prayer, asking God to let me keep working on the cathedral, to forgive me for my sins, not to punish me too badly for missing church. But my prayers had turned mostly empty by that point, just an old habit, almost a superstition.

When I was most of the way through the book, I heard the popping sound of tires on the gravel driveway, but I didn't hear the usual backfiring and rumbling of my father's pickup. Thinking it might be my aunt come to check on me, I hid the book under the pillow and stepped into the main room of the house. My mother was locked in one of her trances and hadn't moved. There was the sound of a car door being closed. I went nearer the window and looked out. I saw a plain black car in front of the house—the police, I thought, at first—and a man standing next to the driver's-side door with his back to me. But then, before the man even turned around, I realized it wasn't a policeman. Pastor Schect stood still for a minute, arms hanging at his sides. He turned his head left and right, left and right again, raking his eyes across the neat stacks of stove wood and the patches of spring grass that marked our bare yard like an infestation. He turned around and as he started toward the house he looked straight at the window.

"What on?" my mother said, lifting her head and blinking like a person awakened from sleep.

Before I could answer, there was a staccato knocking.

"Open it, you Majie you," my mother said in a sleepy voice.

I couldn't make my feet move. I said a prayer under my breath. The knocking started up again.

"I'll boy you for sure you don't open it."

I went to the door and when I pulled it toward me, Pastor Schect was there on the step, his face knitted and puckered as if someone had taken a needle and sewed the cheeks to the lips and the eyebrows to the forehead in five bad stitches. I looked at his dyed hair, his nose that widened like a horse's when he breathed. His eyes belonged to a man who was starving to death and hallucinating, seeing me as a piece of food. From where he stood, the open door blocked his view of the couch, and so, after seeing the empty driveway, he must have thought I was home alone. He'd already started toward me, excited, eager, and I'd already taken a step backward, when my mother blurted out, "Who the God would bang doors on us for this hour?"

I watched the surprise wobble across Pastor's face. He straightened up, breathed through his nostrils once, and strode into the room exactly the way he strode around in church: legs thrown out in front of him, chin back, neck stiff. A wind-up doll playing preacher. I noticed for the first time that he had on a suit, a rumpled brown suit over a white shirt and red tie, and his work boots. "I have come to cast out demons, say," he yelled as he stepped far enough forward to see around the door and make eye contact with my mother. She stood up and bent forward in a sort of awkward bow and then didn't seem to know what to do. We weren't used to having visitors. The awkwardness lasted a few seconds before there was the sound of a pickup in the driveway, another slamming door, and then my father yelling crazily, "Nah! Nah! Nah!" He came running toward the open door and I could see he had the chain saw still in his hand, and sweat and dirt on his face. He'd told me more than once that whenever he left us alone he worried about someone coming to the house to rape my mother and me. He'd kill the man, he promised. He'd cut the man true in half. For one second I thought my father was going to run right up the sagging steps and start the chain saw as he crossed the threshold, and part of me was hoping he'd cut Pastor Schect into pieces. But when he saw who it was he stopped short, breathing hard, and let the heavy saw hang down by his side so that the veins stood out under the skin of that arm.

Pastor Schect dropped his eyes to the saw and lifted his arms overhead and fluttered them there. "Satan from this house go!" he shouted.

My father squinted at him, took two more fast breaths, and said, "We dint ain't do it."

"We dint," his wife echoed.

"I dint do it," I said. "My aunt did."

I felt, at those words, that I would be sick. I felt that Satan surely was in the house then, and had crawled up inside me and taken hold of my tongue. I watched as Pastor stomped around the living room, slapping his hand on various surfaces—the table, the sofa, the walls. My parents had one picture on the wall—a kitten in a basket; my mother had brought it home from the dump in a sentimental moment and my father had banged in a nail and hung it there to please her. When Pastor Schect hit the wall the second time the picture bounced loose and fell. We heard the sound of glass breaking. My father put the saw down at his feet and looked at my mother. He was well into the house now, and Pastor Schect was moving toward my room, ignoring the breaking glass. "Here is the demon's place, say!" he shouted in his high, raspy voice, standing at the door of my room, looking in. "The demon bed! The demon clothings! Cast them out, say!" Hearing those words, my father turned to me and took half a step but I wasn't going to wait to see what happened next. I swerved around his arm and ran out the door and past the two vehicles, sprinting for the road. "You Majie you!" I heard my mother yell behind me. "Girl, you come! Douse you!"

But I kept sprinting, turning onto Waldrup Road and not looking back.

I ran as far as my legs and lungs would let me, listening for the sound of a truck engine over the harsh sawing noise of my breath. When I couldn't sprint anymore I slowed to a trot, my breath coming in big heaves and the soles of my sneakers scuffing the dirt. A coyote crossed the road in front of me, its coat dirt-red and ragged, its long fluffy tail dragging. The animal turned its head once toward me, then slunk into the trees. I angled into the woods on the other side, crossing a rocky stream, breathing hard. Beyond the stream the ground sloped up. I kept going at a fast walk, brushing aside low branches and dodging between the tree trunks and blackberry bushes, listening, listening. In the distance I heard a car engine. A short ways farther up the hill I came upon a boulder with a cleft in it and I laid myself down in the damp cleft and tried to force my breathing into a quieter rhythm. I could hear something through the trees—a car horn being sounded at regular quick intervals, almost in time with every third heartbeat. Beep . . . Beep . . . Beep . . . Beep. I tried to lower myself farther down between the sides of the stone. In my mind's eye, I could see my aunt talking to me across the seat of her car, saying she loved me, and then I heard what I'd said in the house a few minutes earlier, and my own betrayal seemed like the fingers of Satan reaching up the insides of my breasts, taking hold of my lungs, and throat, and tongue. The horn kept beeping, a sound like geese in the fall sky. I heard the car coming along the road and slowing, then stopping, then the engine was turned off and I heard a door. I tried not to move.

"Girl!" I heard after a few more seconds.

God, God, God, I prayed silently. God, God, God save on me now. Forgive me.

"Girl!" Pastor Schect shouted again. His voice came through the trees like a searchlight. "Let the Satan be taken out from you! Girl, let it now! Come down and let it be taken!"

I didn't move. I tried to draw slow shallow breaths but I could feel my heart like a drum in my chest, and the rock pinching my back muscles, and a dampness there as if I was sinking down slowly into a swamp.

There were footsteps, a rustling in the bushes at the side of the road.

"Girl!"

I kept my eyes open, wondering if he'd cross the stream. Above me were spruce branches and beech branches and a weak sunlight filtering through. God, God, God, I mouthed.

"You can't hide from the Lord of Gods," Pastor Schect yelled up the hill, but I could tell from the sound of the words that he hadn't come any farther into the woods. I listened. If there was a truck in the background, if my father was coming, then the streambed and the woods wouldn't stop him. He'd take hold of me by the hair and lead me down to Pastor Schect and there would be nothing to save me then.

But there was no truck engine, just the sound of another car going past the other way, tires in the dirt, the ping of small stones against the undercarriage. I imagined Pastor Schect turning and waving to the driver like a man of God in his rumpled suit and dark-tinted hair, meditating on the glory of nature. He did not shout again. After a time I heard his footsteps on the road and then the car door closing, but he sat there a long while before starting the car, and then several more minutes before he drove away, and during that time I lay still and let the rock cut into the muscles of my back, and the dampness spread on my shirt and pants. I kept my eyes open and steady and I concentrated on the sunlight and wished and prayed with all my force that he'd leave me alone and not go back to the house and wait. I could face my parents, but I didn't want to be looked at that way ever again by Pastor Schect, or touched by him, or killed by him.

In time, he drove off down Waldrup Road, away from our house, but still I lay there, waiting for him to return, my back muscles cramping. When I was sure there were no other vehicles coming, that Pastor Schect wasn't playing a trick, and almost sure my father wasn't standing down there, silently watching for me at the edge of the woods, I sat up. I peered through the trees. Nothing. Another minute and I stood, pushing myself out of the cleft in the rock and looking down at the road. Besides a few coins and two one-dollar bills in my pants pocket I had no money with me. I pictured myself walking the rest of the way down Waldrup Road and all the way into town . . . and then what? Going to Sands at the rectory and asking for money so I could take a bus to Watsonboro? It was Sunday. He wouldn't be working. He'd be off in the country on one of his drives, or down visiting Aunt Elaine, or going to Boston or New York, to a museum, maybe with a girlfriend. I was hungry and thirsty and chilled from the dampness at the back of my shirt. What if Pastor Schect was waiting along Route 112? Or my father decided to go to Weedon's and saw me walking past? I thought, briefly, of taking the risk anyway, sleeping at the work site and waiting for Sands to show, but the idea of him finding me there like that, hungry and dirty and afraid—that was too bitter.

When I'd waited a long time, I walked down the hill and across the stream. After a minute or two, I turned left, back toward our house. I prayed as I went, not asking for anything but forgiveness for my moment of treachery, just speaking to God in whispers and asking that.

My father's truck was still in the driveway, but I didn't see him. When I came through the door my mother's eyes hit me like pointed fingers in the face. She was leaning back against the kitchen counter with an open bottle of wine behind her arm. She was wearing a certain expression, something I'd seen several times in the past, a concentrated fury that seemed to say there was nothing, absolutely nothing, she wouldn't do. "Who's now gonto be willow-whipped," she said, and it was the farthest thing from a question.

I stood still and faced her.

"Who's now gonto," my mother repeated.

"You and Pa go ahead to whip me," I said, meeting my mother's eyes. "Go to whip me and I'm to move out to live at Aunt Elaine. No more of money for you and Pa then. No more of help on a baby." My legs were shaking. My shirt and pants were wet in back. The hunger seemed to be crawling up and around inside my middle.

My mother stared at me a long time, stunned, I think, that I was talking back to her that way. And then quietly and deliberately, with just two corners of a smile on her mouth, she said, "Kill you then, you Majie."

"Then no all money for you then," I shot back. A gigantic anger was shaking my lips and making my hands into fists. "Then Pa and you for a baby and no money from me and from at Aunt Elaine. Kill me, go. I'm not afraid of you killed me as you of no money."

I wanted to step into the kitchen and grab one piece of bread. I believed I could smell it in its plastic bag there on the counter. But if I did that I thought my mother would take hold of me, hit me with the bottle, cut me with a knife, maybe kill me right there, so I turned and went into my room with her eyes burning into the back of my skull. I changed out of my wet clothes and left them on the floor. I put two pairs of pants and two shirts and one sweatshirt on the bed. Underwear, socks. No one had touched the cathedral book, so I set it on top of the pile of clothes, not caring if anyone saw. Then I lay down on the bed with one hand on the book and I waited. I listened the way my father had taught me to listen in the woods, long before, when I was a little girl and there had been a different feeling in the house. I listened for the smallest sound, a whisper of air, a twig crackling, a word. After a time I fell asleep.

I was awakened by the sound of the front door banging open. My stomach throbbed. I felt the hard edges of the book against my fingers, and I heard my mother and father talking but I couldn't make out the words. His low voice. A space. Her voice, higher, insistent, as if she was trying to convince him of something and for once he was resisting. His voice again. I waited for them to come into my room and take me out for my penance, but then there was quiet. The light was changing to late-afternoon light. I heard the front door again, then the truck doors, one after the next, then the engine backfiring and spitting as my father's pickup went out the drive. Still I waited, expecting some trick. When darkness fell, and I was sure my mother and father had both gone, I got up and went into the kitchen, where I opened a can of beans and ate it with a spoon, without pouring the beans into a bowl and without heating them. I drank three glasses of water and had two pieces of bread, then a Coke, and then I walked outside and around back and threw the two empty cans far into the woods. I went back to my room, took the hidden stash of money and put it in my pants pocket, and sat on the bed for a long time, staring into the open closet. My parents didn't come home. I thought of what I'd said to Pastor Schect about Aunt Elaine and what it would be like to go to her for help now, after having said that. I imagined looking into her face and having her say she loved me. And then I took the clothes and the book and set them on the floor in my closet. I pulled off my pants and shirt and crawled under the covers and slept.

In the morning, my parents were still not there. I stood in the shower a long time without using the timer. I made myself two pieces of toast with butter. I took my backpack, put the book and my school papers into it, then two cans of Coke from the kitchen, and set off down Waldrup Road toward the highway.

Twenty

Riding the bus to school that day—we were close to the end of the year—I nearly told Cindy about Pastor Schect. It would have meant breaking our unspoken agreement, but I'd kept so many secrets for so long by then that they seemed to have swollen to the bursting point. Cindy and I sat together as we always did, and for a little while we had the middle part of the bus to ourselves, with the boys yelling and wrestling some rows behind. Cindy—short, plump, blond-headed, and barely able to manage her schoolwork in the lowest division—was bubbling over with news. There were two parts to her news. First, she'd heard over the radio the night before that another girl about our own age had disappeared, this one over in the middle of the state, not far from the highway Sands and I had taken on our way to Boston. She hadn't heard this part on the radio, Cindy added, but her mother had told her there was a witness this time, and the witness claimed the abductor had been a black person, or at least someone dark, dressed in dark clothes, driving a dark vehicle. "I have a feeling it's going to happen to me or you next," she whispered when other students had come onto the bus and sat not far from us. "I'm taking a knife with me now everywhere. You should, too." She reached into the pocket of her dress and pulled out a small hunting knife with a three-inch blade. "My dad give it to me."

"They would take it away on you, while they see it in school."

"My dad showed me how to wrap it up in the finger of a work glove. Lookit." She tugged a leather glove finger out of the same pocket and slid the knife into it. "He said they can't know it then."

I gazed out the window at the new green on the hills and thought about the look on Pastor Schect's face when he'd come into the house, and what amount of good a knife might have done if he'd found me there alone, or if he'd climbed all the way up to the big rock in the woods. "Of what time was it?"

"When they took her? Early in the night. She was maybe coming back alone after staying at her friend's house after church or something."

"We didn't go yesterday," I said. I was trying to make myself tell her about Pastor Schect, but I couldn't seem to do it.

"Why? You always."

"My mother was felt sick. She came better now, today."

"There's something else, too . . . about me and Carl." Two boys came down the aisle, shoving each other and laughing in a rough way. "I'll tell you later," Cindy whispered.

When school finished, instead of taking the bus home or getting a ride with Carl and his friends, Cindy said she'd walk with me as far as the cathedral. She wanted to see it up close, she said, and Carl was going to meet her at the doughnut shop in his friend's car and take her riding. We walked from the school down Mitchell Avenue to where it intersected with North Main Street, and we turned and walked down the long slope there, past old Victorians that had once belonged to the factory owners and that stood, some of them freshly painted, behind large front yards. On the long bus ride to and from school, of all the objects made by people, it seemed to me that those houses were the only beautiful thing to see. Maybe the cathedral would change that. Maybe Sands was going to start a trend in town, making things look good for no reason at all.

Before we even reached the commercial strip, Cindy said, "Me and Carl went the full way."

"Did it to hurt?"

"A little at the first and then it felt nice like nothing you could ever do by yourself."

"Do you want to be p.g.?"

"I don't. But if I did I wouldn't care that much and Carl wouldn't neither."

"They might make you to go from school."

"I don't care that much."

"The kids could laugh on you."

"They do already."

It seemed that Cindy wanted me to be excited about the new adventure, and so I pretended I was. It took some effort. All day I'd been replaying the sight of Pastor Schect coming across the threshold of our house. Even by the standards of our family life, it was something odd and horrible, a new level of trouble. And with the news about another abducted girl, I was finding it more and more difficult not to tell someone about the look on Pastor's face when he'd thought he'd found me alone. The question was: who to tell? Cindy? Aunt Elaine? Sands? My father? The police? There were problems in each case, and I couldn't be sure if it would mean more trouble for me or less, if it would help anything, if the look on his face had anything at all to do with the abductions. His car was dark but he wasn't. And, compared to the other men I knew, there was a weakness about him in the arms and hands, not the kind of thing you'd expect in a person who was grabbing teenage girls from the roadside and killing them.

"There was no feeling ever like it," Cindy repeated when we were in the middle of downtown.

I was pretending to be interested, keeping a curious, admiring look on my face. We walked past the storefronts as if carrying between us the weight and thrill of all the world's secrets.

"You should let Aaron do it so you'd know the way it feels," she said as we came within sight of Sands's cathedral.

"Maybe I would soon."

"You should."

When we reached the cathedral property, I saw that Sands was already at work. I waved to him and he waved back. "My boss," I told Cindy.

"It looks like a small church."

"His own private one. This part he wants of making this summer and then more parts for later."

"Is he black?"

"Partways."

"Really?"

"Sure."

"Is he weird?"

"He's nice. You can to talk on him if you want that."

Cindy shook her head. "Watch out for everybody," she said. "My dad can get you a knife, you know."

"My dad could to get me one. I might to ask him."

Cindy nodded in a worried way and said good-bye, and I stepped onto the work site and felt, as I always did there, a small lift of good mood under my feet. At home, in school, with Cindy, I almost always felt younger than my age, as if I'd learned to play a role, hiding my real thoughts and abilities, tamping down whatever intelligence and maturity I possessed as if they were ugly, threatening things. For just the first few happy minutes with Aaron in his truck and talking with Aunt Elaine, and when I worked—those were the times I felt like what I thought a seventeen-year-old girl should feel like.

I changed into my boots. Sands was standing, hands on hips, working out some puzzle in his mind.

"The walls are getting pretty high," he said when I stood beside him. As he spoke, he was looking at the work, not at me, so I understood he was having one of his shy moods.

"It's not hard to build the staging up that high," he went on, scuffing one boot on the old church foundation and punching the glasses back against his nose with his gloved index finger. "But how to get the stones up there is what I'm wondering. I could buy a chain fall, I guess—that's a tool for lifting heavy things—but I kind of like lifting them up by hand. . . . It slows us down, though. Now it's going to get even slower. I can't picture putting them one at a time in a knapsack or something and hiking up the ladder, can you? It would take forever."

"You could to use small stones," I said.

"*We* could, Laney. It's not just my project."

"We could of."

Sands turned and looked at me, as if he'd heard something different in my voice. He ran his eyes over my face then turned back to the walls. "It would look funny. Plus, another few feet up and we'll be at the top of the walls for this section. And that's where we have to put a notch for the roof rafters. They're going to bear the weight of the roof, and the more mortar there is—the higher the ratio of mortar to stone, I mean—the weaker the walls will end up being."

I walked over to my backpack and removed the book he'd given me. I checked to see that I'd been careful enough with it, that there were no marks on the hard cover, no bent pages. Then I carried it over and stood next to him, paging through. Without exception, the stones near the tops of the walls of all the great cathedrals were the same size as those on the bottom. "How did they do for it those days then?" I asked him.

"Ropes and pulleys and ramps, from what I've been able to read."

"Then we could of the same."

Sands was shaking his head. "They had teams of men rolling or sliding the stones up the ramps, or using ropes and pulleys to lift them up in big wooden crates."

"What about to make steps like for the sill ribbons and to lift on them up like it?"

"We could. It would be very slow."

After a minute, I said, "I'm not strong, aren't I? Because that's what's wrong."

"You're fine," Sands said, but I could tell he didn't mean it. I wondered if he would hire a man to help us, or even to take my place, but I'd noticed that he wasn't particularly comfortable around men. Whenever we went to Warners' with an order, or when someone came to make a delivery, I saw that the shyness in him blossomed out. He could shake their hands, and even sometimes make a joke with them, but there was something else running under the skin of his face, a kind of fear or discomfort or defense that reminded me of myself at home.

The largest stones we needed to lift were about two feet long and a foot high, cut square and flat on their four edges, but front and back they were "beveled," to use Sands's word. I looked at the wooden staging already in place and the straight walls. We were almost ready to fit the windows into them; just another few courses of stone and we'd reach the tops of the window holes, where Sands said we had to make arches like the Romans did—from stones he'd ordered special at the quarry in Barre. Another few courses beyond that we'd be ready for the roof. "What if we made high ramps up?" I said. "Of a kind you could make to higher when you wanted. And then what if we had a little kids' cart on it, wheels, and we put one of the stones to the cart and pulled on a rope to get it high? When we got it high what if we slid the stone over in a line at a shelf there, and then put the mortar, and then slided them on?"

I'd never said so many words to Sands at one time. When I was finished, when he kept his eyes straight forward, I wondered if he'd turn an angry face to me, tell me I didn't know what I was talking about. Everything that had happened at my house the day before sat inside me like a pile of dry brush. It seemed to me that one spark, any kind of spark, would set it ablaze.

Sands turned to face me, but I couldn't read his expression.

"Probly we could do for one whole course in one day," I added nervously, and then I told myself I wouldn't speak another word.

Sands kept looking. After a time he turned and examined the walls and the staging. I could see something in the muscles near his mouth. He said, "Let's go get the wood for the ramps and find a place to buy a wagon."

We drove first to the lumberyard and then to the mall where he'd bought me boots, and we came back with heavy planks on the truck's rack, and thick rope in loops on the seat between us, and a red wagon, large enough to hold two big stones at a time, in a cardboard box in the pickup bed. While we were on these errands, and having a snack at Art and Pat's, and then building the first of the moveable ramps, I found that if I focused on what we were doing, I could keep myself from thinking about what awaited me at home. I expected Sands to say something about the latest abduction—everyone in school had been talking about it; there were extra state police cars on the roads outside town and local police parked on the corners, and I'd heard a report about it on the radio news in Sands's truck—but he held to his shy mood the whole day, working at a steady pace as he always did, never too fast or too slow.

When we'd finished the ramp, he said, "Tomorrow we can try it out. Why don't you come by, even though it isn't a workday, and just put in half an hour or something? We'll do a test."

"Okay."

"It's too late to try it now. Plus, your boyfriend's here."

I turned and saw that Aaron had come to the work site in his ugly truck. He was parked at a little distance, standing outside, leaning against the gray door. I waved to him and he nodded, without smiling. He didn't come over to talk.

"Not for really," I told Sands. "Not like a boyfriend true."

"Good. He doesn't look smart enough for you."

We stowed the wheelbarrows, extension cords, and tools in the rectory basement, and he carried the cardboard box inside, too. "We'll see you tomorrow then," Sands said. "I'll wait for you before I try it out. We'll need both of us anyway."

"I could for the whole afternoon work."

"No stuff to do for school?"

"School could be finished not long."

"No exams to study for?"

"Sometimes at night I can."

"All right. But just for an hour or so."

I walked away from him, almost completely happy.

On Old Quarry Road, Aaron pulled his truck into the trees, kissed me in a rough way, and ran his hands up under my shirt and sweatshirt. I thought he would want me to do what I'd done before, and I had started to do that, but Aaron was pulling at my zipper and tugging the pants down below my knees, and pulling my underwear down and putting his hand on me and then pushing me back on the seat and crawling on top. He was kissing me harder than usual, working his fingers in a funny way, and yanking down his jeans with the other hand. At first, with Cindy's words sounding in my mind, I decided I liked the feeling. It was something new, something grown-up women did, something to make me believe I could change my life. Behind Aaron's roughness and hurry I thought there could be a real affection. But then he hurt me a little bit, poking with his hand. My mind turned. I remembered what my mother had showed me with the cigarette, and I remembered something Aunt Elaine had said, and how upset my father had been at the news of my mother's pregnancies. And then—it was the way Aaron was touching me—I just didn't like the idea of doing what he wanted to do. I felt it in my body, in the center of myself, that I didn't want to. I pulled my mouth away from his and said, "No."

Aaron kept kissing at my face and neck and working to get his pants down around his ankles, and trying to pry my legs apart with his knees.

I said no again, but I could tell he wasn't listening and then it came into my mind that it would be all right, it would hurt a little at first and then be all right, and I should just let my legs go loose. Still, something in me didn't want that. I twisted my hips toward the back of the seat as much as I could with Aaron's weight pressing on me. I reached down and put a hand between my legs. Aaron took hold of my wrist and wrenched it away. I put it back. "Stop," I said, but he wouldn't. My legs were strong from all the walking I did. Even with him trying to push them apart, I could squeeze my thighs tight to my hand, and I turned my face away so he couldn't kiss me, and using all my muscles I tightened my body up into a knot I didn't think he could untie.

Aaron tried for another minute or so, then stopped. He lifted the top half of his body away from me and made his hand into a fist. I went to the place I went when my father was dousing me, squeezed my legs together with all my strength. Aaron spit into my face, and I tried to go tight down into myself for what would happen next. But instead of hitting me with the fist, he opened it and scratched his fingernails across my forehead, trying to pull me to look at him. I wouldn't look, wouldn't stop squinting my eyes. I felt him pushing me then, sitting the rest of the way up and shoving me hard out from under him and toward the door of the truck. I was trying to pull up my pants and wipe the saliva off my face and grab hold of my backpack all at once, with Aaron pushing and pushing. My forehead stung. He was cursing. He reached across and pulled the lever that opened the door and he pushed me once more and I tumbled right out, clutching the backpack. The ground there was soft against my shoulder and hip. I rolled away from the tires. With one of his long puppet arms Aaron pulled the door closed and then started the truck and spun the tires in reverse and backed out fast onto the road, sending up a spray of dirt onto me. I watched to see if he looked at me as he sped away but he didn't. I sat up and breathed, wiped the spit off my face and one spurt of tears from my eyes, tried to shake the dirt out of my hair. I stood and pulled up my pants and wiped the sleeve of my sweatshirt across my forehead. Three thin lines of blood on it. I picked up my backpack and looped it over one shoulder, and stood just breathing deep for a few minutes. Then I went down to the end of the road, turned right where it met the highway, and I walked along there with my head lowered, feeling the push of air against me as the trucks drove past.

Twenty-one

From time to time as I walked, I would reach my fingers up and touch the scrapes on my forehead. There was only a little blood. I prayed as I followed the familiar route, prayers that were shaky and unsure. A combination of things—the way Aunt Elaine had spoken to my parents, the facing, Pastor Schect's visit—had taken my dependable picture of God and erased half the lines on his face. In the best moments then, I felt I might be sketching it over again in a new way, but painstakingly, slowly, and without the kind of neatly drawn plan Sands had for his cathedral. My running away from Pastor Schect had been one of the new lines. My talking back to my mother. And now my saying no to Aaron. I felt like I was starting to build a new kind of person in me, to please this new God. But it was a job so full of pain and doubt, something I knew would bring such a flood of punishment onto me, that it seemed impossible to imagine it would ever end up in any tidy, finished shape. All my school life I'd seen teachers and some students who seemed to be made differently from my parents and Pastor Schect, people who were kind and calm, who dressed in nice clothes, and weren't mean, and talked about good things that had happened in their families. Whenever I saw Aunt Elaine I had another glimpse of that kind of life. During all those years there was a way in which I believed people like that were a different species. There had been an invisible wall that stood between their lives and mine, something impossible to climb over or break through. And now in only a few weeks that had changed. I'd come to see that those people were different only because they knew something about being alive that my parents didn't know. I was beginning to believe they worshipped a different, kinder God. The invisible wall had crashed to the ground in a million bits of old belief and now I felt as though I'd taken two or three careful steps into the territory beyond it—a nice feeling, but look at the price I'd already paid.

It began to rain as I walked, drops tapping in the tree branches and wetting my face and hands. A trickle of diluted blood fell into my right eye; I wiped it away. I worked to brush the dirt off my clothes and make it seem as though no one had tried to take them off me. As I came within sight of our house—the patched roof, the slanting walls, the stacks of stove wood—I realized that the invisible wall had been made of fear. Fear stones. Fear mortar. It was still there, lying in pieces, but I believed I could walk over those pieces now. I thought I might be able to endure whatever my parents or Aaron or anyone else decided to do to me.

My mother was sitting on the couch reading the copy of *True Home and Country* that must have arrived earlier in the afternoon. When I came through the door, she lifted her eyes briefly, then went back to reading, then lifted them again and looked at my face. At that moment my father came out of the bathroom, straight in front of me. He was wearing just a T-shirt on top and his hair was wet and slicked back. Sometimes when he first saw me, in the house or the yard, he'd look at me in the eyes, and sometimes he wouldn't. This time he looked. "Who done at you?" he said. From the day he'd found out about the baby he'd been going around as if someone was cooking his mind on high heat. I could see the boiling inside him then as clearly as if it was water in a pan on a stove. "At work there?"

I shook my head.

"Satan done it," my mother said from the couch.

"Pastor shook Satan away of in us," my father said out of the side of his mouth. He hadn't taken his eyes off the scratches on my forehead.

"No he dint to her. She ran."

My father was stubbornly shaking his head. "Who done?" he demanded again.

On the walk up the driveway, I'd told myself that if they asked I would say I'd slipped and fallen against the staging. But the newly built parts of me didn't want to do that. I didn't want to feel young anymore, or to lie anymore, or to be afraid of saying certain things in my own house anymore. My father didn't seem like he was going to hurt me. There was the boiling beneath the skin of his face, as bad as I'd ever seen. His bare arms hung at his sides, the fingers were curling and straightening, the muscles flexing and going loose, but he didn't seem angry at *me*. "Aaron Patanauk," I said. And then, "He tried to of force me."

"I could bet that," my mother said, without looking up from the pamphlet.

My father stepped in closer. He reached out and touched the scratches on my forehead and I winced and shut my eyes but didn't pull away. I could hear the rain on the roof.

"Patanauk?" he said. I opened my eyes and saw a smear of blood on his fingers. He was rubbing them together, smearing it more. "Tell, you girl."

"In his truck he tried to of force at me to hurt. He was just only mad is all."

"Didn't get what," my mother said, "the boy wanted."

"Shut, you!" my father screamed then, a real scream, with the tendons of his neck straining and his body leaning forward from the waist. It was a scream an animal might make. He seemed to grow larger then for a few seconds, and my mother shrank into the cushions of the couch and couldn't look at him and didn't dare to make one of her remarks.

My father spun back to face me. "Done that? Done it? Patanauk?"

I nodded.

"And you dint give on?"

I shook my head. "But he—"

By the time I'd spoken the second word my father was out the door. I couldn't keep myself from going to the window and watching him. It was raining harder by then, and he was wearing only the T-shirt on top, but he ignored the rain, went to his truck and flung the door open, then changed his mind and hurried over to the toolshed. When he appeared again he had the chain saw in his right hand and was holding it away from his body as if proving to himself how strong he was. He set it in the front seat and climbed in after it, and in another second he was splashing the truck out of the driveway and speeding off down Waldrup Road. He had forgotten to take his cane.

"Might go for the store and call your boyfriend now," my mother said. "For a warning."

But I had no inclination to do that. I waited near the window a long time, watching for the truck, part of me hoping my father would hurt Aaron, or at least scare him, and part of me not wanting that. When darkness fell, my mother stood up to make supper and I left the window and went over to help, listening to the rain beat on the roof. It was a time of the month when we had enough money for meat. My mother took out some hamburger and pounded and shaped it into five small patties, two each for the adults and one for me. I put them in the frying pan and opened a can of peas. I made lemonade from the powder, buttered five rolls and set them next to the stove for my mother to put in the oven. She was smoking in a nervous way. We didn't speak. Over the drumming rain, I listened for the sound of my father's truck.

As if by some magic of husband-and-wife timing, just as the hamburgers were well done, the rolls browned and the peas set into a bowl at the table with a thick pat of butter melting into them, we heard the truck in the driveway. When he came through the door, I saw that my father had a bright red stain on the front of his T-shirt. He looked wet and very tired. Without saying anything, he went into the bathroom, and he spent so much time in there that the food went cool. Then he stepped into his room and changed his shirt, and sat down with us.

"For the Lord of God and this the food," my mother said. My father nodded, and we ate. It seemed to me the air was alive with words, buzzing with them, but no one could grab hold of one and make it be still. Every time I opened my mouth to take a bite I was afraid a question would fly out.

Afterward, I washed the dishes, listening to my parents talking softly to each other in their room—where I was not allowed to go. I did my homework, washed the scratches on my forehead for the third time with hot water and soap, and went and lay under the sheet. I prayed for a long while, sending quiet words up into darkness. I prayed that Aaron hadn't been killed, that my father wouldn't go to jail, that I wouldn't lose my job. And then, when I grew tired of praying, I listened to the rain and tried, as I sometimes did, to hear God's thoughts behind it, to imagine my way into his mind.

Twenty-two

Certain things that would have been settled elsewhere by the law were settled, where we lived, in other ways. Enough people there had served time ("been time" was the way my mother and father put it) upstate, or had brothers or uncles, or sometimes wives or sisters or mothers, who'd served time upstate that they weren't anxious to pick up the phone and call for the police when they encountered trouble. They were particularly wary of the state troopers, as if their beige Stetsons and forest green cruisers were the mark of some tribe that wanted to wipe people like us off the earth. What Aaron had done to me wasn't a matter for the police—my parents and I understood that without having to discuss it. Even if he had succeeded in raping me it wouldn't have been a matter for the police.

In spite of the rough way he'd treated me, the next day I was happy to see Aaron's square head on the other side of the high school cafeteria. Seeing him there meant that my father hadn't gone and killed him, or sliced off his arm, or something else. I watched, but there seemed to be nothing wrong with him. At the end of the meal he swiveled his eyes at me, and I stared back. In his face was something I recognized. Fear has a color to it, and no kind of face can really hide that.

After school, walking toward the cathedral, still wondering what had happened and then turning my thoughts to the new rope-and-wagon system and wondering if it would really work, I made the corner onto North Main Street and saw Aaron's truck parked and idling at the curb. It was too late to turn around, but I wouldn't have turned around in any case. If I ran then, I would only have to face him another time, and then another and another, for the rest of my life in that town. As I drew closer to the truck, the door opened, and where I expected to see Aaron step out, I saw his uncle instead. Cary Patanauk. On his left forearm and hand he wore something resembling a huge white mitten. The bandage went most of the way to his elbow.

Mr. Patanauk stood in front of me on the sidewalk, blocking my way. I stopped a few yards away from him.

"You tell your father," he said to me, "that he's just a crazy man. No one's afraid of him no more."

"You on to tell him," I said as calmly as I could manage.

Patanauk spat on the sidewalk next to his feet then scuffed at the spit angrily with his boot sole and looked back at me. He swung the arm with the bandage on it. "You tell him, he comes for my nephew and I'll call and tell everything."

"Call to which person?" I said, "And tell to what?" because I could hear in his voice that he never would call anyone, and I could see the same thing I'd seen behind Aaron's eyes in the cafeteria.

"The states."

"Call to, then," I said. "Call to, and before he of goes on away he'll to slice you up both. That's the way how he is."

Patanauk was half-bald, with a giant's shoulders and neck and a small mouth all puckered up. I thought he was probably one and a half times the size of my father, but it wasn't size that mattered in things like this; it was which person had a line they'd stop at in an argument or a fight, and which person didn't. There was no line for my father and never had been, and I suspected everyone in town understood that.

"Whore like your mother," the small mouth said.

I stood still. Cars went past on the street. My heart was banging in my chest and I could feel a small trembling, like an electric current, in my arms and legs. "I'll tell him you of told me for that," I said, but it came out with a squeak of breath in the middle of it, so that the little mouth in front of me flexed into a smile.

"Do that," he said. "Little whore moron who can't talk good. And when he comes to my shop again looking for my nephew I'll have my rifle loaded."

"You'll need of it oncet I tell."

For a minute then the fear came up strong in me, cold and blue as an old frozen berry in the woods. I had the idea that if it hadn't been daytime, and if we hadn't been standing there with cars going past, then what I saw in Cary Patanauk's face might be set upon me like a rabid coydog on a house cat. I thought I understood then who he was, and what kind of a man he was, and why my father had taken along his chain saw instead of going to the welding shop with just his hands and strong arms and no line to stop at. I could taste something like warm metal in my mouth, and I knew it was the same as it had to be with Aaron: If I showed fear to this man, then for the rest of my life I'd have to worry about walking along Route 112 alone in the dusk, and if he was coming by in his pickup, or if he was watching out his shop window. So I leaned one inch closer to him and steadying my voice I said, "My boss has a friend at the states. They knows it was you what of kidnapped that girl acrost the river."

It was a wild thing to say, a wild shot that came from an odd intuition. But when I had spoken the words I watched something change in Patanauk's face, a small change, the twitch of a muscle beside his right cheekbone. "And you'll been time forever upstate for that. So go, give at me something I can tell now. Go head."

Without waiting for him to answer, I started walking, my legs wobbly, my course only five or six feet to the right of where he stood. I didn't look at him as I went past, but I waited for his good arm to reach out and take hold of me. When it didn't, when I was beyond him and couldn't see him, I felt as though cold-legged insects were scampering along the skin at the back of my neck. I forced myself not to turn and look and not to change my stride. I heard him say, "Whore," again, but quietly, and then I was well past him, my hands were shaking, and I was walking into the center of the town where I knew he wouldn't follow.

That afternoon, Sands and I put the finishing touches on our long ramp, three feet wide, strong enough to hold the weight of the wagon and two stones, but light enough that we could move it along the wall from front to back. At the top of the ramp Sands put together a small wooden frame and there he set up the pulley wheel. The last step in the process was to build a kind of shelf of two-by-tens, adjustable to various heights, on the indoor side of the wall. And then, after bracing everything, we were ready to give the system a tryout.

"It's been an hour and a half," Sands said. "Don't you need to get home?"

I waited a few seconds, watching him. He didn't seem to want me to leave. I shook my head.

We removed the wagon's black handle and tied a heavy rope through the bracket there. For the first trial run, we put only one stone in the wagon, then rolled it to the base of the ramp. Sands climbed onto the staging and slowly pulled the rope through the pulley wheel while I walked alongside the ramp, holding the wagon steady with my hands. This worked well until the wagon reached the top of the ramp, at which point I could no longer stretch high enough to steady it, and when Sands tried to pull it up the last few feet, the weight shifted, the wagon turned sideways, dangled off the ramp, and the stone came crashing down, with the wagon following close behind.

Sands just stood there, looked at the ramp and down at the dented wagon for a few seconds, then he went for more wood. I loved the way he could think through problems and come up with ideas to solve them, and I loved the fact that, instead of spitting and grunting and throwing tools when something went wrong, he just stopped what he was doing, looked at the work, and reasoned it through.

With me helping, Sands built a set of guide rails out of two-by-fours, attached them to the high end of the ramp, and we tried again. This time the wagon wiggled at the top but only bumped the rails and didn't go over the edge. He took hold of it there and sent me down a big smile. I held the dangling end of rope so it couldn't slip backward. Sands lifted the stone out and set it on the shelf, only a foot or so from its final resting place. He rocked back on his haunches and smiled at me again, this time in a way that made me forget Cary and Aaron Patanauk for a few minutes.

Soon we felt confident enough to put two stones at a time in the wagon. The stones fit as tightly into the bed as if it had been designed and measured just for that purpose. Sands learned how to pull the rope from a certain angle so the wagon didn't wobble as much as it made the climb. And I knew just when to walk around to the other side of the wall and take hold of the dangling rope, just how much pressure I needed to keep on it, exactly the right moment to change my downward force as the stone was lifted out. I loved the teamwork and timing of it. Sands asked me again if I needed to get home. But I didn't care about home then; I could have stayed there working all night.

Once we had twenty stones on the shelf—enough for about half the length of the wall—I mixed some mortar and Sands let me trowel it out in a smooth layer, like gray frosting, on small sections of the top of the wall. Then, one by one, he transferred the stones from the shelf onto the wall, tapped them into place with the butt end of the trowel, and filled the gap between with more mortar. It was my job to trim away the excess with something Sands called a "pointing tool"—basically a short, flat metal stick attached to a wooden handle. We didn't stop to rest until the whole bucket of mortar had been used, the waste scraped away, and the bucket and tools sprayed clean with a hose. By then I'd been there nearly three hours. We stood in the churchyard eating the blueberry muffins Sands had bought at Boory's and drinking chocolate milk.

"I saw the scratches on your head," he said when we were about halfway through the snack. I could tell he'd been holding the remark inside from the first minute he'd seen me. "Is that something you want to talk about?"

"Not way much."

He nodded and pushed his glasses back and looked out at the street. It was easy to keep him from talking about certain things, but that time, after he fell silent, I wasn't sure I really wanted to.

"My mother went p.g.," I said. "Gone to, you know, make a baby."

"Planned?"

I lifted my shoulders.

He gestured with one hand at my forehead. "Did she do that?"

I shook my head.

"Your dad?"

I shook my head again. "He went upset, but over the way my mom is to be. We don't have money for another baby, that's sure."

"Why doesn't he work?"

For a moment then I thought that if I gave the wrong answer, Sands would offer my father a job on the cathedral, which would have been, for me, like a death. "Back goes bad for him," I said, and the words brought up the sour feeling inside me I recognized from other lies. "Permanent disable forever, he tells."

Sands turned his eyes away and went quiet. There were crumbs on the front of his T-shirt. After a minute he brushed them away. "Having a child," he said, in what I'd come to think of as his God voice, the voice he used when talking about church and praying, "is the most sacred act in life. The most important work."

I wanted to ask him how he knew that, since he didn't have any children. I thought about Aunt Elaine, and then about Cindy. I said, "There would be times better and not so better for it, though."

He smiled in a sad way. "It's going to be hard for your mom now. You should try to be kind to her even more than you already are."

"Ma's not that easy for a person to be kind at."

"Well, you and your father should try. . . . And you should say 'kind to,' not 'kind at,' okay?" He looked out at the street. "She doesn't smoke or drink much, does she?"

"Not that much."

"Because that would be bad for the baby's health. You know that, right?"

"Everybody knows it," I said. I waited a few seconds to be polite, then pointed toward the ramp with the empty milk container in my hand. "I think we could might finish on this wall."

I worried he'd remind me that I was only supposed to have worked for an hour, and had already worked more than three. But he said, "Thanks to your great idea," and I was happy.

That evening on the walk from the 112 Store, much later than I should have been coming home and a little worried still about the Patanauk men, I made an attempt to set all the pieces of my situation in a neat line in my mind—Aunt Elaine and Sands, my father and mother and Pastor Schect, Aaron and his uncle. The baby. Going over it all, I had a sense there was a missing piece. Or several missing pieces. Why hadn't my parents punished me for running out of the house when Pastor Schect paid his visit? Why had my father cut up Aaron's uncle and not Aaron himself? What had the police said to Pastor Schect and why had he come to the house in spite of that? Why had Cary Patanauk gotten that look on his face when I'd mentioned the abducted girl? With all those unanswered questions, I could feel that events were gathering into a new shape, the way clouds knit together in a summer sky before a thunderstorm, and I felt I almost knew what kind of storm was coming. Almost.

We were into June then, my favorite month. There must have been a steady breeze that evening, because I have no memory of the last of the blackflies bothering me as I walked. I noticed that wildflowers were growing in the band of grass between where the dirt of Waldrup Road ended and the real woods began. When I was nearly to our house, I went into the weeds there a few steps and made up a bouquet of flowers, blue, yellow, and white.

At the house, I took what was in the mailbox—just the supermarket flyer I knew my mother would throw away, no bills, no check, no *True Home and Country*—and went inside. My mother was standing at the stove with her back turned. "Late, you," she said, and it seemed to me there was something sneaky about her, something she was hiding with her back turned like that.

I set the mail on the table, then found a tall plastic glass in the cupboard, filled it halfway with water, put the flowers into it, and tapped my mother on the back. She had a cigarette in one hand and was stirring some kind of stew. She turned and looked over her shoulder. I held out the flowers. "These go for you," I said, thinking that Sands would approve. "For to being p.g. and everything."

My mother squinted at the flowers and then at me. Our faces were at exactly the same level but I felt much stronger than her then, much healthier.

"Broughten them for you," I said, pushing the bouquet a bit closer.

My mother took her hand off the pot handle and put her fingers around the glass. She placed the glass on the counter next to the stove and looked at the flowers again, shot her eyes quickly over at me and went back to cooking.

"I saw to Cary Patanauk today," I told her, because I wanted her to speak to me then, not a kind word, necessarily, I just didn't want silence. "Come after me for what Pa done."

She turned her eyes to me, squinting through the cigarette smoke. "He had something to say on you?"

"Called on me 'whore.' "

"Curse word."

"I wasn't who said it."

"Still a curse word. You been forgetting God these days, don't you."

She turned back to her cooking and I waited another few seconds, glanced at her belly, and walked away.

I was lying on my bed doing homework when my father came and knocked. It was the usual signal: three fast knocks on the doorjamb, a pause, three more fast knocks. When I looked at his eyes, the empty place inside me where the fear had been began to fill up again. There was no way to run this time, no other door to duck out of, nothing I could say that would work against all the hours the penance had been growing in my father's mind. I stood up and went to him. He took my ponytail in his hand and marched me out the door, and as we went past, my mother gave me a look I couldn't read. Pity, it might have been. Or victory. So I thought: Dousing now. But the water was getting warmer every day. At that time of year, dousing wouldn't be bad enough.

As we went down the front steps and across the yard, my father didn't speak. Everything was the same as it always was when he doused me so I thought he'd stop walking at the stream, but, holding to my hair, he made me step on the rocks while he waded across, soaking his boots and pants almost to the knees. On the far side of the stream he broke his silence. "Pastor told to," he said. "Pastor told to do." We went farther into the woods. By then I understood it wasn't going to be an ordinary penance. There was still some sunlight on the leaves. "Hunger you now," my father said, but it didn't make sense because I had been hungered before, and it was always done inside the house where I could smell food, and watch my parents eating, and so give a better payment for my sins.

Far from the stream, at the very edge of our land, my father stopped next to an ash tree. I saw that he'd left a rope there, and I knew that he'd been thinking about what to do with me probably from the minute I ran out of the house. Or, more likely, my mother had been thinking about it, planting ideas, working him. All that time they'd been planning how to punish me for embarrassing them in front of Pastor Schect, for my disobedience, for the church being closed, for the sin and disapproval I'd brought upon us all.

But then my father said something strange—it was as if he were talking to himself—"Flowers at for your mother from Cary Patanauk."

It took me a minute to understand. "No, Pa! I gave the flowers her! For to Ma being p.g. No! Not him!"

I tried to turn and look at my father but he jerked on the pony-tail once, hard, and let go. I started to cry. He picked up the rope and looped it around under my breasts and pulled me back tight against the rough bark. He looped the rope around my middle again and tied it off behind me and by then I couldn't stop shaking. He ran it down around my ankles, circled them twice, and tied it off, then took my hands be-hind me and knotted the end of the rope around my wrists. "Hunger you now, you," he said. "Bad. For bringing us the trouble."

"Pa!"

"Shut!"

"Not of from him! He came and see me today. He said—"

"Shut, girl! And don't never turn your back on a pastor never again. You broughten the devil on us now, girl you."

I pressed my shaking lips tight against each other. I was breathing hard. "She said, she said it, she said he on done it," he was mutter-ing over his shoulder as he turned. "Slice him on up now, too." My fa-ther walked off through the trees the way he always did, his feet never stumbling on the uneven ground, one shoulder sloped down, his arms hanging straight, his legs going. The bottom of his pants were wet and his boots made squishing sounds that I could hear for a time even after I could no longer see him.

At night in the woods the noises come up. Owls hooting through the darkness. Turkeys making their choking, screeching sounds. Some-times, even from inside the house, we would hear a moose crying, or a bear snorting, or coyotes howling in a pack. I was used to those sounds. But as the last light went out of the woods around me, the world there turned quiet in a bad way. Full darkness came in like smoke around the high part of the trunks of the trees, and then I could sense the moon rising, the light it cast changing minute by minute. There were a few large moths fluttering around near my face, as if they knew how much I feared and hated them—on summer nights they would bang against the screens in our house, some as large as a fist—and knew I was helpless, and had come to pay me back for the times I'd slapped at one with rolled-up newspaper and killed it. Now and again one of them would brush against the skin of my neck as I stood there, or flutter along my arms, and I'd let out a yell. The mosquitoes buzzed and bit. I didn't have to go to the bathroom but I knew I would have to at some point. And then what? My father had tied me so the ropes didn't hurt, but after a time it became hard to stand up. The bark scratched me through my shirt, just at the clasp of my bra. I tried to work myself loose, but I made that effort only once, and without much hope: Ropes and traps and chain saws were things my father knew.

In the years my parents had been reading *True Home and Country* I had been hungered half a dozen times. Of the various penances, it wasn't the worst. In the woods, with the insects and cool darkness, it felt harder, though. There was no food to smell, but it grew cool quickly at that time of year, and I didn't know if my father was coming back for me that night, or the next day, or ever. I wondered if Pastor Schect would come himself to administer the final penance, running an arrow into my side the way it had been done to Jesus, or nailing my hands to the tree. I wondered if Sands might come looking for me if I didn't show up to work. Or if Aunt Elaine might sense I was in trouble. I wondered if you could freeze to death in early June or die from being bitten by too many mosquitoes, but I told myself I wouldn't be afraid until something happened to make me afraid. I wouldn't let my mind move more than a few seconds into the future. I wouldn't imagine things that hadn't yet happened. I told myself to listen hard and concentrate on the changing light, and not to think about food or the moths or the mosquitoes. But as the moon moved higher, my shoulders and middle back started to hurt, and I needed to pee, and the hunger gnawed at my insides, gently at first, and then with a sharper edge.

An hour passed. Another hour. At one point a moth fluttered around my nose and lips and I spat hard to make it go away. My mind went from the hunger, to my bladder, to the fear, and then from those things it turned and circled back to Pastor Schect and his God, a punishing God, an angry man in the sky.

But those thoughts were soon washed away by the pure hurt of standing there. Another hour passed. My legs started to shake. The mosquito bites on my neck and arms itched. The sharp ache between my shoulder blades made me try to move against the rope, and I let out small sounds, crying against the pain, distracting myself from it.

And then, well into the night, against the background of small forest noises, I thought I heard a rustling in the leaves. The sound stopped, started again, stopped. I peered into the darkness and thought I saw a shape there, moving toward me. Another minute and I understood it was a person, not an animal. I saw a glint of moonlight on metal. A knife, I thought it must be, and then I knew my father had come to kill me. And then, three more seconds, and I saw that it was my mother. Walking, turning her head, searching.

"Ma!" I called out, wondering if I should.

My mother's face turned to me and she came walking straight at me with the knife held in her right hand. I looked at the very small bulge above the top of her pants, another life there, another mouth to feed.

"Don't kill of me, Ma. To have only one in now the house."

My mother laughed her smoky laugh.

"Don't, Ma. Kindly don't."

She laughed again and stood in front of me, dangling the knife and watching me strain against the ropes. She swatted her free hand at the insects. She said, "I come to let you off, to eat and that."

At those words, a big sound came out of my mouth, one huge loud breath that had a note of something terrible in it.

My mother went behind me and took hold of the ropes, trying to make sense of them with her hands.

"Don't cut," I said. "Just to untie. Or he'll know was you who done."

"Hah," my mother said. "Smart Majie."

But she seemed to hesitate again, for too long a time. Instead of untying the ropes, she reached around the tree, put a hand on my shoulder, and left it there, and I couldn't understand what she was doing. It was like being touched by something that had no feelings, by a machine, by a cold branch of a tree.

"Ma. Kindly."

My mother didn't speak. She moved the hand back and forth once near the base of my neck so that the small hairs stood up there and on my arms. Then she said, "God and the moon have those times," and waited, and waited, and then at last began to work the ropes.

The moment I was free, I scratched at the mosquito bites furiously, then stumbled away a few steps—my legs weren't working right—pulled off my pants and underwear and crouched in the leaves with my feet spread wide. My mother laughed at the sound. When I was finished, I put on my pants, and my mother and I started back toward the house. At first I led the way because she said she couldn't see in the darkness, but soon the moon was a bit higher, and the trees not as dense, and she moved up even with me and then a step ahead on the path. My legs were slowly coming to life, the pain in my back partly fading. I was hungry, but all I could think about was what my father would do to me when we got home. I said, "Pa told me you said Patanauk broughten the flowers."

"Hah."

"You dint say it?"

My mother walked on without answering.

I could hear the stream in the distance. The path was visible in the moonlight. I worried my father would be waiting in the yard and that they had something else planned. Hungering at home. Or worse.

"Tell you," my mother said, then she fell quiet again, and then she stopped walking. I came up even with her. She glanced over at me, then away. She slapped herself on the shoulder to kill a mosquito. "A time before you," she said, then she started walking again and I had to hurry to keep up. "Time before you, your pa was off away, been time for a little bit." She went a few more steps without speaking and seemed to me to be wondering whether she should go on with the story or cut it off. "Been time upstate. Six month." She shifted the knife to her left hand and reached into her shirt pocket with her right, as if there were a package of Primes there, but her hand came away empty. "Cary Patanauk forced me . . . almost forced me. Your pa come back from upstate and learned it. Wanted to kill Cary Patanauk then. But didn't want to go back upstate though. See?"

"Yes."

"Now so . . . Cary Patanauk will be always at his mind. Why he says, 'Hurt, hurt, hurt,' when he does me. Never forgets one thing, your pa."

"You didn't tell to him Patanauk broughten the flowers?"

"You broughten me those."

It seemed to me she was avoiding the truth, the way she sometimes did, without actually lying. I said, "So he's for just to thinking it then? In his mind?"

My mother didn't answer, seemed not to have heard the question. She walked on quickly, and at last she said, "So okay? See, Majie?" in a distracted way.

"Was it me born from when Cary Patanauk forced you?"

She didn't answer.

"Ma?"

Over her shoulder my mother said, "The baby what died it was. A curse."

"Not me then?"

She stopped and glared at me. "Did you die? Was you the baby what died?"

"No."

"Is you a nigger baby from China?"

"No, Ma."

My mother looked away in disgust and started walking again and said nothing else as we stepped single-file across the rocks in the stream and went past the woodpiles and up the front steps. Inside the house, she went straight to her room and closed the door there as quiet as ice melting. On the counter was half a pan of corn bread, which I thought she'd left out purposely for me. The flowers were gone. Very quietly I poured myself a glass of water and drank it and ate the corn bread standing up. Then I drank another glass of water, trying to make no sound at all. When I was finished I went into my room, which was faintly lit with moonlight. I set my backpack on the bed and unzipped it. I put one pair of pants into it, one shirt, two changes of socks, and underwear. From the hiding place in the closet I took my money and the cathedral book.

I didn't lie down on the bed, though I wanted to. I sat on the floor with my back against the bedpost and my small clock sitting between my knees. Most days my father got up early, sometimes as early as five. Dozing off a few times, I waited until four o'clock, then put my clock in the backpack and put the backpack over one shoulder and crept into the main room and out the front door. To avoid making a sound, I didn't close the door all the way.

I could see the outlines of Waldrup Road, and I walked along it at a steady pace, hungry again, feeling tired and weak but sure of what I was doing. I walked on, past the houses, past C&P Welding and Warners'—all dark—and the 112 Store, which had a light on in the back room. By the time I was crossing the bridge into town the first daylight was showing in the eastern sky. I wanted to go and have one look at the cathedral, but decided against that, too, and went straight to the pharmacy where I knew the bus stopped, though I didn't know its schedule. Twenty minutes later the bus arrived in a wave of engine noise and smoke, BOSTON in white letters on the front display. I asked the driver twice did it stop first in Watsonboro and he told me it did. The ticket cost nine dollars and fifty cents. I paid him, sat in the front seat beside my backpack, and watched the light change out the window as we went across the river and then south, the hills going slowly from black to green, the highway winding between them, the silvery Connecticut coming into view and then disappearing again. I thought that, since the driver was taking the interstate, my father would most likely not be able to catch me.

Twenty-three

For a minute after I stepped off the bus, I was confused. For one thing, I had barely slept. And, for another, the one other time I'd run away, the bus had left me in a different part of Watsonboro. Either the bus stop had been moved or I was remembering wrong.

A few steps from where I stood I saw a diner. I walked there, went in through the blue metal door, sat on a stool, and ordered eggs sunny-side up because my mother never cooked them that way, and sausage, and toast and orange juice and home-fried potatoes and a blueberry muffin. The waitress looked up twice from her pad and said, at last, "Somebody joining you?"

I shook my head. When the order had been placed, I went into the bathroom, glanced in the mirror, spent a long time washing the sweat and dirt from my face and hands, scratching the mosquito bites, and trying my best to straighten out my hair.

I ate slowly, scraping every bit of egg from the plate, every last piece of potato and crumb of muffin, drinking every drop of juice. By the time I finished, I didn't care so much about the way the waitress was looking at me. I asked for a phone book, found my aunt's name, and called from the pay phone outside the front door. "It's Majie," I said when I heard my aunt's voice. "Marjorie."

"Are you all right, honey?"

"Sarno's Diner," was all I could make myself say. I was staring at the words on the front of the building, and holding the phone in both hands, and looking down the street at every pickup that came through the intersection from the north. "Near of where the bus puts you. I can walk if you tell to me the way."

"You stay exactly where you are," my aunt said. "You don't even go two steps from there. I'll be there in four minutes. If you're hungry, go inside and eat and I'll pay when I get there."

"I ate plenty," I said, but by then she was no longer on the line.

Twenty-four

Aunt Elaine's house was not large, a yellow bungalow on a corner lot with a porch in front and a flower and vegetable garden out back. In addition to her own bedroom, a living room, a kitchen, and a bath, she had a small sewing room with a couch and a chest of drawers in it, and I moved into that room. I slept most of the first day. That night at supper I wasn't in a mood to talk about what had happened. Aunt Elaine wanted to, I could tell, but I kept trying to steer my mind away from the house in the woods, as if thinking about it would create a kind of magnetism and draw me straight back, or bring my father and mother to the door with a chain saw and a knife. That night I couldn't get to sleep and stayed up very late, thinking about them.

On my second day in Watsonboro, Aunt Elaine took me to two different stores and bought me clothes and toiletries—I hadn't even taken my toothbrush. After three days, when it seemed my parents wouldn't come looking for me, at least not right away, she and I fell into a routine that was nice enough but like a silent dance: The subject of my home life, of exactly what had happened to finally convince me to leave, sat like a hill of dirt in the middle of the dance floor. We maneuvered around it.

I was very agitated then, but our routine helped me calm down a little. She made breakfast early every morning, then drove me to the bus station so I could ride north to school and keep to my work schedule. In the evening, Sands sometimes drove me back to Watsonboro and sometimes took me only as far as the bus station and waited there to be sure I got on the bus without any trouble.

Walking from the bus station to school—only about a mile—and, later in the day, from school to the work site, I was constantly alert. I expected to see my father's truck come spluttering around a corner and pull up to the curb, or have him step out of a doorway in front of me; I expected to reach the cathedral and find both my parents there waiting for me, new penances whirling in their minds.

In the first week, especially, I was sure my father would simply appear at Aunt Elaine's house one day, the way his own father, Dad Paul, used to appear at our house in the woods. I'd come out of my room early in the morning, and Dad Paul would be sitting there at the table like a ghost in flannel shirt and suspenders. The first twenty times I stepped out of Aunt Elaine's sewing room I looked nervously around the kitchen and living room. I knew the lock on the door would do nothing to stop my father, but I locked it anyway when Aunt Elaine was out of the house. Once my father realized there would be no more eighty dollars a month coming to him from my work, I thought there would be nothing to keep him away. But day after day I didn't see him on the streets of the town, or at the house, and little by little the fear started to drain out of me.

Aunt Elaine worked from three in the afternoon until eleven. I made supper for myself, and often made something for her, too, and kept it in a covered pot on the stove or in a covered dish in the refrigerator in case she was hungry when she got home. At night, I locked the door and did my schoolwork. It was past the middle of June. There was only a week of school left. We'd finished the exams and reports, and the rest of the work wasn't taken seriously; I did it for myself, mostly. With the sunshine pouring through the windows, and the summer air whispering at us, it was all my teachers could do to keep the kids from breaking into celebrations in the classrooms and halls. I had one more encounter with Mrs. Eckstrom, who called me into the office to tell me I was going to be promoted, my work was satisfactory, even strong in some classes, but there had been discussions among my teachers at a recent meeting and it was going to be "exceedingly difficult" for me to be awarded a diploma if I didn't do something about the way I talked. "You won't make a very good advertisement for the school system, will you, if you walk around town talking like you do."

"No," I said. "I won't of."

"Won't. Not won't *of.*"

I nodded and acted in as agreeable a manner as I could and she waved a hand and told me to leave. The conversation had some effect on me, though, I have to admit. Being away from my parents had some effect, too. Once or twice I experimented with saying things to Sands that were a little different from the way I usually said them. He didn't seem to notice.

On the first two Sundays, instead of going to church, which was what I expected her to do, Aunt Elaine slept late, then suggested we walk into downtown Watsonboro. We had breakfast both times in a place where there were ten different kinds of tea in boxes on the shelf, and things on the menu that I'd never seen before. Whole wheat pancakes. Eggs Benedict with spinach. Yogurt drinks. I asked my aunt about all of them but was content to keep to foods I knew: eggs and sausage and juice.

Afterward, we walked to a small bookstore that opened at noon. Since moving to my aunt's, in addition to eating as much as I wanted, I was allowed to stay in the shower as long as I wanted—an unimaginable luxury for me—and I'd started washing my hair every other day, and spending a long time brushing it, and my clothes were not used clothes from the shed at the dump but new jeans and colorful short-sleeved shirts, and even a pair of sandals, something I had never worn but took an immediate liking to. There was a young man working in the bookstore, not much older than Aaron, and he showed me

where to find books about stonework, and recommended other things
he thought I might like to read. On our second visit, when I was sitting
in a corner paging through the books, he came over and stood near me
and asked why I was interested in masonry. Was my dad or my boyfriend a bricklayer? Was I working on a project at school?

"No, I'm for making a cathedral with a friend I'm having," I said,
and he nodded and blinked his eyes fast and soon drifted back to the
front desk. He hadn't said anything about the way I talked, but it was
easy enough to read the confusion on his face. That small moment with
him had some effect on me, too, but I wasn't yet ready to let go of the
shield of my broken-up speech. I didn't feel I could just all of a sudden blend into the normal world, as if I'd always been welcome and
comfortable there. I couldn't let myself trust people, not completely,
not even Sands and Aunt Elaine. Ask someone who was in prison for
seventeen years what it's like when he first gets out, how easy it is to
put on a good shirt and pants and go order dinner in a nice restaurant.

When we were walking home from the bookstore that day, Aunt
Elaine asked if I was happy. It wasn't a question I ever remembered
hearing and not something I often thought about then. With the exception of the first minute she'd seen me, in front of the diner, and one
attempt on that first night, she'd been good about staying clear of the
hard subjects. We talked about everyday things: the weather, items I
should pick up at the market, errands I might do, gardening, the progress of the cathedral, whether Sands was coming for dinner on a certain
night or staying up at the rectory. Then, on that walk, she suddenly
said, "Are you happy?"

"I don't think about being it," I answered. We were on the sidewalk, going past the front yards of tidy wooden houses. People were
out in some of those yards planting flowers, or fixing a front gate, or
washing their cars or trucks with a bucket and a sponge and a hose. I
was surprised at the way those people, who didn't seem to know Aunt
Elaine by name and didn't know me, would greet us as we went past,
smile at us, say something about the weather.

"What do you think about?" Aunt Elaine asked when there were no people nearby.

I think about my parents every minute, I wanted to tell her, but I was still not ready for that conversation so I shifted to another truth. "I think about to living the life God gives me."

We turned a corner, heading away from the river and the center of town. There, still a twenty-minute walk from my aunt's front gate, the houses were farther apart, some of them with large yards and neat lawns. Walking side by side, we climbed a long slope, and it was much easier for me than for my aunt. I knew she had cigarettes in the house, and I wanted to tell her she didn't have to sneak them, that I was used to people smoking.

"Is that what the pastor told you to do?"

"In the start. Now I want to do it for my own. Do you think on that? On going to church and God and that?"

"Not much."

"Why?"

"I don't know why. I think about what I have to do around the house, or someone we're taking care of at work, and about you and your life, and Sands and his life, and wanting you both to be happy." She fell silent for a few steps and then added, "I think about your parents."

"I do," I admitted. "My mother special, getting big with the baby and that. And then what it could be like there now."

"Do you want to go back?"

"Do you want that I do?"

"Not at all. I'm just wondering."

"Not all much."

"Do you think that was the way God meant for you to live? I mean with your parents. The way they treated you."

"For then it was. Otherwise it wouldn't of been."

"And for now?"

A man was mowing his huge lawn, riding back and forth in even lines on his mower, and for a few minutes the noise made it impossible to speak. I watched two squirrels in the middle of the street, stopping with their tails up, and then hopping across to the curb and scampering up the back of a maple tree, fighting and chirping at each other. I noticed we were near a catalpa tree, my favorite, and that it had dropped its flowers—like miniature orchids—in a white and pink circle on the concrete. I didn't want to answer the question, but when Aunt Elaine asked it again I said, "I have two feelings in me now. One is for good, strong. And one . . . I think God now will to punish me for what I done. Send my father killing me, or some other way."

"For what you did?"

"Leaving away my parents. My mother p.g. and everything. My father wanting for me to help in the woods and to bring in money, and my mother to help at the cooking and that."

We walked along. At the top of the hill my aunt was breathing hard and she couldn't make any more conversation until the road went flat again. Her house appeared in the distance like a small square sun, the pine tree out front, the porch with three chairs on it, where we sometimes sat with Sands at night and drank cold tea.

"What if . . . ," Aunt Elaine said, and then she waited. "What if God wanted you to have a life with a man who loved you and treated you well, and children who loved you, and work you enjoyed, and enough money to buy the things and do the things you wanted, and a house that was peaceful and clean and nice to live in? What about that kind of life? Do you ever dream of something like that?"

"You don't to have that life," I said, because as she was describing it, I felt two fists pushing through my shirt and through my skin and through the muscles over my belly and down far inside me. "Cindy doesn't to have it. Aaron Patanauk doesn't to. My mother and father."

"I have pieces of it. There are people in these houses we've been walking past who have lives like that. Good people. What if God wants that for you?"

"There's a lot of sins inside me. A lot of penances I should to make."

"Do you really believe that, honey?"

"Inside me I do."

"But what if it turned out you'd made all the penances you needed to, and God forgave you any sins that remained and wanted to give you a life like that?"

"It would make you afraid to think of," I said. "You wouldn't want ever to die." I couldn't look at her, because my aunt was raising shades in store windows that had things in there I believed I would never be able to own.

"What if your finding the stonework you love, and moving away from your parents, and leaving the pastor, and starting to read different kinds of books and dress differently, what if all that was God beginning to give you that other life? Asking you whether you wanted to have it or not? Have you ever thought of it that way?"

"Before now never."

"Well, what if it was?"

We turned through the gate. Aunt Elaine stopped there with her hand on the pickets and looked at me. Her face was a nice, clean face, I thought, without any tricks under the skin. Just a mouth and a nose, just eyes on you, just a face that said, "Here I am. A bear sometimes. A mother who let go of her own child. A nice aunt. A person."

"Then he could grab it away off you any minute."

"He could, yes. But what if, at least for a number of years, he really wanted you to have a life like that, and didn't take it away, and offered it to you as a gift, and gave you an opportunity to pass on some of the happiness of it to somebody else, maybe your own children, or your friends, or a husband? What if he was saying that if you worked hard you could keep it, at least for a while?"

"Then a lot of people would have it the wrong way about him," I said. I could feel a balloon inflating inside me and it made me as afraid as anything that had happened in my life. In the world Aunt Elaine was describing I would have so much to lose.

"That's right. A lot of people would. But a lot of other people would have it right. I want you to start looking for those other people. Would you do that?"

"I could," I said.

We went inside and I retreated to my room and quietly shut the door. I sat on the couch with the book on stained glass windows that I'd bought with my own money from the friendly boy at the bookstore. I tried to concentrate on the pictures and words, but my mind kept returning to the conversation with Aunt Elaine, and the feelings it had raised in me. I went out onto the porch and sat there, and tried to read the book where it was warm and sunny, but I couldn't do it.

Twenty-five

Sands called it "the Laney System," the way we lifted stones up to the top courses of the walls with the ramp, wagon, and pulley. It made me happy to hear him say that. I was beginning to believe I had some real value to him, as a worker. And, as the worst of the fear lifted a little ways away from me, I was beginning to see—slowly and against strong waves of doubt—that he had some interest in me that went beyond the cathedral project. Sometimes I'd lift my eyes from the work and catch him looking at me, and he'd quickly try to pretend he hadn't been. When he drove me into town at the end of the day and waited to see that I got safely onto the Watsonboro-bound bus, I had the sense that he might be a person who could protect me from my father, or Cary Patanauk, or Pastor Schect. I could feel that he enjoyed my company, enjoyed sitting across from me when he had dinner at Aunt Elaine's. When he drove me to Watsonboro on those nights, he put music on his radio and said very little, but I was accustomed to that in people and preferred it to Aunt Elaine's talk, which was pleasant enough, but, as the weeks went on, would veer in close to subjects I didn't yet want to think about—my parents, my future. I felt a warmth in the middle of my body when I was with Sands, and I see now that it was something more than sexual.

Once in a while, even with the rails he'd attached to the upper part of the ramp, and even with our adjustments to the system, the heavily loaded wagon would flip over the side. Depending on the way it fell, and the way the stones fell with it, the wagon could be slightly dented or completely ruined, so we bought a second, and then a third, to keep in the rectory basement as a spare. But even with those small failures the Laney System worked. Soon we'd reached the tops of the side walls and the front wall, and two of the small angular connecting walls, and we were putting together the arches above the windows—the most interesting job yet. By then it was time to make a trip to Vermont to talk with the man who was building the windows.

We went west from downtown and over the long bridge that crossed the Connecticut. Out the side window I studied the men fishing there to see if one of them might be my father. But they were unfamiliar men in jeans and baseball caps, standing close to each other and talking. My father would have been off alone at the rail with his cane propped conspicuously beside him, not acknowledging anyone else, just staring down into the water, willing a fish to take his hook and then jerking it up in the air with a violent motion. Even with the possibility of a legal threat from Aunt Elaine—who had, she told me, managed to permanently close down Pastor Schect's church—it seemed strange and worrisome that, in two, three, and now almost four weeks, my father had never driven by the work site, or come and bothered me there. It didn't make sense that he would have started a penance like that and not finished it, or that he'd passively accept the end of the income from my work with Sands. I wondered if he'd found an under-the-table job, or moved away, if Aunt Elaine had sent them money or a threatening letter, if Cary Patanauk had gone to the police after all and filed an assault charge, or if Sands was too frightening a figure for my father to face a second time. I wondered how my mother was feeling, well into her pregnancy, but I didn't speak of those things with anyone.

We crossed the river and climbed into the hills on the Vermont side. The road there brought us through the hamlet of Hensonville, which had been in the news a few months earlier. As we were passing through the tiny town center—a general store, a gas station, a pizza place—I thought of mentioning it to Sands. This is where the girl was coming home to, I wanted to say. Somewhere right along this road was where the police found her bike. But I held my silence, as if I believed that speaking about something so evil and horrible would invite it into my own life. I looked at the houses we passed, wondering if the girl had lived in one of them and what her parents thought about when they drove by the place where their daughter's bicycle had been found. What they thought when they got into their bed and it was dark all around them, and the room where their daughter had slept was empty, night after night, morning after morning. One body had been found— the most recent disappearance—and there was a rumor that the police had clues from it and were close to arresting someone. I looked carefully through the newspaper that was delivered to my aunt's house every afternoon but saw nothing beyond those few facts and letters to the editor from fearful citizens. Why, they wanted to know, after two years and what seemed to be five murders, had the police detained only one suspect—who turned out to have an alibi, at that. With all the state troopers in town, all the police overtime, why hadn't the killer been caught? What tormented me more than anything was the question of whether or not I should go to the police and tell them about Pastor Schect. But, in our family, voluntarily going to the police had always been the near equivalent of spying for the Russians or defacing a statue of Christ—something done by traitors, sinners, or crazy people. And, in any case, what would I tell them? That the pastor had come to our house, one time, and I thought I'd seen something evil in his eyes? The same kind of thing I'd seen in Cary Patanauk's eyes, the blaze of lust, a desperate hunger for a female body? No, where men like that were concerned, the best thing to do was avoid talking and thinking about them, keep them as far away from your mind as possible. Finding the kidnapper was a job for the states, for people like Sands's friend.

Still, I was sometimes touched by a nibble of guilt.

The man who was making the cathedral windows carried a bush

of white hair on the sides of his head and had a kind of name I'd never heard before. There was something about him I immediately disliked. I was used to men we met—at the hardware store, at the lumberyard— staring at me in a certain way; it wasn't the way of Pastor Schect and Patanauk, it wasn't bad. But the window maker shook Sands's hand and barely acknowledged me, as if I couldn't be a true worker, just a girl. Being ignored like that, after all the work I'd been doing, lit a familiar fuse of insult in me. Dad Paul had been that way: I'd been invisible to him.

Close beside the man's house stood a small log cabin that served as his workshop and was as tidy inside and out as the cab of Sands's truck. The man was nearly finished with the first set of windows. He'd laid them out on a long workbench for Sands's inspection. Four of the windows were rectangles with curved tops, seven feet by three, and one was a circle four feet across. Sands had told him not to put images of saints or Christ in them, and no words, but to make them so just the colors and shapes gave a feeling of peacefulness. When we opened the door and stepped in, there was sun pouring into the log cabin, and even though it wasn't shining through the stained glass windows, it was falling on them, and I could see that the white-haired man had done his job. The windows showed curling vines and green leaves against a background of clouds, and the designs were lit by a light that was somehow mysterious. Looking at the colors and shapes, I even had the sense that the kindhearted God Aunt Elaine talked about might have sneaked in and touched the windows with a finger and then sneaked out again before there could be any trouble. I could see how much Sands liked them. He kept pushing his glasses up, glancing at me, walking back and forth in the shop so he could examine the windows from different angles. He stood still finally, ran his fingers along the lead solders, looked at the designs again the way he had looked at the paintings in the Boston museum, met my eyes.

He wrote the man a check and shook his hand enthusiastically, but I could see that he didn't want to leave. He asked the man about the delivery schedule, and how we were going to lift the windows into the spaces in the wall and hold them there, and how we were going to seal them to keep the rain and snow and cold out, and if it was better to put the roof on first or not. The man answered in short sentences, always smiling at Sands and ignoring me. I noticed that he seemed odd or different in a certain way, and that Sands seemed more comfortable with him than with some of the other men we'd had dealings with.

At last, Sands shook the man's hand again and we got back in the truck and headed down toward the river.

Just at the place where I imagined the girl had been abducted, I said, "Are you a Q?"

"What?"

"A Q."

"How did you know?" he said. We were winding down the road, and I could see that the girl probably couldn't have ridden her bike up a hill like this unless she'd had very strong legs. It would have been natural for her, especially if she was late or tired, to leave her bike in the weeds and start to walk, or to stick out her thumb and hope for a ride. It had been a mistake to do that, but the size of the punishment didn't fit the mistake at all, so why had God let that happen?

A piece of the river, like a ribbon of green metal, showed between the hills below.

"How did you know?" Sands said again.

"Because you don't to have a girlfriend ever."

"I'm a little . . . what are you talking about?"

"Q," I said again, vaguely disappointed. "Queer."

"Gay?"

"That's the same. The kids say 'Q' now."

"You're asking me if I'm gay?"

"Never a mind. You just said. It doesn't make a lot of matter to me."

Sands was laughing in a quiet way I didn't like. He looked across the seat at me when I thought he should have been watching the road.

"I'm a Quaker," he said, laughing, and then smiling in a way that made me twist in my seat. "I thought that's what you meant. Q. For Quaker. I thought your pastor wouldn't let you say the word or something."

"He's not anymore."

The road bottomed out, then came, after a ways, to the old two-lane highway that ran along the river. We turned south on that road, went along a few hundred yards, and made a left onto the bridge.

"Do you know what a Quaker is?" Sands asked over the noise the tires made on the steel roadway.

"It means you don't like boys or girls but you like to hurt with birds. Crows you like so much. Kissing on sparrows is your fun."

He was smiling and watching the road. "You're a joker now, all of a sudden."

"I was before. You just didn't see of it."

"I just didn't understand you, I think."

"The girl what talks funny is why."

"That's what they call you in school?"

I decided not to answer. Since school had let out, ten days after I'd moved to Aunt Elaine's, I'd been making more and more of an effort to change the way I talked. Tiny steps in the direction of the polished world. But I was nervous then, on that ride, and the old words bubbled out of me. "You don't to having girlfriends, don't you," I said.

"Not at the present moment."

"What about the state police girl?"

"Just a friend."

"Why not? Because of to be a Quaker?"

"Because I'm waiting for the love of my life."

"God might to send her someday."

"I hope so." Sands watched the road for a few minutes and then turned to me again. "You have a boyfriend, you said, am I right? That boy with the truck? A girl who looks like you, I'd think you'd have a lot of boys asking you out."

"I think, probably, he's a went-away boyfriend for now. I think most of likely his uncle made him not be my boyfriend anymore, and other things."

"Why?"

"I think because my father tried at cutting his hand over."

"Cutting his hand off, you mean? Your boyfriend's hand?"

"His uncle's."

"Why would your dad do a thing like that? Did he try to hurt you?"

"He wanted to hurt, sure, but it was really because my father knows his uncle forced my mother once in the long away when he been time."

"You lost me."

The truck turned into town and stopped at a light there.

"There's a lot, in this town here, of people who know other people's people, and might of, in the years long away, had trouble on them."

"Still lost."

"I don't have for one, that's all."

"And I don't have for one either," he said, but he didn't seem to be making fun. "There's the shyness factor, I suppose. There's the dirty-clothes-every-day factor."

"There is it both," I said, and I watched two people crossing at the light. They were holding hands, and there was something in the way they walked with each other that raised a whole cathedral of hope inside me. But *hope* isn't exactly the right word. *Possibility* is better. And right beside that possibility I felt a new kind of fear. It had nothing to do with my father and mother coming after me. It was bigger than that. Deep down inside I was used to fighting a solitary battle—to stay alive, to stay sane, to protect a part of myself that my parents and Pastor Schect, and even God sometimes, seemed to want to suffocate. In order to do that, I'd developed all kinds of strategies and built all kinds of walls between myself and other people. I remember watching the young couple crossing the street and imagining, just for one minute, what it would be like to let go of that.

Twenty-six

We went through the middle of that summer, working five and a half days each week and watching the first section of what Sands had taken to calling the Connecticut River Cathedral take shape. The blackflies had disappeared, replaced first by deerflies—slower, larger, with a stronger bite, but easier to kill—and then a second hatching of mosquitoes. The days were hot and the nights cool and good for sleeping.

Aunt Elaine let me work in the garden with her. Sands let me help him build the window and door arches—they were a kind of miracle that defied gravity—and, after the conversation on the ride home from Hensonville, we seemed to get along more easily. With every new stone we cemented in place I buried the past a little deeper. Food, clothes, speech, some television now and then—everything was new.

When the crane and the man with the puffy white hair arrived to put in the stained glass windows, a small crowd gathered on the sidewalk to watch. From time to time I'd turn my eyes to them, expecting to see my mother or father there, but I didn't see them. I saw Aaron's truck go past but couldn't catch a glimpse of his face, and I didn't really care very much. In spite of my admiration for his work, I didn't like the window man any more than I had on the visit to his shop. I had a vague intuition that he was not as kind and meek as he pretended to be.

Once the crane work started, I stood in a safe place in the middle of the cathedral floor and watched how the sun poured colors through the stained glass, how the windows seemed to light up with a life they'd only been hinting at in the man's workshop, golds and yellows and the green leaves in a combination of shapes that suggested something hopeful. Seeing the windows go perfectly into their places one after the next, slowly, methodically, without trouble, I was almost convinced that the cathedral might stop being a weird curiosity or a demon place in the minds of the people in town and that, instead of being just another local eccentric, Sands might be lifted up to the status of semi-celebrity, the young brown-skinned guy with a ponytail who'd built himself a beautiful church.

Once he noticed the small crowd, Sands put up ropes and sawhorses to keep people off the site and away from the sweep of the crane. I could see that he was shining inside and that the creator of the windows was proud, too, strutting around here and there, sending hand signals to the crane operator, watching carefully to see that Sands and his invisible girl helper caulked the windows tightly from their places on the staging and didn't smudge the glass.

The job took the whole day. When it was finished, we toasted with cartons of chocolate milk from the rectory refrigerator. The window man looked at me, finally, but as if I was a stranger to the human condition, an alien of some sort, a brown-haired robot in overalls who didn't speak like anyone else and who shouldn't have been allowed to work on a project that showcased his glorious glass. He drove away in his dark van and I was glad to see him go.

Sands had decided to keep the crane a second day and use it to set the beams in place across the middle of the nave, resting the thick pieces of oak in notches on the tops of the side walls. On the second afternoon two men he called "specialists" came all the way from Keene to supervise the setting of the precut roof rafters. That evening, when the crane and the specialists had gone and Sands and I had put away the tools, we stood back and admired the work.

"Now it's starting to look like something," he said proudly.

"You can start to see what it would be," I agreed. I slanted my head behind me at a small collection of onlookers that had stopped by after work. "People come for watching it now all the time."

"Your dad came by," Sands said after a minute.

I tried to pretend the news hadn't hit me like a two-by-four swung against my ribs. I took a breath, kept my eyes on the cathedral walls, which looked now, suddenly, like something unconnected to me.

"It was the other night, late. Just when it was getting dark. I came out to make a last check of things and he was standing very still on the sidewalk, staring. He looked at me for a minute, and I looked at him, and just when I was about to say something, he walked off."

I couldn't seem to move or speak.

"Don't worry," Sands said. "If he was going to bother you, he would have by now."

"You don't know it."

"Just don't worry, okay?"

The next day—Sands had promised to give me the afternoon off— we covered the windows with heavy tarpaulins to avoid accidental breakage and to reduce the temptation to stone-throwing passersby. A truck with a noisy engine drove up onto the site. It was loaded with the heavy oak boards that would sheathe the rafters, and when we'd helped unload it and piled the boards neatly on the site, and when Sands had taken me into town for a shared pizza and salad, he wrote me a paycheck and told me to go have some fun, we'd meet at the site at six o'clock and he'd drive me to Aunt Elaine's.

I hadn't seen Cindy since school let out, so I'd brought my new bathing suit and planned, after a quick stop at the bank, to spend the afternoon at the quarry. She was there, as I'd expected, and she greeted me on the stony shore, looking tanned and happy. She wasn't yet preg-nant, she said when we were out in the water and floating around, but all she seemed to want to talk about was what she and Carl did with each other and how it felt. The song in her voice made me think they'd found a kind of heaven for themselves.

"You still haven't done it yet?" Cindy asked me quietly.

"No."

"Aaron tells everyone you did, with him, and he didn't think it was no good so he busted off with you."

"I didn't."

"Your talk's a little bit different."

"A little."

"It's good now."

"Thanks."

"Pretty soon you'll be too smart to be friends with me."

"No, I wouldn't."

We swam over to the bank and sat on the rocks there, watching boys and girls jump or dive from the highest ledge. It seemed that all my life I'd been hearing stories about the quarry, about young people who'd drowned there during a night of drinking or hurt themselves diving from the top rock. There were stories of my father as a boy, performing the wildest acrobatics—somersaults, backflips, long looping swan dives—and staying under so long that other boys would dive in, thinking they had to save him. I couldn't imagine my father doing anything like that, couldn't picture him making a graceful dive the way these young boys were doing, or coming to the surface like them, spluttering and laughing. I couldn't imagine my aunt and my mother swimming here as sisters and walking home together. I tried, but no picture of it would form in my mind. I wondered if having a child was what took all the laughing out of a person.

For a time, as we sat there drying in the sun, I thought about telling Cindy what had happened with my father and mother on my last night at home, and why I'd moved away and was living with my aunt, but Cindy was asking about the cathedral, and complimenting me on my muscles, and saying I should get more sun because my stomach and legs were pure white and looked funny against the brown of my face and neck and arms. She asked me what I thought about possibly getting back together with Aaron.

"Aaron and me I don't think are friends no more."

"You want me to fix you up with Carl's brother so you can try it?"

"Maybe after the summer is done."

"You sure?"

I nodded.

"I seen your mother at the 112 a few days ago. She didn't look too good."

"She doesn't never."

"Fat and thin at the same time, kind of."

I stood up and dove from the low ledge into the water and swam a hard crawl stroke back and forth until I was out of breath. I could hear and almost feel the splashes when the divers hit the water, and then a silence would fall over the people around the edges of the quarry, and then, when the diver surfaced, a group of nice-looking boys drinking beer on the far end of the bank would cheer and yell out, "Ten! Ten! Ten!" if they thought the dive had been a good one, or another number if they thought it was bad.

Afterward, walking back into town to where Sands would meet me, with my hair wet and my shirt rubbing against my breasts, I remembered the noise of my parents' bed hitting the wall on the nights they had sex. When I was small, I'd thought someone was knocking, wanting to be let in, and I'd gone to my bedroom window and looked out to see who was there.

Sands drove me home that night, talking a little bit about his mother and father and how happy they'd been together, how kind they'd been to him, how he'd tried to pay some of that kindness back when they were sick. "They had some troubles in the marriage, like everybody, but there was a friendship there that you don't see a lot. They ended up dying within about two months of each other, my dad first. It was like my mother couldn't imagine being alive with him not there." I listened to the feelings running through his voice, and I tried to picture his mother and father and imagine what a marriage like that would be like. When we were at Aunt Elaine's I asked him to stay for dinner but he said he couldn't that night, no reason. I imagined he was going off to see a girlfriend somewhere near Watsonboro and just didn't want to tell me. The next day we started to put the boards on the roof, sixteen-foot tongue-and-groove boards, inch-thick oak that was as hard and heavy as iron. We had to lift one end at a time up onto the staging shelf and then climb up and lay the board across the rafters just so. "If you put the first one on crooked," he told me, "there will be trouble the whole rest of the way up. That's really the first law of construction, you know: Get the beginning right."

By the end of the day we had set only two courses in place on one side of the roof, but Sands measured with his long yellow tape at the front and back, and from bottom to the peak the numbers were exactly the same. "Now it will get easier, instead of harder," he said. "You'll see."

When we'd finished putting the tools away, he surprised me by inviting me into the rectory to see his work. Except for going in and out of the basement for tools, or stepping inside to use the bathroom, I avoided the rectory as much as I could. I knew he slept there. I knew that, on days when we weren't working—Sundays, rain days—Sands spent his time fixing up the interior, which had been damaged by weather coming through a hole in the roof and basically left to rot once the church was no longer used.

"I think I should just to catch the bus," I said.

"I'll drive you again tonight. Your aunt insists I have dinner there at least twice a week."

I noticed that he never said "my mother" but always called her "Elaine" or "your aunt."

"I just want you to see what I've been doing, Laney. Give me your professional opinion on the quality of the work."

There were two floors to the rectory. Up to that point, Sands had been working only on the bottom one. He'd completely renovated the kitchen, bathroom, and two bedrooms there, and I could see that everything he knew how to do with his hands—stonework, carpentry, painting, electrical, plumbing, tiling—had been put into the project. The hardwood floors—"These are all maple," he told me, as if I didn't already know—shone like gold. And the bedrooms, to me, were like something out of museum paintings, so orderly and colorful, with new beds covered with quilts and clean white pillows, the walls painted a deep green in one room and salmon pink in the other. I wondered if his state police friend had helped him with the decorating, because it didn't seem like a job a man could do. I ran my hands over the window trim, the miter cuts made so well and nailed up so tight I couldn't have fit a pine needle into the forty-five-degree joints at the corners. The wood was painted a glossy off-white, every surface so clean it seemed Sands had spent hours going over it with a washcloth and toothbrush.

"I don't have anything to do at night," he told me. "So if I'm not too tired I do this for an hour or two."

I walked slowly through the rooms, looking at the work, wondering if I should have taken my boots off, if my hands were too dirty to touch anything, why he seemed to want so badly for me to see it, and why right then. It reminded me of the time he'd taken me to Boston, and I wondered if I'd done something wrong on that trip and that was why he'd never invited me anywhere again.

"No place else can be the same as this," I said when we were standing in the kitchen after the downstairs tour and he was looking at me expectantly. "No perfect place could be better."

Instead of seeming pleased at my comments, Sands appeared uncomfortable. He was fidgeting again, pouring himself a glass of water at the sink and pouring one for me, fiddling with his glasses, looping his eyes around in a way I recognized from other awkward moments. "You could live here if you wanted to," he said at last, without quite looking at me. "Until the cathedral is done, I mean, at least. It would save a lot of travel."

I pretended not to hear. I drank the glass of water down without moving it from my mouth. Sands waited, and when I didn't answer, he started telling me about his plans for the upstairs, where there were two more bedrooms, a study, and another full bath. I could feel an echo of his nervousness in myself.

"There will be lots of space for guests," he was telling me, still not making eye contact.

Instead of "guests" I thought he had wanted to say "children."

"And there's a whole big room up there—I'll show you next time—that I'm going to turn into a study where I can work on my designs. There'll be a big drafting table, and I'll have a phone, and file cabinets, and a computer, so when I go into business once the cathedral is finished I'll have a regular office. The cathedral is going to be a kind of advertisement. People will see what I can do. I'm going to put a skylight in there, too, upstairs I mean, and Italian tile in the bathroom. I've already picked it out. I'm going to hire somebody to take pictures and put together a portfolio."

I held the glass for a few seconds then set it down on the counter. I glanced at the door behind me. Sands had stopped talking but he was taking small sips of water and looping his eyes around. He finally settled them on me. I was all dirty and sweaty from the work. There was sawdust in my hair.

"What about staying here instead of at your aunt's?" he asked, as if he was forcing himself to say it and would never again find the courage if I didn't answer this time.

I looked at him. In his square, rugged face, with the eyes peering out through the thick glasses, I believed I could see what the minister had done to him as a boy. I could see it as if it was painted there, just below the skin, a layer of old-man sadness underneath the boyish face. I thought this layer of pain might have grown smaller since I'd first met him, and I guessed that, maybe, if things went the right way for him, if he could have a little time every day to sit in his cathedral and talk to the God who loved you, if he could start calling Aunt Elaine by the name he should use with her, if the cathedral did, in fact, bring him regular work with his skilled hands, and if the people of the town got to know and appreciate him, then maybe the pain would almost disappear. It might even be possible, I thought, that when he woke up in the night it wouldn't be the minister's face he saw or the minister's voice he heard.

Sands was looking at me across the kitchen.

I said what I didn't mean to say, in a way I didn't mean to say it, a young way, holding a young, not-so-smart Majie doll out in front of me as a kind of shield. "You want to be with me in a bed the way Cindy and Carl do."

I watched something ripple across his face and couldn't tell whether it was hurt feelings or surprise or another burst of anger.

"How old are you, Laney, really?"

"In April I'm being eighteen."

He looked away and then back. I felt then that he had put up a shield of his own. I wanted to go back outside then and didn't want to. I was thinking about how nice Sands's face was, and how clean the bedrooms were, and how long the bus ride seemed some days, and about other things. And then about what people in the town would say if I moved in. I was thinking that probably never again in my life was I going to be asked something like this by a man as kind as this man.

"There are two bedrooms finished," Sands went on. "There's going to be four or five."

I looked at him.

"It could be just for the company," he said.

But I knew it wasn't just for the company, and I didn't want it to be, and I had to stop myself from reaching up and shaking the dust out of my hair and straightening it. I was thinking about what I had done with Aaron in his truck, and it is a measure of the person I was then that I was wondering whether or not I should tell Sands about it at that moment.

"I always rush things, I guess," he said when he saw I wasn't answering. "There's something about my timing that is just off. I've never been good at these kinds of things." He took a step toward the door and so I moved, also, too quickly, and we went outside and got into his truck. Before driving away, Sands looked through the windshield a last time at the roof rafters and crossbeams, the covered-over windows and sturdy walls. I looked, too, but the pleasure of it was shadowed, and I was working to understand what I could do to change that, to open up another part of myself to him. As he started up the truck and turned to back out of the lot, I said, "What would Aunt Elaine say about it?"

"About what?"

"For me to move here."

"I'm twenty-four," he said, turning the wheel and heading up toward the bridge and the interstate on-ramp.

That was all he said, and I couldn't be sure how he'd meant it. That he was too old to care what his real mother thought? That he was ashamed of being alone at that age? That he was regretting what he'd asked me and emphasizing the distance between us?

For the rest of the way to my aunt's house we didn't say anything more about it.

Twenty-seven

That night Aunt Elaine wasn't working and for supper she made grilled salmon with mashed potatoes, broccoli, and corn bread. We set the small table on the front porch and she, Sands, and I ate outside in the summer air. There weren't so many mosquitoes in Watsonboro, and very little traffic on the streets that bordered her small yard, and it seemed to me that we'd reached the point where the three of us were almost comfortable with who we were to each other, something partway between family and friends.

Aunt Elaine talked for a while about a sick boy she was helping in the hospital, a brave young child with a disease I'd never heard of. Sands talked for a while about the cathedral and said he'd had requests from some friends of his, who were Quakers, to rent it every week for what he called "meeting," once the job was finished, and another request from someone to do stonework on their house when he had time. I ate my meal and listened to them, half my mind somewhere else. When we were finished I carried the dishes inside and scraped the leftovers into a plastic bin my aunt used to make compost for her garden. The corn bread made me think of my mother, and the smell of the fish cooking had made me think of my father and the walleye he'd sometimes bring home. Standing there in the kitchen, with the last of the day's sunlight filtering through the curtains over the sink and the voices drifting in from the porch on the summer air, I imagined my parents having dinner at the old scratched-up table, the trees keeping out most of the daylight so the room was decorated around the edges with strange shadow shapes, and the mosquitoes buzzing at the broken screens and sneaking through. I told myself that now, if there was any talk there at all, it would center around the bitter taste of not having enough money, no meat, no way to fix the truck. I thought of what it would be like for a baby to come into that house, without me there to watch over it. When the child grew old enough they would douse her and hunger her. If Pastor Schect's church remained closed, then probably my parents would find another one similar to it, or at least keep receiving *True Home and Country* with its recommendations for discipline and Ancient Way of the Lord penances. Probably they wouldn't allow the boy or girl to go to school. Possibly, I thought, if things got bad enough, by accident or on purpose they would kill it.

My aunt had baked a chocolate cake with vanilla frosting, Sands's favorite. When I finished clearing the plates she came into the kitchen and together we carried out the cake and cups for coffee (I had started to drink it then, one cup after supper; it never kept me awake) and cream and sugar, and Sands stood up and served us, his ponytail grown longer, his arms like tree trunks made of muscle, and his face, in the evening light, showing his mixed heritage and the little-boy happiness I liked underneath the shadow of a one-day beard.

We had started in on the cake when I said, "I want of visiting my mother and father soon, if we could."

Aunt Elaine set down her cup and looked at me. Sands went on eating as if he hadn't heard, but I was sure that he had.

"I don't know if that's a good idea," Aunt Elaine said.

"It could be hard for them, not with money, with a baby coming on."

"They'll manage," my aunt said.

"You don't know it."

"You're right, I don't. But I know they're very upset that you left.

I met your mother and father in town two weeks ago and tried to talk
to them and it was as if I were the devil, literally. They're furious with
me, very upset with you. They're bitter about the church closing, about
everything."

"You didn't tell me."

"I'm sorry. I didn't want to upset you."

I swallowed a spurt of anger. "I want that we should do it," I said.
"I have a present I ordered for the baby. In town."

"You didn't tell me that."

"We should have to think for that baby now, not for us. When a
baby is being born, the grown-up people have to think for that and not
themself."

My aunt ran her eyes back and forth over my face, then looked
down into her coffee cup as if something was hurting her inside. Sands
had stopped eating; it seemed to me he wished he wasn't there. Since
I'd been staying at my aunt's house, it was the first time I'd felt a strain
among the three of us.

"Aunt Elaine," I said, and the words felt strange on my lips. I was
still unused to calling adults by their name. My aunt looked up at me.
"I think now I'm old enough to saying what I want, and like that. I
think now that I am. You couldn't to stop thinking about"—I paused,
glanced at Sands—"your son. I can't stop to thinking about my brother
or sister."

"For what it's worth," Sands said, raising his eyes to his mother,
pressing his mouth closed for a moment then going on, "I think Laney's
right."

Aunt Elaine stood up abruptly and went into the house. I heard her
in the kitchen, opening and closing a cabinet. I looked at Sands. "She's
on upset now."

"She'll come back in a minute," he said, but we sat for several minutes in a silence that was broken only by the weak notes of some kind
of party music from a house on the next block.

When Aunt Elaine rejoined us, I could see that she'd been crying.

She couldn't look at me. I surprised myself by reaching out and putting my hand on her forearm. She put her own hand over mine but still couldn't look up.

Sands tried to shift position in his seat but his legs hit the table leg and jostled the liquid in the cups. Some of it spilled onto the table. "You know," he said, and then he stopped. I wished he'd said, "You know, Mom," but he wasn't ready to do that. "You know," he repeated, wiping up the spilled coffee with his napkin, "maybe from now on everything shouldn't be guilt and sin and punishment for us."

Into my inner eye came a vision of Pastor Schect with the children lined up in front of him. I squeezed my aunt's arm and let go.

"Maybe," Sands said, not looking at either of us, "we should go visit Laney's mother and father and let them see we're making something new, the three of us, over what was wrecked and ruined in the past. Maybe the baby that's coming is a chance for them to start something new, also."

I was glad to see my aunt's face change and lighten at those words. Though it made no sense, really, though I knew better, I let a little candle of hope go on inside me, one little impossible light. I think that's what happens in families like the family I grew up in: You keep telling yourself it will be different. Year after year, time after time, you keep telling yourself things might change. It's what makes people go back to people they shouldn't ever go back to.

Twenty-eight

By the end of the workday on Saturday, Sands and I had almost finished attaching the oak boards to the lower half of one side of the main roof. At four o'clock, an hour before we usually would have put the tools away, Aunt Elaine drove up and parked at the curb. I remember that she was wearing new jeans and a copper-colored short-sleeved shirt with a collar. As we drilled and screwed into place the last of the long boards for that day, she walked around the cathedral the way she'd done on her previous visit, running her hands over the stones, stepping beneath the arch where the front door would be, calling compliments up to us. When we finished our work and climbed down, she helped us loop the orange extension cords and carry them into the cellar, and then, while I put away the rest of the tools, Sands gave her a tour of the rectory's first floor. I could hear more compliments through the screen and then the quieter notes of a conversation that wasn't meant for my ears.

But when my aunt appeared again, there was no sign that we wouldn't go, no late change of plans. I sat in the backseat of her car, behind Sands, and we set off through the town and east on the two-lane highway. We passed Weedon's Bar—I looked for my father's truck in the lot there and didn't see it. Then Warner and Sons Gravel and Stone, then the 112 Store, then C&P Welding and the bus shelter at the corner.

And then, on Waldrup Road, the skin of my arms and neck felt the way my legs felt just after I shaved them. I was caught, for just a minute, by a wave of nausea. We rolled and bounced slowly down the dirt road and turned into the driveway. I saw my mother's face in the kitchen window, and then my father, off at the far end of the yard, sitting on a boulder fishing the stream for six-inch trout for supper. He turned his face to us, but I could see nothing there. I made myself get out. Sands and Aunt Elaine got out. For a moment I imagined my mother closing the lock on the door and my father continuing to fish or walking off into the forest. But Aunt Elaine opened the trunk, and I lifted out the present. I had wrapped it in pretty paper of my own choosing, neither blue nor pink because I didn't know if the child in my mother's body was a boy or a girl. I lifted it out and held it in front of me against my chest. Aunt Elaine had a present, too, but hadn't wrapped it.

My mother opened the door, reluctantly it seemed. She had a belly. In the corner of my eye I saw my father set down his fishing pole. "Ma," I said, standing at the bottom of the steps with Aunt Elaine and Sands close behind me and my mother close in front, "we broughten some things for of the baby when it's come."

My mother stared, a wisp of cigarette smoke circling up beside her face. I thought we wouldn't be admitted to the house then, and I was about to say we'd brought some money, too. But at that moment my aunt said, "Emmy, aren't you going to let us in?"

My mother pushed open the door. "Good to see ya," she said with the hoarse-voiced sarcasm I instantly remembered. I could hear my father's footsteps on the dirt near the shed, and with those two familiar sounds I had a moment of thinking I'd made a terrible mistake. I had forgotten what it was really like to live here.

Inside the house, with all of us crowded near the front door, Aunt Elaine turned to my mother and said, "This is Sands," and then, a little quickly, as if forcing the words out, "my son."

When my mother understood what she meant, she let out a laugh. She seemed happy to have the news, but it was what I thought of as a wrong happiness, the kind that grew in the dirt of someone else's trouble. The laugh twisted my mother's mouth up high at the corners. Her eyes moved from Sands's face to Aunt Elaine's, back and forth twice, and then to the face of her husband, who had taken one step in over the threshold and was standing there with his fingers drumming on the cloth of his overalls. After a moment, she put her hands on her belly, the cigarette smoke now twirling up in front of her, and she said, "This here's *my* son. Hah."

I couldn't look at my father. I said, "Ma, this here is a present to him. A little cradle so because he won't have to—" I stopped short there. I'd been about to say, "so he won't have to sleep in a cardboard box"—which is where I had slept as an infant, a box with a blanket on a table in my parents' room. They'd told me that themselves, proudly. "It's soon, but we had a want to give it now."

"*She* wanted to," Aunt Elaine said. "She bought it with the money she's made. This"—she held up the unwrapped box that had baby bottles and some formula in it—"is from me. I didn't think you would want to breast-feed."

My mother's one-note laugh knocked against the ceiling.

Aunt Elaine put the box down on the table. I set my large package next to it. "You don't of have to want to open it and look now if you don't," I said, and felt my face go red because I was caught between the way I had once spoken in that house—without self-consciousness— and the way I was trying to speak with Sands and Aunt Elaine. When I looked up, my father was shooting his eyes into me. I could see the hairs on his beard shaking. I was a traitor, and in his way of thinking, nothing, not even a murderer, was worse than that.

I was about to mention the money when he shifted his eyes to Aunt Elaine as if Sands was not there and spat out, "You stoled her on away."

From all those hours of working with Sands, I could feel that he didn't like my father any more this time than he had on their first meeting. I guessed he didn't like the smell of smoke and old cooked food and mold either. I looked at his arms and shoulders. Next to my father's twitching fingers, they seemed enormous and too still.

Aunt Elaine turned to face my father. "Really?" she said. "The story I have was that you tied your daughter to a tree. In the woods. At night. And left her there, hungry and in pain and eaten up by mosquitoes. I seem to remember writing you both a letter about that a little while back. Maybe you've forgotten, Curtis. Maybe this will remind you: Attorney Robert Baker. Does the name ring—"

"Not'n yourn business," my father said. His eyes flicked once to Sands, an appraising glance, a naked evaluation.

"Is that so?" I noticed that Aunt Elaine had gone very quickly from being polite to looking like she was going to start yelling at them again. I had another moment of thinking I shouldn't have come, or should have come alone.

My father bumped his chin down one time in an angry nod.

"The trouble with you, Curtis," Aunt Elaine was saying, and I wanted to tell her to stop then. I knew, I could feel, that years of anger had built up inside my aunt and were about to spill out. She was brave as a bear, but she didn't know certain things, seemed to have no idea of the kinds of actions her brother-in-law was capable of, seemed to think words had equal force to a chain saw or a knife or a willow whip. "The trouble with you has always been that you aren't smart enough to separate the people who want to be kind to you from the people who want to hurt you. You think everybody wants to hurt you so you live in your little hard shell out here in the woods. When you come out of the shell it's so you can hurt somebody first before they hurt you. We came here—your daughter, your child, came here bringing a gift for the baby in your wife's womb. She wants to give you money, too—because you still pretend to be unable to work—though I told her several times that she's given you enough money over the years. I bet you haven't even taken your wife in for a checkup once in her pregnancy, am I right? You don't know about things like that. You don't pay attention to things like that, do you, Curtis? The health of a woman and an unborn child. But you know how to tie your grown daughter to a tree."

Except for his nine fluttering fingers, my father's body had an odd quietness about it. But in another second I saw that the skin of his face was moving the way the top of a pond moves when a breeze runs across it. His eyes flicked over to Sands, and one chip of a smile went flying across his lips. It was the smile of a person who knows he is going to get hurt and in a strange way likes it. The hurt confirms something in him, some expectation about how the world works, some sense of his own ability to bear pain, if nothing else. He made the chip of a smile— I realized then that I'd told Aunt Elaine but never told Sands about being tied to the tree—and then he turned his eyes to Aunt Elaine and said two words very quietly. "Little whore." He was starting to say something else, "Get out," I thought it would be, when Sands, moving faster than I'd ever seen, grabbed him by the front of his T-shirt, lifted him off the ground, and pushed him back hard against the doorjamb. I heard a sound like "hunhn" when the air came out of my father's body. His eyes were fixed unblinking on Sands's face. I saw no fear in them at all. Sands's other hand hung at his side but he had made the fingers into a fist.

"Cut you," my father said, looking into Sands's eyes.

"All right, then," Aunt Elaine said. "Stop that now." She put her hand on Sands's back but he didn't seem to feel it. For about two seconds my mother had a smoky smile drawn in pencil on her face, then it fell away. There were a few times when I'd listened to Sands talk about nonviolence, how wars were wrong, how killing was wrong. He seemed to mean what he said, but I could see that there was another part of him where those words didn't come from. His left arm was held out almost straight, bunching the fabric of my father's T-shirt against his throat. I could see that he was pressing forward and that if my father moved down off his tiptoes he wouldn't be able to breathe.

"Cut your whore mother, too," my father squeaked out, and when I heard those words, and saw Sands's other hand swing up, I thought that if he hit with a fist, my father's head was going to fly right off like a bearded doll's head, like the plastic head of the figure outside the plumbing shop. But when Sands hit it was with an open hand, and so hard the noise was like a gun going off in the room. My father went flying over sideways, caught himself on a chair for a second, and then the chair fell and he fell with it. In an instant he'd scrambled to his feet, his eyes like the eyes of an animal, blood on his mouth. My mother was watching with two hands spread on her belly, a cigarette pinched between the fingers there, a twirl of smoke rising as if from the fetus itself.

The words that came out of Sands's mouth then were like air being forced out between his teeth, like steam from a kettle. "Saytheword-againPastor," I thought he said, though I have never asked him about it and I might have heard it wrong. "Saythewordagain." He was facing my father with his hands in fists now, a different man than the man I had been working with, completely different. A killer, I thought. And I thought that my father, who was also a killer-man, knew it. In my father's eyes I saw that he expected it would be like two animals in the woods, one of them a catamount or a coyote, and the other a raccoon or a fox, with no amount of mercy there. No rules. No forgiveness. None at all. It seemed to me that my father knew about things like this from far back in his life, from his early years with Dad Paul or when he'd been upstate, or both. There was no hatred in his face, and no fear. It was almost as if he was looking at something related to him, the way one animal looks at another, not seeing it so much as feeling its existence through its own existence. There was blood running from my father's mouth, a good amount of it, but he seemed not to notice and he was holding the chair in one hand in such a way that I knew he would swing it if Sands came at him.

"Enough," Aunt Elaine said, in what was meant to be a strict voice. "There's a pregnant woman here. This isn't a bar."

But the men weren't listening. My mother took a drag from her Prime as calmly as if she was watching a scene on a street corner from out a third-floor window. She said, "Yeah, we all are none of us a saint here," in the way she had, a crazy way almost. It was almost as if she was trying to make fun of someone, Aunt Elaine probably, but the joke came out crooked. I tried to think of her walking out into the dark woods to untie me, holding in her hand a knife four sizes too big for the job of cutting rope.

Before my father and Sands could say or do anything else, I took the money out of my pants pocket and set the folded green bills, two hundred dollars, on the table near the packages. For a minute a new silence fell across the room. I said, "I want of to give you money for the baby now and I want to go." My mother and father were looking at the money. I stepped across and put my hand on Sands's left arm. Without speaking to him or looking into his face, I moved him gently back one step away from my father. I had my back turned to my father—I didn't have the courage to look at him then—but I could feel his anger like smoke on my neck.

"I don't care about any of the rest of this now," I heard Aunt Elaine say nervously. "I don't care about you, Emmy. Or about Curtis. If you ever were sister and brother-in-law to me, that's finished now. But if you have trouble with the pregnancy, the smallest trouble, you come get me immediately. You get to a phone and you call. Or you drive to the church they're building and you tell them to get me. Do you hear? That's what I care about now, about that baby, and about this young woman here who you've treated worse than an animal. You and Curtis just come and get me, that's all." She turned to my father and for a moment I thought she would step across the room and attend to his bleeding mouth. But she looked back to my mother. "And stop drinking and smoking, for God's sake. Just for these months. And if one little thing seems not right, you—"

"Gittin' you all out now," my father spluttered. I turned to look at him, saw that blood had sprayed onto the front of his shirt when he spoke. He didn't reach up to wipe it and had not taken his hand off the chair or moved his eyes from Sands's face.

Aunt Elaine looked at him. Everyone was looking at him. The blood ran into his beard.

"We're going," Aunt Elaine said. She moved so that she, too, was between Sands and my father. She looked at her stepsister one last time. My mother smiled a crazed, mean smile back at her, a bitter good-bye, and then we were going out the door, Sands beside and a little behind me, walking backward. Another second it seemed like and we were in the car. At the end of the driveway I turned and looked out the back window. The door was open but I couldn't see anyone there.

Twenty-nine

Through the heart of the summer, the only season of real heat in our part of the world—though even then the nights are usually cool—I stayed living with my aunt, rode the bus to work most days, and struggled not to think about my parents too much. Sometimes I let myself imagine that my mother and father had sold the house and land and gone off somewhere in the truck with the money, or taken a bus to Canada or Florida and were never coming back. Other times I felt they were standing on the sidewalk, watching me, waiting for me, and I had to force myself not to turn and look.

As if they knew I didn't want them to, Sands and Aunt Elaine never talked about my parents. And Sands never again brought up the idea of my living in the rectory, which made me believe that, after seeing the kind of parents I had, he'd changed his mind about the invitation. Maybe he didn't want a person from a family like that living with him. Maybe he didn't want to worry about my father showing up some night to, as he used to say, "make a revenge."

On Sundays, my aunt and I would ride up along the river on the Vermont side and have lunch in one of the towns set into the hills there—the Windsor Diner was a favorite of ours—or drive south into Massachusetts, where she knew a few nice places to walk in the woods.

Sometimes I paid for lunch on these outings, as a gift or a thank-you, because I was never allowed to pay for anything else. Twice, Sands came along, pleasant enough but very quiet, as if he had seen something in himself he was so ashamed of he'd made a vow never to speak again, or as if he was working out plans behind his eyes—for his cathedral, for his future. He touched his mother once in a while, and she touched him, but I waited for him to use a certain word and he never did.

Something was happening inside me in those weeks. Years later, when I was pregnant for the first time, I recognized the feeling. I moved differently, looked at the world differently, felt a kind of power growing through the middle of me. I thought about my parents, but I was no longer so afraid of them. I saw Aaron in town once and said hello, but, though I could tell he wanted me to, I didn't stop to talk. The cathedral still filled my life, but I felt this new strength even when I was miles away from the work site. I remember—and this may seem like a trivial thing—going into a women's clothing store in Watsonboro and, for the first time in my life, buying underwear that wasn't plain white.

Board by board we finished sheathing the two sides of the main roof. As much as anything I had ever done, I liked standing high up on the boards and looking out over the town. From the top of the cathedral I could see the roofs of all the buildings nearby, the white steeples of two churches, and, beyond them, a piece of the Connecticut with hills folding down to either side. Sands had told me that when we finished screwing the oak boards into place, and then finished with the small connecting side-roofs, a team of men would come to put hundreds of small squares of slate over them—one of the few things he seemed unable to do himself. We still had the three doors to hang, he said, and metal gutters to run along the roof edges above them, and then a patio and walls to build before the landscapers came to smooth the grade. If we timed it right, he said, we'd finish the outside work just as the weather started to turn cold. We'd have a new furnace installed and could spend the long winter on interior work: figuring out how we wanted the inside walls to look, laying down smooth concrete and then a wooden floor over it; putting in some kind of seats or pews or furniture, he hadn't decided yet.

I didn't ask where the money for all that would come from. I didn't want to think about those things. I felt that new strength inside me, but, having lived for so many years in a universe of complete unpredictability, I didn't much trust plans, especially plans that made the future look like a happy place. While I was on the job, I tried to bring my thoughts only to the task at hand—the hot black plastic of the drill handle after it had been sitting in the sun, the sound the bit made as it bored through the dense oak, the way Sands and I had to always lean in against the roof to keep from falling over backward and sliding all the way down onto the top of the staging, the way we'd use a crowbar to pry a slightly crooked board in tight against the one just below it. I tried to concentrate on those things, but Sands and his elaborate plans were like a sugary tongue licking against the skin of my arms and face.

As time passed, I thought of my parents a bit less, but I never stopped worrying about the baby. The summer went on; the days began to shorten and the nights to grow cooler. Aunt Elaine often brought a newspaper home; I scoured it for news of Pastor Schect and his church. But there was nothing, no news from the woods or West Ober, no evidence that those people still existed at all. Once, without my aunt knowing, I put twenty dollars in an envelope and mailed it to my mother and father at the Waldrup Road address and included a note saying they should use it for the baby. The letter was never returned or acknowledged, and I never saw my parents in town, and neither Cindy nor Sands nor Aunt Elaine offered any word of them. It was as if, wounded yet again by the world of people, my mother and father had retreated still farther into the north woods and were living there off the small trout my father caught in the stream, the deer he poached with his bow and arrow, the berries and ferns my mother picked.

And then one day in August, just at the point where I had started to believe I would never see them again, I was on a ladder struggling to fit together the pieces of metal gutter over the front door when I heard a familiar rumbling and backfiring. I looked up to see my father's truck racing down Main Street toward me. Sands was working at the peak of the roof, caulking the last joints there before the slate workers came, and my first thought was that my father had come to kill him. The humiliation of our visit had festered and swollen and burned in his mind all those hot weeks—I'd suspected that would happen; I'd suspected my life had gotten too peaceful to be real—and at last something, a remark my mother made, a few days of having no money for meat, had blown the smoldering coals to life, and he'd gone out and borrowed or stolen a shotgun, and here he was, speeding like a crazy man down Main Street, about to jump out of the truck and start firing.

I tried to call a warning to Sands, but before I could accomplish that the truck skidded to the curb and I could hear a panicked yelling. The passenger door swung open. My mother put one foot gingerly to the ground and I saw her large belly and then, a second later, blood all down the front of her jeans. For an instant I thought my father had cut her. But then he, too, was out in plain view, trotting in a wide circle as he came around the truck, his face torn open by what were almost screams. "Help!" he was trying to say, but what came out of him was "Heh! Heh! Heh!" And then, "Heh, Majie you! Heh me! Heh! Heh! Heh!"

By the time I climbed down and ran to the truck, with Sands two steps behind me, my mother had managed to get both feet on the sidewalk. She was leaning back against the edge of the seat with her arms spread, one holding the armrest of the door, one the body of the truck. Her face was painted in fear, too, but the colors were different, a palette of various off-whites: cheeks, forehead, chin. Her eyebrows were arched and her nostrils flared and her mouth stretched, and everything was stuck in that position as if she was trying to let the pain pour out of her through her face. There was blood everywhere—on the step of the pickup, the seat, the sidewalk. It soaked the inside halves of the legs of her jeans. Without the smallest hesitation, Sands picked her up and carried her to his truck. I held the door open. He set my mother in and propped her upright until I could climb in after her. Neither of us even looked at my father. Sands backed the truck around and sped out of the lot too fast, bumping down over the curb so that my mother let out a tortured groan. Her head sank down toward my lap and I held it in both arms.

We went flying down a side street to the river road, then over the bridge, my mother making small cries, "God, God, God," as the truck bounced over the uneven surface. We shot up the ramp onto the interstate and went along there in the fast lane, over a hundred miles an hour, I was sure. Once, I glanced in the side mirror and thought I saw my father's truck shrinking in the distance. I worried about the police, but Sands just kept the accelerator down, both hands on the wheel, eyes fixed on the road. Shortly before we reached Watsonboro, I felt my mother lose consciousness in my arms, and I began shaking her head lightly between my palms. "Ma, Ma. Go awake, Ma," I said. "Go awake."

Sands skidded up to the emergency room entrance and snapped off the engine. He took my mother under the back and behind the knees, the blood dripping, her belly looking like a huge egg about to break open, and he ran with her through the automatic doors and into the emergency room. I was a few steps behind. Sands yelled to the nurses that he had a pregnant woman, that she was in trouble, but he didn't have to do that: Just the belly and the blood showed what was happening, a thin trail of it from the truck into the waiting area, and then in big drops on the linoleum there. A nurse came out and hurried us through a door and into one of the treatment rooms.

In seconds, a doctor stepped into the room. I looked at my mother's pale face and closed eyes and begged the nurses to let me stay, but Sands and I were made to leave. We went and stood in the waiting room at first, our clothes crimson and wet, everybody looking at us. "Elaine Archimbault," I said to the woman who seemed to be in charge. "A nurse here. She's the sister to that woman all blood. Elaine Archimbault. She's here working now, a nurse. My aunt."

Another patient—an unconscious man with an enormous body and huge, bald head—was wheeled through the entrance. Five or six people who must have been family members crowded in after him. Sands and I stepped outside. Sands moved the truck away into the parking lot, and we stood out there next to it, keeping our eyes on the entrance. I was praying. I watched the nurses in their white uniforms come out and stand not far from the door on their cigarette breaks. I watched ambulances come up to the door, twice, the attendants calmly removing a stretcher from the back and wheeling a patient in. I looked for my father's truck but didn't see it and I wondered if he'd run away, or been stopped by the police for speeding, or gotten lost.

Finally, Aunt Elaine appeared at the automatic door and looked for us. Sands waved a hand. We walked toward each other and met in the middle of the tarred road that led out of the parking lot. "Your mother's in surgery," Aunt Elaine told me. She had a hand on my shoulder and was looking up into my eyes and speaking partly in a nurse's voice, and partly another way. "The doctors are taking the baby by cesarean. They're both still alive. It's going to be a while before you can see her, so you should go home and get into some other clothes and maybe have something quick to eat and then come back. Don't be too long. When you get here, come in the main door and go to the desk there and tell them to call me first before anything else. All right?" She looked up at Sands, and I could tell she wanted to hug both of us but was holding herself away because of all the blood. She squeezed my shoulder with her hand and looked into my eyes. "All right?"

"Yes."

"There are good doctors here. Don't worry too much, honey. Pray if you want to. I can't tell you to do that, but if you want to, pray now."

The seat of Sands's truck was sticky. We had no choice but to sit on it and make the short drive to Aunt Elaine's. Sands stayed outside while I went in and showered, put my clothes in a plastic bag and threw them in the trash, got dressed, and came outside with a thick blanket. I laid the blanket on the seat and we drove into town and I went in and bought a pair of pants and a shirt and some underwear for him while he waited outside. He had to go back into the store to change. When he came out he was carrying the bloody clothes in a plastic bag, which he threw into the Dumpster. "They thought I'd just murdered some-body," he told me as I was unfolding the blanket to go under him. "I had to show them my ID, if you believe that, before they'd let me out of the place."

At the hospital, I went up to the volunteer at the main desk and said, "Elaine Archimbault," and waited. In a little while I saw my aunt coming out of an elevator, and I knew just from the first look at her face what the news would be. "Come up," Aunt Elaine said, putting an arm around my waist. And to Sands, "Could you wait?"

The hospital elevator was all shining metal. Aunt Elaine had an arm around me, but there were other people in the elevator so we didn't speak. On the floor where I was to see my mother, I followed my aunt into a small waiting room—four chairs and a table with old magazines on it, no people—and there Aunt Elaine turned me and put both hands on my shoulders and looked up into my eyes. "The baby was born," she said. "A girl. It might live or it might not. It was born too early and there was some trouble. . . . Your mother is . . . There is internal bleeding that they haven't been able to stop, and she lost a lot of blood before she got here. If she lives it would be a miracle. You can see her but she's very weak. If you have something you want to say to her, say it this time, all right, Marjorie?"

"All right."

Walking down the hallway, Aunt Elaine held my hand and I didn't mind that. We turned into a white room. My mother was in the bed there, and beside her stood a nurse doing something with a tube that was snaking into my mother's arm. My mother was small and thin in the bed. Her face and arms and hands were the color of wet paper, and her hair looked damp and was pushed back from her forehead in a way she never wore it. I moved in front of my aunt, walked up to the bed, and put the fingers of both hands on my mother's arm. The nurse finished what she was doing and left. Aunt Elaine left. My mother's eyes opened, closed, opened again. There was a small wrinkle at one corner of her lips. "You Majie," I thought she said.

"Ma."

Another little twist in the mouth muscles.

"Ma, the baby's a girl."

It was almost as if she laughed then, a bump in her chest and throat, a faint "huh" escaping from between her lips.

"Pa . . . where?"

"I don't know it, Ma."

There was another bump of sound.

For probably a minute we didn't say anything else. My mother was using all her concentration just to breathe. Her eyelids fluttered. I could see that she was afraid, but not terribly afraid, not panicky, not terrified, just struggling to breathe.

"You were a good ma . . . to untie me."

My mother's eyes had nearly closed but when I said that she managed to push them open for a few seconds. She didn't exactly shake her head, but she moved it half an inch to one side, said something that sounded like "Don't know" or "You don't know," then let her eyes close. I stayed there, keeping my fingers on her arms and my eyes on her pale face. She seemed to have fallen into a deep sleep. I watched her chest, waiting for it to stop moving, but the breathing went on and on, shallow but steady. I waited there an hour or more, praying in whispers, unable to make myself say anything else though there were things I wanted to be saying. Aunt Elaine came back in and stood quietly for a time, then told me it was all right if I wanted to leave. My mother couldn't hear anything, couldn't know we were there. I shook my head and stayed.

My aunt left and came back again twice. Another nurse came in, then a woman doctor, and I was edged away from the bed and toward the wall so they could work. For a long time I stood there, catching glimpses of my mother's face over the doctor's shoulder, feeling Aunt Elaine's arm around me, praying and praying. "There's nothing you can do, honey," Aunt Elaine whispered. "It would be all right to leave."

But I stayed, watching my mother, listening to the beep of a machine at the far side of the bed.

I turned my lips in between my teeth. The sound of the beeping machine changed slightly; my mother twitched but kept breathing. One of the nurses stood back away from the bed like she was giving up, but the doctor was still leaning over my mother, the machine still going along. I listened to it for a few seconds with my eyes closed. Aunt Elaine squeezed my arm. My mother twitched again and let out a groan. I went up to the bed, pushing a little bit to get beside the doctor. I put my hand around my mother's wrist, looked at her one last time, and then turned away and went out the door. I took the elevator downstairs and sat with Sands in the larger waiting room. After a time he reached out and put his big callused hand over mine, and I turned my palm up so I could put my fingers between his. It wasn't much longer before Aunt Elaine came out of the elevator and toward us. She asked if I wanted to come say good-bye to the body. I said that I did not.

"The baby is alive," she said. "You could see her. Do you want to?"

Upstairs we went again, Sands with us this time. We stopped at a different floor, and turning and walking along the hallway, I felt as though I was carrying a huge stone weight in my middle.

In a glassed-in room, in a glass box with tubes running into it, there was a pink girl so tiny it seemed to me she could fit inside a winter hat. It was warm and light in the box. Dressed only in a tiny diaper, the girl seemed as fragile as a robin's egg, with miniature hands and feet, and eyes that opened from time to time but didn't focus on anything. A tuft of damp dark hair showed at the top of her head. She had wires attached to circles of white tape on her chest. I stared at her, felt Sands put his hand on my back. I leaned in for a closer look at the girl's wrinkled face and heard my aunt say, "The doctor thinks she's going to live." And I tried to say a prayer for that, tried to picture a God you could ask for something good like that.

Late that night the three of us sat at the table in Aunt Elaine's kitchen and ate Chinese food we'd bought on the way home. Sands had taken a shower. He and Aunt Elaine were drinking beer; I had a glass of Coke. After a while Aunt Elaine got up and poured some beer into another glass and set it in front of me and I took a sip and held it in my mouth a moment before swallowing. As he had been from the time he'd carried my mother into the emergency room, Sands was like a statue of a man, barely speaking. I had a few bites of chicken wings and a few sips of the beer but it was hard for me to eat then. Part of it was because of my mother, but I also had a sense, from my aunt's silence, and from Sands's, that there was something else in the air around us. I waited, and waited, and wouldn't let myself ask. At last Aunt Elaine said, "Your father was stopped on the highway for speeding. When the police saw the blood in the truck they thought something about him that isn't so, and they arrested him."

"Okay," I said. I had suspected it was something like that. It was as if some other stream of knowledge that had nothing to do with words was already inside me.

A memory came over me then of my father walking with me up to the north end of Waldrup Road, to the state park line there. This was before Ronald Merwin lived in the only other house on that section of road and before Pastor Schect had come into our lives. I was five or six. My father knew a trail there that led to a very small pond. It was a hot day. He let me take off my clothes and swim and when I came out—naked and cool and happy—he took off his shirt and dried me with it. I remembered how he'd kept his head turned away and then left the shirt over my shoulders so I wouldn't shiver.

Sands ate the Chinese food slowly, bite after bite, as if he was very hungry. He didn't talk and couldn't make eye contact with me. Aunt Elaine said that she knew it was hard to lose a mother—she'd lost her own mother, too, a long time ago—but I could tell she was only trying not to say anything bad. Very late, Sands said he had to go, and Aunt Elaine asked him to stay and sleep there on the couch but he didn't want to. "I'm going home to pray a little," he said. "After a day like this." We all stood up. Sands hugged me against him for the first time, and hugged and kissed his mother, and then he asked for another blanket for the seat and went out the door and we listened to his truck starting up.

I cleaned up the food scraps and brought the glasses to the sink in a kind of trance. Aunt Elaine came into the kitchen and put a hand on my shoulder and turned me around. "You come and get me in the night if you want to," she said. "Think of a name for the baby if you can. Think of a good name for your sister."

Thirty

For a while after that terrible day, we didn't work on the cathedral. We buried my mother in a cemetery in Watsonboro, without delay and without any church service or any friends in attendance. My father couldn't be there. It seemed wrong to me, to have a human being go into the ground with so few people watching. I half hoped that someone—even Mrs. Jensen from the 112 Store or a person from Pastor Schect's church—might suddenly appear as my mother's casket was being lowered into the ground, but no one did.

The baby had to remain in the hospital for several weeks, and I went to see her whenever I could. Aunt Elaine let me choose the name. Lillian was what I decided on, after a lot of thought, because I liked the music of it, and liked the nickname she'd have, Lily, and because I didn't want the girl to have a name that was connected to anyone— not my mother, my father, my aunt, or anyone we knew. I wanted her to have a fresh start in life and not be linked to anything I had lived through or anything about my parents. That was foolish, probably— she was born with so much of my mother and father in her, so much of their confusion and stubbornness. I have seen that over the years. I have lived in the knowledge of it and dealt with the trouble from it. But that was the way I felt at the time.

The other thing I felt then—this might seem strange but it is true—was an overwhelming sense of relief. I find now that when I think of my mother, I picture a darkness, as if the center of her was a shadow. Even then, before I knew some of the things she'd done on her rides in the country with my father, I thought of her that way. I've met plenty of people now whose mothers were loving, caring, giving souls, and I've seen, in Sands, how the gift of a mother like that echoes down through the generations, deep in the hidden inner life of sons and daughters. With every ounce of my strength I have tried to be a mother like that.

But my own mother was a dark ghost who had rare sparkles of tenderness. The rest of the time she sucked the world into herself and turned it to ash. Not that my father was so much better, but in him at least there was a simplemindedness that could occasionally look like compassion. He wasn't so eager to raise his hand when Pastor Schect asked for a child to be faced. He let it happen, yes, but he wasn't eager for it to happen. He did evil things, and he would pay for doing them, as he should. But my mother had some other dimension to her, and in the deepest part of me I knew that.

In the days after her burial, I sometimes found myself wondering if she would pay for the harm she'd done. And if so, how? What did Sands's kindly God do with a spirit like that?

Two days after my mother was buried, with Lily still in the hospital, I was sitting on the porch of my aunt's house when Aunt Elaine came outside with a newspaper clutched in her two hands. She didn't sit down. She said, "There's something in here about your father being arrested. I didn't know if you wanted to read it or not, honey. It's not easy to read. We can talk about it afterward if you want, but I won't say anything unless you do, okay? If you don't want to talk about it for now, I understand. If I can, I'll try to make it so people don't come here, and no one calls you, but I might not be able to."

My aunt handed over the newspaper and retreated into the house. For a long time I sat holding it and not looking at it, watching people

go past on the sidewalk, studying the leaves to see if they were turning yet, smelling the end of summer in the air and feeling a thin film
of sweat forming on my palms because that stream of knowledge
was working again, and I had a good idea what the article might say.
I knew they wouldn't have kept my father so long just for speeding,
or just for having blood on the seat of his truck. At last I took up the
paper and opened it. I read the first part of the article, which was on the
right-hand side of the front page, and then, after thinking about what
I'd read and building up my courage, I turned to a page inside and read
the rest. There was a photograph of my father there, taken at the police
station, but not one of my mother.

When I finished, I left the newspaper on the porch, went to my
room, and closed the door. I lay down on the bed, faceup, and I began
to weep, trying not to make any sound my aunt could hear. I wept for
a long time, the tears streaming down and into my ears, and my body
trembling and the fingers of both hands clutching the fabric of the quilt.
On and on it went, as if all the trouble and pain inside me had turned to
liquid and was pouring out my eyes. When my aunt came to the door
and knocked, I tried to stop myself from crying and be as quiet as a
girl sleeping, but I couldn't do it. Aunt Elaine called my name, twice;
I didn't answer. She knocked again later and asked through the door if
I was hungry, but I didn't answer then either. When I finally stopped
crying, I fell into a swamp of thoughts. I pulled out a hundred memories and turned them this way and that in my mind. My parents leaving
on their overnight outings. My mother holding the knife and coming
for me in the woods. The way she could work my father and work him
until she convinced him to do what she wanted. The different looks I
could see on my father's face. The times he had talked to me kindly,
taken me into the woods and taught me things, taken me to Weedon's.
The times there had been some peacefulness in the house. The things
that had been said at Pastor Schect's church and the hunger on his face
when he came across our threshold. I fell asleep with my clothes on
and had the most terrible dreams: girls' bodies broken into pieces and

scattered in the trees, and then a longer nightmare in which I was alone in a house like Aunt Elaine's, unable to move, and it was dark and there was the sound of footsteps out front. I awoke in my small dark room, shivering. I sat there for a moment, running my eyes over the ceiling and walls, then I went to the kitchen, made myself a piece of toast, and sat there with the light on, looking at it.

The next day I wandered around the yard in a stupor, replaying the memories again and again, searching through them. When people from the local newspaper and the TV stations came and parked in front of the house and started pointing their cameras at me over the fence, my aunt called me inside. We stayed in the kitchen with the front door locked, and she finally had to call the police to get the reporters to stay off the lawn. She waited until the end of the day to ask if I wanted to talk about it.

I told her I couldn't talk about it then. The tears came up almost as strong as before.

My aunt reached across the table and covered my two hands. "The police want to interview you, to get some information."

"I couldn't now."

"I told them that. They asked if you could write some things down, what happened in the house, what your parents did and when. Sands could do it for you if you'd rather talk to him. You could just talk and he would write it. That might keep you from having to go to the police or having them come here. At least for a while."

I sank my chin down on my chest and felt my aunt stand up and hug me. I reached up and held her arm against me tight. I felt small then. All the new strength had drained out of me.

Thirty-one

I waited as long as I could. I stayed in bed a lot, making sketches of buildings and sometimes trying to read.

Sands went out and bought a new truck, different color, different make, nothing in it to remind us of what had been there. On the afternoon when I'd agreed to talk to him, I stood at the edge of the porch and watched for it. One of the neighbors was peeking out at me from her backyard but I pretended not to see her. The press people had come again and again, but we wouldn't talk to them and eventually the police came and told them to leave and they'd gone somewhere else and, except for phone calls we didn't answer, mostly stopped bothering us. Aunt Elaine took time off from work, and she and I basically hid out in her house, with the TV off and the newspapers out of sight, leaving there only to visit Lily in the hospital and to buy food. One time the reporters followed us all the way to the hospital and back.

When I saw Sands's truck—dark green, shining chrome, beads hanging from the mirror—stop in front of the house and saw him get out, despite what I had been telling myself all morning, I thought I would be able to do what everyone seemed to want me to do. It would be better than being called to speak in court, better than facing the police (who were being very kind to me, thanks to Sands's friend,

I imagine). It would be hard but it would be better than talking to strangers.

Sands wasn't dressed for work, sneakers instead of boots, chinos instead of jeans. He came up the walk and stopped in front of me and the first thing he said was, "I haven't been to the cathedral since your mom died. I've been sleeping in the rectory but I haven't set foot in it, haven't worked on it, have barely looked at it. Will you take a ride with me up there?"

"I could," I said.

On the way up the highway—out of nervousness, I could tell—he began to talk. He came at his story sideways, telling me first what he remembered from his own childhood: his house and neighborhood; the kind ways his parents had treated him; the way they had told him about the adoption and the way that had made him feel; the times his father had taken him hiking in the mountains of western Pennsylvania and showed him how to pitch a tent and make a fire and track animals by their footprints; his mother's flower gardens and strawberry pies. He talked and talked, about the river near his house, his love of baseball, his love of going to church and saying prayers. When he reached that point he stopped for a while, then squeezed the steering wheel in both hands and went on, not looking at me, telling me what church had meant to his family and what the minister had meant to him, and then, step by step, how the minister had slowly tricked him, and what he had done to him, and made him do, and how he'd frightened him into not saying anything to anyone, and how he had felt, alone in his room afterward, and for years and years, and even sometimes now. When he was finished with that part he stopped, as if the story of his life ended on the day that man was moved to another city. I had been facing forward the whole time, watching the highway rush toward us, focusing on every word and listening to every feeling behind the words. I waited until he took the exit for the town, and then I said, "And you have that in your mind now always, thinking those things?"

He shook his head. "I've learned how to wash it out. Mostly. Or, at least, to let it be there and not matter so much."

"Teach me for that then," I said.

"I will."

"That part is part of the cathedral, I think. Why you would be sitting in there quiet those times."

"That's right."

"Teach me for that and I'll try to talk right if I can."

When he pulled up to the cathedral we got out and walked around it separately for a little while. I was glad that, for once, there were no reporters nearby to bother us. I didn't look at the work or touch the stones, I just walked around the outside and then went in through the front door and stood in the cool interior, glancing up at the way the sunlight came through the small corner of one stained glass window we hadn't covered all the way with the tarpaulins. Sands met me in there and stood a few feet away. "Turned out pretty good," he said. "So far."

I nodded but didn't look at him.

"Come into the rectory," he said, and I followed him there.

I sat at the kitchen table and drank from the glass of water he poured me. Being in the cathedral had lifted me a little ways out of the darkness I had been living in, but I still wasn't sure I could talk about some things.

"We can go see Lily on the way home," Sands said. He hadn't sat down with me. "She'll be ready to come out of the hospital in a week or so."

"Me and Aunt Elaine are taking her back to us."

"That's the right thing."

"For all the three of us."

"Four," he said, and then he seemed to wish he hadn't said it. After shifting his weight for a while, looking at me, then pacing back and forth a few steps in the kitchen, he went to the room where I supposed he slept and he came back with a pad of paper and a pen. He sat opposite me. "My mother told me you read one of the articles," he said.

I nodded and looked straight at him. I liked being with him there, liked it in a new way. I liked the way he'd led up to talking about what we had to talk about. "It said they caught him for going speeding on the interstate behind us, and when they did they saw the blood."

"That's right."

"He told them it was of my mother's."

Sands nodded. "It was."

"They wouldn't let him go to the hospital though. He was asking if they could."

"They had a sighting of the truck, or a truck like it."

"I didn't know it."

"Someone near where one of the girls had disappeared—that last girl—had seen a truck like that about the same time she was taken, so as soon as they stopped him, even before they saw the blood, they were suspicious. He was agitated and yelling about his wife and a baby but they couldn't understand him very well. They saw the blood and they wouldn't let him go anywhere, not to the hospital, not anywhere. They held him in the local lockup until they did some tests, and then they moved him to a jail an hour or so north and east of here."

"They have those new tests now. Even here."

"DNA. You've heard of it, haven't you? In school? Or seen it on TV."

I nodded. "Not on a TV."

"The police found one of the girls, the last one. They found her body, you knew that."

"Yes."

"And they had something—even my friend isn't saying what it is—that was left there by the person who killed her. They had blood or a hair or a cigarette butt or a fiber from clothes or something. That's all they need now."

"But it was from my mother, what they found."

"That's right. What they found on the girl matched the blood on the seat of the truck."

"Then it was my mother who . . ."

"They don't know. They won't know until the trial. They might never know, because your father isn't talking. But your mother was there, they know that much. If your father did it, he didn't do it by himself."

I was shaking my head. "I don't think he was who did it. Not the worst part, anyways. I just have a guess it wasn't." I sat for a long time looking at my hands on the water glass, trying not to let myself imagine exactly what my mother and father had done, and how. But I couldn't stop my mind from going to those places, imagining those girls tied to trees and my mother behind them, imagining their bodies buried in places no one would ever find. "I think Pastor Schect might to know something," I said at last.

"I'm sure they'll talk to him and call him to talk at the trial."

"Tell them now to get him, can you? With your friend at the states? Can you ask?"

"Of course." Sands waited until I looked up again. "I'll do that as soon as we finish. They'll call you, too, unless we can get enough down on paper and convince them they don't have to."

I looked into his eyes through the thick lenses, trying to search behind them for any more surprises, any more of the world collapsing around me, any more of things being the worst way they could possibly be. "I like it that you told me . . . this way," I said. "And Aunt Elaine like she did."

"Are you afraid?"

"Now I am. More than I was."

"You shouldn't be now."

"But I am, though. I worry what's inside of me . . . from them."

"It doesn't work that way."

I sat there looking down and sideways at a piece of door trim where the cut had not been made just right.

After a while Sands said, "Can you tell me something so I can write it down?"

"Yes."

He picked up the pen. He pushed the glasses back against his face and waited for me.

I drank some water and started talking. I said, "When I had a birthday—seventeen—my mother and my father they told me to go out for full-pay work. So I did."

"I think we have to go back before that," Sands told me. "I think . . . just start with the first thing you remember."

I felt like I had been holding very tightly to my mind for that past week, not letting it go places. But I knew then that I had to release it, and when I did that the memories came flooding back over me fast and bad and I just let them out. "I remember," I said, "watching my father to make the old shed burn. I remember the feeling it made inside my mother. That she was happy."

Thirty-two

We went back to work the following week. It was the day before Lily came home. A team of four men from Keene arrived and put the slate on the roof of the cathedral, hundreds, maybe thousands of pieces nailed through two holes into the wood. Sands and I watched for a while and then started work on a low wall that was going to surround a flagstone patio. Sands had drawings for what he wanted to do with the interior of the building, he said as we set out the stones, but he wasn't ready to show them to anyone yet, not even me. There would be surprises, he said. It wasn't going to be an ordinary church.

Even just bare and clean, though, with the stone walls and wooden ceiling and big oak beams going across, I could feel that the pain and evil and craziness of the outside world would have a hard time reaching into a building like the one we had made. It wasn't very large, but, even so, I'd started to think that maybe cathedral *was* the right word for it after all. People like Pastor Schect wouldn't ever stand at the pulpit in a place like that. Angry gods like his god wouldn't be able to breathe there.

When I told him I was ready, Sands took me inside at the end of one workday and taught me what he said was a Quaker prayer, though people who weren't Quakers used it, too. You were supposed to sit quiet and bring your mind back to a secret word or a picture. "Your mind will wander away in all kinds of directions," he said, "and you bring it back. Just like you would with a puppy. Never angry at it, just gently carrying it home. If you keep doing it every day it will get easier. For some people, it starts to make every bad thing inside you have less and less power."

I chose "Lily" for my secret word and tried to do the prayer, but a hundred pictures and thoughts crowded in. Still, I kept at it the way I kept at a lot of things in those days, as if my life depended on it.

"That's all right," Sands said when I told him I was having trouble. "The thing is not to give up."

"I'm not a giving-up girl," I said.

"I kind of know that by now."

When we brought Lily home to Aunt Elaine's, I sat next to her in the backseat. She was facing backward—the safe way to ride—and I kept one hand on her small knees. It made me so happy to have her there, to have something else to think about than my father and mother and the dead girls, but I admit I looked at her pinched face and tried to see if there was any visible damage from my mother's smoking and drinking and the way she'd been born. After a while of thinking about it, I realized who she looked like, through the eyes. Dad Paul, my father's father.

For a time, as September approached, Aunt Elaine tried to convince me I should go back to school, but I was stubborn about that and I refused. She was right, and I would pay for being stubborn, later on, when I had to go back and finish at an older age. But that wasn't a time for me to be with other kids. It just wasn't something I could do then, and eventually my aunt understood. In the mornings I stayed home and took Lily for walks in the stroller, changed her diaper, fed her, and held her when she cried, and made up songs to sing to her. I was good at it. Safe and happy and clean and never hungry was what you wanted a baby to be, I told myself, with no trouble in its mind. I made that kind of a world for my sister and I was happy to do it because in some way it was like I was doing it for myself, long in the past. When she slept, I found a quiet place to sit close by and tried to do Sands's prayer or read a little bit. In the afternoon, Aunt Elaine would come and I would take the bus north and work with Sands, and he'd drive me home at night, and we'd always have Lily there on a blanket on the table, sleeping while we ate. Or we'd put her on a soft blanket on the carpet in the living room, or in a crib in my room, and then Sands would drive all the way back and sleep in the rectory.

Because of what had happened, I thought there might be some trouble from the kids I'd known, that they would come by the cathedral and bother me. I avoided the school and the quarry. It was another reason I liked living in Watsonboro then, a safe distance. For a while, after the first newspaper stories, I'd sometimes see people walking slowly past the work site, or driving slowly past in a car, looking at the building, maybe, but probably more curious to see the girl whose mother and father were killers. In spite of everything, I still couldn't believe those words; even now, there's a small small part of me that can't really imagine them doing what they did. I feel guilty about that. I have gone to the graves of the three girls whose bodies have been found and left flowers. I've prayed for them many times, on lunch breaks in the cathedral, before bed, when I first wake up. I've thought of writing to their families, but I've never had the courage to do that. There are some kinds of sorrow that words can never reach, certain kinds of things you can never hold in the box of your thoughts, certain kinds of pain you can't soften in other people.

On her days off, Aunt Elaine brought Lily up to see the cathedral. We laughed at the way her noises echoed inside. Sands and I were mostly working out back on the patio by then, or, if it rained, indoors. People from the newspapers and TV still called occasionally (it got much worse when the trial started) but we told them I wasn't talking to anyone, and after a while they let us be. I remember Sands saying to me then that if you thought about yourself from the outside, if you looped thoughts out through other people's heads before bringing them back into your own, then you'd never be happy.

Cindy was going to have a baby. She came to the cathedral several times on Saturdays and had lunch with the four of us, not showing yet but as happy as I'd ever seen her. I let her hold Lily for a little while. We'd talk about how to care for an infant, and Cindy would tell me what the kids and her parents were saying about my father and mother, but not in a mean way. There was a simple goodness about her, there always had been, and that was what I needed then. In spite of every-thing—getting pregnant when she was so young, losing her husband a few years later, having another child with someone else—she's more content than a lot of people I know, even now. She cooks breakfast and lunch at Art and Pat's, and cares for her son, Willie, and her daughter, Jess. She has a talent for both jobs and sometimes now I'll go visit the cathedral and she'll come and sit with me there for half an hour, so we can make our quiet prayers together. No amount of distance be-tween the way we live our lives has ever really been able to damage our friendship, and I'm grateful for that.

One important thing that happened in those first weeks was that, after the detectives worked on him and worked on him, and after hours of being alone in his cell, my father finally broke and told them what he knew. That's how they were able to find two more of the bodies. Pastor Schect had been under surveillance and he was ar-rested the same day, and then Cary Patanauk, on lesser charges. It turned out that, very early on, from the larger group of his congrega-tion, Schect had chosen my parents and Aaron's uncle for a kind of inner circle. With his satanic intuition, the pastor had sensed some-thing in them—a mix of lust and anger in Patanauk's case, and a mix of eagerness and bitterness in my mother's. And in my father, I think, just the trait that so many evil leaders have counted on over the centuries: a willingness to be convinced that their worst impulses are actually the word of God. It would come out at the trial that this small group had met a half dozen times at Patanauk's shop, where Pastor Schect began to take his twisted ideas about the punishment of children and bring them, week by week, to a new level. There were girls and young women, he said, who God had sent to earth as sacrificial lambs. Wasn't it then their own God-given work to accept these girls as offerings?

Patanauk—who testified to all this in exchange for a reduced sentence—was tempted at first, he said. He hosted those first few meetings, then opted out and left the church. Which gave my mother the opportunity to pit my father against him, to urge him to be more of a man than her former lover—if that word can be used where Cary Patanauk was concerned. The last thing I want to do is to paint my father as an innocent victim. The fact is, he drove his wife around the back roads of New Hampshire and eastern Vermont, many times, hoping to stumble on a solitary young woman they could trick into the vehicle and then terrify and slaughter. There is nothing innocent about that. But there was always a certain simpleness about him. I think of him sometimes as a kind of donkey who could be led to someone and told to bite. I like to hold on to the idea that if my mother hadn't been mentally ill, if his own father hadn't ended up in disgrace, if the people who published *True Home and Country* had never sent their poison into our mailbox and led us to Pastor Schect, then Curtis John Richards might have lived an unexceptional life, doing what so many other people do around there—cutting and burning wood, making and spending money, eating and chasing small pleasures, growing old. I like to think the connection between us might have blossomed into something like the love that should exist between a father and daughter, a parent and child. In certain foolish moods I like to think that way, even now. Maybe because I want there to be some goodness in myself. Maybe because I worry there isn't. Or maybe only because there is a certain loneliness that comes from being so distant from the family you were born in.

When Lily was about four months old and strong enough, and when Christmas was approaching, and when, finally, the newspapers had gone quiet about the story and all of us were just waiting for the trial, and when I had let the feelings about my mother and father sink a small distance beneath the routine of my new life, I told Sands I wanted to take the baby to see her father. Aunt Elaine didn't like the idea at all, but I insisted.

On a cold day in the middle of December, I wrapped Lily up in flannel pajamas and a blanket, set her car seat between me and Sands, and we drove northeast across the state to where my father was being held until the trial could start. The hills were white with deep snow, and they had a black-brown stubble of hardwood trees on them. A weak, gray sun pushed through the clouds.

Quiet in the best of times, since the death of my mother and everything that had followed it, Sands was diving down into new depths of silence. Sometimes we'd go the whole morning without saying five words to each other.

After a few miles he said, "When the first part of the cathedral's completely finished, sometime around your next birthday, I'm going into business full-time. The cathedral worked out like an advertisement, the way I hoped it would. I've already had three jobs offered that I want to take, and the money will come in handy. Two walls and a small stone house at an apple orchard a ways south of us. Jasse's. Where we got the pies that time with . . . my mother."

I didn't answer. I didn't like to think about the cathedral being done. I looked out at the hills. In her sleep, Lily was holding on tight to one of my fingers.

"I'll need a partner," Sands went on. "Business partner, I mean. If you're interested, you have the job. We can still work on the cathedral in between. I want to make it bigger, build a bell tower, for one thing. I have a feeling I'll be working on it until I'm too old to lift stone."

I looked at him, then away. I studied the cold white fields.

"You could make, I think, about thirty thousand dollars a year or more, if we did it right. Maybe not at first, but it wouldn't be so long until we could each make that much if we worked hard."

It was not a number I could say anything back to. At that point in my life, it wasn't a number I could fold into my mind. I looked over at him once, to see if he might be making a bad joke, but Sands didn't make bad jokes, or many jokes at all usually, and from his face I could tell he was serious. Deluded, maybe, but serious.

"It would be a favor to me," he said. "Because then you could buy your own truck and I wouldn't have to drive you all the time."

Just when you think someone doesn't make jokes is when they start making them, I told myself. I said, "I'll drive better than you someday."

"I hope so." He wobbled the truck from side to side in the lane and smiled. "What about it, though, Laney? The business partner idea?"

"I could do it," I said, but I felt I might as well be agreeing to go up into space or run for governor of New Hampshire.

"If you're going to raise Lily, or partly raise her, we could find a way to work that out. Time-wise, I mean."

"I'm going to raise her. She's my own sister."

"You're good at it," Sands said. "Anyone can see that."

Out of all the mess of emotions inside me at that moment—going to see my father, feeling my sister clutching my hand, listening to talk about a thirty-thousand-dollar-a-year future—I was trying to think of a way to ask Sands if he would help raise Lily, too, if that was something he might think about. But just then she stirred and started crying. We pulled into a rest area, where I changed her diaper and fed her from the warmed-up bottle I'd put in a heating pack before we left. I walked her around in the fresh air, but just for a minute, because it was too cold for a baby to be out longer than that, and I was starting to worry we wouldn't make it in time to see my father.

We got back in the truck and drove another half hour. There were few houses. Lily slept and slept. When we saw a sign for the correctional facility, Sands put on his blinker and said, "What do you think about when you're quiet all the time lately? Your parents?"

I shook my head. I felt a twist of something in my belly, and, after hesitating for so long, I hoped the words would come out right when I was finally able to speak them. At the bottom of the exit ramp I said, "What living in the rectory would be." Then I thought a moment and added, "But some men don't have a like for children that near."

I could see I'd made him happy. He said, very proud and happy then, some of the little boy still showing, "Some men aren't me."

The prison was set back from the road on a flat, ugly stretch of land with hills in the distance and no houses nearby. From the banks at the sides of the road, I could see how much more snow had fallen there than in our river valley—it looked to be deeper than my waist in the flat fields. We came to a sign and turned onto the prison access road. There was a guardhouse with a long metal arm across the road and, a few hundred yards beyond it, two rows of tall chain-link fences with razor wire on top, and beyond them, the guard towers and high gray walls. There wasn't the slightest chance that even a man like my father could escape from a place like that, and for a minute I pondered the drudgery of endless days leading only to old age and death, and I felt a drip of pity for him, and for my grandfather in another building not far away. The feeling lasted only until I thought about the fear he and my mother had passed on, the sorrow they'd draped over the girls' families, the terror. Inside my mind, to let those thoughts drift away, I said my sister's name.

We parked and walked toward the building in the frigid air. I held Lily tight against my breast, adjusted the pink cap on her head. I lifted the blanket up around her cheeks. At the door there were guards with guns, and a man and then a woman checking us, asking us questions about what we were carrying, making us take everything out of our pockets and leave it there on a table. And then more doors, so loud and gray and cold seeming that I held the baby close against me and rocked her. Finally, there was a room where Sands couldn't enter. I went in—another female guard checked me everywhere and checked to see there was nothing inside Lily's clothes and inside her diaper or blanket—and then finally I stepped into another room and up to a wall, half-glass, where there was a row of stools with torn gray cushions glued onto the top of them. I sat on the one the guard pointed to, and I waited there, rocking the baby and murmuring to her so she wouldn't be afraid.

In a short while I saw my father come through a door. His clothes were orange, a color he hated; his beard was gone and his hair cut shorter than I'd ever seen it. He looked small and too white-faced there. I could tell nothing from his eyes. He sat on a stool on the other side of the glass and at first he kept his gaze turned down and away from me. I spoke into the microphone but he wouldn't look and wouldn't look and wouldn't look, and then he did. His eyes went quickly over the baby and then up into my eyes and remained there, still and dark. There was something in them that I remembered. It was something most people would not see. I remembered him telling me not to look away when the squirrel had been caught in his trap, and so I didn't look away then.

"Pa, this for here is Lily," I said, finding our language coming into my mouth again, automatically. I turned my sister so she was partly facing him. "Your girl."

My father kept his eyes up on my eyes and wouldn't look down. I shook the baby a bit, gently, lifted her a few inches, moved the blanket and cap away so he could have a better view of her face. My father blinked and kept his eyes up and looked at me like I had come all that way only to torture him.

"I just wanted for you to see on her," I said. "How the way she's growing up. Near to Christmas and everything I just had a thought to want to."

My father looked away and down, a movement that, in the past, would have been accompanied by spitting. But there was no spitting in that room.

"Is it too bad on you here?" I asked him, because I couldn't say anything else of what I had planned to say to him.

"Enh," my father answered, jerking his jaw down and to the side the way he always had.

"Good then. I'm happy of that. I just wanted for you to see on her is all. I could to bring her again if you wanted of it, so you can see when how she grows."

My father looked at me for a long time then. He looked at me out of the dark confusion of his innermost self, as if there was one enormous, impossible question there that occupied him night and day. Behind him the guard shifted his weight from one foot to the other. My father's eyes went down to Lily for less than the time it would take to count to two, and I saw something wobble and almost break in him. I thought, almost, that he would burst into tears. But then a crust formed over those feelings. I could see it very plainly. His eyes came up again. "Enh," he said, and he stood up quickly without saying good-bye or anything else to me, and then all I could see was the back of him, one side tilted down, the shoulders rounded, going away. Something wobbled and broke in me then. I could feel it break inside me like a dead branch snapping off a tree in winter.

Thirty-three

Leaving the prison, I felt as though I had an emptiness in me that started on my skin and went in and in and didn't stop. Sands and I had coffee in a town not far from the highway, in a place where they had moose and deer antlers on the walls and one stuffed fox. I gave Lily the rest of the bottle, still warm, and we ate something, too. I went to the bathroom and stayed in there a while, trying to breathe and pray the prayer Sands had taught me, trying to let everything go, to let it be what it was, to let my life be the life I had been given. It was very hard.

When we were back in the truck and had been riding for a while, Sands saw that I'd been crying and he said, "You've had a rough growing up, compared to a lot of people."

I looked over at him. His face was a nice face, I thought, compared to the faces of most of the men I knew, a kind face with a little winter light on it just then. His way was a good way compared to theirs. He didn't try so hard to protect himself, to keep all the hurt of life away. He had the courage not to do that, and I remember thinking then that I wanted to find that same courage in myself.

I folded back the edge of the blanket far enough to see that Lily was asleep. She seemed so peaceful there. I wondered, as I often did then, how you went about keeping a life that way in this world. How you kept the pain off it, at least for a while. How you stopped the river of the past from flooding over your present-day feelings. She twisted around, let out a small cry, and then fell back to sleep.

"Do you ever think it's unfair?" Sands asked me.

"You can't ever know what might come later to fair it up."

"Right, but do you ever wonder why things happen to some people and not others?"

"My father and mother used to say there's a penance for them to pay. My mother said it even about herself."

"You really believe that?"

"I don't know." I was looking out at the porcupine hills.

"Maybe we've finished paying now," Sands said, "both of us."

"There's a place where you do," I said. "A time when you finish it off, I think. Heaven, maybe. Or before."

It fell dark not long after we turned onto the smaller highway. A sliver of a moon came up behind the clouds, and I saw a bright star I re-called my father telling me was Venus. We passed near the edge of the town where I had gone to school, and though we didn't say anything, both of us looked in that direction, as if we might see the roof of the Connecticut River Cathedral there, behind the hills. We went across the river and up onto the interstate.

Near Watsonboro there were more houses on the hillsides, more lights, and then we took the exit and were going along the old two-lane highway not far from the river, with houses on both sides, some of them lit up with Christmas lights and plastic Santa Clauses and plastic angels. Lily cried a bit. I lifted her out of the car seat and rocked her and told her it wouldn't be long now until we were home, and she'd have something warm to eat and another clean diaper, and be able to sleep in her nice bed all by herself. Sands stopped the truck at a red light. I moved the blanket away from my sister's face and turned her so she was facing out the side window and I said, "Look, Lily. Look at those houses. There are nice people living in those houses. A lot of good people living there."

When I said those words that way I felt Sands turn toward me. I put my hand on the downy top of my sister's head, very gently, and I held it there, so the girl would know what someone in the world felt for her.

Epilogue

My father was given a sentence of life in prison without parole, Pastor Schect eighteen years, Cary Patanauk five years' probation. Aaron enlisted in the marine corps and was sent overseas. Sands and I were married when I turned twenty-one. I've never visited my father again—he doesn't seem to want me to—but I've seen Patanauk once or twice in the town, on my trips up there. Older, weaker now, he still stares at girls' bodies the way he always did, though he pretends not to recognize me.

In the years since my mother's death and my father's sentencing, we did our best—Sands, Aunt Elaine, and I—to raise Lily well. But it didn't turn out the way we wanted. As if by some unlucky spin of a roulette wheel, there was, in my sister, just too much bad weight handed down. Even having people around you who are kind and loving isn't always enough to balance off something like that. For a long time—until I reached my middle twenties—partly because of what seemed to be happening with Lily and partly for other reasons, I was afraid to have children of my own. Sands convinced me we should try. Among many other things, I'm grateful to him for that. I became pregnant almost right away, and then again a few years later. We named our first child Audrey Elaine, in honor of my aunt, and our second in honor of Sands's father, Robert Arthur.

By the time Robert was born, Lily was in fifth grade and already causing a great amount of trouble. This wasn't a surprise to any of us. We'd first taken her for counseling when she was in second grade. She chose bad friends, did poorly in school, was unhappy at home. From sixth grade on, she seemed drawn to larger troubles the way animals are drawn to the smell of food. We left the rectory and moved to Watsonboro, hoping a new place and new friends would make the difference, but nothing really changed.

By the time Lily was sixteen there were days at a stretch when we wouldn't see her. I'd leave Audrey and Robert with Sands and go out looking for her at all hours of the day and night. If I found her, I'd try to convince her to come home, I'd buy her a meal and try to talk, but it was like talking to a tree in the woods in winter. She had discovered that certain kinds of drugs—easy to get where we lived—could temporarily blot out the pain inside her, and no amount of sisterly affection was a match for that. I tried and tried—bailed her out of jail when she was caught shoplifting, paid for more counseling, paid to have her sent away to a residential treatment center for teens that Aunt Elaine knew about.

Finally, when Lily was seventeen, just the age I'd been when I went out looking for full-pay work, Sands said to me, "You have your own children to think of now, Laney." That was all he ever said about it, but I understood what he was getting at and I knew he was right. I began to let go of Lily then, and Aunt Elaine began to let go. She left school and we didn't try to stop her. She lived with friends not far from the cathedral and then moved away altogether. For a while we'd get collect calls from her, always when she was in trouble and needed something. She was in New York City. She was in North Carolina. She was in Fort Lauderdale. She'd be angry sometimes and lonely sometimes and trying to get us to send her money most of the time. Eventually the calls stopped, though I expect someday I will hear from her again, if she is still alive.

Audrey and Robert are good children, eleven and eight now,

normal children, able to show love and receive it. We take them to the weekly Quaker meeting at the cathedral, and sometimes they can sit still through most of it, and sometimes not. So much joy has come of our life with them. So much good to set against the bad that came before. I struggle with that bad part, though. Even still. Sands struggles, too, inside himself, in a different way. Sometimes the ordinary trials of daily life just turn in a certain direction and call up the hurt of the past, and there you are, living with children of your own, surrounded by echoes of the things you went through. Those echoes were what sent me back to try and understand my own life better, to wring a lesson out of the past. All that bruise and confusion, all that guilt and shame and buried anger: I wanted to go back and hunt it down and close the hurt-museum for good, though I discovered you cannot really do that. What you can do, what you have to do, is not pass too much of it on. If you can stop that trouble from flowing through you onto your children and husband and other people, or even if you can dilute it, then it seems to me your life ought to be pleasing to whatever kind God it was who made you.

June 22, 2009–January 26, 2011
Conway, MA

The Corporate Mystic

Contents

Contents

Chapter 1
Integrity:
Leadership by Inspiring Authenticity

Chapter 2
Vision:
Leadership by Inspiring Clear Intention

Contents

Contents

Contents

PART THREE

The Disciplined Mystic
Four Ten-Minute Practices for Enhancing Integrity, Vision, and
Intuition

The Last Word

The Seven Radical Rules for Business Success

About the Authors

Acknowledgments

We are deeply grateful to the following men and women for embodying the Corporate Mystic ideal and for enriching the lives of so many thousands of people in the process. An exhaustive list of the people we have admired, interviewed, followed around, or consulted with would fill a separate book. Forgive us if your name does not appear on this list, and know that your contribution is appreciated.

Larry Boucher, CEO, Auspex
Ron Bynum, corporate consultant
Kenneth Casey, President, Professional Investors'
    Financial Services
Paul and Elizabeth Cotulla, entrepreneurs

Acknowledgments

Stephen R. Covey, author and consultant
Carlene Ellis, Vice-President, Intel
George Fisher, Chairman, Eastman Kodak
Bob Galvin, Former Chairman, Motorola
Chris Galvin, COO, Motorola
Glenn Gienko, Corporate Vice-President, Motorola
Heath Herber, president, The Herber Company
Portia Isaacson, founder, Future Computing
Les Isbrandt, Vice-President, Warner Lambert
Kathryn Johnson, CEO, The Healthcare Forum
Jerry Jones, President, The Jones Corporation
Bill Klimpton, Chairman, Kimpco
Philip Knight, Chairman, Nike
Barbara LaTour, Vice-President, Adia
Kathy Mankin, Executive Vice-President, Heller
    Financial
Darshan Mayginnes, cofounder, Performance Coatings
Ed McCracken, CEO, Silicon Graphics
Richard McNeese, former CEO, First National
    Bancorp
Joyce Russell, Vice-President, Adia
Ken Schroeder, President, KLA Instruments
Bob Shapiro, Chairman and CEO, Monsanto
Gary Tooker, CEO, Motorola
Jack Unroe, President, Judicial Arbitration and
    Mediation Services
Virginia Weldon, Senior Vice-President, Monsanto
Bill Wiggenhorn, President, Motorola University

You must have a room, or a certain hour
or so a day,
where you don't know what was in the
newspaper that morning, you don't know who
your friends are,
you don't know what you owe anybody,
you don't know what anybody owes you.

This is a place where you can simply
experience and bring forth what you are and
what you might be.
—JOSEPH CAMPBELL

Often people attempt to live their lives
backwards; they try to have more things, or
more money, in order to do more of what they
want, so they will be happier. The way it
actually works is in reverse. You must first be
who you really are, then do what you need to
do, in order to have what you want.
—MARGARET YOUNG

Prologue

HEART AND SOUL AT WORK

*Work can provide the opportunity for
spiritual and personal, as well as financial
growth. If it doesn't, we're wasting far too
much of our lives on it.*
—JAMES AUTRY

Corporations are full of mystics. If you want to find a genuine mystic, you are more likely to find one in a boardroom
than in a monastery or a cathedral. Surprised by this notion? We were, too. But over the past twenty-five years we
have been in many boardrooms and many cathedrals, and we
have discovered that the very best kind of mystics—those
who practice what they preach—can be found in the business
world. We are now convinced that the qualities of these remarkable people, and the principles they live by, will be the
guiding force for twenty-first-century enterprise.

Prologue

In preparation for writing this book, we spent a thousand hours in conversation with several hundred Corporate Mystics. As a result, our business and personal lives are forever changed. We will share with you the practical details of what they taught us: how to do soul-satisfying work in a way that empowers, heals, and profits. We have distilled their learnings into brief bits of "just-in-time" wisdom that you can draw on to help you in every minute of your work life.

We are consultants to corporations and to other corporate consultants. From working with eight hundred executives over the past twenty-five years, we make a prediction: Successful corporate leaders of the twenty-first century will be spiritual leaders. They will be comfortable with their own spirituality, and they will know how to nurture spiritual development in others. The most successful leaders of today have already learned this secret. Corporate Mystics know that an organization is a collective embodiment of spirit, the sum total of the spirits of the individuals who work there. Those who think spirituality has no place in business are selling themselves and those around them short.

What is a Corporate Mystic? The dictionary says that mystics are those who have been initiated into esoteric mysteries. It says that mystics intuitively comprehend what is true. The people we call Corporate Mystics seem to operate at a level of effectiveness that appears esoteric until you understand the principles they are drawing on. In addition, the mystics we have known definitely have a strong connection with their intuition and know how to use it where it counts. We go further in our definition, however: Corporate Mystics are those who operate from a base of integrity, pursue their visions with passion and compassion, and evoke the full potential of those with whom they come in contact.

Genuine Corporate Mystics live life from a spiritual base. They are in business for their hearts and souls as well as their wallets. They are in business to support the hearts and souls of the people with whom they work. We have done consulting work with many different types of organizations, so we have a basis for comparison when we say: There is more careful and conscious application of the Golden Rule in business settings than in any other institutions we have visited, including church, university, and government.

> *Dad once looked down an assembly line of women employees and thought, "These are all like my own mom—they have kids, homes to take care of, people who need them." It motivated him to work hard to give them a better life because he saw his mom in all of them. That's how it all begins—with fundamental respect.*

—BOB GALVIN,
SPEAKING OF HIS FATHER, FOUNDER OF MOTOROLA

Many of us have a deep sense of spiritual connection when we are young, only to have it erode as we enter the bottom-line world of adulthood. Childhood photographs often show us feeling wonder and delight. It looks as if we are spiritual

Prologue

beings having a physical experience. By adulthood we often look very different, like physical beings having, if we're fortunate, an occasional spiritual experience. The people we call Corporate Mystics have managed, through good fortune and diligence, to maintain their connection with the spiritual nature of themselves, other people, and the world around them.

A Corporate Mystic we interviewed for this book shared a story with us: "In my late thirties I felt like I was dying. I had been working in the corporate world for ten years, and though I had experienced quite a bit of success, I somehow knew I would never go all the way to the top. My office was on the tenth floor of a twenty-some-story building, and I remember looking out the window thinking that this was the story of my life. I was stuck on the tenth floor, halfway to the top. As I looked out the window I asked myself why this was true. After all, I worked hard and seemed as smart as everybody else. Then it hit me: I was split in half. Outside of work I was one way, but at work I was trying to be another person entirely. Outside work I was fascinated with human behavior and spent hours browsing in the psychology sections of bookstores. At work, though, I pretended to be this hard-driving fire engine of a person who was single-mindedly focused on numbers and productivity. I had the thought, 'The split is over; the way I am is the way I am, wherever I am.' I actually felt something shift in my body, like I was coming back together again. Looking back, I think what I was doing was accepting both halves of myself and making a bigger container for me to be all of myself. Now, as CEO, I try to emphasize a message of being your full, undivided self whenever I talk to the younger people in the company." This is an example of a spiritual awakening that had profound implications for this person's life and career.

When we talk about spirituality in business, we are talking about experiences, not religious beliefs. Religion usually refers to the organized aspects of spirituality: the rules, beliefs, and traditions that shape how spirituality shows up in the world. The Corporate Mystic demonstrates a type of spirituality that lives in deeds, not words. The Corporate Mystic is primarily interested in the benefits of spirituality, not in beliefs about it.

Corporate Mystics move easily between the spiritual world and the world of commerce. Corporate Mystics are visionaries with their feet on the ground. They celebrate the oneness of everything, yet at the same time they are able to focus on details. They look at a mountain peak and a spreadsheet with the same eyes. They treat the janitor and their biggest client with the same attitude.

What follows is the distilled voice of our own learnings, influenced by the wisest men and women we have ever known. The Corporate Mystic is the mentor of our dreams, the voice that we wish had been coaching us through the tough times of life and business.

There is a Zen monastery near Tokyo that attracts many powerful executives from the nearby industrial cities. One day the master said: "There is no room in my monastery for mushy mystics, dreamy folks who leave their dirty teacups everywhere. Here we meditate and we wash our teacups. Both are equally important. We teach our students to be ruthlessly demanding of themselves and their colleagues. Expect the best!

Prologue

If people cannot function with clarity in the often-tough real world, their meditations and practices have been for nought. You must master two realities: You must revel in that vast inner space, the emptiness that is connected to all the emptiness everywhere. And at the very same time, you must give your full attention to the present moment, whether you are buying a train ticket or kissing your wife or reading the stock quotes."

We offer this book with respect to the hidden saints and mystics of the business world. May this wisdom enliven and enlighten all your hours, at work and at play.

Introduction

How to Recognize a Corporate Mystic:

Twelve Characteristics of Twenty-First-Century Leaders

The less effort, the faster and more powerful you will be.
—Bruce Lee

Corporate Mystics have certain identifying characteristics. In this introduction, we will describe those characteristics as they appear from the outside. Then, in the rest of the book, we will show you the specific attitudes and action steps that will help you adopt these winning strategies for yourself.

We believe that these qualities will become crucial in the century to come, when change occurs at a rate that may be hard to imagine even in our speeded-up present. Here is an opportunity to check yourself out against these qualities, atti-

1

tudes, and operating strategies. Find out how many of these characteristics are part of your life already.

In describing these traits let's make it clear that Corporate Mystics are perfectly human and therefore full of imperfections. These are street saints, front-line visionaries who have a hundred opportunities to mess up each day. They would be the last to say they have mastered the following traits. But we have seen with our own eyes that they are all in a serious inquiry into these characteristics every day they live and breathe.

ABSOLUTE HONESTY

Every single mystic we interviewed said the same thing: The first secret to success in business is to say only things that are true and to say them with total consistency. Businesspeople get into trouble when they say one thing to the banker, one thing to the customer, one thing to the board. We have facilitated many emotionally charged sessions in which company executives admitted lies, distortions, and concealments to people who had believed them. Yet even though these meetings were often loud and long, we have never seen a situation where absolute honesty did not pay off. People cannot relax and produce at their finest in an atmosphere of distortion and concealment. Honesty brings out the best in everyone. In other words, integrity is not just a noble idea, it's a tool for personal and corporate success.

Corporate Mystics are also honest, even brutally honest,

with themselves. They want to know the truth, even though that truth sometimes is personally painful. In his first major consulting job, Gay had the sweaty task of delivering a litany of bad news to the president of the world's largest corporation of its kind. Not only was the news bad, but it involved one of the president's own pet projects. "I had been engaged to measure the success of the project and instead had found that practically everything was wrong with it," he recalls. "I went into the session feeling fear and trepidation. After all, I was a freshly minted psychologist, barely thirty years old, and he was a multimillionaire who frequently dined at the White House. I was worried that I would get blasted if I told him what I had concluded, but I decided to call it as I saw it. I had learned the hard way the consequences of soft-pedaling the truth, and I figured the worst he could do was fire me. But I soon found I had nothing to fear. When his attention focused on me I was treated to the best listening I had ever experienced. His interest did not waver, even during times I was telling him things he could not have possibly wanted to hear. There was never a trace of blame in his voice, either. His first move, upon hearing the bad news, was to reflect on whether anything was amiss in his own intentions and visions. He did this with the same attitude of blameless inquiry that he focused on the staff of the project under consideration. His attitude was: What actually happened? What can be done? Fix it or fold it? I had walked into the meeting expecting to be grilled and possibly dismissed from my contract. I walked out feeling completely valued. It was the first time in my life I was certain I had been in the presence of greatness."

Introduction

How do you demonstrate respect? Through the integrity of the message you communicate. It sounds simplistic, but we found that the easiest way of getting things done was by being straight. It's in our self-interest to be straight and treat people "square."

—BOB GALVIN, MOTOROLA

FAIRNESS

Scrupulous attention to fairness distinguishes the Corporate Mystic. They do what they say they are going to do. They don't do what they say they're not going to do. And all of this is carried out with across-the-board fairness and consistency. A high compliment often applied to the mystic is "Tough as nails but always fair." Everyone wants to be treated fairly, but many of us forget this under the stress of decision making. One of the mystic's edges is the ability to apply the question—Is it fair to all concerned?—even when the pressure is fully on.

For the Corporate Mystic, fairness goes beyond a moral injunction. In other words, they are not fair because they should be fair. They are fair because they see that equality pervades the universe. All of us are equal, all of us at the core are the same. As one person put it, "Fairness is the way everything hangs together in the world. When I act unfairly I disturb the actual workings of the world. When I am fair I participate in the way the world is woven together."

When Ken Levy of KLA Instruments was leading his firm through a tough time, he opened a meeting like this: "I'm announcing today across-the-board pay cuts of 10 percent for officers. Because I make more money than a lot of people in the company, I'm taking a 20 percent cut." People at the meeting, instead of grousing about their own cuts, tried to talk him down to 10 percent. He held firm, and the corporate grapevine hummed with this radical approach to fairness. Morale soared instead of plummeted.

SELF-KNOWLEDGE

Human beings are born learning, and the moment we stop learning we start to die. Corporate Mystics are particularly concerned with learning about themselves. They recognize that our minds, bodies, and spirits are the instrument by which we carry out our actions, so they put a great deal of attention on examining their motives, history, and feelings.

Corporate Mystics are committed to their own learning and at the same time committed to helping others learn. The attitude of inquiry, of wonder, is sacred to the mystic. Few things anger them more than people claiming to be right, to have all the answers. We have not yet met a truly successful person who wasn't actively learning about themselves every day.

Introduction

It's what you learn after you know it all that counts.

—JOHN WOODEN

As consultants, we are most often hired by an executive to work with his or her colleagues. A chairman will hire us to work with the company president, or the president may hire us to work with a management team. We can think of fewer than a dozen instances in which executives have sought our services for their own development. Yet in each case, they were extraordinary. Among them: The head of an entertainment conglomerate, a woman who is on her way to becoming the head of a *Fortune* 100 company, the chairman of a $20 billion company, a high-tech start-up entrepreneur. Our conclusion: The more talented you are, the more likely you are to go out of your way to learn and improve, even if you are phenomenally successful by the world's standards.

Corporate Mystics gain self-knowledge in three crucial ways. First, they acknowledge and appreciate their emotions. Although businesspeople have the reputation of being controlled and unemotional, and some certainly are, we have not found this to be true of the leaders we call mystics. More often, they simply deal with their feelings without dramatizing them. Mystics never hide their feelings, even their painful fears, angers, and griefs; they can report them to you with the same clarity as they can tell you the time of day.

Second, they understand their programming from the past, and hence are less likely to be blindsided by it. The mystics' edge is a thorough and deep knowledge of their own story—its limitations and glories—so that those limitations do not hold them back or overshadow the present.

Third, they are open to feedback, even when it is expressed as criticism. Kate was once invited to spend an evening working with CEO Ed McCracken and the executive team of Silicon Graphics. This company is responsible for many innovations, including special effects for many hit Hollywood movies. Ed McCracken, who has also taught meditation classes, meets every month or two with the executive team for an evening of leading-edge learning. On this occasion, the focus was on getting 360-degree feedback from people close to you.

Kate: "I gave out colored sheets of paper, one color per person. I invited them to pick one area that needed improvement in themselves and in each of the other people present. Each person wrote his or her own area of improvement on a colored sheet, and peers used that color to select an area they felt that person needed to improve. Thus, every person gave themselves feedback, got feedback from the others, and gave the others feedback. It was a very rich evening of learning for all concerned, but two aspects stand out vividly in my memory. First, nearly every person picked out areas they needed to improve which were considered by the others to be strengths already. In other words, they were harder on themselves than the others were on them. Second, everyone was eager for the feedback! Nobody got defensive throughout the whole evening. I had done this activity with groups of middle managers at other companies and had seen a great deal of peevishness, put-downs, and general defensiveness. But Silicon Graphics had built a corporate culture of openness to personal learning. It was heartening to see a roomful of powerful executives who had such a high commitment to self-knowledge."

A FOCUS ON CONTRIBUTION

Jokesters and cartoonists often depict business leaders as greedy, but we have very seldom met a high-level leader who was motivated by greed. Most were deeply concerned with the well-being and empowerment of other people. Contribution was at the forefront of their intentions.

Early in his executive development work, one of Gay's clients was a CEO who had been uprooted by the shifting winds of corporate politics. Gay recalls, "I asked him point-blank why he didn't just retire right then in his early fifties. After all, I said, you have more than enough money to live on for the rest of your life. You could play golf, enjoy your grandchildren, get to know your wife. What would you miss that would be worth getting back into the fray for? He looked at me with a total incomprehension. *'The contribution,'* he explained, as if he were showing a child how a clock worked. 'When I retire I want to be completely satisfied that I have made my full contribution. I'm not finished yet.'

"At that moment I realized that I had never fully understood why people work. They work for contribution, for the opportunity to serve. Ultimately they work for love. I felt as if I were looking directly into his soul, into his deepest and highest motivation. This conversation allowed me to open up more to my own soul-level commitment to contribution."

NONDOGMATIC SPIRITUALITY

The four characteristics we have described—honesty, fairness, commitment to self-knowledge, and focus on contribution—are in themselves the ground of a perennial, universal spirituality. Corporate Mystics tend to be allergic to dogma, and often remain at a distance from religion in its more structured forms. Rather, they attempt to live their lives from the universal sources of spirituality that underlie differing beliefs. Bob Galvin once said that it is important for business-people to stay out of theology and potentially divisive beliefs about spirituality, and instead to focus on the unifying benefits of spiritual practice.

Above all, spirituality means deeds, not words, to the Corporate Mystic. They have an ability to see through the particulars to the universal connection points of us all. This ability to look beneath differences to the essential core frees up the mystic to focus on how spirituality expresses itself in action.

> *Spirituality cannot be something a person toys with, a little compartment of their lives. It has to be at the core, in a way that affects every other part of their lives.*
>
> —STEPHEN COVEY

Introduction

*My objective in life is not to have a spiritual
part of life that is separate from
the rest of my life.*

—ED MCCRACKEN, CEO, SILICON GRAPHICS

THEY GET MORE DONE BY DOING LESS

An executive of a West Coast corporation describes his first morning as an aide to his mentor many years before. "He had an apartment in the corporate headquarters, and that's where I was asked to meet him that first morning. He came out of the door at seven A.M., greeted me, and took me into his office with him. An hour later, I excused myself to go to the bathroom. When I got in there, I just stood there shaking and trying to catch my breath. He had gotten more done in an hour than I had ever done in two weeks! And yet he did it all effortlessly; one thing just flowed into another. He never even looked like he was working. He focused all his attention on what he was doing right then and there, then he went to the next thing and gave it that same attention. It was remarkable to see someone so centered in the present. I felt like a U-Haul trailer being pulled along behind a Ferrari. I vowed then and there that if I ever found myself working too hard or looking busy, I would take it as a sign that I wasn't working smart."

Introduction

Man: I'm a hard-driving businessman. If I learn to meditate, won't it take the drive out of me?

Zen master: No, no. It will simply make you an easy-driving businessman. Who ever said the drive had to be hard?

To get more done by doing less is a credo and a key operating style of Corporate Mystics. They put a great deal of attention on learning to be in the present because they have found that this is the only place from which time can be expanded. If you are in the present—not caught up in regret about the past or anxiety about the future—time essentially becomes malleable. When you are in the grip of the past or the future, there is never enough time, because you are trying to be in two places at once. If you are standing in the present while your mind is somewhere else, there is a fundamental split that produces pressure and tension. Only by coming into the present can the mystic master time. Corporate Mystics study carefully how time feels to them. When time pressures begin to creep in, they use this as feedback that they are not centering themselves in the present.

Move like a beam of light,
Fly like lightning,
Strike like thunder,
Whirl in circles around a stable center.
—MORIHEI UESHIBA

THEY CALL FORTH THE BEST OF THEMSELVES AND OTHERS

M ost mystical traditions speak of a clear space at the center of ourselves, whether it is called soul or spirit or essence. It is what some call the higher self and represents who we really are at the core. Corporate Mystics know how to stay focused on this essence in themselves and in their co-workers, and how to bring it forth reliably.

At every moment you choose yourself, but do you choose your self? Body and soul contain a thousand possibilities out of which you may build many "I's." But in only one of them is there congruence between the elector and the elected, only one which you will never find until you have excluded all those superficial feelings and possibilities of being and doing with which you toy out of curiosity or wonder or fear and which hinder you from casting anchor in the experience in the mystery of life and the consciousness of the talent entrusted in you and the wonder of you which is truly your "I."

—Dag Hammarskjöld

Introduction

Essence is distinct from persona. Persona, coming from a word that means "mask," is the act we wear to survive in the world. You may have learned the persona of "appeaser" or "dominator" to survive in your particular family, and you may still run that act in your workplace today. Mystics know that we all have personas that are wrapped around our true essence, but they also know that we are not our personas. They know that underneath the blustery facade of the tough supersalesman may be a terrified little boy. But the boy, too, is a persona, and both may obscure the true self of the person beneath all the masks. The true self is often characterized by wonder, curiosity, and openness to resonance with others, qualities that often become obscured in the growing-up process. Once we become fully identified with our essence, we feel at home wherever we are.

Corporate Mystics develop a kind of double vision, at once able to see the mask and the essential person inside.

This skill has a high payoff in confronting difficult people. Because Corporate Mystics see and honor the person's essence, they can say things like "You can be a total jerk sometimes, Harry," and have it meaningfully received. Without respect of the person's essence, the same comment triggers resistance. Kate recalls the breakthrough moment of an executive development session with Linda Smith, a senior vice-president of a multinational company: "With no malice intended, I referred to her as a 'political boob.' She got to laughing so hard at this description of her that tears poured down her face. I think I could get away with saying something like this because I could see her essence—her pure nature—so clearly, and because she knew her own essence nature so deeply. Hearing this feedback from someone who saw her essence deeply triggered an important behavioral shift in her toward increased political astuteness."

It is as important to challenge people about their personas as it is to love and cherish their true essence. In the business world it is dangerous to ignore people's personas. Genuinely caring for people means seeing them as they are, not blithely overlooking possibly fatal flaws.

OPENNESS TO CHANGE

Mystics have a respect and even a fondness for change that reaches down into their cells. They know that everything is change—that's the way life works in this part of the universe. As one Corporate Mystic put it: Everything in the universe is subject to change and everything is right on schedule. At times they may have unpleasant feelings about the direction of change, but they are careful not to let those feelings limit their ability to respond.

One of the major talents Corporate Mystics develop is the ability to let go of being right. Attachment to one's own point of view is a make-or-break problem for many people because it blinds them to the need for change. In the course of our work with over eight hundred executives, we have invited twelve thousand of their co-workers to fill out surveys rating their performance. One survey item asks if the executive is willing to let go of no-win situations or goals. The responses indicate that this is a problem for about 50 percent of the executives.

Depending on the circumstances,
You should be hard as a diamond,
Flexible as a willow,
Smooth-flowing like water
or as empty as space.
—MORIHEI UESHIBA

Gay has traded commodity and stock index futures for many years. He has learned the hard way about letting go. "If I buy a contract for a thousand barrels of oil at $20 a barrel, I have reason to believe that it will go up. If it goes down to $18 a barrel an hour after I buy it, I am faced with a dilemma. Sell out now and take a $2,000 loss, or hold it and hope it comes back up? If I hold on, it could keep going on down. This nerve-wracking moment is the one that keeps most people out of the game, but I have learned to savor it. It comes down to admitting you're wrong. The winner will say: 'Okay, I'm wrong. It's going down. I'll get out, take my loss, and maybe sell a contract instead of buying one.' In other words, winners play it the way it's going. Losers say: 'I know I'm right, darn it, even though the market says otherwise. I'll just stay in a little longer and I'm sure I'll be proven right.' Some truly colossal disasters have come from thinking this way."

When Coca-Cola changed the formula of their flagship

product some years ago, there was a large hue and cry from their loyal customers who liked the old formula. Apparently there was a faction of executives within the company who wanted to stick with the new formula and ride out the uproar. Another faction took the "go with the flow" approach and voted to bring back the old formula. The second group prevailed, indicating that the company would rather listen to the customer than be right. Corporate Mystics learn to flow with change and even thrive on it. The non-mystic gets seasick amid change by trying to pretend he's still on dry land.

A SPECIAL SENSE OF HUMOR

Corporate Mystics laugh a lot. They are quick to point out the quirks of life and the human animal, and they are quick to include themselves in the joke. They can laugh at themselves and do because they have embodied a basic duality: the sacredness of life and the utter absurdity of it at times. Kate, who has observed dozens of corporate cultures, says, "The single best way to judge the health of a team or a company is by how much humor there is."

In our twenty-five years in the presence of corporate leaders, we have seldom heard jokes or remarks that relied upon cruelty, humiliation, or ridicule for their humor. This in itself is remarkable, but it gives an insight into the viewpoint of the mystic: We are all in this together—let's laugh ourselves out of this fix we're in.

KEEN DISTANT VISION AND UP-CLOSE FOCUS

Corporate Mystics have a gift for engaging people in big dreams. They can stand in a future that does not exist and map out the details of how to get there. (We will tell you exactly how they do this in a later chapter.) At the same time they can look steadily at right-now reality. Many people have a grasp of the nuts-and-bolts reality of the moment. They can look at the way things are and not flinch. On the other end of the spectrum, there are also people who can see the possibilities on the horizon. But often these two skills—keen distant vision and equally keen up-close focus—do not come in the same package. In Corporate Mystics, they do. One of the striking characteristics of the mystics we've met is their comfort with this twofold vision.

Twofold vision also includes the ability to focus on the separateness and the way everything is woven together. People at the top of companies have a feeling for the wholeness of the organization, the people in it and the way it all fits together. Decisions made from this sense of wholeness tend to be sound and fair. One observation we have made is that there is more ecological awareness at the top of companies than the casual observer might suspect. News reports of, say, the logging industry tend to play up the "bottom-line" mentality of corporate leaders in contrast to the "natural" concerns of eco-activists. But, like most gross generalizations, these obscure the truth. Contrary to public opinion, business leaders tend to be quite mindful of the big picture. It is just that the big picture for them includes the families of the people who work for the company in addition to the aspects of nature with which the company is in conflict.

The head of a Rocky Mountain communication company reminisced about the first time he saw this quality: "My high school football team was coached by a fine man named Coach Ford. Sometimes he would call me over to give me some bit of individual coaching. All the while he was talking to me, his eyes would be sweeping the field where the rest of the team was practicing. He had the skill of carrying out a detailed conversation with one person while covering the whole scene in his vision. I couldn't have put it in words at the time, but what I was learning from him was how to stay firmly in the present and in my vision of how the future could be, all at the same time."

During an interview over lunch for this book, Bob Galvin interrupted a visionary discourse about twenty-first-century business to point out something we hadn't noticed. The waiter was setting up for dinner in another section of the restaurant, and our (long overstayed) presence was getting in his way. This is an example of the twofold vision of the Corporate Mystic: to be concerned simultaneously about the visionary future and how to make someone's life easier right this minute.

The Corporate Mystic carries this respect into other dimensions. They cultivate an ability to live in multiple "time zones," with a respect for past, present, and future all at once. It is a kind of moving-average approach to life in which past, present, and future are all factored into the equation. Those who get far out in the future often underestimate the time and resources necessary to get there. Those who are stuck in the past cannot meet the present or the future effectively. It takes a keen grasp of the present situation, a respect for the past, and a sense of the future to work effectively in this current age of sweeping and rapid change.

Mystics can enroll and engage others in their vision of what is possible, even though these visions at first seem like "impossible dreams." John Kennedy, at his inauguration in 1961, not only described the impossible dream of putting a man on the moon. He seemed effortlessly to enroll everyone else in it as well. A few people said it was a kooky, expensive idea, but nearly everyone got on board. This feat was a classic example of the mystic at work.

AN UNUSUAL SELF-DISCIPLINE

Corporate Mystics are fiercely disciplined, but it is a discipline born of passion. They generally do not rely on the kind of authoritarian discipline that is driven by fear. They motivate themselves through a clear sense of purpose, not with the shoulds and oughts of a fantasized ideal. This type of discipline makes them flexible and adaptable rather than rigid.

Corporate Mystics are passionate people. They play to win, of course, but more importantly, they play to play. We have had the opportunity to go from boardroom to golf course to family dinner with many mystics, and have been deeply impressed with their ability to be passionately present in each situation. Ken Casey, head of Professional Investors' Financial

Services, is one of the most passionate participants in life we've met. Ken said: "I retired in my early forties with the vision of having plenty of time to run on the beach with my dog. After running on the beach with my dog for two or three days, I sat down to rest and wondered—'Is this it?' I realized I loved what I'd been doing, so I went back and stepped back into leadership again." But that's not all. As we got to know him, we found that he spends considerable time raising money for a home for abused children. Then we found out that he also sings in the chorus in an opera company. Then we discovered that he is one of the top whitewater rafters in the world. One of his latest exploits was to open up the Upper Zambezi to rafters for the first time, during which his team was attacked by crocodiles between sixty and seventy times! He is also a world-class soccer player. This is clearly a person who plays passionately in every area of life.

To play with passion requires discipline. There is no other way to generate the tireless source of energy that passion runs on. You set high standards and you hold to them. The act of making good on your commitments to yourself and others is what generates the high level of energy needed to run a successful life.

BALANCE

M ystics keep a keen eye on balancing their lives in four main areas: intimacy (including marriage, family, and close friendship), work, spirituality, and community (including social and political life). The balance between work and intimacy is usually where problems occur. A considerable amount of our consultation time has gone into helping extremely busy people achieve a harmonious balance between work and home.

> *It is your work in life that is the ultimate seduction.*
>
> —PABLO PICASSO

Corporate Mystics strive for balance in each of the key areas of life. Many people mess up by trying to get their home needs met at work, and vice versa. A person who is hurting because he does not know how to communicate with his kids becomes a blustery communication obstructor at work. Another person walks in the door at night so full of undigested work issues that no one in the family can get through to her. This problem, unless corrected, becomes a self-fulfilling spiral downward. He or she spends more time at work to get away from home problems, which creates more conflict at home, which causes them to withdraw into work more.

Stephen Covey is one of the few major voices emphasizing the need for balance in order to achieve genuine success. One of the reasons for the enthusiastic reception of his books and seminars is a deep hunger for balance in the corporate world. In our consulting work, we often must deal with the fallout from imbalanced lives: problems with children, marital strains, psychosomatic illnesses. Part of the problem is time management, but more fundamentally it is a matter of commitment to balance. Logic and emotion, home and work, future and now: all of these can be sources of deep division, splits within ourselves that can destroy us. But with the proper commitment and some practice, they can also be sources of unity in the healed wholeness of ourselves. This is the territory that the mystic walks, not unfalteringly, but with commitment and passion.

"Master," said the student, "where do you get your spiritual power?"

"From being connected to the source," said the Master.

"You are connected to the source of Zen?"

"Beyond that," said the Master, "I am Zen. The connection is complete."

"But isn't it arrogant to claim connection with the source?" asked the student.

"Far from it," said the Master. "It's arrogant not to claim connection with the source. Everything is connected. If you think you are not connected to the source you are thumbing your nose at the universe itself."

PART ONE

The Mystic as Leader:
Becoming the Source

Leadership is going where nobody else has gone.

—Bob Galvin, Motorola

If you will open up to being a source of integrity, vision, and intuition in your organization, you step into leadership regardless of what niche you occupy. Many people wait to be instructed or reminded to take full ownership of these powers. The Corporate Mystic knows that real power and real fun comes from being a source. When you are the source, you take full responsibility for bringing into being the corporate culture you want. Everyone can be the source, and when they think they are, they are.

If you are willing to let go of your resistance to being a source, you claim a type of spiritual power that others can feel.

Leaders are comfortable with being a source of integrity, vision, and intuition. They seek to be producers, not consumers of these three rare commodities. Inspired leaders, though, have something extra. They are committed to everyone else being a source. In other words, they are committed to being a source of sources. This takes them out of the power game. If you set yourself up as the source of something while disempowering those around you, look out. It may feel great for

27

a while, but the costs are enormous. You risk playing Daddy or Mommy to people who are still looking for someone to take care of them. Boardrooms are not immune to this problem.

Imagine what could happen in your organization if everyone were trained to be a source of integrity. In a work space in which everyone felt connected to the source of integrity, miracles would happen every day. All the energy usually wasted on cleaning up integrity breaches could be channeled into creativity.

The same thing is true for vision or intuition. Imagine the power of an organization where everyone was empowered to be visionary. In our corporate training workshops we get to see this happen week after week, but it never fails to move us. A typical situation is that one person in a room of twenty will be the only one operating in the visionary role at the beginning of the workshop. Usually this is the CEO or highest officer; frequently it is the person who arranged for the training to take place. After three days of work, though, the picture is very different. All twenty are now taking responsibility for being the source of vision for the company. The energy in the room is humming with shared excitement. Everyone is on the same frequency because everyone is source.

Source is where the creativity comes from. It is also where the profits and the fun come from. People who connect with source get to inspire creativity, profits, and fun. Everybody else gets to sit on the bench and grouse. In this part we will explore how to go about becoming the source of integrity, vision, and intuition in your organization.

1

INTEGRITY:

Leadership by Inspiring Authenticity

I'm sometimes too blunt, but it's most important to be open and straightforward and tell the truth. This helps with bureaucracy and turf battles: As soon as you're open and listening and willing to dialogue, people are remarkably receptive and changes speed up rapidly.

—MORT TOPFER, VICE-CHAIRMAN, DELL COMPUTERS

Integrity creates a force field of aliveness, energy, and creativity around you. An integrity breach clouds the field around you, making creativity impossible. Lack of integrity leaches energy from you, your colleagues, and the company.

29

Taking a stand for integrity will create a stirring of energy throughout your organization. It will also create a stirring inside yourself. Committing yourself to integrity flushes to the surface any aspect of yourself and your organization that is not committed to integrity. The moment after you take a stand for integrity you might suddenly start thinking of some lie you told sixteen years ago. That's because your commitment to integrity is penetrating your body, flushing out anything in its way. The same thing happens in organizations. One person's stand for integrity will have a ripple effect. It will cause some people to move toward integrity, others to resist it. But the power of an integrity stand cannot be denied. You cannot ignore it.

Bob Galvin, former Chairman of Motorola, tells this story: "In the early 1950s we had the opportunity to get a huge contract with a South American country, installing a microwave radio system. The first part of the contract was for $10 million worth of work, which in the context of our overall revenues in excess of $100 million represented a very large possibility. One of the executives came in and told me that we had won the order but that he had decided not to take it. The reason: The generals who ran the country wanted the contract to read $11 million so they could skim the difference off the top. I told him that I was sorry that this had happened, and to refuse the contract even if they dropped their demand for padding and wanted to do it at the original price. Further, I told him that we would do no further business with this country until there was a change of leadership." When you take strong stands like this, people come to understand that you mean what you say. And the results speak for themselves: The generals are long gone and Motorola is doing very well.

There is a deeply personal and highly visible reason to focus on integrity: Your face will light up when you act with integrity or correct an integrity breach. Your mood will drop like a rock when you commit an integrity breach. If you are not feeling fully engaged throughout your workday, it's likely you've cut a deal somewhere that's robbing your energy.

When businesspeople stop and consider it, they are always shocked to discover how much time, energy, and money are wasted by integrity problems. But the positive flip side of this is also true: Creativity is unleashed by attending to integrity. If you feel like something isn't being said in a conversation, for example, stop right there and say so. If you are on the wrong track, you'll find out soon enough. But if you don't say something you will carry the incomplete interchange away with you. Then a small portion of your mind will still be occupied with it, the same small portion that you need for creative breakthroughs.

Integrity allows you to make an authentic connection with people, especially those you want to be close to. Without integrity, there is no relationship, only entanglement. The dictionary tells us that an *entanglement* is "two or more things enfolded upon each other so that the freedom of each is compromised." That's what happens when people fall out of integrity with each other.

Integrity is the great simplifier of life. As Henry David Thoreau said, the three things we all need to do to be happy is "simplify, simplify, simplify." As Gay's grandmother put it,

"If you always tell the truth, you don't have to remember what you said." If you are a student of integrity, you don't have to waste thought, energy, or time looking for where the problem is. You know that when things aren't working to look at integrity.

Mystics know a secret: Integrity works. It is not just a noble idea, it is a crucial set of operating principles. It takes a great deal of energy to be out of integrity, to live in a state of separation from the wholeness of life. This wasted energy is a poisonous force for destruction in personal and corporate life. If we pretend that our actions have no consequences—if we think we can get away with anything at all in these speeded-up times—we are setting ourselves up for the rudest of awakenings.

Many people have never been members of an organization—be it a family, a club, or a company—that operated in a state of full integrity. We can tell you that the feeling is exhilarating. We have had the great pleasure of helping many organizations dig themselves out of pits caused by integrity breaches. Sometimes it has taken months—and even years—of hard work for them to go from a culture of nonintegrity to a culture of integrity. The results have been well worth it in every case we've seen.

In our travels in and around the corporate world, we have found that people are basically well intentioned. There will always be bad apples, but that's never the real problem. The problem is that people are unclear about just what integrity is. They don't know the navigational principles of integrity and how to make it work for them in the corporate environment.

In this chapter, we endeavor to take some of the mystery out of integrity.

Character is what you are in the dark.

—DWIGHT L. MOODY

WHAT INTEGRITY ACTUALLY IS

The mastery of integrity comes down to three things: being authentic with yourself, being authentic with others, and doing the things you have said you would do.

If you will commit to this kind of authenticity, you have a chance to embrace the ultimate in integrity: owning your own soul and making it unsellable. By knowing yourself completely, you become immune to self-deception.

Before looking at these three areas, though, we need to confront something even more fundamental. Are you committed to your own full development and the success of the organization you're in?

Inside each of us there are two strong pulls. One pull is toward complete independence—becoming our own person through and through. But there is also a strong pull to commit ourselves in something larger: communion with other people, a company or family, the universe itself. Both pulls must be honored and developed fully. Some people are tugged too far in one direction and are thrown out of balance. One imbalance is to stay so independent that you never have the deep joy of surrendering yourself to something larger. Another imbalance is to surrender yourself so thoroughly that there's nobody home when you wake up one day and ask, "Who am I?" Corporations are full of people with each of these imbalances. There are those who hold back and never really surrender to full participation. And there are those who are swallowed up by the company so that they have no life of their own.

Corporate Mystics study this problem carefully, knowing that both strong pulls must be developed in themselves. They know that they must surrender fully to the team enterprise while at the same time being completely committed to themselves as separate individuals. Neither one commitment nor the other will do; both must be fully honored.

> *When we create advertising from a place of integrity—when we tell the truth about a product or service dramatically in a way that doesn't seek to motivate people to buy from a place of fear—that advertising is the most successful for both the client and the agency.*
>
> —MARK HORN, VICE-PRESIDENT AND CREATIVE SUPERVISOR, WUNDERMAN CATO JOHNSON

INTEGRITY INCREASES VITALITY

Integrity feels good. When you come from integrity, there will be a streamlining of resources throughout your body. Check it out for yourself. Next time you clear up an integrity breach—"Jim, I told you I would return your call at noon but I didn't get back to you until 1:30"—notice what happens in your body right afterward. Usually, you will feel an energetic sense of relaxed alertness. Suddenly you can bring all of your attention to bear on the moment. Because you pay attention to integrity, you have free energy that will amplify your power to accomplish whatever you want.

One mystic put it this way: "When I'm in integrity I feel full-contactedness with the world and with others. I can let go instead of holding myself. I feel an openness in my face and skin, a pleasant kind of fullness—the way I feel after I've taken a shower. I feel an activation in my body that is relaxed and alert. I feel curious and very calm. My intuition is heightened. I make leaps and see images more clearly. I listen better, because I'm not listening through a filter of 'Are they gonna get me?' I feel happy for no reason when I'm in integrity."

The certain test of sanity is if you accept life whole, as it is.

—Lao-tzu

THE THREE PLACES TO LOOK FOR INTEGRITY PROBLEMS

Nearly every personal or corporate disaster begins with an integrity problem, and often a small one. Left untended, like a tiny shimmy in your front wheels, a small integrity problem can escalate quickly to shake loose anything that's not tightly connected. When things are not going well and you cannot figure out why, assume an integrity glitch. This is not because people are fundamentally bad but rather because true integrity is hard to master. Here are the three key questions to ask yourself:

Are you being authentic with yourself?

The first question to ask is whether you are out of integrity with yourself. Are you genuinely at ease with the path you are on? Many of us learn very early to tune out inner signals, and the long-run costs of this are enormous. We receive a signal that says "Don't do this," and then we go ahead and do it anyway. Nearly everyone we have talked to who was involved in large integrity breaches felt uncomfortable at the very beginning. They overrode that feeling and rationalized it away.

Being human, we often need a number of trials to get this lesson right. Even if you have been avoiding the subject, begin the learning process this minute. Pause right now and ask: Are there any places now in my life where I'm lying to myself? Happiness flows from a clear spring: You need to have a totally honest relationship with yourself.

Your feelings are a key part of the equation. There are three feelings you need to become comfortable with, so comfortable that you can talk about them calmly. These are fear, anger, and sadness. To be in integrity with your feelings, you must be able to know when you are scared, angry, and/or sad, and to be able to say "I'm scared" or "I'm angry" or "I'm sad." Many interpersonal problems come from hiding feelings from ourselves or each other. These can only be resolved by knowing ourselves intimately and being able to speak the truth of our emotions to each other.

Our bodies are where our feelings live, not our minds. Yet very little training is ever given in body awareness as we're growing up, so many of us have to start from scratch as adults. In a saner world, first-graders would be taught the difference between anger and fear, for example, and where those feelings live in their bodies. As adults, we often have a great deal of confusion about feelings. We get scared, perhaps, and instead of saying "I'm scared," we hide our fear and lash out in anger. We get angry and instead of saying "I'm angry," we burst into tears.

If we are out of integrity with ourselves—not knowing who we are, how we feel, what we want—it sets up a rattle that throws everything off. But when we take this rattle out into the world around us, real trouble, even dangerous trouble, begins to occur.

Are you being authentic with others?

The second question to ask is whether there are or have been any distortions in your communications to others. Bluntly put: Where are the lies in your life? If you find a lie, first acknowledge it to yourself: "I told Company X that Company Y was buying our brand of software. That was a lie, but I was scared I wouldn't make quota unless I made the sale."

This step is essential; otherwise you throw your own system out of kilter. Next, square yourself with the relevant people. A ten-second communication is usually what it takes: "Jerry, I told you that Company Y was buying our software. The truth was that they hadn't bought it yet, but I wanted to sell you our software and I thought knowing Company Y was buying it would inspire you." The big fear, of course, is that your listener will get mad and punish you in some way. Trust will be destroyed (forgetting, of course, that we have already destroyed the trust). Occasionally it happens that way, but more often your listener will be grateful and trust will be enhanced in the long run.

Sigmund Freud was asked to summarize his life work in one sentence. He replied, "Secrets make you sick." Lies and secrets can make companies sick, too. There is no faster way to poison the community well than to stir lies into it. Of course, we are not talking about "healthy" secrets, such as the patent to a computer chip or the secret to the Coke formula. The kinds of lies and secrets that hurt companies usually involve withholding information—the president is having an affair with the vice-president—in order to protect someone.

> *There is no such thing as a minor lapse of integrity.*
>
> —TOM PETERS

Are you doing the things you said you'd do?
The third place to ask when things go wrong is whether you have broken any agreements. Often the agreement is tiny,

the breach slight. But it isn't a matter of size. Look how much shimmy you get from a tiny front-end misalignment. The mystic knows that there is only one thing to be done when an agreement has been breached: Stand and face it. State it clearly: "Jim, I said I would have the report to you by 5:00 P.M. It's ten past now and it's coming off the printer. I regret any inconvenience." Then, pause and listen. Maybe the other person has a reaction, maybe it doesn't matter a whit. Winners cop to it and hear out any reaction. Losers are too busy with fancy footwork:

> making excuses,
> laying the blame elsewhere,
> promising to do better, and so on.

Corporate ditches all over the land are littered with habitual excuse makers.

> *I contend that dishonesty will create a failure*
> *force that often manifests itself in other ways—*
> *ways not apparent to the outside observer.*
>
> —JOSEPH SUGARMAN

TAKING HEALTHY RESPONSIBILITY

Integrity culminates in the ability to take full, effective responsibility. The ordinary definition of responsibility: Whose fault is this? The successful person's definition: How can I respond to this so that everybody wins?

All the best responsibility is taken. In other words, genuine responsibility—the kind that changes your life—does not begin until you actively take it. There is no magic age when you become responsible. Some people go to their graves avoiding responsibility. Corporate Mystics surf on the edge of responsibility, always asking themselves how they can take healthy responsibility for the issue at hand.

If your definition of responsibility focuses on fault and blame, you are pointed in three fruitless directions: It's their fault, it's my fault, it's the world's fault. None of these directions lead to effective action.

The mystic knows there are only two relevant questions: What can I learn from this? and What needs to be done? The first question opens you to infinity itself, because there is that much to learn from any situation, and the second question focuses you on the infinitely practical.

Responsibility is to keep the ability to respond.

—Gustav Mahler

Here is an example of the power of responsibility. It shows how one person who steps into full responsibility inspires others to do the same. When these events took place, Ron Bynum was the leader of a training organization that used a former summer camp as one of its facilities. One night he was reading at home when his phone rang with dramatically bad news: One of the buildings at his training center had caught fire and burned down quickly. Someone had left a towel near a heater in a dormitory where some of the staff lived. The old wooden building had gone up in flames like a bundle of kindling.

When he got to the center the staff of nearly one hundred was in an uproar. Everybody, even the site manager, was in a tumult of blame and self-recrimination. Our mystic called a meeting in the main hall and took the stage. His words went like this:

"I want to raise the question of who is responsible for this situation." He paused as the group went into an uproar of finger-pointing. He waited for it to die down. "The answer is very clear to me," he said. "I'm responsible." Dead silence filled the room. "Wait a minute," someone said. "You weren't even here. How come you're responsible?"

"I'm responsible because I'm claiming responsibility. That's all that really matters. If you're looking for details, I've been in that dormitory a dozen times this summer, and I could have noticed that the towel rack was too close to the heater. But I didn't. So that's one reason I'm responsible. But the details are irrelevant. How about if we all take responsibility rather than blaming ourselves or somebody else? Then let's find out what needs to be done." The atmosphere in the room shifted in a second. Blame and recrimination stopped cold; the conversation turned to solutions. By stepping into responsibility, he got everybody heading in a productive direction. What more could be asked of a leader?

Problems begin to dissolve the moment someone steps into being a source. Leaders deserve to be leaders not because they are always the source of integrity but because they can step into it quickly when they see they have stepped out of integrity. In other words, Corporate Mystics are not saints who are above it all. Rather, they are nimble at seeing when an opportunity arises to claim their connection with the source.

> *Taking personal responsibility is the part of our corporate culture we honor most. If there's ever a choice between corporate policy and personal responsibility, we tell people to go for personal responsibility.*
>
> —ED MCCRACKEN, CEO, SILICON GRAPHICS

A NEW DEFINITION OF RESPONSIBILITY

Kathlyn Hendricks, corporate consultant (and Gay's wife), stands in front of a group of about twenty people, all top-level executives of one of America's largest companies. She holds a hundred-dollar bill aloft, then passes it around the room for all to touch. Even though all the people in the room make million-dollar decisions on a regular basis, and many of them are themselves millionaires, there is still something attention getting about a hundred-dollar bill. There are quizzical looks as the bill goes around.

She attaches the bill with a clip to an easel.

"Who is responsible for this bill being here?" she asks.

There is silence, punctuated by a few snickers. She repeats the question, carefully keeping the wording the same.

"You are," someone finally says.

Integrity

"Why?" Kathlyn asks.

"It's obvious. Because you put it there," the person says.

"Okay, let's look at that," says Kathlyn. "One way we think about responsibility is 'Who did this?' Many of us first became acquainted with this question when Mom or Dad saw something amiss and said, 'Who's responsible for this?' "

There are chuckles around the room as people remember their experiences with this kind of responsibility.

Kathlyn writes on the easel, making two big columns. One column is entitled: Familiar Definitions of Responsibility. The other column is entitled: Breakthrough, Life-Changing Definition of Responsibility. She writes "Who did it?" under Familiar Definitions.

"We'll put it in that category because we're all familiar with it, and because knowing who did it does not often generate a creative breakthrough or change lives."

Kathlyn asks again. "Who's responsible for this hundred-dollar bill being here?"

Silence prevails, then someone says, "We all are."

"Why?" Kathlyn asks.

"Because most of us touched it when it went around. And even if you didn't touch, at least we all saw it."

"Let's look at that explanation," says Kathlyn. "When you think about it, though, this is an elaboration of the first definition we came up with. Instead of 'Who did it?' we have 'Who participated in the chain of events that led to things being the way they are?' This definition of responsibility gets a lot of press when things like Watergate or the Iran-contra scandal happen. The president and whoever else can muster the power try to depict themselves as being out of the loop.

Meanwhile the opposition tries to prove that the president was definitely in the loop. But, really, this is another way of saying 'Who did it?' " She writes "Who participated in the Chain of Events?" in the column entitled Familiar Definitions of Responsibility.

"Aha!" someone says. "The U.S. Treasury is really responsible."

"Why?" Kathlyn asks.

"They printed the bill," the person says. Many murmurs of agreement rustle around the room.

"Okay," Kathlyn says. "Let's look at it that way. Isn't that really an extension of the Familiar Paradigm? It's taking that paradigm to the source. The Treasury is responsible because they started the chain of events that led to things being the way they are." There are murmurs of assent, and she writes "Who started it?" in the Familiar Definitions column.

Now there are many frowns and crossed limbs in the room. They are, in a word, stumped.

Kathlyn lets them endure a long silence, allowing the creative tension to build.

Suddenly someone bolts upright.

"I'm responsible for it being there," the person says.

"Prove it," says Kathlyn.

He steps quickly to the front of the room and takes the hundred-dollar bill from the easel.

"I'm responsible because it's not there anymore. I took responsibility for changing it."

Kathlyn smiles. "He took responsibility for changing it. Regardless of who started it. Regardless of who touched it. Regardless of who participated in the chain of events. He stood up and did it. Congratulations. That's the breakthrough, life-changing definition of responsibility."

She leads applause for him. He goes over to her and tries to give her the bill back.

"Keep it," she says. "Responsibility has its rewards."

HOW TO MAKE AND KEEP AGREEMENTS

A simple definition of an agreement is anything you have said you would do, or anything you have said you would not do. Part of the art of successful living (and working) depends on learning how to make and keep your agreements.

If you say the report will be on someone's desk at 5:00 P.M., you have to have it there or agree to change the agreement. By making the agreement you have created a new entity in the universe. Before you created this entity there was no such thing as "The report being on Jim's desk at 5:00 P.M." By making this agreement you joined forces with the creative power in the universe, the same power that makes oak trees where no trees were before. Having stepped into unity with the creative force in the universe, you need to make good on the creation or cancel it out cleanly. Otherwise you are bucking the greatest power there is.

Here are the bare essentials of the art, learned by many difficult trials and errors.

1. Think carefully before you make an agreement. It is much easier to not make an agreement than it is to get out of one you no longer want to keep. Just ask a good matrimonial attorney if you have any doubts about this point.
2. Make only agreements that you feel a heart connection with. If you don't have heart behind the agreement, whether it's your child's baseball game or attending the annual shareholders' meeting, why bother? Agreements that are unimportant to you, but that you make anyway, have a tendency to come back and haunt you later because some intuitive person will perceive that you are not really there.
3. Scrupulously keep the agreements you make.
4. If you have a life any more complicated than, say, a sheepherder's, be sure to write agreements down. Taking them out of your mind and putting them on paper frees up more of your creative energy. A frequent component of business squabbles is the sentence "I wasn't sure we agreed to that. . . ." These can be entirely avoided.

Honesty isn't the best policy.
It's the only policy.

—HARLAN RANDOLPH

HOW TO CHANGE AN AGREEMENT THAT ISN'T WORKING

There's only one way. Communicate about it. Take a deep breath and tell the truth. The other person may or may not go along with the change. There may be an emotional explosion. You may not get what you want. But you'll never know until you talk about it.

The more you can tell the absolute truth about the situation, the better it will work. For example, if your big meeting with the boss coincides with your child's baseball play-off, tell the details about the conflict to the relevant person. How do you feel about it? Are you afraid, or confused? Give the raw data, the unresolved stuff inside you. People appreciate hearing it. It gives them the "real you" instead of the packaged version, and often allows a creative solution to emerge.

INTEGRITY IS A MATTER OF PHYSICS AS MUCH AS MORALITY

Although integrity sounds like a moral issue, it is even more fundamental. Integrity is a physics problem, and to fiddle with the laws of physics is to invite rapid disaster.

If you get out of step by not making good on your agreement, a domino effect is set in motion. Catch it quickly enough and you're usually fine. Ignore it or try to cover your tracks and watch what happens. The universe will not be messed with. Many people think of this as a moral issue, but long before there were morals—a human construction—there were the fundamental laws by which the universe was running itself. No doubt these laws will be operative long after the human experiment has run its course.

> *In the battle between you and the world,*
> *back the world.*
>
> —FRANK ZAPPA

There is a cosmic and yet highly practical reason all the mystics we interviewed for this book showed up on time for their interviews, no matter if they were coming from across town or across the country. They know that to make agreements is a sacred covenant between them and the universe. They know better than to mess with the forces of creation. They also know that to keep agreements is a statement of how much they value themselves and the essence of the person on the other end of the agreement.

STANDING ON ONE LEG: HOW NON-MYSTICS HANDLE AN INTEGRITY PROBLEM

When confronted with an integrity breach, non-mystics typically do one or more of several things:

Make Excuses: Like the fancy footwork of the matador, an excuse is an attempt to sidestep the consequences of having tempted fate. But most businesspeople are smarter than bulls; they don't fall for the fancy footwork.

Pretend It Never Happened: Some ignore the integrity breach and proceed blithely as if things are all right, thus postponing the inevitable. Next time the message comes in, it comes in louder.

Execute the Messenger: Mystics thank the people who bring up the integrity breach. The ordinary person shuns them. In the Nixon inner circle all the truth tellers quit, got demoted or were fired, until all that remained were the liars. And we all know how that ended.

Get Defensive: Some people, particularly those of low self-esteem, stonewall or bite back because they misperceive the message as an attack. Their self-worth is fragile at best, so they think that being reminded of a broken agreement is a barb directed at their personhood rather than a wake-up call.

Send Up a Smokescreen: Caught in an integrity breach, some people fire off a barrage of complaints they've been nursing inside. They don't like the way the message was delivered or they've been mad about something else that they used as their excuse to break the agreement. Sometimes they are successful at getting people to fall for this shift of focus.

Compound the Felony: Others compound the felony by saying "The check's in the mail" when it still hasn't made it off their desk. Caught in one integrity breach, a step out of synchrony with the universe, they take a further step away from integrity, standing alone on one leg out where the high winds blow. Look out.

These moves are all the stuff of soap opera, but they happen all too frequently in the corporate realm. To walk the mystic path, study them carefully, and do the exact opposite: Thank the messenger, get the message, take action.

HOW MYSTICS HANDLE AN INTEGRITY PROBLEM

The surest mark of mystics at work is how they handle integrity lapses. Remember, mystics are not immune to integrity breaches, but they are quicker to fix them than the average person.

Part of the mind-set of the mystic is to greet feedback gracefully. Mystics take care to appreciate both the message and the messenger. They thank and often reward the person who says "You've broken an agreement" or "This isn't fair." Most people do not get this kind of direct feedback because the messenger is afraid to give it. Mystics typically place a higher value on truth than they do on their own comfort.

They are quick to acknowledge lapses they have perpetrated. They can say things like "I realize that I broke our agreement" and "I was not telling you the truth when I said. . . ." Although they may make far fewer mistakes than the average person, they are quick to say "I made a mistake here" or "Looks like I was dead wrong on that issue." People with low self-esteem cannot admit mistakes or cop to a broken agreement: Being right is all they've got. Corporate Mystics will tell you they made a mistake as quickly as they'll tell you the time of day.

Mystics do not waste time with regret; they put their energy into solutions. Sometimes it's as simple as telling whatever truth wasn't told the first time around. Other times you must handle the wounded feelings of the person on the other end of the perpetration. An agreement may need to be renegotiated or an apology issued. Whatever the action, you won't know until you raise the question: "What needs to be done here to fix this and move on?"

Once you have determined that a painful phone call has to be made, it is wise to do it before you do anything else. Integrity problems fester faster once you know about them but before you've acted on them. Usually, what is required is a communication or an action, and sometimes both. If your employee has been stealing from Widow Smith's account, you have to replace the money, fire the employee, and give the widow a full accounting of the story. Act quickly and leave no loose ends.

The mystic's response can be broken into four steps.

First: Face squarely what happened.

The number one cause of integrity disasters is looking the other way, not facing them straight on in the early stages. Some of us postpone it for a lifetime. An example: A man who headed one of America's largest companies was having an affair with a charismatic woman, a vice-president some years his junior. As the buzz began to spread through the organization, his top aide told him that he needed to face the situation squarely. The aide later said that his boss literally looked out the window and changed the subject! The cost of not facing it squarely escalated quickly. Soon, with the board of directors on his back, the boss issued a heated denial, saying that he and the vice-president were "just friends." Nobody believed it, and time showed why. Later, after the ax had fallen, the two were quietly married.

The question remains: Why not just face things squarely and cop to them? The answer is the fear that most of us carry with us from junior high school on: We don't want to get caught and look stupid. Mystics know a secret that cures them of this fear: By the time we start getting scared of being caught and looking stupid, we've already been caught and we already look stupid. We have caught ourselves. Might as well admit it cheerfully and get on with it.

Second: Accept the situation.

Suppose you have cheated on your taxes. The first step—facing squarely what happened—means that you drop all the denial, excuse making, rationalizing, and avoidance. You admit it: You cheated.

Accepting goes deeper. It allows you to have a deep-body experience of reality. You haven't accepted something until you feel a shift deep in yourself. This may take time. It means giving up your final resistance to the truth. You accept the part of you that is a cheater. You acknowledge your greed, your irresponsibility, and whatever else motivates your cheating. You accept your cheating history, assuming it's happened before, and you open up to learning everything you need to know about the role cheating plays in your life. Accepting is a very comprehensive action. It may take months, not minutes.

However, the moment you truly accept something, no matter how long it takes, you create an open space from which to create a new way of being.

Most of us are kept from genuine acceptance by two barriers. First, we often do not want to accept unpleasant or unsavory aspects of ourselves. But until we have faced and accepted these aspects—"I'm an alcoholic" or "I cheated"—there is no clear space from which to generate change. Second, many people think that if they accept something they will be stuck with it forever. There is a rich paradox here. Not accepting something as it is keeps it in place. Accepting it begins the change process. We have it upside down. We need to understand that a full, deep-body acceptance of reality, exactly as it is, provides the springboard for change.

Third: Make a choice.

Now you must choose. Choosing has enormous power, especially if it comes from a clear space of acceptance. Failure to choose a new path of action causes as many integrity breaches as not facing or not accepting. The ordinary person thinks that not choosing keeps lots of options open. The mystic knows that not choosing keeps us mired in confusion and energy-draining drama. Perry Barlow faced a difficult choice when he took over as CEO of an Australian land-development firm. The preceding six months had been tied up in a dispute of whether to proceed with a resort-development project that violated an Aboriginal sacred site. The previous CEO's reputation had been eroded in the struggle, and Perry had been called in to bail out the company. He called a news conference his first day on the job and announced that the project would be scrapped. He became a hero overnight to the environmentalists, one of whom steered him to a piece of land that was beautifully suited to the project.

Fourth: Take action.

The fourth step sets you free. It asks you to focus on action: What do you need to do right now to set the situation right? Suppose you have faced and accepted that you cheated on your income tax. You have taken the third step, choosing to pay the money you owe. What is your fourth step? Is it to write the check and mail it? Is it to write the IRS and tell them what you've decided? You don't get back into integrity until you complete the necessary action step.

HIGH-FIRING AS A STEP TO INTEGRITY

As you increase your ability to tell the truth and keep your agreements, you will find yourself held back by people who are not willing to play at a high level of integrity. You need to consciously free yourself from these entanglements. Whether or not you are in a position to actually terminate their employment, you can benefit from "high-firing" these people from your business and personal life.

High-firing takes guts, but it pays off very quickly. The rules for high-firing are simple: If you tell the truth reliably, you stop spending time with people who don't. If you keep your agreements, you avoid people who don't. You "fire" people who aren't functioning at your level, and by so doing you establish a free zone into which you can invite people who are.

Integrity

High-firing requires you to look at your end of the relationship. You must be honest with yourself about the reasons you enrolled this person in your life. For many of us, the brutal truth is that carrying low-energy associates is a way of holding ourselves back. As long as we're saddled with energy-draining people, we have a good excuse for not being as successful as we might be.

Most firing done by non-mystics is not high-firing. One person simply gets mad at another, usually for some totally unconscious reason, and there is a noisy breakup. There is no intention to create integrity for each person. In high-firing, you work out your intentions first, before you sever your connection with the person. If you are kindhearted, you will probably want to give a warning. You sit down with the person and say, "I'm taking a major stand for truth and keeping agreements in my life. We haven't had a relationship in which we've had high integrity. Would you be willing to base our relationship on integrity from here on out?" Watch carefully the other person's reaction. If they get defensive or negative in any way, this predicts that they are not capable. You can give them a chance, if you want, but you may be disappointed. Most people, in retrospect, wish they had fired the person earlier and cleaner.

A fellow consultant shared this high-firing story with us: "When you challenged me to look at who was draining energy around me, I was resistant to it. As I checked out why I was defensive I uncovered a loyalty issue stemming from protecting my mother from my father. Dad was frequently abusive, and I took my mother's side in protecting her. But siding with her meant overlooking some of her bad habits, especially her hypercriticalness toward me and my sister. It was a lose-lose situation for me, putting myself in the middle. I realized I was doing the same thing in my organization. There was one contract employee who was a real energy drain. He produced a lot of revenue for me indirectly, but he also had a lot of bad habits I wasn't confronting. He was cheating on his wife in a particularly flagrant manner which had involved some unpleasant calls to me from two women in his life. I realized that failing to deal squarely with this situation was a replay of the pattern with my mother and father.

"I called a meeting with him and said we weren't going to work with him anymore. He became angry and abusive, using language that was eerily similar to my father's. I stayed pretty cool throughout, though, and at the end I walked out feeling light and free.

"The real magic happened just after the high-firing. I had been trying for a year to get on a national talk show to call attention to my book. Even though the book had been out for a year, suddenly two national shows booked me within three days. Although there's no way to prove it, my gut tells me that firing him made the space for this burst of good luck."

THE ULTIMATE PAYOFF

When you are in integrity, you are in step with the universe. If you say you will be at the corner of Vine and Ninth at twelve noon, you step into the creator role in the universe. You designate a future that does not yet exist and create an image of yourself there. If you actually show up on that corner at twelve noon, you are in a perfect time-space relationship with the universe. If you don't, you are out of step with time and space. So, the ultimate payoff for integrity is mastery of time and space. After acting with integrity for a while, you always seem to be in the right place at the right time. The universe seems to bend to your wishes.

The following true story will illustrate how the high-integrity person can move unimpeded through a universe fraught with danger, difficulty, and uncertainty. This example comes from corporate consultant Susan Snowe. Susan was leading a workshop on integrity in southern California. One of the agreements for the seminar was radical and stringent: If, at any time during the week, you were late for a session, you were out of the program. Period. No matter what the reason or the excuse. Since it was a very expensive training program, the motivation for integrity was high.

Susan tells the story: "Upon returning from a dinner break one evening a woman stood up and related the following experience. She had taken care of an errand during the break and was running tight on time. As she hurried out of a market with a bag of food, a man with a knife accosted her and demanded her money. Without thinking about it, she looked him in the eye and blurted out, 'I don't have time for this now. I have an agreement I can't break. I've got to go.' She ran to her car and sped away, leaving an astonished robber in the parking lot, staring at the departing car.

"She got to the seminar on time for the evening session, unrobbed and in integrity."

2

Vision:

Leadership by Inspiring Clear Intention

The only limits are, as always, those of vision.

—James Broughton

If you can dream it, you can do it.

—Walt Disney

Integrity must precede vision. History has shown us the awesome cost of vision without integrity. A charismatic leader such as Hitler gets his people excited about a vision but leads them to doom because the vision is unsupported by integrity, rotten at the core. If your vision does not have a strong integrity base, expect disaster down the line. Begin by focusing on integrity, and your visions have a great deal of positive power in the world.

Integrity has a beneficial effect on the ability to see the future. It produces alignment in yourself, and just as in a well-aligned car, steering becomes easier. If your integrity is unshakable, you have a clear grasp of present reality—and this helps you see where things are going. Particularly, you can see if the direction you're heading is causing the spirits of the people involved, you included, to contract, wither, or shrivel. There is no more powerful early warning that you are heading in the wrong direction. If you aspire to be a Corporate Mystic, combine your mastery of integrity with a careful study of visioning skills.

If we don't change the direction we're going,
we're likely to end up where we're headed.

—ANCIENT CHINESE PROVERB

Most business failures are failures of vision. By contrast, a clear vision often is the first step on the road to success. Many of the successful people we have encountered began their journey to success with an act of vision. Sometimes it was a simple act, like asking themselves that radical question, "What do I really want?" For others it was a more formal procedure of mocking up a desired future in their imagination.

Visionaries often have difficulties in corporations unless they are at the very top (and sometimes even then). Some of the most visionary people we encountered were often frustrated because they had to deal with two or three layers of noncreative, nonvisionary managers. Managers often do a thorough job of squelching ideas, but not such a good job of nurturing creative input from visionaries. Visionaries must bear some of the responsibility here, too. We have met many visionaries who were too thin-skinned to keep their visions flourishing when they encountered resistance.

There are several good reasons to develop visioning skills. Without vision, you have no proactive direction in which to organize the resources at your command. Vision allows you to create reality, not merely to react to it. Another major advantage of conscious visioning is how setbacks are perceived. If you have a clear vision of your goals and purposes, you will experience the inevitable setbacks as barriers on the path to something grand. If your vision is big enough, you'll view barriers as challenges rather than obstacles, to be studied with care as you navigate. Some people fall apart when setbacks are encountered. That's because their vision is not grand enough.

Every Corporate Mystic we interviewed for this book was a skilled visionary. Although the mental techniques they used were very different, they all knew how to transplant themselves into the future and describe the steps necessary to get there. Some of our mystics had these skills from early in their lives, while others had consciously worked to develop them. Corporate Mystics are also masters of something broader we will call intention. We will begin there.

WHAT IS INTENTION?

Intention is a powerful force. Coming from a Latin word that means "to stretch toward," intention is the initial bending of your mind toward a target. It is the force that permeates the journey and the goal. A story from the medieval Christian tradition illustrates intention: A traveler came to a worksite and saw two men carrying stones. One man was working listlessly, with a sullen expression on his face, while the other man was cheerfully singing as he busily carried stone after stone. "What are you doing?" asked the traveler of the sullen worker. "Laying stone" was his reply. "What are you doing?" the industrious worker was asked. "Building a cathedral" was his reply. This is intention at work.

Intention precedes and inspires vision. Intention lives in the zone between potential and action, organizing the diffuse energy of potential and bringing it toward reality. Intention is also the ability to hold a visionary context in which all of your specific visions are organized. Inspired leadership is the ability to work from the zone of intention, so that your very being brings forth visionary thinking in your colleagues. This is important because great leaders do not want to have followers, they want to spawn more leaders. The old formulas such as "Management thinks up the job and workers carry it out" are clearly out of date. Ideally, everyone should have the ability to add his or her own unique visionary capabilities to the job at hand. But many of us, even the best and brightest, are handicapped by a lack of training in the skills of intention and visioning. You will need to bootstrap yourself and your colleagues up to a functional level of skill.

Think of intention as your overall way of getting to a place, not your map of the details. It is a vast goal that is at once measurable yet so large that it inspires people to become themselves visionaries within it. An intention is how you want the game to come out, both in content and process. It sets magic in motion. If you will make the decision, the saying goes, your subconscious will make the provision.

Cross-disciplinary teams at Monsanto worked on their intention diligently before refining it down to something everyone could support: "Abundant food and a healthy environment." Teams at Komatsu, the Japanese maker of earthmoving equipment, spent a great deal of corporate think-time working to express their intention succinctly. Finally, they got it down to two words: "Encircle Caterpillar!" This intention says how they would like the whole enterprise to come out. It also expresses the sense of competition they will use to get there. With two words they formed an intention that also worked well as a rallying cry. Your intention can and should be expressed this concisely. Another good model, developed by a team at Coca-Cola: "A Coke within arm's reach of everyone in the world." Whether or not you like Coke, you experience movement in your mind and body when you hear that intention.

If your intention is clear, you create an electric field of possibility that actually pulls creativity out of yourself and those around you. This is the real power of intention. It inspires you in ways you could not predict. When Komatsu developed their intention—Encircle Caterpillar!—they did not know exactly how they were going to do it. Far from it, in fact. One of the hallmarks of a good intention is that it should be bigger than your current abilities. As their clarity with this intention grew, they found themselves devising technology and marketing strategies commensurate with the size of their intention.

If you know exactly how to get to your goal, you need a bigger intention. Growth and excitement in individuals and companies come from stretching to achieve things that may not have seemed possible even a week earlier.

The secret of life is to have a task, something you devote your entire life to . . . and the most important thing is—it must be something you cannot possibly do!
—HENRY MOORE

What we need is more people who specialize in the impossible.
—THEODORE ROETHKE

HOW TO CREATE A POWERFUL INTENTION

Kate was once in charge of a large project that brought together executives of six major semiconductor suppliers and their eight largest distributors to pool some of their data for the common good. Kate: "I was very excited because of the groundbreaking nature of this cooperative project. After we were under way I got a call one day saying that the largest distributor was backing out. I was deeply disappointed. Although the project would still be useful, having the largest player pull out would weaken the paradigm-shifting collaborative effort. My heart actually ached because I so much wanted them to pull together.

"We went ahead, though, and I set the intention in my heart of having the project yield the breakthrough we were looking for regardless of who played and who didn't. I held the intention that it be a win for the players and even for the company that had dropped out. I resolved to share the findings with them, even though they weren't sharing with the others. After a few months we had processed most of the data, but we uncovered a software problem that we couldn't figure out how to correct. As we were puzzling over it I got a call from the head of the company which had backed out: They had decided to play! Everybody was elated, and even agreed to wait six weeks for the new data to be integrated so that we could present a unified set of findings. During the six weeks we got our software problem fixed, so the delay turned out to be a blessing for all concerned."

BEWARE OF COVERT INTENTIONS

M ost of us have values that are sacred to us, values like passionate commitment, complete integrity, and warm regard for others. Yet we do not always act in accordance with these high intentions. The road to hell, the old saying goes, is paved with good intentions. Why is that?

It is because we have covert intentions, hidden from the light, that trip us up when we move in our chosen directions. The only way to clear ourselves of these covert intentions is to bring them out into the light and openly acknowledge that we carry them.

A Corporate Mystic we interviewed shared this story: "Throughout the development of [a new technological device] I missed one deadline after another. The CEO kept calling me on the carpet and I kept saying, 'This isn't like me' and 'I've never missed deadlines before.' Finally one evening after one of our consulting sessions, I let go of being defensive and acknowledged the negative intention. I said, 'Okay, I'm committed to missing deadlines. That's what the results say. I have an intention to miss deadlines.' Now why would I have that intention? About two seconds after I asked myself that question the lightbulb came on in my head. This was the biggest project of my career, and I wanted desperately to succeed in the eyes of the CEO, who was a father figure to me. But at the same time I was putting the face of my father's criticalness on him, too. It was as if I was trying to set it up so I failed in his eyes. I realized I was carrying a conscious intention to succeed and an unconscious intention to fail. Because I had failed so often in the eyes of my father, I had embodied an intention to fail that was getting in my way."

One of our clients was a peace activist of national reputation who had founded a political organization. His conscious intention was nonviolence and world harmony, yet his organization was in trouble because of his violent explosions of anger. His wife had also left him because he hit her on several occasions. It was obvious from his actions that he carried a covert intention to harm others that was sabotaging his stated intention to promote peace.

He was very comfortable expressing his intention to promote world harmony—he could make that speech at the drop of a hat—yet he became angry at us when we asked him to acknowledge his intention toward violence. He could easily say, "I'm committed to world peace," but he had trouble admitting, "I'm committed to getting my own way even through violence." Yet this intention was the one that was ruining his life.

There is only one way to find out what your unconscious intentions are: Look at any negative results you produce. Every Corporate Mystic needs to know this principle in his or her bones. In the case of our peace activist client, the results said, "I'm committed to expressing violence." After several sweaty days of consultation, he was courageous enough to acknowledge both his violent and his peaceful aspects. He confronted the roots of his violence in his tortured relationship with an alcoholic and abusive father. He also discovered that he had become a peace activist partly in reaction to his father, an "I'll show you!" intention.

Only when he acknowledged all this did the violent out-bursts cease. His organizational and marital problems smoothed out once he cleared his covert intentions.

> *The first peace, which is the most important, is*
> *that which comes within the souls of people*
> *when they realize their relationship, their*
> *oneness, with the universe and all its powers,*
> *and when they realize at the center of the*
> *universe dwells the Great Spirit, and that this*
> *center is really everywhere.*
> *It is within each of us.*

—BLACK ELK

THE INTENTION OF WHOLENESS

If you would operate in the mystic realm, you must operate from a clear intention of wholeness and connection. In words, the intention might be expressed like this: "I consciously intend to have [this project or enterprise] benefit the wholeness of ourselves and the environment around us." If you build in a metavision of wholeness at the beginning, projects will work more smoothly. If you pretend you are not connected to the whole, that doesn't stop you from being connected. It just stops you from feeling connected. Mystics have a nearly reflexive ability to ask questions like: How am I not participating in the whole? Who else is not operating from an appreciation of the whole? Where is connection being broken or impeded?

Motorola executive Rick Younts: "Before I moved to my international role and started interfacing with so many other cultures, I was reasonably myopic. Until I sat in forests with trees that were four thousand years old, I didn't understand how long life really was and how fragile it was, how important it was to get our lives to fall in harmony with nature." This is an awareness of wholeness, and one can see how powerfully it might shape the future visioning of this executive as he works on new projects.

THE INTENTION OF BALANCE

Balance is the Corporate Mystic's second key intention. As we proceed toward our chosen visions, we need to keep ourselves and our enterprises in a state of balance. The notion of balance pervades the mystic worldview. For Taoists, yin and yang are in eternal balance throughout nature itself, and it is our task as humans to harmonize ourselves with this balance. A pinnacle concept of Navajo metaphysics, *hozho,* says that we must walk in harmony with ourselves and the earth, lest we do damage to both.

Businesspeople go out of balance in several common areas.

Logic and emotion. Nature has given us logic, which resides in the neocortex, and it has also given us emotion, which lives beneath the cortex in the limbic system. Logic is indispensable for success in business, but businesspeople get in trouble when they leave behind their feelings. Feelings were here long before logic evolved, so extra attention must be given to staying in communication with them. Emotions like fear, anger, and sadness flicker across the screen of our consciousness all day long. You don't have to report each one of them to the world, but you do know what you're feeling when you're feeling it.

Home and work. No matter what rung of the corporate ladder you're on, constant vigilance is required lest the demands of the workplace eat up your home life. The higher you climb, the more imperative it becomes to walk in and out of your front door each day with a clear mind and an open heart. In our consulting work, we find that imbalance between home and work is often the most common subject of conversation among executives. Single or married, living in a mansion or a studio apartment, we all need a life outside work. It is easy to get out of balance, given the demands of the contemporary corporate environment.

Striving versus enjoying. The tightened jaw and the furrowed brow are signs not of zeal but of imbalance. Are you so focused on outcome that you are not enjoying the process? If so, find out how you can lighten up and have a better time. You might even discover, as many have, that they get more done when they ease up a little. As consultants, one of the quickest ways we diagnose the health of an organization is by the amount of fun people appear to be having. They are getting the job done, and they are having a good time doing it. There is a feeling we call the "fun-buzz" that successful organizations have. The fun-buzz is made up of relaxed busyness, pleasant interactions, laughter, and engagement. One of the most exciting things as organizational consultants is watching the fun-buzz begin and build as the health of the organization improves.

The intention of balance changed the life of John Fine, a real estate developer and entrepreneur based in California and Colorado. "During the first ten years of my working life I was so focused on my projects that I hardly stopped to take a breath. Even when I was hiking in the mountains I was planning projects in my mind. Then I had two wake-up calls in the same week. While jogging (and of course discussing a real estate project with the guy I was running with) I developed chest pains. I went to the doctor in a panic, but it turned out to not be a heart problem but an emotional one. My wife had been telling me for a year that I needed to open up to my emotions more, so I could find out why I got into such rages when things didn't go my way. When I came home from the doctor and told her my heart was okay, she said it was not okay at all. In her opinion I was hiding so much anger and sadness that it didn't matter how many shopping malls I built. I was never going to be happy unless I took a look inside. Further, she said she had been thinking about leaving the relationship because I was never really there. She said, 'I didn't marry you just to show up at public events with you. I want a real marriage.' I was stunned, and I sat down on the floor in the living room to mull it over. About ten seconds after I sat down, I burst into tears. I don't think I'd cried since I was a kid. I couldn't have stopped crying even if I'd wanted to. I found myself babbling to my wife about how cheated I felt about not having a childhood. My father had a heart attack when I was eleven, and I took over his role in the family. I had as many wrinkles in my brow at fourteen as I had now at forty-four.

"Thank goodness Annie didn't try to stop me from crying or tell me it was all going to be better. When I got through, which was maybe twenty minutes later, I got up and wrote some new 'vows,' as I thought of them. I vowed to play as much as I worked, love as much as I worked, smile as much as I scowled. I actually put these on the wall in my office and my den. I asked Annie for six months to make good on these vows. If I wasn't making progress on them that she could see, we would amicably divorce. One of the proudest days of my life was when that six months was up. I said, 'Well?' She hugged me and said that I had changed my life. That was twenty years ago, and we're still together."

One direct outcome of this personal transformation was that John instituted an intention of balance in his organization. Friday mornings started with "balance" meetings, to which he invited guest speakers from different backgrounds to address the issue of wholeness and balance. The working retreats held once a year took on this theme, also. Significant others were invited for the first time, and off-site locations were chosen with the idea of balance in mind.

THE INTENTION OF GRATITUDE

Your visions will become real more smoothly if they emerge from a context of gratitude. Many people have gratitude backwards: They are willing to express it only after something good happens to them. Corporate Mystics know a secret: Express gratitude first—lead with gratitude—and you will get gratitude back in double measure. Each new step toward the future is taken in gratitude for the way things are now. And what if the way things are now is not to your liking? All the more reason to appreciate them, for the beginnings of change live in a deep acceptance of the present reality. The Corporate Mystic thinks: Things are the way they are; now let's go about changing them. The ordinary person thinks: Things can't possibly be the way they are! or Whose fault is it that things are the way they are? Denial and blame have no place in the mystic tool bag. A clear-eyed look at the present and a vision of the future: These are the tools the mystic uses to steer through an ever-changing universe.

A good question to ask is: What could I do in my life and in my organization to foster a pervasive tone of gratitude? If you were going to honor each person you work closely with in a singular way that moved them, how would you do it? For example, in one of the authors' organizations, we put considerable attention into gratitude. Gay: "We have a diverse group of people who work with us, so our challenge is to express our gratitude for them in ways that are particularly suited to them. One of our people loves travel. At the end of one very good year, we gave her a bonus of a trip to Hawaii. Another person has a high value on education. In her case, we help her financially with her schooling, and we also make time available to her for it. We come up with ideas based on the question, 'What could we best do to express our gratitude?' and then we consult with them about the details."

Begin with a moment of reflection: Who in your life are you most grateful for? How could you best show your gratitude for the people around you? Take a few seconds right now to feel appreciation for them.

THE TYRANNY OF IS

Some visionaries may be born free from the tyranny of "is." But the rest of us have to break free of it. What is this tyranny? It is a view of the world that keeps you trapped in a limited set of options. Here's how it works. Many people act from a vision-killing superstition: that their interpretation of reality is the same as reality itself. When the steam locomotive was new, a breakthrough in technology made it possible for it to exceed thirty miles an hour. With the speed of forty miles an hour in sight, a debate broke out, even in the medical literature of the time. One learned doctor said that it was common knowledge that the human body would explode at forty miles an hour. That's the way it "is," he said.

Usually the tyranny has its stranglehold on companies when everyone agrees on the interpretation of current conditions.

"This company is in decline."
"We are in a recession."
"The president is an ineffective leader."
"This problem is unsolvable."

When we are in the grip of the tyranny of "is," there is no possibility for change. We see the condition, whatever it may be, as intractable.

> *Notice the difference between what happens*
> *when a man says to himself "I have failed*
> *three times," and what happens when he says*
> *"I am a failure."*

—S. I. HAYAKAWA

Visionary leaders break free of the tyranny, and they get others to break free. They look carefully at all the places they are operating out of "is." They step back, separate out their interpretation from reality, and find out what needs to be done.

Begin by changing your verbs. Avoid "is" and "are." Instead of "The president is an ineffective leader," try "I disagree with the president's choice to . . ." or "The president didn't produce a successful labor negotiation when he said he would." When you take the "is" out, you open up the possibility for change to occur. "Is" and "are," since they are statements of being, do not point to actions that can be taken. When you unfreeze your perceptions from "is" and "are," you move toward action: What can the president do to move the labor negotiations along? What can you do to help?

THE TYRANNY OF BECAUSE

There is another tyrant you must battle in your company and in yourself. It is the tyranny of "because."

"I was late because my alarm clock didn't go off."

"Profits are declining because of the recession."

"I am getting divorced because my spouse is too critical."

"Women make poor leaders because they are too emotional."

"You can't be honest with people because it will damage the relationship."

When you say "because," you claim that you know the reason something happened. You justify your course of action because of an extraneous factor. And you know what? Sometimes you're right. However, more often than not the reason you claim is not the sole reason or even the most important reason for something. If you think you are late because your alarm didn't go off, you are overlooking other interesting possibilities. You might be late because you have a self-sabotage program operating. Or because you don't really want to be doing what you're doing. Once you lock in on a certain "because," you don't go any further. When you say "because," you stop the inquiry process.

"Because" is a vision killer. One of the most common phrases heard in early visioning sessions with companies is "We can't do that because . . ." There can be a dozen reasons: not enough money, not enough resources, not enough time. Another common one these days: "My plan was sidetracked because I wasn't willing to play politics." "Becauses" are dangerous because they keep us from looking inside ourselves. A "because" stops the inquiry process, which must be ongoing for individuals and companies to succeed.

Here is how a Corporate Mystic handled a potentially troublesome "because." As a newly appointed vice-president, she had difficulty getting people on the executive team to listen to her ideas. As she tells it: "At first I blamed it on the usual reasons, like 'They don't listen to me because I'm a woman.' But as long as I held that point of view, nothing changed. So I shifted my strategy. In the meetings I observed the vice-president who had the most power. I respected him enormously, plus he had the ear of the president. When I simply observed him instead of envying him, I learned several crucial things. First, he presented his ideas in a bottom-line format; he gave supporting details only when he was asked. He didn't present a flurry of data, as I had been doing. Second, when he encountered resistance he didn't argue with the other people. Rather, he asked them a lot of questions! In other words, he was genuinely interested in understanding their concerns. What often happened was that people would talk themselves out of their concerns as he listened carefully to their points of view. Looking back, I can see that my career took a major upturn when I quit indulging in 'becauses' and started looking for people I could really learn from instead of envy."

Visionary leaders put all "becauses" under the microscope, especially the ones everybody agrees on. Often the biggest breakthroughs come from finding the "because" that underlies the most intractable conditions.

> *If you've always done it that way, it's*
> *probably wrong.*
>
> —CHARLES KETTERING

THE ZONE OF COMPLACENCY

Corporate Mystics learn to work outside the zone of complacency. Non-mystics live in the zone, and usually die there. Your zone of complacency is that complicated batch of thoughts, feelings, beliefs, and convictions designed to keep you from becoming uncomfortable. Most of us have one, whether we are flush with success or broken and battered. It is worth our careful attention because it has slain more good visions than a million critics.

Many people think that their discomfort is all the reason they need not to do something. Corporate Mystics look at discomfort completely differently: It is something to be met squarely on the way to wherever they've chosen to go. One of our corporate clients calls now and then to get a phone consultation on some project she is working on. Often she begins by saying, "I've hit a couple of speed bumps here lately, and I want to find out what I can do to smooth things out." She views obstacles as speed bumps—just a minor feature of the road—and by slowing down a little and being careful, she can get back up to speed.

The zone of complacency develops a life of its own inside us. When it is challenged, it throws several types of feelings at us. These feelings are smoke screens, designed to discourage us from going outside the zone.

The first smoke screen is fear. Wired into our bodies hundreds of thousands of years ago, fear programs us to run, fight, faint, or freeze. That is just what the zone of complacency would have you do. You come up with an outrageous vision of yourself—"I'd like to start my own business instead of working for Fred"—and the zone kicks in with fear. It wants you to run from this vision or better yet, freeze where you are. Our zone of complacency thinks that safety comes from running or freezing. Once we're in fear, the whole world looks different.

> *When we're afraid, everything rustles.*
>
> —SOPHOCLES

When we dream of a bigger future for ourselves, we invoke its fears as well. We need to look unflinchingly at those fears if we are going to design a better future. Even a question that seems relatively straightforward—"How will Fred and I get financing?"—can have its roots in a much more fundamental fear: of aging, death, poverty, diminished capacity, criticism, loss of love, ill health. If we have not dealt with such fears, our ability to see the future is clouded. This act of averting our eyes, even slightly, will keep us from the level of comfort with the future that is required to make our home there.

The second smoke screen is guilt. You make a move that takes you out of the zone and you start to hear voices like:

"Who do you think you are?"

"If you're successful you'll outdo your dad."

"If you're successful nobody will like you. It's lonely at the top."

Guilt is really based on anger that was directed at you long ago for being gifted. It is the burden the gifted person drags into adult life. Long, long ago, someone—usually a parent or a sibling—drummed these negative messages into your mind. The drumming was so subtle and successful that you now think that these thoughts belong to you. They don't, except that you've internalized them and let them rattle around in your head. Now is the time to take a deep breath and let them go.

The third smoke screen is a lingering sense of our own unworthiness. If you have a shred of this left over from childhood—and most of us do—the zone of complacency will find it and use it to keep you locked in the zone. At least a dozen top-level Corporate Mystics have told us that they are flooded with a deep sense of their unworthiness just before they launch a big, new vision and just after they've tasted a big success. And you can see why: They are operating outside their zone of complacency.

Although it seems to work against us, let's not make the zone of complacency an enemy. Befriending the zone of complacency is the healing maneuver. To befriend the zone, let's first acknowledge that we are powerfully attracted to the comfortable and predictable. It's safe and secure, and wouldn't that be nice for a change? There is one part of us that is a comfort seeker, pure and simple. Accept and love that part of you, just as it is. But we also need to honor the risk taker within us. Most creative people have a strong drive that challenges the zone of complacency. It is the drive to explore the unknown, to bring into being something that never existed before, to soar into the high reaches where the air is thin but the big breezes blow.

The real trouble with the zone of complacency is that it expands very quickly. The zone gets bigger every time we make a decision to sacrifice an adventurous vision in favor of comfort. Unless we're very careful, pretty soon the zone of complacency has taken over our living space. We retreat to the zone a few times to avoid the risky business of life, and one day we wake up to find we can't get out of it.

But the zone can also shrink in the wink of an eye. All you need to do is make a few decisions outside the zone and—poof!—you're a player. No longer in thrall to the seductions of the zone, you are free to form visions that are uncontaminated by it.

Vision

Vision starts from the answer to a simple question: What do I really want? or What do I most want for this organization? One day the answer might be a new quality of personal interaction around the office. The next day you might get an entirely different answer, one that launches a new product line. Corporate Mystics live in this question, asking it so frequently—even unconsciously—that their presence inspires others to start asking it.

> *The indispensable first step to getting the*
> *things you want out of life is this:*
> *Decide what you want.*
>
> —BEN STEIN

Questions of this nature—What do I most want for this company?—are powerfully transformative. When you ask them in a genuine state of inquiry you get brand-new information from your creative mind. But even when nothing comes, you are still doing something important. You are taking full responsibility for the creative direction of the company. You are becoming a source of creativity.

A mystic recalls a thrilling moment in the evolution of his business: "I had been on the bandwagon for creativity within the company for a long time, trying to get everybody inspired to think of creative ways to improve their particular area. One moment made it worthwhile. I was passing by the mailroom and stuck my head in to say hello. One of the staff, a minimum-wage part-timer, was writing a memo to her supervisor. In it she was proposing three changes in the mailroom operation. When I asked her where she'd gotten the ideas, she pointed to the question I'd asked everyone to post on the wall of their area: What do I most want for this company? She said she'd gone to bed the night before thinking about the question, and the three ideas had been floating through her mind when she woke up.''

Kate organized a team-building retreat for a high-tech executive and the eight people who reported directly to him. One of the activities asked them each to draw a picture of themselves doing something that represented who they were at the core. Two of the managers were men in their fifties who hardly knew each other, yet they drew almost identical pictures. Both drew themselves working with older people in an elder-care facility. This represented the core heartfulness that was important for them to express. Of course, they and the whole team were dumbfounded that this shared vision had emerged; it did indeed bring the team closer together. More importantly, though, the bond between these two men increased with several rewarding outcomes. They began to meet midway between their two facilities, first to deepen their friendship and ultimately to find ways to express this passion in their current jobs. They also brainstormed a special project that would allow them to get more familiar with the actualities of elder care.

Wherever you are in the corporate hierarchy, you are in a perfect position to look around and find out what you want, both for yourself and for the company. Often it only takes a few seconds to come up with an answer. Then, expand your horizons by asking other people: What do you most want? Many people have never been asked that question; to ask it could change someone's life for the better.

> *By believing passionately in something that still does not exist, we create it. The nonexistent is whatever we have not sufficiently desired.*
>
> —NIKOS KAZANTZAKIS

DEVELOPING NO-LIMITS VISION

What if there were no limits to what you could create? What if you could bring things into being through the powers you already possess? Well, this actually seems to be the way things work. Up until a hundred-and-some years ago there was no such thing as right and left shoes. If the shoe didn't fit you had to wear it anyway. There was even resistance to the idea at first. Why bother? Who cares? Shoes work okay the way they are! But somebody had a vision: Somebody hatched an idea in the mind, then transformed it into physical reality. Now just about ten billion feet walk around in an idea that nobody had even thought worth thinking before the last century.

Mystics know that they can't have everything they want: There is not enough time to manifest and enjoy everything you want. The mystic knows this and is careful to choose deeply desired heart-wants. Part of maturity, both in spirituality and in business, is to realize that you can't have everything, but that if you choose carefully you can have anything.

> *"One can't believe impossible things."*
> *"I daresay you haven't had much practice,"*
> *said the Queen. "When I was your age, I*
> *always did it for half-an-hour a day. Why,*
> *sometimes I've believed as many as six*
> *impossible things before breakfast."*
> —Lewis Carroll

On a corporate level, this idea applies a thousandfold. As we travel on our consulting rounds, we find that the successful companies are doing a great deal of work on refining and narrowing their focus. They are selecting their customer demographics very carefully, and they are listening—really listening—to what those people want and need. The days of the corporate dinosaur are numbered; the large companies are often so unwieldy that they cannot respond to changes rapidly enough. The same problem faces individuals. If we have not narrowed our focus to choose carefully what we want, we cannot focus energy in the laserlike fashion that today's environment requires.

The key is really two keys in one: choice and focus. You

have the power of decision with regard to your wants. The word *decide* comes from the Latin and means "to cut off," as in cutting off your other alternatives. Once you've done that, your job becomes to focus on your chosen goal until you get the outcome you want.

STEP OUTSIDE THE BOX

Corporate Mystics take care to have visions that are grand enough to keep them inspired. Your goals should always be stretch goals, ones that you have no ready-made strategy for achieving. If you are always inside the box of known possibilities, you don't give your imagination the stretch it needs each day to keep it flourishing.

You must always do the thing you think you cannot do.

—ELEANOR ROOSEVELT

Mystics hone the ability to be in the present and in the future at the same time. Paradoxically, the skill of relaxing into the present opens up greater power to envision the future. Some people experience pain or despair when there is a gap between where they are and where they want to be. The mystic has learned to relax in the gap, to hold the goal lightly yet with unwavering intent. Corporate Mystics know a secret: Success is possible only when you are fully present—being there, wherever you are. They put their attention on their wandering attention, bringing it back to the present, here where I am. By doing this over and over again, they learn to relax into the gap. If your goals are big enough, there will always be a gap. Might as well enjoy it.

Take a step or two outside the box. What would be the most unreasonably positive future you could imagine for yourself? For your organization?

Think six impossible things before breakfast tomorrow.

> *I am looking for a lot of men who have an*
> *infinite capacity to not know what can't*
> *be done.*
>
> —HENRY FORD

DEALING WITH IDEA-SLAYERS

The truth is this: The better the idea, the more resistance it is likely to stir up. The best strategy is to expect resistance and try to bring it to the surface at the first presentation. While much of the resistance will be based on fear of change, some of it will contain valuable feedback. Visionaries who shrink from conflict often try to keep the resistance under the rug, only to find that it surfaces later covertly. If possible, confront every concern, ridicule, excuse, and fear up front. Provide counterarguments to these concerns, and expect that these counterarguments will flush up even more resistance. In a better world there would be fewer pigheaded people, but meanwhile visionaries need to cultivate their ability to handle resistance to new ideas. If you get stonewalled completely, thank your colleagues for their input and ask if they would be open to hearing a refined version at a later date. Usually they will say yes to help you save face; they will be shocked when you actually come back in a month or so with a revised plan.

It would be easier if the only resistance we met came from outside. The real problem, though, lies within. The source of much of the resistance that stops us comes from our own beliefs about our limitations.

> ### *We have met the enemy, and it is us.*
>
> —WALT KELLY

The stubborn obstacles we encounter outside ourselves are best regarded as signposts pointing to our own internalized resistance. The Corporate Mystic sees resistance as a friendly part of ourselves that is trying to point out risks and refine our communication skills. By honing our skills we can deal with the vast array of different people out in the world. If we see resistance as "out there," it locks us into an us versus them model that can be very destructive.

The real message here is that enlightened perseverance is necessary to bring about change in the corporate world. Visionaries must learn to expect resistance, both inside and outside themselves, and surf on the edge of it rather than letting it overwhelm them. Your own passion and dedication have to be bigger than other people's attachment to the way things have been, their fear of change and of losing control.

FUTURE-VISION

C orporate Mystics have an ability to stand in the future and take a look around, then to use the power of this imagined future to pull themselves and their organizations toward it. Most people, trapped unknowingly in their conditioning, sit in the past, which causes them to create a limited present and very little vision of the future. If you are sitting in the past, you may even resent the present and try to sabotage those who are committed to the future.

The difference between Motorola and AT&T is that we pictured people walking around with phones, not simply talking on phones in their cars.

—Bob Galvin

If you want to become a Corporate Mystic, stand in the future and look back toward the present. Get yourself thoroughly grounded in the future. Be there, and get comfortable seeing the world from that perspective. It is not important for you to have a detailed picture of the future, but it is crucial to plant one foot there so that the other foot will be motivated to follow.

Imagination is more important than knowledge.

—ALBERT EINSTEIN

John F. Kennedy enjoyed telling the story of small boys in Ireland who, when they came to a fence they were afraid to climb, would throw their hats over first so they would have to go after them. Throw your hat into the future, and you will be inspired to do whatever you can to follow it.

Another reason to become skilled in future-vision is so that you won't sabotage success when it begins to happen. If you step into the future and try it on, your body and mind have an opportunity to get comfortable with it. Once you've developed comfort with a positive future, you are less likely to trip yourself up when it unfolds. We are all conditioned to be afraid of the unknown, and even a positive unknown can rattle us. Future-vision allows you to establish yourself comfortably in an imagined positive future.

Now, in your imagination, locate yourself in the best future you can think of. Go out five years. What are you doing? What is your organization like? From the future, look back toward today. What did you do to get to that positive future?

What would you attempt to do if you knew you could not fail?

—ROBERT SCHULLER

3

Intuition:

Leadership by Calling Forth Full Potential

*People with high levels of personal mastery
do not set out to integrate reason and
intuition. Rather, they achieve it naturally—
as a by-product of their commitment to use
all the resources at their disposal. They cannot
afford to choose between reason and intuition,
or head and heart, any more than they would
choose to walk on one leg or see with
one eye.*

—Peter Senge

Intuition

$\int$ ome call it a "gut feeling," while others speak of an intuitive "flash." The dictionary says that *intuition* is "direct knowing of something without the conscious use of reasoning." It is what you might use to:

- Make a personnel decision.
- Tune in to where the problems are in a particular project.
- Get your timing right on an investment.
- Come up with a new market for an existing product.

Intuition is a natural gift, something to which we all have access. It is also a talent, something we can fine-tune with practice. The main reason intuition is so important is this: It is a clear sign that you are connecting with your inner spiritual guidance system. Intuition is a direct signal from your deepest self that you are navigating from your true center. When intuition is not working for you, it is a sign that you need to refresh your connection with your center. As an archbishop of Canterbury once said, "When I pray, miracles happen. When I don't, they don't." The same is true with intuition. When it's there, you can rest assured that you have been nurturing your connection with your own soul in some way. When it's not there, it's time to spend some time in meditation, or by a waterfall, or in your office with the door closed.

Intuition is a high-skill area of Corporate Mystics. As leaders, they must be in touch with the intuitive as well as the logical aspects of themselves. When the heart and soul connection is missing, no amount of data will fill the gap. As Father Theodore Hesburgh, former president of Notre Dame, once said of leaders, "You cannot blow an uncertain trumpet." The combination of intuition and logic gives the corporate leader a stance of unity from which to lead.

> *The leader who would create a vision*
> *sufficiently compelling to motivate associates to*
> *superior performances must draw on the*
> *intuitive mind.*

—JOHN NAISBITT AND PATRICIA ABURDENE

Integrity and vision are precursors to the full use of your intuition. Intuition works better when you are in a state of integrity. When you are out of integrity, the noise from all your integrity incompletions tends to drown out the subtle signals from intuition.

Intuition also works better when you know where you're going. Vision is a great liberator of intuition. Creative detours appear most benignly in the journeys of people who are already on their way to somewhere important. As Louis Pasteur said, "Chance favors the prepared mind." Echoing this, one of our Corporate Mystics said: "Intuition favors the quiet, open mind." Integrity helps quiet the mind by eliminating the noise caused by lying and breaking agreements. Vision clears the mind by giving it a general focus and direction.

Intuition is not something you can learn from a book; you need to practice it experientially, experimentally, and frequently. Even our best information about intuition will not ultimately make you more intuitive. Spending time in the vast spaces of your own mind is what will do it. The last section of the book—"The Disciplined Mystic"—includes a very reliable method of opening to intuition that has been tested thousands of times. We encourage you to turn to this exercise after mastering the information in the present section, and give yourself plenty of practice time to get comfortable with it.

None of the ideas in this chapter is theoretical; all come from real people who use them in the heat of action. Keep in mind, though, that intuition is not an exact science for the best of its practitioners. Take what appeals to you, try it out experimentally, and feel free to modify and reject anything that doesn't work for you. At the very least you will experience the satisfaction of opening up an often mysterious realm for your own learning.

> *The intuitive mind will tell the thinking mind*
> *where to look next.*
>
> —DR. JONAS SALK

INTUITION PLUS LOGIC: THE CORPORATE MYSTIC'S WINNING FORMULA

Chance does indeed favor the prepared mind, so we are not suggesting throwing out logic and doing everything by gut. But logic is only part of our mind's capabilities; since we've got intuition, why not learn to use it? The great value of intuition is that it helps us come up with solutions that cannot be seen by the clear light of logic. It is a way of tapping the vast riches of the unknown. If logic is the sun, intuition is the moon. Both can be appreciated by the thoughtful leader.

Many corporate leaders we know have a harmonious working relationship between intuition and logic. When we ask them how they got it, some of them say it's always been there. They say that their thinking strategies have not changed since childhood. Others tell us that they had to make a conscious commitment to using all of themselves. In many cases, the imbalance was originally in the direction of logic. They received feedback that they were too data-oriented and made a decision to open up to more of their intuitive capabilities. In a few cases, highly intuitive people had to balance themselves in favor of more logic and reasoning capabilities.

YOUR CREATIVE THINK-TIME IS YOUR MOST IMPORTANT DAILY BUSINESS ACTIVITY

As one Corporate Mystic put it: "If I take twenty minutes a day of pure think-time, my day runs smoothly. If I get 'too busy' and forget to take my magic twenty minutes, things often feel slightly off all day. I've learned to notice when I'm drifting off course. Then it's time to go in my office, close the door, and look out the window for a little while."

Some of the mystics we interviewed for this book took ten minutes, others an hour. Some looked out the window, while others closed their eyes and hummed a mantra. But almost all of them had a way of building creative think-time into their day. They referred to their creative think-time in different words:

"Integration"
"Digesting data"
"Recharging my batteries"
"Accessing the creative zone"
"Resting and roaming"

But they were all talking about a similar process: going inside and drawing on their own inner resources. One manager put it bluntly: "Most businesspeople would not mess up half as much if they just took a few minutes to think. Just close the door and do nothing for a little while. A lot of the busywork that clutters up the business day is just a symptom of not enough think-time."

It takes discipline to make time in your day for creative thinking, and even fiercer discipline to protect this time from the ever-present demands on it. Those who do will reap rich rewards, both in increased productivity and a greater sense of working from one's true depth.

The really valuable thing is intuition.

—ALBERT EINSTEIN

GETTING A BETTER INTUITIVE HIT RATE

Your intuitions will improve to the extent that you can step outside your beliefs, opinions, and biases about the way things are. Think of biases as the noise that you hear instead of the clear signal of greater possibility. You might notice that your intuitions are very clear in one area of your life but very poor in another area. One mystic put it this way: "My hits were very accurate about work, but in the area of relationships I seemed to have little or no intuitive skill. As I studied this problem I came to see that I was carrying a lot more baggage with me about relationships than I was about work. At work I could look dispassionately at a situation and say 'That's the way it is,' but in relationships my head was too full of expectations and programming to see clearly."

If you want to boost your hit rate, begin by studying yourself.

Notice how your intuition communicates with you. Intuition seems to come in on three channels: word, picture, and body-sense. Most of us receive better on one channel than another, so it helps to find out what your best channel is. For example, think of a question like "Where do you want to be five years from now?" A word-channel response to this question might be a sentence flashing across the mind: "I want to be chief financial officer." A picture-channel response might be an image of yourself sitting in a particular office. The body-sense channel might be a warm, pleasant sensation in your abdomen that carries with it a meaning, the good feeling of success.

No channel is better than any other; they all come from the same place—the intuitive capability that we all seem to be born with. You just need to find out where your strong channel is.

In helping several thousand people improve their intuition, we've noticed that the majority get their intuitions in the form of pictures and gut feelings rather than on the word-channel. Everybody's a little different, though, so you have to do some research inside yourself to find out. Check it out right now: Take ten seconds to imagine yourself at your most successful in your career. When you imagine yourself that way, do you see a picture in your mind or get a feeling in your body? Do you see or hear some words?

Now go to a finer level of detail. If you saw a picture, where did it occur? If you got a body-feeling, where did it occur? If you received words, where did they appear in your mind? Listen to a description from a highly intuitive person: "My most accurate intuitions seem to happen about one-quarter to one-half inch to the right of the area between my eyes. The ones that aren't accurate seem to come from behind and to the left of that place." By zeroing in on the body location of your intuition, you get a clearer sense of where to go for the best information.

Once you're familiar with your inner patterns, start to practice on everyday events. In our Integrity/Vision trainings we practice intuition-sharpening exercises with real-life experiments that give immediate feedback. For example, we tune in to weather changes and fluctuations in the price of gold, coffee, and other commodities that bounce around a lot in price. Often by the end of the training, people are predicting rain, sunshine, and price movements with unerring accuracy.

Kate has used intuition from the beginning of her business career, and she has also interviewed many Corporate Mystics to learn their secrets: "I have always been fascinated by the ability to see the future accurately. By 1981 I had begun to do everything I could to increase my intuition, so I decided to set up personal practices and experiments that would help me learn.

"In the early eighties my office was in a magnificent old building in San Francisco. I worked on the second floor, while many of the managers I worked with were on the eighth floor. This meant I spent a lot of time waiting in front of a bank of six elevators. Putting this time to good use, I began checking inside to let my intuition tell me which elevator to stand in front of. When I started I was right about half the time, but within several months my elevator hunches were proving right nine out of ten times. This let me know that intuition was something that could be learned, sharpened, and improved experimentally. One week I went twenty times without an error.

"As my intuition got stronger, so did my trust in it. Although there had never been a layoff at this company, and the CEO had said publicly many times there never would be one, my intuition told me differently. I began spontaneously to think of how a layoff could be handled gracefully and to develop ideas about the implementation of one. On the surface these speculations seemed totally out of sync with reality, until one lunchtime. This day I had a hunch not to go out to lunch (a no-lunch hunch?), but to stay at my desk. Out of the blue the CEO dropped into my office, which he had rarely done, and told me that there would need to be a 40 percent layoff. He asked me if I had any ideas on how best to proceed! Without blinking I gave him a whole plan, with accompanying organizational diagrams. Needless to say, my stock rose in the company."

BECOMING BIGGER THAN THE PROBLEM

When Bob Marshall took over as CEO at Silicon Optics, he was faced with a crisis his first month. Practically the first piece of paper put in his hand was a report saying that a major new product, a piece of technology he had been hired to shepherd into the market, was not working as it should and that nobody knew how to make it work.

Bob recollects: "At first my head was swimming. This was about the worst news I could imagine. Fortunately I hadn't had to relocate my family, so I had the freedom of treating it purely as a business problem. But what should I do? Leave? Stay? Bring in consultants? Because I'd had training in the use of intuition at my previous company, I shut the door and asked that my calls be held for an hour. As it happened, I didn't even need the whole hour.

"I put my feet up and got comfortable. For a few minutes I just closed my eyes and let myself feel all the emotions pouring through my body. I did my best not to resist or censor them. Anger at the board . . . fear that I'd been lied to . . . fear that my career was about to take a plunge . . . fear that I wouldn't be able to pull it out . . . fear about what my wife would think when I told her I might be out of a job . . . After a few minutes my mind and body settled down, and I began counting my breaths to get very still inside.

"When I got into the quiet place inside, I posed a simple question: What was the best course of action to take at this time? I asked the question and let go of any need to answer it. I just got receptive and let the images come. I'm strong on the visual-channel, and I saw a clear path open up, just like I was looking at a photo slide of a clearly marked path through difficult terrain. My next question was: What's the first step? Quick as lightning, a piece of information appeared in my mind: It said 'Be a listener.' It came in on the word-channel, a sentence that said 'Listen to yourself and listen to them.' As I tuned in further, the sense of the message was that I needed to be absolutely truthful with myself and everybody else, particularly the board. I saw in my mind that as long as I behaved with impeccability I had nothing to fear.

"The whole process took less than fifteen minutes, and I came out feeling great. I still had all the same issues to face, but suddenly everything had changed. Now I knew I was bigger than the problem was."

The upshot was that Bob met with the board, aired all his feelings, and listened while they aired theirs. He went into the meeting with a little piece of paper he kept in front of him the entire time. It said, "Listen to myself and listen to them." At the end of the meeting the board decided to fold the project and scale down, which meant hiring a much less expensive person than Bob. They cut him a check for $100,000 in sever-ance, and he went back to work for his former company, where he is now CEO. Interviewed a few years later, he said, "Intuition really saved the day for me. I could have gotten into a loop with the board, making them wrong and duking it out with them. Or I could have stewed in the whole situation for a year and driven myself crazy. Instead, by listening to myself and them, by following my intuition, I got out cleanly. The clear path turned out to take me back to where I'd been, to my old company. But while I'd been away they found out how much they missed me. I don't think I could have become CEO without that few months over at Silicon Optics."

> *The mind, when it is quiet, delivers up*
> *phenomenal intuition which can then be*
> *focused to design a next-generation product or*
> *to understand what's driving particular*
> *customers.*

—ED MCCRACKEN, CEO, SILICON GRAPHICS

DEVELOPING GOOD PEOPLE-INTUITION

Have you noticed that some people—maybe a manager, a teacher, or a friend—seem to be able to read your mind? Somehow their sensory radar seems to work better than other people's. Although some people may be gifted in this area, we know for sure that people-intuition can also be learned. The real problem is not in learning a new skill but in learning how not to overlook what you've been seeing all along. People are organically intuitive; we come factory-equipped that way. In fact, it takes effort not to be intuitive.

Here's how we learn not to be intuitive. Let's say that one day early in your career you notice that your boss looks uncomfortable when he talks about last month's sales figures. You, in your unpolished enthusiasm, blurt out: "I notice you looked uncomfortable when you talked about the sales figures. What's up?" If people are open and in a good mood, they often receive these kinds of communications readily, even gratefully. But let's say your boss is mad about the sales figures and decides to take it out on you. He blasts you and tells you to worry about your performance, not how he looks.

These kinds of events first happen in childhood, where we are asked or forced to overlook things we see to preserve the status quo. In our Integrity/Vision trainings, we find that in a roomful of fifty people as many as thirty will remember experiences of being punished for some intuition, hunch, or observation they shared as a child. Sometimes it only takes one negative experience to snuff out our inborn sense of intuition. On the positive side, human beings are famous for their resilience, so it is possible to overcome these early learnings and give your intuition room to flourish again.

Ed McCracken of Silicon Graphics tells a remarkable story about the power of people-intuition: "We were in a complex negotiation worth hundreds of millions of dollars. We were stalled out, about $75 million apart, and everyone was getting tremendously frustrated. Finally, we called time-out and took a break to reflect. During the break it occurred to us that the issue didn't have anything to do with the technical aspects of the deal. It was really about the other side wondering if we liked them. We were trying to pour on more and more details, when it was actually an emotional issue. So, when we got back together we focused in on how much we liked them and wanted to work with them. The deal was resolved very shortly."

Intuitive managers have special skills that are likely to become more valuable in tomorrow's rapidly changing environment. They are likely to be the people who dream up the new products of tomorrow. They are the people who have a feel for what the consumer wants and how much he or she is willing to pay for it.

—WESTON AGOR

INTUITIVE HIRING

Lou Ann Scardino, vice-president of a cosmetics firm, made a key personnel decision using her intuition, one that later proved to be accurate and highly profitable: "We needed a new leader for our new-products division. We interviewed half a dozen people and narrowed it down to two. They were both highly qualified but about as different as two people could be. Larry was articulate, handsome, and a charmer, down to the cuff links and the Armani suit. He also had a fine track record with another company, so it was clear that he wasn't just appearances. Andy, who had worked for our company for years in a different division, always dressed like he was put together by a committee. He looked like a grown-up Goofy the Dog, a bit of a bumbler. I had many conscious considerations about both of them, but what finally helped me was using my intuition.

"One Sunday afternoon at home, I took a glass of wine out on the patio and spent a few minutes opening up my intuition to solve the problem. I centered myself and posed the question, "Which of these two guys would be best for the company?" It was fascinating and somewhat scary, because every time I tuned in to Larry, I got alarm signals and physical pains in my body, like someone screeching chalk on a chalkboard. When I tuned in to Andy, I felt calm and centered, and I had images of what a calming influence he would be on the team.

"Monday I made the decision and gave the job to Andy. At the same time I offered Larry another position in one of our marketing divisions. He took it and things went well for about two months. Then he got embroiled in a difficult divorce and his performance went downhill very rapidly. He got a DUI ticket, then another one which resulted in losing his license. We let him go and got him into a treatment program. I have since heard that he has changed careers and become a drug and alcohol counselor. Andy is doing extremely well as team leader. My big regret is that I didn't listen to my intuition all the way, which would have probably meant not offering Larry any sort of job. I think my personal response to his charms clouded my ability to trust my intuition completely."

FEAR CLOUDS INTUITION

Intuition must be nurtured. At first, it is important simply to uncover it so that it can live and breathe. Since intuition is wired in, a natural gift, nothing has to be attained in order to be more intuitive. Rather, the process is one of clearing away the things that block its use and appreciation. Fear is the main thing that must be cleared away.

Fear breeds projection, a killer of intuition. We know, for example, that several hundred people rushing toward O'Hare Airport on any given morning may have pictures of their airplanes crashing. Almost never do these "flashes" turn out to be valid intuitions. These images come from their own personal fears and are being projected onto the airplane flight.

As you work to sharpen your intuition, learn to distinguish the voice of fear from the voice of intuition. You might have a thought of not going to New York for a sales call. Is this thought coming from a fear that you won't be able to make the sale? Or is it a genuine intuition that your trip will be unproductive? There is only one way to find out: Acknowledge your fears first. Find out how your fear-thoughts look and feel, and learn to appreciate the difference between them and genuine intuitive hits. It takes practice.

Businesspeople often suffer from a particular fear that limits their creativity and intuition. To put it bluntly, it is the fear of looking foolish. Let's face it: We've all embarrassed ourselves at least a few times in our lives. This implants a fear of looking like a fool deep in our bodies. Anybody who has passed through the educational system has many years of training in trying not to look foolish.

To access creativity and intuition, we must drive out this fear. Fear keeps us trapped in the realm of the predictable. While we are in thrall to the fear of looking ridiculous, our colleagues who have cleared up this fear are busily designing new equipment, dreaming up outrageous campaigns, and coming up with ingenious personnel assignments. Sure, some of their designs and campaigns may look stupid and prove utterly unworkable. When this happens, they just take a deep breath and go back to the drawing boards.

> *The greatest advances in man's*
> *understanding of the universe are made by*
> *intuitive leaps at the frontiers of knowledge,*
> *not by intellectual walks along well-travelled*
> *paths.*
>
> —ANDREW WEIL, M.D.

A company president told us: "When I get stuck, I like to leaf through the notebooks of Leonardo da Vinci. Many of his designs were totally ridiculous and still are. But some of his inventions were ridiculous only in the context of his time.

His designs for the parachute and the helicopter were basically correct, although they were five hundred years ahead of their time. What I respect, though, is that his commitment to his creativity was bigger than his fear of looking stupid. He was willing to play with his creativity, a sure sign of mastery."

To get to the zone of intuition many people have to walk through the gate of another fear: being crazy. Some people are afraid to open up to the unknown in themselves, for fear that some monster slumbers deep within. Some of us grew up around people whose intuitiveness became mingled with irrational acts, so that later we came to resist intuition because we feared our own inner voices. Both of the authors had family members or acquaintances who fit this category. Gay: "As my paternal grandmother slid into senile dementia, her telepathic abilities increased in direct proportion to her paranoid fantasies. Sometimes she would get a great intuitive hit and predict the arrival of a letter from a distant relative. These accurate intuitions were mixed up with wildly crazy ones, like her conviction that my mother was having an affair with Franklin Delano Roosevelt. I think this gave the whole family a fear of the intuitive." Kate: "I had a neighbor who was lobotomized when I was growing up, and that gave me a fear of what might happen if I opened up to my inner voices. Also, children's books were full of witch archetypes, which didn't inspire little girls to open up to their magical powers."

If you discover any of these fears, understand that they are normal and natural. Many people have had to move through them in order to get on a congenial basis with their intuition.

Just as jumping in the water the first time can be scary, so can a jump into the vast ocean of your intuitive powers. Once you get comfortable there, some real and useful pleasure can be yours.

REMOVING THE INNER CRITIC

Most of us by adulthood have acquired a severe inner critic and an internal hanging judge. These mental marionette masters keep us frozen or jumping through hoops not of our own conscious choosing. There is only one way to acquire the judge and critic: Somebody told us there was something fundamentally wrong with us. We were wrong because we were the wrong color, the wrong sex, the wrong socioeconomic class. Even if you've risen above this, you can still have remnants of it buried deep in your cells. You might feel that acknowledging a mistake is the same as acknowledging that there is something fundamentally bad about your being itself. Nobody likes to face that, so we often defend ourselves against it by needing to be right all the time.

In our consultations with executives, we have often seen great breakthroughs in leadership come when they are able to let go of the need to be right. Letting go of the need to be right is also crucial to turning on the power of intuition. Intuition is best accessed with a nonjudgmental mind, a mind that says, "Let me just take what I get from my intuitive depths as it comes, and I'll evaluate, judge, and edit later." This is a correct use of the judging and evaluating mind.

Intuition often turns dreams into demonstrable facts.

—BUCKMINSTER FULLER

WHAT WE FEAR IS OUR OWN POWER

The dominant human fear is the fear of the unknown. It can severely limit your ability to open up to your intuition. This fear causes us to live in the zone of complacency, where creativity and intuition do not dwell. As long as we are in the grip of the fear of the unknown, no great leaps of mind are possible.

When we fear the unknown, what we are really fearing is the depths and heights of our own power. If we open up and connect with the powerful creativity of our intuitive mind, we are at once opening to the creative power of the universe that resides in microcosm within us. This is strong stuff, so strong that there is a widespread tendency to avoid contact with this creative potential. We delude ourselves into thinking that it is safer to stay in the zone of the predictable. This, however, can be a bad bargain, especially if we want to go all the way to full success in life. The moment we choose to stay in the predictable zone is the moment we sign our death warrant as a creative individual.

We also fear the great responsibility that goes along with great power. The intuitive is our connection with our ability to make and remake the world. We may have an intuitive flash of how the atom is constructed, but along with it comes a sense of responsibility for how this knowledge might be used. Instead of resisting our intuitive powers and resisting the responsibility, the mystic embraces both.

INTUITION IS A PHENOMENON OF THE GAP

Intuition dwells in the gap between ordinary thoughts. Much of the time our thoughts seem jumbled together so tightly that there doesn't seem to be any space between them. But if you look carefully, you will see that there is open space between and behind all your thoughts. Intuition occurs in this gap.

The gap is the province of the mystic. Mystics are comfortable in the gap, while non-mystics experience fear when they're there. Non-mystics are comfortable only in the predictable territory of their known thoughts. Mystics cannot live in the zone of the known for very long without feeling stultified. To find intuition and make it your friend, you must enter the gap.

The gaps are the thing. The gaps are the
spirit's one home, the altitudes and latitudes
so dazzlingly spare and clean that the spirit
can discover itself like a once-blind man
unbound.

—ANNIE DILLARD

There are formal ways to enter the gap, such as through meditation. Part Three of this book contains a short, effective means of entering the gap and turning on your intuition. There are also informal ways to access the gap. The simplest way is to pose a question, then let go of the need to have an answer right away. It is a seeding technique; you sow the question, then let go of it to await the surprise of an answer later.

As an experiment right now, pose a question that has significance for you. Just ask it in your mind and let go of it. If you notice, the question is surrounded and embraced by a vast space. That's the gap. Just relax into it and get comfortable there. That's the comfort zone of the mystic: the friendly unknown, the zone of all possibilities. From somewhere in the gap, when the time is right, you may be surprised by an answer to your question.

CONTROL CRAMPS INTUITION

If you want to live in the zone of intuition rather than just visit it, cultivate the skill of letting go of control. This skill is difficult for businesspeople, who often think they have gotten where they are through their ability to control. But to go all the way to full success, you have to master controlling what is controllable and letting go of everything outside your control. There is a specific way to do this.

Imagine you have two boxes. Box 1 is labeled "Things over which I have absolutely no control." Box 2 is labeled "Things over which I have complete control." Mystics learn to assign all the elements of life to the correct box and to then focus all their attention on Box 2.

Box 1 is surprisingly large, and gets larger the more you think about it. Among the things you cannot control are:

- The feelings and actions of other people.
- Anything that has already happened—the past.
- Anything that hasn't happened yet—the future.
- Most of what goes on inside your own body.

You cannot control other people, the past, or the future. But what about that last item on the list? Many people think they can control what goes on inside their bodies. Forget about controlling your poor liver, which every minute is doing several hundred things, most of which are unpronounceable. Think about controlling your feelings. Imagine being afraid just before making a speech. If you had control over your fear you would be able to make it go away. And we all know how well that works. That's why the wise mystic counsels: When you're feeling scared (or angry or sad), simply acknowledge it, resonate with it, tell the truth about it. Trying to control it is like squeezing the middle of a garden hose while water is flowing through it.

Or consider your weight. Even the most perfect physical specimen has no control over his or her weight. Don't believe it? Go step on the scales and check your weight. Then try to make it go up or down. Did it? No. You have no control over it. But what do you have control over? What can you put in Box 2? You have complete control over what you put in your mouth. You have complete control over whether you get up right now and get on your exercise bike. What you can control and what you cannot: It's a key distinction. The mystic focuses on what can be controlled and accepts the rest just as it is. From this deep acceptance of reality, exactly as it is, comes the possibility of choosing to make it different.

Relationships with other people? That's where we really come up against our lack of control. The harder you try the worse it gets. Just ask any former despot. Mao once had everyone in China reading his Little Red Book, to convince the citizens of the superiority of communism over capitalism; now the book is a novelty item, found in the souvenir shops along the Great Wall. Mao's picture is widely available on T-shirts, which the Chinese are very happy to trade for capitalist blue jeans.

The mystic knows the difference between control and influence. While you cannot control other people, the past, the future, or much of anything about yourself, you can certainly influence them. Control comes out of fear; influence is exercised consciously with a goal and a plan. Control is the offspring of desperation; influence is carried out in a businesslike fashion.

Letting go of control is the first step; it frees up the energy you will need. There is a simple, powerful strategy for dealing with all the contents of Box 1, the things you cannot control. Face them and accept them, just as they are. Many people tie up all their energy in resistance to things they cannot change. This same energy, freed up, is the stuff that fuels miracles.

THREE MILLION DOLLARS' WORTH OF INTUITION

Kate, who describes herself as a very risk-aversive person, used intuition to deal with her fear of risk and start an enterprise that has since yielded an impressive payoff: "I took January 1991 off for rest and relaxation, as a reward for my first year of billing half a million dollars as a consultant. I spent most of it with my daughter, enjoying the outdoors. For a year I had been toying with the idea of creating proprietary software for conducting personnel assessments and other surveys. Every time I thought about this I got the special flurrying feeling in my chest that I get when I have an intuition that I ought to move on rapidly. The glitch was that these developmental projects are costly, and I would have to dig deep into my own pocket to do it. Also, I talked to several companies to assess enthusiasm for 360-degree assessments. It was lukewarm at best, because no one knew that such assessments would become popular until a few years later.

"I decided to run the idea past Ken Schroeder, president of KLA Instruments, who had been a mentor and coach to me in the mid-eighties. Ken strongly recommended that I go ahead. I mounted some resistance, arguing that my daughter was just starting college and I didn't have extra money to spend. In spite of what my inner critic said, I trusted Ken, and I trusted my own body-sense of intuition. Even though I had little support from my potential customers I decided to go ahead with the project. I spent $20,000 in 1991 on developing the product. After I had committed my own money and time, Intel gave me $15,000 to customize the software for their company, so in actuality I invested only $5,000 of my own money. To date, the product has brought in $3,000,000 in revenue. I'm tremendously grateful to Ken for helping me believe in the project and my own intuition."

Never lose a holy curiosity.

—ALBERT EINSTEIN

PART TWO

The Practical Mystic: Spirited Solutions to Everyday Business Problems

Manifest plainness, embrace simplicity.

—LAO-TZU

In this part we will present solutions Corporate Mystics have applied to some of the most common business problems we have encountered in our twenty-five years of consulting. These examples all show mystics at work, drawing on the principles of integrity, vision, and intuition. In our travels we have seen four main areas in which problems occur.

The first area is commitment. When people are not committed, little productivity is possible. The cultures of many corporations are cultures of noncommitment. There is entitlement, apathy, and downright sabotage at work in some of the largest and oldest companies we have visited. In order to turn these companies around, radical work had to be done in the area of commitment.

Communication is the second area, and a large one it is. No matter how many books are written about communication in corporate settings, we keep seeing the same old communication breakdowns over and over again. As one of our frustrated colleagues put it at the end of a long meeting, "The level of communication in most corporations is approximately equal to that of the average junior high school. And that may be generous to corporations and an insult to junior high school students." What is really required is courageous practice of certain fundamental communication principles, and we have laid out the principles that we have seen to be of most benefit.

The third area is in managing projects. In any dynamic human enterprise there are going to be unexpected twists and turns. In fact, corporate life is a daily experience of the unexpected. It is likely to become more so in the twenty-first century. What will distinguish successful companies, perhaps more than anything else, will be a comfort and even enthusiasm for change, coupled with a reliable way of handling the unexpected.

The fourth area is the creation of wealth. While most people do not work only for money, they seldom work without it. Most people in corporate life are concerned with creating wealth for themselves and for others. In our consulting work, we have had the opportunity to ask many self-made millionaires how they went about creating wealth. They have shared a cornucopia of ideas with us, and while these principles are intrinsically fascinating, their cash value is that they work. We have personally tried each of the tools described in this section, and our wealth has increased as a direct result.

> *In our era, the road to holiness necessarily*
> *passes through the world of action.*
>
> —DAG HAMMARSKJÖLD

4

Inspiring Commitment

Five frogs sat on a log. One decided to jump. How many frogs were left?

Five. There's a big difference between deciding to jump and actually jumping. The inspired leader knows how to get total commitment, so that no frogs are left on the corporate log. Zero-frog leadership.

Getting "buy-in" is essential in every area of life: family, play, work. Have you ever tried to play a game—whether tennis, business, or marriage—with a partner who didn't really want to be there? All it takes to destroy a game is one person on the team who doesn't want to play.

A multimillion-dollar failure shows what can happen when buy-in is overlooked. We came in on the tail end of this fiasco to attempt a bailout, but by then it was too late. Because it was such a costly failure for the company, we took pains to "backward-map" the various steps that had led to the debacle. Here's what happened.

A new venture was put together within one of America's largest communication companies. A brilliant innovator had designed a new telecommunications product. Speed was of the essence because the technology was also under development in at least two other firms. The financial side of the house promised an eighteen-month deadline to the people who were funding the project. When the managers went to the creative people who would actually build the product and get it out the door, the eighteen-month deadline was greeted with derision. "No way" was the basic message.

Under this resistance were several layers of fear: the fear of losing jobs, the fear of being away from families for evenings and weekends, the fear of being in an adversarial relationship with management. Management, in their zeal to develop the product, overrode this resistance heavy-handedly, offering promises of great rewards if the deadline was met. The resistance went underground. The one misstep that seemed crucial in retrospect was that the feelings of all concerned never got an airing. Everyone gave lip service to the deadline, but the design team never fully got on board.

A sense of mistrust soon permeated the project. Everyone had both a public and a private version of their feelings. The main topic of whispered conversations in the lunchroom was the Deadline. Eighteen-hour days and six-day weeks became the norm, with many people coming in on Sunday afternoons. Finally everything came to a head a couple of months before the deadline, in the form of an emotional blowup between the head of the design team and the head of the financial side of the company. Everyone's feelings came pouring out in the kind of messy confrontation that engineers, especially, do not relish. The deadline was exposed as unfeasible, threats were made, three people went home sick.

From then on a pall lingered in the air, which cleared only when a new deadline was set, with a five-month extension. Meanwhile, Company B delivered a version of the product to market a few months early and soon dominated the field. Company A brought theirs in under the new deadline, but by then the energy was dead.

All of this could have been avoided. The rest of the chapter shows you how.

RECOGNIZING THE MOST COMMON COMMITMENT PROBLEM

As consultants, the commitment problem we have seen more than any other is this: People do not buy in to a project, assignment, or vision. The leader does not perceive this lack of buy-in, or chooses to ignore it. Instead of speaking up and voicing whatever the resistance is, people swallow their communication and act as if they have bought in. They file dutifully out of the meeting, and then the troubles begin. They passively resist, perhaps not completing work on time. They gossip about the project or the leader or the people who have bought in. All of the problems have stemmed from a lack of up-front commitment.

A related problem is that people will make an agreement, perhaps to meet a certain deadline. Some event, often outside their control, will get in the way, and they won't know how to change the agreement. Feet will be dragged, sick days will be taken, the project delayed.

The solution is obvious but not easy to implement. Leaders have to get skilled at recognizing the signals of noncommitment. The best way is to watch body language. Notice the averted eyes, the glance at the watch, obsessive fiddling with the coffee cup. There are dozens of ways people telegraph their feelings. The savvy leader must be willing to find out what is behind these fidgets.

"Bill, I notice when we set the deadline you looked uncomfortable. I'd really like to know how you actually feel about it." These can be tough moments for leaders, who often want to hear what they want to hear. In these moments people might be feeling:

- Fear that they won't be able to deliver.
- Anxious that resources won't be available.
- Fear that a time-consuming project will disrupt family life.

The important thing for leaders is to look for signs of noncommitment in the first moments and hear people out. It is also important to create a climate in which people can talk about their authentic feelings without fearing punishment. Timing is often crucial in such confrontations. Some people do not like to speak out in meetings; they can be contacted later over a cup of coffee. Sensitive leaders study the styles of their key people so that an effective avenue of approach can be designed for each person.

An ounce of this sort of attention up front can prevent a ton of problems later on.

KNOWING YOUR PURPOSE

Your first step in getting commitment is to know your ultimate purpose. It is hard to inspire commitment unless you can speak your purpose in one clear sentence. It is hard to get committed to something if you don't know what it is. It is hard to get others committed if they're not sure of what they're committing to. One thing you have absolute control over in life is where to put your focus.

Members of a Yale graduating class in the 1950s were surveyed periodically throughout their lives to assess their well-being, happiness, and financial abundance. All of them were bright, many of them were wealthy. But 3 percent of them had an edge that later proved significant. When first contacted, 3 percent of them had developed written goals for their lives as they left college. Thirty years later that 3 percent was worth more money than the other 97 percent put together.

Purpose.

What you most want.

If you figure out your purpose you won't wander aimlessly and you won't settle for side steps that take you away from your purpose. Without a clear sense of your purpose there are a thousand and one sidetracks to seduce you. A great advantage of knowing your purpose is that it becomes easier to make decisions. You know at a glance whether a specific path serves your purpose or not. Many people, in a misguided attempt to keep more options open, fail to make clean decisions and suffer for it.

THE PURPOSE OF PURPOSE

There are Big Life Purposes and there are small daily purposes. Both are equally important. The function of both is to give shape and definition to your actions.

Your Big Life Purpose is the answer to questions like: What, above all, am I really here for? What do I most love to do? At the end of my life, if it had been a total success, what would I have experienced and accomplished?

Small daily purposes are the answer to questions like: What do we want to accomplish with this project? What spirit do we want to lend to this enterprise? What feelings and accomplishments do I want to walk away from this meeting with? What emotional state do I want to be in as I go about my tasks?

An inspiring leader knows how to connect the small, incremental (and often irksome) steps with the Big Vision. When you see someone doing a trivial but essential job, pause by the person's desk and say, "I appreciate the care you're giving this job. It's obvious you remember the purpose, why we're all doing this."

There needs to be harmony between your Big Life Purposes

and your daily purposes for you to be happy. If there is conflict between the two, expect rattles and bumps along the journey.

INTEGRITY IS CENTRAL TO COMMITMENT

Nothing deflates commitment faster than broken agreements. One broken promise can erode trust in a moment, and can take years to straighten out. If you really want to complicate your life quickly, don't keep your agreements. At the bottom of most corporate disasters is a small pile of broken agreements. Sometimes just one. If you break an agreement and show up a minute late for a meeting, others will use this as justification to steal paper clips. Someone will see them stealing paper clips and get inspired to embezzle the pension fund.

Deadlines are a kind of agreement that is worth paying careful attention to. Deadlines are crucial to corporate life. The mystic solution to deadlines is: Never make a deadline you don't intend to keep. People get sloppy when deadlines are extended or swept under the rug. Don't let people in your organization waste a second trying to figure out if a deadline is real or not. If you don't mean it, don't do it.

The rules are simple: Don't make agreements you don't want to make. Keep all the agreements you make. Tell the rock-bottom truth if you find you are not going to keep an agreement. Cop to it immediately if you fail to keep an agreement.

Hold yourself responsible for a higher standard
than anyone else expects of you.

—HENRY WARD BEECHER

DOING WHAT NEEDS TO BE DONE

How many people do you know who can be counted on to do what they say they are going to do? If they were counting, would they count you? Pros are people who can keep showing up day after day, doing a good job even when they don't feel like it.

How do you know what most needs to be done? Look and see. Ask. On the battlefield, doctors use the art and science of triage: They separate the wounded into three categories. The first category are those who are going to live, with or without medical treatment. The second category are those who are going to die, with or without treatment. The third category are those who will die unless they receive treatment. The last category gets the priority on the doctors' efforts. We have seen many executives benefit from developing a triage system for their daily activities. There are always paramount activities that will cost you and the company if not attended to. Too many executives waste time and energy on activities that are not crucial.

Corporate Mystics often employ a trick: They do the thing they would least like to do first. Then the rest of the day is like vacation. Who are you most dreading talking to? What decision are you painfully aware that you haven't made yet, but which absolutely needs to be made? Whose phone message keeps staring you in the face?

Everything begins with a commitment. In the beginning was the word. There is a tiny club that truly deserves to be elite: those people that know what their purpose is and who can be counted on to do what they say they are going to do.

Sit, walk, or run.

Just don't wobble.

—ZEN SAYING

WHY PEOPLE DON'T HONOR THEIR COMMITMENTS

The moment you make a commitment, you are pulled rapidly in the direction of your goal. This increased velocity brings to the surface your barriers to being completely effective. If you make big commitments, you will often face big barriers. If you ever find yourself thinking "I didn't ask for this kind of trouble!" just look back at your commitments. You will often see that big barriers follow hot on the heels of big commitments.

There are three barriers that most of us are likely to encounter. The first is wrong information. If we are misinformed about ourselves, others, or the world, making a big commitment will usually expose where our errors lie. Not long ago, a bright, young star ascended to a corporate presidency. He was articulate, hardworking, and charismatic. Soon, corridors were buzzing with the rumor that the president was having an affair with another charismatic young star, a vice-president in the organization. The corporate culture had a taboo against such relationships; the new president chose to stonewall, denying there was anything more than a friendship. In doing this, he fell prey to a fatal piece of misinformation: that no one notices when you sweep a lie under the rug. The more he denied, the bigger the uproar got. Finally, he was forced out and quickly revealed his hand by marrying the woman.

In analyzing this situation, we would say that his ascendence to the presidency was a deeper commitment on his part. At the higher level, which surely represented a lifetime dream of his, everything was required of him. The deeper commitment exposed the flaw that he had been able to conceal or manage at lower levels of commitment.

Now let's turn to the second barrier.

HANDLING FEAR, DOUBT, AND CONFUSION

The moment you declare a big commitment, another barrier may rise up to hinder you: uncomfortable feelings. Take, for example, the perennial problem of dieting. Millions of people every day make a commitment to follow a diet. Most diets fail for a simple and powerful reason. Within minutes perhaps, certainly within hours, they are feeling uncomfortable emotions like fear and hunger. These are the very same feelings that their bad eating habits are designed to squelch. The only way to make a diet succeed is to handle those feelings, perhaps by experiencing them deeply, breathing through them, going for a run. Unwilling to be with these feelings, they eat their forbidden foods again. Unwillingness to go through the gate of uncomfortable emotions causes people to sabotage their commitments.

If you are doing anything big and worthwhile in life, you are going to flush up uncomfortable feelings. The bigger the commitment, the bigger the bundle of feelings that is likely to come up. Big commitments mean big wins and big losses. Both wins and losses stir up the pot of your feelings. The mystic knows that big commitments are often followed by big fears, doubts, and confusions. Imagine the feelings that must have surfaced as Columbus's ship lost sight of the European shore! Veteran Corporate Mystics know about the second barrier and give themselves and their co-workers plenty of opportunities to tell the truth about their feelings. They make a space of safety in which to feel all feelings, but keep everyone reminded that feelings pass through like gusts of wind. Feel whatever you feel, says the mystic, and keep focused on doing what needs to be done.

There's no choice about whether you are going to have the feelings; the only choice is how you are going to participate with them. The mystic knows that peace of mind flows from total participation, with fear, with sorrow, with joy. With feelings, all you can do is see them, feel them, and keep on moving. The worst thing you can do is deny them and hide them.

Once you have chosen a path and committed to it, regard all your doubts as noise. Fear plays a useful role only until you are committed: It is the energy of choice. Once you have committed, most fear will disappear. If any remains, regard it as a cue that you are not taking action fast enough.

MISPLACED LOYALTIES

When you make a deep commitment, a third barrier arises—misplaced loyalty—and it is often the most difficult to cross. The moment you declare, "My goal is to make $300,000 a year" or "I would like to have a loving marriage," you invariably expose the hidden bonds that keep you shackled to the past.

The mystic knows the power of invisible loyalties. For example, many people do not rise to the full level of their potential out of unconscious loyalty to a failed and wounded parent. It is for this reason that Corporate Mystics work carefully not to confuse their own personal story/dramas with what needs to be done. Everybody has their story/dramas: Some of us are betrayals waiting to happen, others of us are misunderstood geniuses, still others are hidden heroes afraid to take the leap. Regardless of whether your story is a comedy or a tragedy, it absolutely needs to be distinguished from what most needs to be done. These are two separate categories: your story, and what needs to be done in every given situation. Many of us sabotage our enterprises by getting our stories muddled up with what needs to be done.

Remember the young president who was having the affair? He got his own story/drama confused with what needed to be done. His story, based on his history with his authoritarian father, was about "How much can I get away with?" What he needed to do—lead the corporation—was to be authentic about his affair to the employees and the board, and to choose consciously between the love relationship and the presidency.

Corporate Mystics know that everyone's story is sacred to them, whether it is about betrayal or heroism. The Corporate Mystic's edge is being able to see how his or her story is clouding what needs to be done and to do what needs to be done anyway. If the mystic is a manager, he or she learns how to acknowledge people's stories but keep them focused on what needs to be done.

When we get confused about what needs to be done, it is often because we are in thrall to an ancient version of ourselves. The same is true for any organization. Corporations often stay fixated on a limited version of themselves. There are frequently loyalties to old visions, former leaders. Corporate Mystics confront this issue head-on. They ask: "Who are we being loyal to by not doing what needs to be done?"

RECOGNIZING AND REWARDING COMMITTED PEOPLE

Keeping people committed is a high art, part of which is finding ways to recognize their contributions. Money is the obvious way, but most people don't work for money alone. Creative leaders find ways of stepping into the shoes of other people and asking, "How would I feel and what would I want if I were this person?"

Bill Wiggenhorn, president of Motorola University, one of

the most innovative organizations we have ever seen, found a unique way of compensating a unique individual who reported to him. From his conversations with her he knew that money played a very small role in her life. She, in fact, lived simply and gave most of her money away to charity. He wanted to increase her compensation in a way that would recognize and benefit her, and he knew if he gave her more money it would not have that result. So, he stepped into her shoes and asked himself what he would want if he shared her spiritual values. More education and training, he thought. Instead of increasing her salary, he put aside funds for her professional development and offered her some flextime to pursue it. These contributions allowed her to complete her doctorate, which had been unfinished for several years.

Somebody ought to tell us, right at the start of
our lives, that we are dying. Then we might
live life to the limit every minute of every day.
Do it! I say. Whatever you want to do,
do it now.

—MICHAEL LANDON

5

COMMUNICATING WITH PEOPLE

*Put your heart, mind, and soul into even
your smallest acts. That is the secret of
success.*

—SWAMI SIVANANDA

Corporate Mystics know a secret: Genuine communication is possible only when you are fully present—being there, wherever you are. Mystics put their attention on their wandering attention, bringing it back to the present, here where I am.

At its best, work is play. When you are fully engaged, when your full capacities are in use and creativity is flowing, there is no such thing as work. Then you are just doing what you are doing. If you watch children at play—fully there, completely earnest, engaged—you will see the exact attitude that Corporate Mystics cultivate at work.

Jim Jarman took over the presidency of an undercapitalized biotech start-up on the West Coast: "My first week on the job I was confronted with a dizzying number of problems no one had told me about. Some were financial, others were technical, many were personality related. I remember playing with my daughter in the family room on Friday night after my first week of work. My daughter suddenly said, 'Where are you, Dad?' and I realized I was in a trance. I was nowhere near being where I was. In fact, I was running through my financing options for getting a cash infusion for the company. I felt guilty as heck for letting my work get in the way of my relationship with my daughter, so I got down on the floor with Andrea, who was in kindergarten at the time. 'Teach me how to play, honey. Show me how you play.' She didn't bat an eyelash. She grinned at me and said 'okay,' and for the next hour I got reacquainted with playing. I just did what she did, and when she went from one thing to the next I followed right with her. What I noticed was how she paid total attention to what she was doing. When she played with the dolls, she was right there with them, completely engaged. But when we switched to trucks, she gave her full attention to them. I saw that my mistake at work had been to go to the next activity while leaving part of my mind behind on the last one. Or farming out another part of my mind to the future. Andrea didn't do this at all. The secret of her play was that she was right where she was. When I went up to join my wife later, she asked me what I had been doing down there that had kept Andrea so engaged. 'She was teaching me how to do my new job,' I said.

"When I got back to work Monday I posted a sign on my

wall that said, 'Remember Andrea's Secret.' Probably fifteen times that week somebody asked me what Andrea's secret was. And I told it over and over until I got it."

> *The secret of success is nonattachment to results; doing your best at the moment, and letting the results take care of themselves.*
>
> —J. DONALD WALTERS

BEING AUTHENTIC

Good communication starts at home, inside yourself. Is your communication with yourself clear and direct? One thing they don't teach us in school is how to listen to and honor all our feelings. It is left to life to teach us, often painfully, how to listen to the signals from our inner selves. One of the main messages of life is: Don't lie to yourself. Lying to others will get you in trouble, but lying to yourself will make you sick. And fast.

> *What are you pretending not to know?*
>
> —GRAFFITI IN A HARVARD BUSINESS SCHOOL RESTROOM

The problem becomes obvious when we are trying to communicate with others and they can clearly see we are not communicating with ourselves. Bluntly put, life gets painfully complicated the moment you lie to yourself or to someone else. Enlightened leaders tell the truth to themselves and the people around them. The Buddha said it plainly: Unhappiness comes from not facing some reality that you need to face squarely.

> *The first step to becoming a leader is to stop pretending, especially to ourselves.*
>
> —AN ANONYMOUS CORPORATE MYSTIC

Sometimes this reality is inside, sometimes outside. Sometimes the reality is in the past, sometimes in the present. Kate worked with two vice-presidents who were locked in a power struggle: "The CFO of a high-tech company in Silicon Valley was a black man named Dan. A white woman, Gracie, was the vice-president of sales. They got into a communication breakdown so extreme that they would not even sit in a meeting together without a third party. After looking over the situation, I didn't think it was fixable. I suggested they both look at their individual stories that were contributing to the drama. The level of mistrust seemed way out of the norm. As we worked on their issues separately, suddenly she surfaced a memory of a traumatic early childhood experience with a relative of a black nanny she'd had when she was a child. As we got this sorted out, she found out that Dan was Dan, not some shadow figure from the past. On his end, he uncovered an old program of white women being beyond his reach, and Gracie, who happened to be a "homecoming queen" beauty, seemed particularly annoying to him. Finally, he saw her as

Gracie, not as some archetype of an unavailable woman. Now they're good friends, out from their projections on each other."

The most exhausting thing in life, I have
discovered, is insincerity.
—ANNE MORROW LINDBERGH

I noticed that when people weren't listening
to me it was usually because I wasn't telling
the truth.
—AN ANONYMOUS CORPORATE MYSTIC

PLAIN TALKING

If you make sure you're telling the truth, you won't ever have to worry about people listening to you. When people don't listen, it's usually because the speaker's got something else he or she is communicating besides the truth. Say only true things and keep it brief. Mystics are famous for not making small talk.

If you want one thing to focus on at all times, one thing that will guarantee happiness and success, focus on whether or not every word you say is the truth.

Facts first. Part of learning to tell the truth is getting the facts right. Instead of saying "The other day I was talking to Joe," just go ahead and say, "Tuesday morning I was talking to Joe." Instead of "I've been noticing a lessened commitment on your part, Harvey," give him some facts. Say, "Harvey, you reported late on project A and you missed our Wednesday meeting on project B." A lot of people like to put a little spin on their facts, and it costs them their credibility. So, focus first on telling the truth about facts.

Then, make sure you tell the truth about feelings. If you're angry, don't try to hide it. People can see it anyway. Say, "I'm angry." If you're sad or disappointed, say it right out. Same thing for fear. A lot of people think feelings are a sign of weakness, but the truth is, they're a sign of being human. Nothing gives a leader more power than admitting to having feelings. Hiding your feelings makes you look bad and it throws your timing off. That doesn't mean you have to wallow in them or make a drama out of them. Mystics acknowledge and express their feelings the same way they acknowledge and express the time of day. Then they move on.

Any man who doesn't cry scares me a little bit.

—H. NORMAN SCHWARZKOPF

GET OUT OF THE MIDDLE

When we asked Corporate Mystics what their number one learning had been in the area of communication, many of them said: getting out of the middle. What they meant is this: Bob comes to you with a complaint about Marsha. You immediately ask, "Have you talked to Marsha about this?" Bob says he hasn't. "Go talk to her now. Come back later and give me a report." Many problems can be eliminated by getting out of the middle. If you are willing and have time, you can also say, "I'll call her in right now and we can all discuss it together." Either way saves much time and trouble down the line. It gets you out of perpetuating one of the oldest family dramas humans run. Many of us grew up in families where there was not straightforward communication. Mom would get upset at Dad but would filter it through Brother or Sister. Dad would be mad at Billy, who wouldn't find out until Mom told him. Roundabout communication costs a great deal of energy in human life, and there is only one efficient way to stop it. When it's your turn to play, don't.

LISTENING FOR ACCURACY

Power lives more in listening than in talking. In fact, listening may be the key skill of the successful person. As soon as people feel that they've been listened to, they begin to evolve. They may have been stuck in one position for a long time, but a little bit of listening lubricates the hinge. As consultants, we have taught listening skills to thousands of people and have seen these skills work outright miracles. Take a moment now to ask yourself the question: How do you listen?

There are three levels to the development of listening skills. The first simple step is to feed back to people exactly what they said. This type of listening could be called "listening for accuracy."

Person A, beating on table with fist: "I want the Brooklyn Bridge and the Tappan Zee, or there's no deal."

Person B, a Corporate Mystic: "So you're saying you want the Brooklyn Bridge and the Tappan Zee, or there's no deal."

You might think such a response would come across sounding stupid. It does not. Try it and you will see what a radical move it is. People, especially when they have strong feelings, are so caught up in their own point of view that they are listening for opposition. It completely disarms them when you refuse to play. There is an electric moment of possibility when you listen to another human being with no agenda, no wanting them to see it your way. Pure listening. The Corporate Mystic thrives on such moments.

> *I always thought I was listening, but now I*
> *realize I have been just watching people's*
> *mouths move, waiting for them to stop so I*
> *could talk!*

—PARTICIPANT IN A SEMINAR ON LISTENING

A corporate officer told us: "I never knew the power of pure listening until one day a few years ago. There was a guy that I didn't get along with very well, partly because I had him labeled as a whiner. He bugged me because he seemed to recycle the same upset feelings all the time, particularly his feelings of competitiveness with other people at his level. One day we were having coffee in the cafeteria when he started again. I felt my gut tighten and my blood pressure start to go up. I had just read a book and listened to a tape on listening, though, so I decided to practice on him. Instead of agreeing with him or talking him out of his point of view, I simply restated it. I said, 'You're mad about Hilda getting a bigger salary increase, and you have a strong desire to move ahead in this company.' I did my best to say it with no judgment implied or expressed. After I said this, there was a silence. Finally, he said, 'Yeah,' and that was the end of it. He started talking about something much more pleasant. I don't know to this day if he stopped complaining in general or just to me, but I know for certain that I haven't heard him talk the same way since."

On a humorous note, a friend of the authors' went with his wife to a party where he knew almost no one. He decided to try an experiment: Rather than talking or trying to impress anyone at the party, he vowed to do nothing all evening but listen carefully and restate what each person said to him. On the way home his wife, glowing with pride, told him that several people had remarked about what a powerful, charismatic, and articulate person he was.

The first stage of learning to listen, then, is being able to summarize the content of what you've heard, just the way they said it. Teachers of listening will tell you that it takes about ten minutes to learn this skill and about ten years to master it.

LISTENING FOR EMPATHY

The second stage of learning to listen is to resonate with what the other person is saying, particularly the emotional content. We'll call this "listening for empathy." You do this by trying their emotions on in your own body. The other person says: "I want this company to be the industry leader in quality microchips by the year 2000." The resonant listener tries on what it feels like to have this desire. You resonate with it. That doesn't mean you have to agree with it. Far from it. You might want something entirely different. But understanding—true resonance—comes first, long before resolution. Remember: *Resonance precedes resolution.* The acid test of this skill comes when emotions are in the air. When someone says he's angry, the resonant listener tries on what it feels like for this person to be angry. The power of this move has to be seen to be believed.

Heath Herber, president of The Herber Company, told us: "I would say that listening to the other person's emotions may be the most important thing I've learned in twenty years in business. What I do is tune in to what's underneath the other person's words. It might be doubt. It might be irritation or nervousness. Then I just name it matter-of-factly. I say something like 'It sounds like you have some doubt, and I can sure understand why you might.' I never try to talk them out of it. If I can name it, they start to talk themselves out of it. I caught onto this one time when I was trying to sell a major contract to a car dealer. Things were bogged down and I couldn't figure out why. I knew I had the numbers that made sense to him, but he was stalling around. I saw that he was distracted about something, so I named it: 'You seem distracted, Charlie.' He blinked and shifted gears. 'Yeah, I guess I am. My daughter's getting married Saturday, and I'm having a lot of feelings about it.' It turned out our daughters were about the same age, but neither one of us until that moment even knew we had kids. Five minutes later I had a signed contract and a new friend."

LISTENING FOR MUTUAL CREATIVITY

The third stage of learning to listen comes when two people have done enough of stages one and two to develop an alliance. With the goodwill developed by stages one and two, they begin to listen to each other in a way that sparks the creativity of each to heights they could not have reached on their own. This deep listening—listening to inspire mutual creativity—is responsible for many breakthroughs in the world. Listening for mutual creativity is rooted in two questions: What do you most want? and How can I help you get what you most want? To listen in total support of other people—to be for their goals and aspirations in your own body, mind, and spirit—may well be the greatest gift you can give your fellow human beings.

Susan Snowe, one of the most effective corporate consultants we've met, gave us a great example of this deeper type of listening: "Once I was feeling stuck in my career. I scheduled a session with another consultant to help get me moving. After hearing my story, he asked me two questions over and over. The questions were 'What do you really want?' and 'Is that what you really want?' He gave me no information or advice—just those two questions. After about the third go-around, I realized that I wanted to start my own company. I'd been working for someone else for twenty years; now it was time for me to work for me. To this day I can feel the shift in my body that happened when I realized what I really wanted. It was as if all the stress and tension dropped away and rechanneled itself into energy."

GIVING AND RECEIVING HONEST FEEDBACK

One of the mystics interviewed for this book, Donna Kindl, was at one time head of human resources at Clorox. After a meeting she was taken aside by another woman executive: "The woman told me in harsh, nonsupportive language that I was arrogant and a terrible listener. At first I was shocked, but as she continued talking I wanted to get down on my knees and express my gratitude. No one—not even my manager—had ever given me feedback like this. Even if it was exaggerated or colored by her personality, she was giving the gift of a lifetime by describing in excruciating detail how I came across. When she finished I expressed my thanks. She was so touched by my response that she took me under her wing and mentored me for the next few years."

For many people the most difficult thing in communication

is getting and giving honest feedback. Yet it is the most valuable commodity in the world. Many of the mystics we interviewed can give and receive feedback, even the brutally honest kind, in approximately the same tone of voice as they would give and hear the time of day. Their commitment to getting accurate data is higher than their commitment to being right.

> *People say I don't take criticism very well, but
> I say what the hell do they know?*
>
> —ATTRIBUTED TO GROUCHO MARX

BUILDING A CORPORATE CULTURE OF INTEGRITY

One of the authors has worked as a consultant for two IBM-Motorola joint ventures. Kate: "In one situation I was brought in because the senior management team was involved in major conflict between each other. All the people were veteran executives with IBM or Motorola, and all were imbued with a strong sense of the values and culture of their respective companies. The people from Motorola were accustomed to talking openly about their differences in meetings. Ideas were attacked, people were sometimes embarrassed, and the tone was often confrontational. However, the Motorola people were comfortable with this, because to them it seemed up-front and honest. They felt they could trust each other because they knew where they stood.

To the IBMers, though, this open style of communication seemed disrespectful and at worst, barbaric. They had grown up in a culture where you came into a meeting having worked out the issues one-to-one before the meeting so that there would be no surprises or hurt feelings. Meetings were to present "done deals," never places to flush out issues. You were expected to keep any contrary feelings to yourself and work them out one-to-one later.

The Motorolans saw this style as intensely political, leading to backroom deals and roundabout decision making. They felt they couldn't trust people to tell the truth in the meetings, so they never knew where anyone stood. The groups polarized: The slick Politicians versus the noisy Barbarians."

A look at the growth rates of both companies in the 1990's would seem to favor the Barbarians. Motorola has built a very successful company partly by placing a high value on telling the truth. In their case, integrity isn't a nicely framed value statement on the boardroom wall; it's a living, breathing way of working. The bottom line says that it pays off.

6

MANAGING PROJECTS

Life is either a daring adventure, or nothing.

—HELEN KELLER

Business success often depends on the art and science of course-correction. No one can predict when the next communication breakdown will occur or the next turf battle will erupt. Instead of a crystal ball, Corporate Mystics have an attitude that works wonders: They not only expect the unexpected but savor it.

We have often asked MBAs and others what was missing from their formal education—What did you have to learn "the hard way"? Frequently they have told us that their professors led them to believe that the course of business would be smooth, given careful planning and well-thought-out procedures. Breakdowns were regarded as symptoms, something to be avoided. In retrospect, however, they wish they had been told the opposite: Even with good planning and procedures, breakdowns are the normal and natural state of affairs. That's just the way it goes, and the businessperson who realizes this is in a much stronger position to deal with the vicissitudes of the day.

We begin with the worst- and best-case scenario.

HANDLING BIG WINS AND BIG LOSSES

M ystics learn to pay close attention just after a big success or a big loss. In both situations we are wide open and vulnerable, beyond our usual boundaries. These times are ripe for messing up.

Gay recalls a profound realization at the circus as a child: "A circus set up shop in a field near my house, and I got a job for a dime a day feeding the animals. This was back in the days when dimes were actually made of silver, so I thought I was getting the deal of a lifetime. One thing I noticed was that the elephants were tethered to a tiny peg that the trainer stuck in the ground. I could pull the peg out with two fingers, so I wondered to the trainer why the elephant didn't pull it out. He told me that the trick was to use a bigger peg when the elephant is little. The elephant cannot in the beginning budge the peg, so that it eventually stops trying to pull it out of the ground. The animal grows up with a clear sense of limitation. After a while, the elephant just knows it can't budge the peg, so you can tether several tons of elephant to a peg that a child could pull out of the ground. Most of us have some kind of limitation in our minds that we take as real. We don't realize that it is simply made up."

One of the key moves of life is to notice where we've got ourselves pegged to the ground. We need to look at our limitations and ask ourselves: If this peg weren't there, what would we do? What would we create? This is where the creativity comes from to start up a project or a company.

A big problem emerges right after you have pulled your peg out. Suddenly you're free, but you're also in the zone of the unknown. This is what often happens just after a big success. You've soared to a new level of power in your world and you may not yet have an internal structure to handle this new power. Rock stars are notorious for flaming out in their twenties; Alexander the Great had done all his conquering by the time of his death in his early thirties.

Just after a big success is a time to slow down a little, take a breath, recenter yourself. Do the same in times of loss. Just after a loss is a vulnerable time; there is a strong tendency in most of us to blame ourselves or others at times like that. When a loss has occurred it is very important to feel all of your feelings about it—anger, sadness, fear—then recenter yourself and ask: What most needs to be done right now?

The same wisdom applies to times of big loss. You are in the zone of the unknown, with pain instead of exhilaration in your body. There is a strong tendency to go into a blaming rather than a learning mode. You think: It's my fault, it's their fault, it's the world's fault. That way of thinking is normal, natural, and habitual. Human beings have been doing it that way for years. So don't beat up on yourself for dropping into that mode from time to time. As quickly as possible, though, shift to a learning mode. The questions then become: What can I learn from this? What revisioning is needed? What course corrections?

What most needs to be done right now?

GETTING THE RESPONSIBILITY FORMULA RIGHT

Most successful people are in the habit of taking more than 100 percent of the responsibility in work situations and life in general. This is a key trait, and you might not be where you are without it. So we're not suggesting you become less responsible, but you do need to be vigilant to make sure you're inspiring other people to be 100 percent responsible. In a situation involving two people, there is 200 percent responsibility to be divided up. With three people there is 300 percent. Responsibility goes up in multiples of 100 percent. The more people who are playing, the more important it becomes to have everyone taking their hundred.

Toward the top of companies most people are more-than-a-hundred-percent types. Down the line you get less-than-a-hundred types. For Corporate Mystics, the problem usually is learning to notice when they're operating in the more-than-a-hundred mode. How can you tell? The most reliable indicator is often what is going on in your body.

A budding mystic told us this story a few months after we had conducted a training in her company: "Until the training day when you explained how responsibility worked, I had no idea why I went home from work sometimes with crushing headaches. After the training I started tracking when I was taking responsibility that actually belonged to someone else. The headaches were coming from anger I was storing up about taking too much responsibility. I was angry at other people for not doing their share, and I was angry at myself for not knowing how to motivate them to do so. As I began to set myself the task of giving people room to be 100 percent responsible, I woke up one day and realized I hadn't had a headache in over a month. That to me is close to being a miracle."

How do you motivate others to do their 100 percent? Delegation is the usual answer, and there is no question that it's a crucial skill for outstanding leaders—one that you have to practice until it's second nature. But delegation, important as it is, is not the fundamental issue. It boils down to your basic position in life: Do you feel that people are fundamentally equal? Do you genuinely feel that people are capable of operating at the 100 percent level?

Michelangelo is said to have looked at a raw block of marble and seen the statue of David in it. Do we see ourselves, and other people, as masterpieces waiting to happen?

REAL POWER

Jerry Jones, a Portland developer and first-class Corporate Mystic, told us: "Some of the best deals I ever made were ones I chose not to make. Earlier in my career I would often beat things to death with energy, trying to make things happen that I should have probably left alone in the first place. As I've matured spiritually and in business, I've learned to listen to the flow. If something is taking a tremendous amount of energy—if it hurts to do it—it may be something you shouldn't be doing. I might compare it to sailing. If you watch the winds carefully you can take advantage of the way they're blowing. Sometimes it's fun to beat into the wind, but over the long haul it eats up too much energy.

"On an airplane flight a while back I was sitting next to Philip Knight, head of Nike Corporation. Behind us was a fellow who was a middle-management type. He spent the flight making phone calls, barking orders, generating a tremendous amount of energy and noise. It was as if he was trying to get people to see how important he was. Meanwhile Phil, a billionaire whose company provides jobs for thousands of people, spent his time thinking, reading, napping. There was a tangible aura of serenity around him. It made me realize how much energy gets wasted in business by ego and displays of false power. By contrast, real power comes from your inner contact with yourself and the universe."

As a practical step in this direction, Jerry does two things that all Corporate Mystics might consider. He spends the first hour of his business day in meditation. With his contact with his inner self and the universe refreshed, he then moves into action. His second edge is to spend each Thursday in complete silence. He will send faxes and such, but he does not have any conversations with people. Both he and his staff have found that this "time-out" is extremely productive. They appreciate a day without his verbal input because it gives them a chance to catch up on assignments from earlier in the week. Once, during a busy spell, he thought he would cut out the Silent Thursday for the sake of the staff. However, they begged him to continue because they were so impressed with the value of it for his well-being and creativity.

RETAINING HIGH-POTENTIAL EMPLOYEES

One of the challenges in corporate life is keeping good people. Paradoxically, as corporations mature they often have a harder time retaining creative people. Bureaucracy grows, rules rigidify, communication must pass through more and more levels. Many of the creative people we have met in corporate environments privately expressed their deep frustration with the strictures of their rule-bound workplaces. When Kate was vice-president for human resources at KLA Instruments, she used intuition, listening, truth telling, and good, old-fashioned creativity to keep a valuable employee: "Mark was an engineering vice-president, a creative guy who had probably brought in $300 million with his designs. I didn't know him well, nor did I see him very often because he worked in a different building. But one morning I kept having uncomfortable thoughts about him tugging at me. Following my intuition, I drove my car over to his building and knocked on his door. I found him staring off into space, confused and unhappy. I sat down and asked him what was going on. After a few minutes of evading the issue, he finally spilled it out. He had just received an offer from another company and was thinking about leaving his job with us.

"I was stunned because he seemed so irreplaceable and so much a part of our culture. I've learned, though, that it never works to 'buy people' because people don't work for money. So I pulled out all my listening skills and drew out of him what the problem was. It took a couple of hours to get the whole story. It turned out that he hated his commute and the administrative aspects of his job, which kept him away from his two children and his wife, who was pregnant with a third child. The commute was a real sticking point; it took him an hour and a half if he came during rush hour and an hour if he came early and stayed late. The other company was five minutes from his house, which made it look very attractive in spite of his love for his work with us.

"I cleared my calendar and we spent a day and a half designing his perfect job. At first it was tough, because none of the things he thought of as a perfect job were things he could visualize ever happening at KLA. Eventually we arrived at a creative solution which met all of his needs and those of the company. We rented a small suite for him in an office building down the street from his house, and set it up so that he only had to come into the main office twice a week for major meetings. We brought in a pure management person who took over the administrative aspect of Mark's job, freeing him up to put his attention on his first love, designing new technology. When I left a year later, he was still happy with the arrangement."

USING INTUITION TO AVOID A COSTLY MISTAKE

A Corporate Mystic and CEO of a Silicon Valley firm tells how intuition came through for him in an acquisitions deal: "The chairman of the board was very hot to acquire a company back east that had designed a new technology that he thought would fit our company's long-range goals. I knew nothing about the company and did not have much of a feel for the technology, either, but as I thought about it I kept having the urge to talk to one of our vice-presidents about it. This was an unusual thought, because she normally would not be involved in any project of this nature. Nevertheless I followed my intuition and met with her. We mutually decided to have her fly east the next day to meet with the principals of the company. She returned after the meeting with a nagging feeling that there was something wrong, but she couldn't put her finger on it. She had liked the people but there was something 'funny' about the business. We decided to spend more time and money investigating the company, only to find that there were major problems with their approach to the technology. Essentially, there was no market in the way they had approached it. Listening to my gut ended up saving the company millions of dollars, even though following my intuition meant bucking the desires of the board chairman. In the long run, though, he came to appreciate the choice we made, especially when he saw the waste that would have occurred."

HANDLING COMPLAINERS AND LOW PRODUCERS

When people are not producing, it is usually because they are out of integrity with themselves. They are not doing what they really want to be doing. The post office is full of people who want to be writers, while writers often dream of a simple job like sorting mail. Your task, if you're the kind-hearted sort, is to talk with these people and ask them, "What do you want to be doing?" If you can help them find a way to do it, great. If not, get them out the door as soon as possible. The post office can't do this, but you probably can.

Complainers complain because they are out of integrity, too, but their integrity breaches go deeper. They are out of integrity with themselves first and foremost, but they are usually out of integrity with the organization, too. Sometimes complaints are valid, but people who complain a lot are usually out of integrity and don't want to admit it. Your loudest complainer about office fairness will reliably turn out to be your big paper-clip thief. A mystic manager recalls: "The president hired in a superstar from another company who started complaining practically the moment he arrived. After listening for a while, most of us tuned it out and assumed it was a character problem. One night I got the proof. I was working late, with the holidays approaching, and I saw our man come into his office with his wife. 'That's unusual,' I thought. During the several hours they were there I had to make numerous trips past his office. Every time I passed they were talking to their relatives! They had come to the office to make their holiday calls! Not long after this, our superstar disappeared from the scene."

HOW TO HANDLE AN OFFICE AFFAIR

Sexual affairs can be a difficult problem for all concerned. A Corporate Mystic we know used the integrity tools outlined earlier to clear up an awkward situation that was hindering a major project.

"I was a vice-president at the time, and the company was about to launch a major new product. Everybody was tense and working eighty to ninety hours a week, so when the rumor mill started grinding it sent tremors through the whole operation. The rumor was that a general manager who reported to me was having an affair with a woman who reported to him. Both were married. At first I was stumped; nobody had told me how to deal with this sort of thing in my MBA school, and I had never confronted it before.

"As I sat down to mull over what to do, I realized I was conflicted in my values. I didn't see myself as the arbiter of somebody else's ethics, but on the other hand I knew all about sexual harassment suits, too. I mainly was concerned that the lying and covering up would throw everything off kilter at a critical time in the company's evolution. I decided to take action. I checked out the source, to understand if there were any documentable facts. There were. So I went to see the man himself. In his office I told him that I was hearing the rumor. I told him that I didn't know or need to know if it was true. I explained everything that had gone through my mind and everything I'd heard. I told him what I saw as the consequences if the rumor were true, both for him and for the company. Then I explained the legal risks as well as I could. He didn't say much during the meeting. He looked down a lot as I was talking to him, showing body language that made him look guilty.

"Two days later I heard that the woman in question had been transferred to a different position, with mutual satisfaction all around. The rumor mill died down, and within a year both people had been promoted. The project went off successfully, giving me all the proof I needed that telling the truth had healed the situation."

ENDING TURF BATTLES

One of the main drainers of corporate energy is the turf war. One of the mystics we interviewed for this book put it plainly: "If turf battles were not going on in most American corporations, there would be no trade deficit with Japan. The Japanese have figured out a way to get by without this kind of junior-high-school stuff. Maybe their way is too hierarchical for American tastes, but we've got to figure some way before there's no way."

You've seen it a hundred times. Manager X squabbles with Manager Y over who would do the best job on a project. Or Manager Z won't share his data with Manager A. The message is: This is my turf and you can't come in here. Our monkey cousins do it very directly. Get on their turf and they spit at you or toss something even more unpleasant at you. Anyone who has spent time in organizations will have a healthy respect for the power of this monkey business to limit productivity. One longtime corporate officer told us that ceiling tiles were a turf benchmark in her company. People actually counted their ceiling tiles to determine the exact square footage of their offices.

As consultants, we often are called in when turf problems have gotten out of hand. We have found that most turf wars could have been avoided by ten minutes of authentic, heartfelt communication. Often, when everything resolves, it is because the main parties put together that few minutes of plain talking that could have been there in the beginning.

Turf battles usually backfire to hurt the people who started them. We have seen this happen so often that it has given us faith that there is a type of justice or karma at work in the world. Here is a typical example: A new marketing vice-president (we'll call him Mark) was hired and seemed to be doing a good job at first. After a couple of months he developed a personal animosity toward one of the engineering managers and began blaming all sorts of problems on him. After much politicking on Mark's part, the engineering manager stepped back from an active management role. It looked at first as though Mark had won, but a very different outcome soon unfolded. The CEO had become so disenchanted with Mark's blame-oriented behavior that he was the next to go.

In a turf war, it becomes more important to be right than to do a good job with the project at hand. In Mark's case, his driving need to be right cost him the ability to see the bigger picture, only to get a rude awakening just as he was celebrating his victory over the other guy.

We were called in to help end a turf war that had cost a small fortune in time, energy, and money. It happened in one of America's largest consumer-products companies, and it could have been avoided by that ten minutes of clear communication we mentioned earlier: "During a vision retreat offsite, the whole engineering staff got very turned on about setting a new product direction. As the high of this new direction buzzed through the room, they sent for the marketing vice-president, Perry, to get him as fired up as they were. He had been in a much duller meeting and came in cold, with no preparation as to what the engineers had been envisioning. He became flustered and went into overwhelm. He proclaimed that it was his job to come up with new product directions. Jack, head of the engineering team, tried to explain that they were just excitedly brainstorming and wanted to fill him in. Perry wasn't having any of it and stormed out.

"Jack and Perry were as different as two people in the high-tech world can get. Jack was an honest, technical sort without a shred of political savvy. He described himself as a 'political boob.' The other man, Perry, was a very skilled corporate politician, a honey-voiced salesman in an Armani suit. After the meeting they got into a turf battle that lasted two years. By the time we were brought in, the conflict had spread through three levels of management. We set a deadline, to work two days and into the second night if we had to, but nobody was going to leave until it got sorted out. As the deadline approached on the second evening, they finally made a breakthrough. They saw that there had been a massive misperception of each other's intentions in the original situation two years before. They went back to that moment and talked about their fears and how these fears had colored their perceptions of the events. There was a major meltdown of tension in the room as these two 'worthy opponents' accepted each other."

What to do about turf battles? First, see them clearly for what they are: one primate, living in fear, trying to keep another primate from booting him out of the leadership position. Once you see that it is "gorilla warfare," you are in a much stronger position. You've called the game for what it actually is. The next thing to do is to look inside yourself. Are you participating in any turf-protecting dramas? Naturally, it is harder to see them in yourself than in others. But take a hard look at yourself first.

Next you have to choose your way out of the game. You do this by making a decision not to participate in or support turf battles. You find yourself looking up at those ceiling tiles, and instead of counting them again, you take a deep breath and bring yourself back to the real issue: your resonance with your inner self and your creative contribution to the enterprise at hand.

HOW TO KEEP MEETINGS FROM BEING BORING

I n our role as consultants, we are frequently asked to facilitate meetings. We have noticed that meetings often do not produce results because not everyone is taking total responsibility for the meeting's success. Often, in fact, the only people engaged are the person who called the meeting and the people who oppose that person or the issue. We evolved a strategy to get total involvement, and it really works.

> *If we know the right answer, let's not have the meeting. If we're going to have the meeting, let's talk to each other the way people talk when they have difficult problems to deal with. That means talking openly and honestly and not withholding and not stage-managing.*
>
> —BOB SHAPIRO

We put a ten-point rating scale on the board, with ten being "totally involved" and one being "bored to death." Every fifteen minutes we ask people to rate themselves and to do what's necessary to get to ten. Most people are willing to admit their lack of interest, but they often blame this on the team, the leader, or the content of the meeting.

When they begin to take responsibility—when they see that it is their own boredom that is making the meeting boring—magic begins to occur. The team members begin to see what produces boredom and what produces involvement. They shift toward feeling responsible for producing involvement, and that is sometimes the only shift that needs to be made.

TURNING ADVERSE SITUATIONS INTO BREAKTHROUGHS

What makes a breakdown happen is very simple. You can see it in the corner shoe-repair shop and you can see it at GM or IBM. What happens first is that some event occurs. The event itself could be as small as a delivery not being made or as large as a stock market crash. The event itself does not cause a breakdown. It is the people-reaction to the event that causes the problem.

The winners of tomorrow will deal proactively with chaos, will look at the chaos per se as the source of market advantage, not as a problem to be gotten around.

—Tom Peters

The breakdown is caused by diverting attention into one unproductive line of inquiry: Whose fault is this? Sometimes a scapegoat is found: It's his fault or her fault. Other times the fault is located outside: It's the world's fault. Occasionally you will get lucky, pinpoint a scapegoat, and fire the person. But it's hard to fire the world. The night before committing suicide, Hitler dictated his last will and testament, disavowing any responsibility for the war and blaming it on the Jews. Some people just never seem to get the message.

There is only one productive line of inquiry in a crisis: What can we learn? What needs to be done? Shifting focus to learning and doing what needs to be done always changes a breakdown to a breakthrough.

7

CREATING WEALTH

All the Corporate Mystics we interviewed for this book agreed on one thing: Wealth begins in the human mind. We focused many of our interviews on men and women who had earned their wealth rather than inheriting it. We found that their belief systems about wealth were surprisingly uniform. They had all made conscious decisions to generate abundance for themselves and others. The tools they used were different. Some tapped into the robust stream of wisdom represented by Napoleon Hill, George Classon, and other writers on prosperity and success. Some used techniques of their own devising, learning their prosperity lessons in that most rigorous of business schools: Hard-Knox.

In this chapter we will summarize every key principle we

discovered in our conversations with Corporate Mystics. These are all tools real people have used successfully; we present them for your experimentation. We have also used them in our own successful quest for financial independence. May they work for you as well as they have worked for us.

> *You may be disappointed if you fail, but you*
> *will be doomed if you don't try.*

—BEVERLY SILLS

ENLIGHTENED PERSEVERANCE

The corporate woods are full of what the music business calls one-hit wonders. These are people who have a burst of success, then quickly flame out, mess up, or fade away. If you want to be abundant in money, love, or anything else, you have to show up consistently. Persistence will win out over creativity and talent just about every time. Was John Belushi a better comedian than Jay Leno? Doesn't matter much now, does it?

Gay had lunch with a radiant man of seventy in his mountaintop retreat. This man, a millionaire many times over, had walked from Germany to the coast of France as a teenager to stay a step ahead of the Nazis. He got on a boat and came to America, where he knew no one and did not speak the language. By the end of his thirties he had a wife and a family and had built a thousand houses. Hot with success, he built up a $5 million fortune and sat back to live the good life. Then came an economic downturn. Not only did he go bankrupt, but he was stuck with a vast amount of lumber. Within fifteen years he had gone from penniless to millionaire to bankrupt. Did it bother him? "Hell, yes, it bothered me! But you have to get back up and go again. Every minute you spend thinking about the way it used to be or the way it ought to be is a minute you haven't been thinking about the way I could make it be. I had a couple of things going for me, though. The main one was that once you've walked five hundred miles in the winter to get away from Nazis, dealing with a bunch of angry bankers is like a picnic. The other advantage I had is persistence. I had it when I was a kid and I've got it right this minute. I know if I just keep getting up in the morning and looking for some contribution to make, I'm going to have a good day."

Eighty percent of success is just showing up.

—Woody Allen

This attitude served him well. The Vietnam War heated up as he was trying to unload his extra lumber, and he became one of the primary suppliers of wood products to the war. Soon he was back in the millionaire ranks and hasn't looked back.

If you match creativity and talent with some persistence, you have a powerful combination. Corporate Mystics know that the secret to showing up consistently is to reframe adversity into challenge. If you consider it a setback when you get dumped off the horse, you don't have a very good time learning to ride. If you see it as part of the process, a necessary and fundamental aspect of riding, you have a context for adversity that allows you to keep your eyes on the goal.

> *Nothing in the world can take the place of persistence: Talent will not; nothing is more common than unsuccessful men with great talent. Genius will not: unrewarded genius is almost a proverb. Education will not: the world is full of educated derelicts. Persistence and determination alone are omnipotent.*
>
> —CALVIN COOLIDGE

HAVING WHAT YOU WANT

The first secret to wealth: Wealth is having what you want. The second secret: Wealth is enjoying what you have. You will hear compelling arguments against both of these ideas. Just about everybody will have a good reason why you shouldn't have what you want. The world is full of people who will argue forcefully for mediocrity and settling for less. Don't listen to them. Others will have great reasons why you shouldn't enjoy what you have. There is so much suffering in the world that many people think that's the way it's supposed to be. Don't listen to them, either. It is perfectly acceptable to have what you want and enjoy what you have. From this place it is possible to facilitate others in having what they want and enjoying what they have. That's where the big fun is to be had in life. A wise person once said that a life of total leisure is the hardest career to pursue. Human beings are not built for unrestricted leisure. Contribution is the driving force of the truly successful person. To the Corporate Mystics we interviewed for the book, the desire for contribution to others' lives was a paramount motivation.

Along the way, why not have what you want and enjoy what you have?

One of the authors' friends decided she wanted to go to medical school. "You can't," said everyone from her mother to the dean of the local medical school, "you're forty-four years old!" She applied to several schools and was turned down at all of them. Finally, she applied to a university in Holland. They accepted her. "See you in three months," they said, "and by the way, all the lectures are in Dutch. Be sure you are fluent when you get here." At the time she spoke not a word of Dutch, but three months later she was fluent. She's now a practicing physician in her early fifties, having what she wants.

Gay was resting on a park bench in Paris, sipping a cup of coffee and feeding the birds. "A woman in her late sixties sat down beside me and we struck up a conversation. She mentioned she had just arrived from Portugal. Oh, I asked, how did you make the journey?

" 'I walked,' she said, and told me that she had decided when she retired at sixty-two to walk around the world, starting from Arizona. Friends and family mounted a fierce campaign to talk her out of it, but she wasn't listening. First she walked to California, then she changed her mind and went the other direction. She was on her eleventh pair of sneakers when I met her. Noticing her wedding ring, I asked her where her husband was. Back in Arizona, she said. 'I asked him to come, but he didn't want to. Said he'd rather stay home and watch TV.' But she hadn't let that stop her.''

As consultants, we have had the opportunity to talk to many people who have done the business equivalent of going off for a walk around the world. One man left a corporate job he found stultifying to found his own company. He went from a plush office with a view of the Chicago Loop to a little facility in an industrial park on the outskirts of town. "But, at least, it was my name on the door. There was no one responsible for me but me, myself, and I." After two years his company failed. "But, you know what? I felt happier even dealing with the failure than I had in the previous five years with the other company." Two years after that failure, though, he had bounced back and was one of the industry leaders.

We have talked to fifty people or more who have taken the plunge and started their own companies. Of those fifty, only twenty or so have been successful. But we cannot think of one who has regretted the move. Something good has come out of it, even though it often did not fit the picture they originally had.

ENJOYING WHAT YOU HAVE

Once you have what you want you will be faced with the problem of enjoying it all in a world filled with shame and scarcity. Don't buy into this, either. Go ahead: Have what you want. You'll know if it's something you really want if you're willing to walk around the world for it. But then, once you've got it, you still have the challenge of enjoying what you've got.

A Corporate Mystic of our acquaintance wrangled an invitation to visit a man worth $100 million. The man's jaw muscles clenched constantly as he described his desperate desire to get to billionaire status. He chain-smoked and carped at his wife throughout the discussion, which was carried out in his underground bunker/fallout shelter, four stories beneath where his dream house glittered in the afternoon sun. He seldom left the bunker to go up the elevator to the dream house. He said the natural beauty tended to interfere with the concentration he needed to work. Although all signs said he had it made, he did not have what he wanted and he was not enjoying what he had.

Mystics realize that satisfaction and enjoyment are completely within their control, so they start there. They work on enjoying what they have, exactly as it is now.

*There are two things to aim at in life; first, to
get what you want; and after that, to enjoy it.
Only the wisest of mankind achieve the second.*

—LOGAN PEARSALL SMITH

THE FUNDAMENTAL LAW OF CREATING WEALTH

The first law of creating wealth is this: You can choose
what you think. You can choose any goal you want, and
you can make up any financial rule you choose to live by, as
long as it does not interfere with any fundamental rules of
how the universe works. There is no limit to what you can
think up. To make it live in the material world, you have to
support it with action, but the key moment is taking responsibility for thinking it up the way you want it. If you really
understand the significance of this law, you are in a position
to create genuine miracles for yourself and for your organization.

All wealth comes from the human mind. In Zurich it may
be measured in gold or by blips on a computer screen. On a
remote South Pacific island it may be measured in cowrie
shells. But always and everywhere it is based on pure agreement, constructed by the creative power of the human mind.

The good news is that we all carry that same creative power
within us. If you understand the nature of your own consciousness, you will see how wealth is generated.

The human mind has evolved to the point that we now can consciously perceive ourselves as connected to the infinite. Many of us do not, of course, choose to celebrate this connection or use it to make us happy. But we have the potential, all the same, of opening up to a seamless relationship with all creation.

> *We are what we think. All that we are arises with our thoughts. With our thoughts we make our world.*
>
> —THE BUDDHA

As soon as we embrace our connection with the infinite, we can see that we are connected to the source of creativity. The same creative force that makes oak trees, dolphins, and rainbows also makes us. An acorn is something that was created out of nothingness, and it has the seeds of creation hidden in potential within it. It is at once created and creator.

We are a microcosm of the whole universe. We carry creator and created within us.

You have the power to create something from nothing. You can think up any reality you want. As long as it does not conflict with any laws of the universe, it can manifest, providing you support it with whatever actions are required. In other words, you can make up the rules, as long as your rules don't conflict with the other rules. The thought "I enjoy complete abundance of love and money" does not conflict with any laws of the universe. Put your attention on it, support it with action, and it will come into being. If you make up a rule that says "I can steal without getting caught," you probably won't succeed because it conflicts with other rules in the world. The thought "By flapping my arms I can fly like an eagle" conflicts with a current law of the universe. You can think it all day long and it won't become reality. If you want to argue this point, send us a picture first and we'll get in touch.

Nobody would be harmed by a new rule in the universe that says "I am abundant in love and money." If you are ready and willing to be abundant in love and money, step into the creator role: Go ahead and choose it now.

Say the words and get the body-feeling: "I am ready and willing to be abundant in love and money."

Go one step further. Put it in the present tense.

"I am abundant in love and money." Feel it in your body as a right-now reality.

You can bring into creation anything you want, as long as it's in harmony with the fundamental way the universe works. Some thoughts that have a great deal of power are:

> "My income is always much larger than my expenses."
> "Every dollar I spend comes back to me multiplied."
> "I effortlessly have plenty of money to do everything I want to do."
> "The more people I make prosperous, the more prosperous I become."

There is no limit to what you can think up.

*Money doesn't buy happiness, but that's not
why so many people are poor.*

—Laurence Peter

*The greatest discovery of my generation is
that a human being can alter his life by
altering his attitudes of mind.*

—William James

HOW TO CREATE A MIND-SET OF PROSPERITY IN YOUR ORGANIZATION

You carry your abundance or lack of abundance with you night and day. It is not in your portfolio or bank account. There are many, many people with large amounts of money who are stingy, unpleasant, greedy, and unhappy. There are just as many living in a virtual garden of love who do not open to it or appreciate it. So abundance of love and money begins in our consciousness. We have charge of it. We can say: I consciously choose abundance of love and money in my life.

You can make this choice individually with great rewards, but a more powerful set of possibilities emerges when you do this as a group or as an entire company. We have been in meetings in which an entire executive team opened up to choosing abundance for themselves as individuals and for the company at large. When the individuals coalesced into a team, the shift in consciousness could be felt throughout the room. The late Andrew Carnegie taught that if you could get five people into harmony around a goal, you could generate miracles. It worked for him; he funded fourteen hundred libraries around the world through his philanthropy, with change left over for a couple of universities.

The benefit of abundance consciousness is you can take it wherever you go in the world. If you know that your abundance begins in your mind, you create love and money anywhere. If you do not know this, you can sit in the middle of a pile of money in a garden of love and not know how to access either one.

It all begins in your consciousness. And you invoke it by choosing.

Right now, make the choice.

I choose complete abundance in love and money.

Or not. It is completely your own choice.

If you want abundance, choose it carefully and calmly. Bring it into being by thinking and feeling this idea: *I choose complete abundance in love and money.*

TURNING AROUND NEGATIVE FINANCIAL ATTITUDES

Once you invoke abundance in your life, you will be able to see more clearly where you are operating from limiting beliefs about yourself or about the world. Our most limiting beliefs will not even be revealed until after we have made a commitment to abundance. Right after you choose abundance you may think, "These ideas will never work for me." This is the limiting thought that has been released into the light by the power of your commitment to abundance. Any negative thoughts that surface as you consider these ideas can be regarded as old limits put in your mind by you or someone else. Don't make them right or wrong; just let them move on through.

There is a specific technology that is helpful when those limiting thoughts bubble up: Use a positive thought to replace the old limiting concept. Let's say you find yourself thinking: "I always lose money in the stock market." You wouldn't have a limiting thought like that unless you or someone you identify with had been wounded and infected with scarcity. When you uncover a wound, use the healing power of your own thoughts to soothe it. Think "All my investments are profitable." You might surface a limiting thought like "I could never be financially secure." Apply a more positive thought: Think "I have complete financial abundance." One good way to apply a positive thought is to drop it into your thought-stream as soon as you notice a limiting thought go by.

Applying a positive thought takes your negativity out of the situation. Perhaps your stock market investments will improve or perhaps you'll take all your money out of the stock market. Either way you win. But at least you will not be carrying around that blotch of negativity with you.

Once you have begun identifying your own negativity about money, look around you at the key people in your life. See if they are carrying negative attitudes. The reason this is important is that alignment with two or three key people in your life can produce abundance much more quickly. If you are linked to a life partner who has scarcity programming they won't confront, it makes your journey to abundance much more difficult. Sit down and talk it out. Find out if your friends and family would join you in a mutual quest for abundance.

Definitely find out where your main business partners stand on this issue. Do they understand, believe, and practice the principle that we generate wealth first in our own minds? If they do, great! If not, you need to help tune them up or you will be dragged down by them.

CLEAN UP YOUR UNFINISHED FINANCIAL BUSINESS

A powerful key to creating abundance is to start taking care of any unfinished business in your money life. Start with two main categories: *Money I Owe* and *Money I Am Owed*. Take out a sheet of paper right now and put these two categories on it. List anything you can think of, going back as far as you can.

Gay received the following letter from a woman who had taken his course for consultants: "I committed to complete several pieces of unfinished business in the area of money at our March meeting. The unfinished business included relatively trivial items like $15 I owed someone, up to significant items like $23,000 someone owed me and the unresolved issue of ownership of a house. Within ten days after the training I repaid all the monies I owed people, hired a lawyer to go after the $23,000, and flew to Hawaii to negotiate the agreements about the house. In April I had my first $15,000 month as a consultant, more than doubling any month I'd ever had in the past."

It is important to realize that you don't have to take care of all your unfinished business at once. All you have to do is start the process. You may owe $1,000 and have only $10. It doesn't matter. The important thing is to make a start. Send the $10 to the person or open an account with the intention of putting a dollar a day toward the debt. You'll be surprised at how quickly your actions will be rewarded with abundance.

LEADING WITH GRATITUDE

One of the most powerful tools for creating abundance is leading with gratitude. Here's how it works, as described by Gay: "In the mid-eighties I began confronting my limiting ideas about how prosperous I could be. Soon, I began having spontaneous thoughts of people with whom I had financial incompletions. Two of these were John and Bill, both of whom had loaned me money years before. They had disappeared from the screen of my life, and I had conveniently 'forgotten' about the debts.

"One thing I learned from Buckminster Fuller was to act on an idea within ten minutes of having it (I think he was talking about business ideas, not ones about showroom Ferraris or people to whom you're sexually attracted!). As soon as I realized why John and Bill were appearing in my mind, I started trying to find them. I found Bill with a couple of weeks' research and wrote him to tell him I wanted to pay him back. His circumstances had changed radically, such that he was now nearly destitute. He indicated that the money would mean a great deal to him. John was more difficult; to this day I have not located him. I put his money into circulation by dispersing it to various charities I thought he would approve of.

"My wife, Kathlyn, and I started to work systematically on discovering incompletions and taking care of them. They nearly always turned out to be in the area of things we needed to communicate to people. For example, Kathlyn and I both realized that we had never formally and completely thanked several members of our families who had helped us out financially when we were in graduate school. My mother had sold a piece of property worth about $10,000, and had split the proceeds with me and my brother. Kathlyn's parents had come through with a $2,500 loan while she was working on her doctorate. We wrote several detailed letters of appreciation and gratitude, and were richly rewarded by a tide of good feeling that rushed back our way.

"In addition to the good feeling, this process started us thinking about what we now call 'leading with gratitude.' Many of us are waiting for something good to happen, then we'll express some gratitude. Maybe. It is akin to a gardener saying to the garden, 'Give me some flowers and then I'll water you.' But we found a better way, which was to make the expression of gratitude an ongoing process. Focus on gratitude first: Lead with appreciation. Our practical step was to look for ways we could express gratitude to people in our lives. This, more than any other principle, began to turn our lives toward prosperity."

FACING YOUR INTERNAL ENEMIES OF ABUNDANCE

In our consulting work, we have found several main barriers people face even at the very highest levels of corporate life. In fact, the more successful you become, the more likely you are to encounter them. Those who are not conscious of these barriers often trip over them or sabotage their success because of them.

The first is the fear of rising to your full measure of success because of unconscious loyalties to people in your past. Many of us grew up in families or went to schools where we felt guilty about outdoing others. We had to pretend to know less than we did, or we felt guilty that not everyone could win the prize we won. Later in life, when success strikes, we may not enjoy it fully because we still carry this guilt about outdoing someone else.

There is another version of this fear: By being fully successful we will leave someone else behind. The origins of this fear are usually in our family lives, in our guilt about abandoning someone less capable than ourselves. Perhaps it is a younger sibling or a retarded family member; there is often someone we have to leave behind, and it hurts to do so. Later that hurt haunts us so that we do not go into our full abundance for fear of abandoning others. For example, both Gay and his brother, Mike, were the first members of their family to attend college. "Both of us felt mixed feelings of pride and guilt. We knew people in the family were proud of us, but we also felt guilty that we were doing things they never had a chance to do," recalls Gay. "I felt a strong need to reassure them, when I went home to visit, that I still loved them. I was sometimes hesitant to tell them about stimulating cultural events I attended, for fear that they would feel bad."

Unless you bring this fear to light, you run a risk as you grow in your career. The typical pattern is to commit an act of self-sabotage based on this fear. You have a big win, for example, then mess up in some way or get sick. Family scripts are powerful teachers, for better and for worse. Many successful people come from humble beginnings and have worked hard to transcend the family script. Yet at the same time they may carry unconscious fears that their success is somehow being disloyal to the family. We have worked with many such executives to help them acknowledge and release their unconscious loyalties to those in their past. As the burden of guilt is lifted, successful people find that they can love and appreciate the people in their past more easily.

IS YOUR SUCCESS A BURDEN?

A second internal barrier is the fear that our abundance might be a burden in some way. In today's ecologically sensitive environment, there is widespread concern that the creations of humankind place a burden on the earth's natural resources. There is a great deal of validity to this perception, and each person must face his or her obligation to the planet as part of each corporate decision. However, there is a more personal problem that successful people must face.

As consultants we have often worked with people who have grown up feeling they were burdens to their families. Sometimes this perception was based on realities such as poverty or illness. If you actually are a burden in some way to your parents, you may internalize and carry this feeling into adult life. More frequently, though, the burden was imaginary. Imaginary or real, the net result is often the same: Their success as adults is dampened by a concern that it is a burden to the world. One of our clients grew up in quite a wealthy family, but he was the last-born of five, the last two of whom were accidental pregnancies. Both grew up with a pervasive sense that their very existence was unwelcome, based largely on nonverbal messages they received. Our client didn't make this connection until later in his thirties, when he found that he was not moving as fast as he wanted on his career track. He was also motivated by his older brother's entry into a drug and alcohol rehabilitation program. As he confronted his unconscious fears, he found that he had perceived himself as a burden from the first moments of his awareness in life. When he cleared the issue up, he moved ahead quickly in his career and later went into the family business, which he had always resisted joining.

Related to this is a fear that our abundance might be taking from others. We may think: If I am fully abundant it will cause someone else to suffer lack. It is very rare for this to be the case, but many people suffer from this fear because of early programming. They were made to feel in their families that their existence took love and attention away from someone else.

With all of these barriers, the simple act of awareness takes their power away. Noting them and seeing which ones pertain to you is the most liberating step you can take.

DOING WHAT YOU LOVE

The happiest mystics we have met are those who are doing what they most love to do. Many of them ask this question on a regular basis: What do I love to do that adds real value to people's lives? Gay has based his whole career on this question: "I was sitting at home one evening when I was still in my twenties, thinking about what I really wanted to do with my life. I had recently heard a lecture by J. Krishnamurti in which he said that the sole purpose of education was to help you find out what you, with all your heart, most love to do. With this in mind, I asked myself what I most loved to do. Ten minutes of wondering later, I had come up with several ideas. One was that I loved to write. The act of putting words on paper delighted me. The second thing I loved to do was to sit around with interesting people discussing the most fundamental issues of living. Putting these two together, I dreamed up a career of writing about and consulting with people about the most important psychospiritual concerns human beings face. If I could do that, I thought, I would make full use of my talents while never feeling like I was working for a living.

"Next I found myself confronting my limited thinking: A loud, mocking voice in my head said, 'You could never make a living doing that! Who would pay for that?' At first I took this voice seriously and felt a wave of despair course through me. Then I thought 'Wait a minute!' I recognized the mocking voice as belonging to my older brother. That was his voice and his attitude! He's an air-conditioning and heating contractor, so naturally he wouldn't think much of a career in applied metaphysics. I let go of the negative voice and took a deep breath. Next, an image of one of my Stanford professors flashed through my mind. It was a memory of my saying to him that I wanted to put the powerful learnings of psychology into forms that everyone could use. He sneered with utter derision, 'Surely you're not thinking of becoming one of those pop psychologists!' His tone made it sound like I was going to mass-market bubonic plague.

"I took a few more breaths and let that old painful image go. I realized that what I wanted to do was groundbreaking in my family tradition and my classical psychology background. There was not going to be much agreement there for my goals: I would have to manufacture my own agreement. Right then and there I made a deal between me and the universe that I would go for what I wanted, which was to make a living doing what I most love to do. And that's the way it's been."

PULLING THE PLUG ON DRAIN-RELATIONSHIPS

Unless you are very lucky, you have certain relationships that drain your energy. These relationships decrease your energy, your money supply, and your free time. Usually we put up with them for some other reason, perhaps because they involve family or friends.

These relationships can be changed radically if you are courageous enough to take action. For those relationships where you are not obligated by blood ties or binding legal contracts, we recommend a process we call high-firing. In high-firing, you sever your draining connection with the person, but you do it from a high intention. The intention is that both you and the person prosper through severing the connection.

There is a convenient rule of thumb for determining who needs to be high-fired. Fire anyone who costs you time, energy, or money three or more times.

Take a moment to think of who in your world fits that category.

Listen to a Corporate Mystic describe the process of high-firing: "One day at a meeting my partner and I had a revelation. We realized that we had spent considerable time that week patching up a communication breakdown caused by one of our salespeople lying and failing to keep agreements. We applied the high-firing rule of thumb to the situation: Had things like this happened at least two times before? The answer was a resounding 'yes.' So we decided to high-fire him. To get clear on our intentions, we had to look at why we had kept him around so long. The answer was illuminating. My partner and I had both grown up with alcoholic fathers, so we were used to covering up the messes made by others, out of our love for them. We were treating our salesman like our fathers! That came as a real shocker to realize this, because the salesman was actually younger than we were.

"We wrote out an intention on a piece of paper. It said 'We release our connection to Bob in a way that allows us all to prosper.' Then we called Bob in and told him everything we had decided, including even the part about our alcoholic fathers. To our surprise, Bob burst into tears and confessed that he had been stealing trivial things from the company in a way we had never suspected. He also told us he hated putting on a suit and tie each day because he liked to spend time outside. The upshot was that he ended up thanking us as he left. Later we heard that he had set up a small lawn-care outfit. The bottom line to us was that it seemed like our whole company breathed a sigh of relief."

Everything in the universe is subject to change
and everything is right on schedule.

—A CORPORATE MYSTIC

PART THREE

The Disciplined Mystic: Four Ten-Minute Practices for Enhancing Integrity, Vision, and Intuition

L earning the information in this book is useful, but mastery becomes possible only when you practice it in key situations. It is easy to have integrity, vision, and intuition when things are going well, but only practice will keep them in place when the pressure is on.

The following practices are designed to be done in ten minutes or less. If you have more time, they can be amplified with great value.

The Basic Centering Practice

M any of the Corporate Mystics we interviewed are staunch advocates of meditation in some form. Not all of them call it that, but they are really talking about the same thing: a method of clearing and quieting the mind so that it becomes refreshed, creative, and productive. We were surprised to find that quite a few top corporate executives have been trained in one of the formal approaches to meditation such as Transcendental Meditation, Zazen, or Vipassana; others have invented a practice for themselves that works.

In our seminars and consultations with corporations we began to teach meditation twenty years ago when it was much less accepted than it is now. We did so with trepidation, because we feared that it would be met with resistance. Indeed there was resistance on occasion, but much less so than we imagined. Once people practiced meditation, they immediately recognized how beneficial it could be. The Basic Centering Practice, which follows, has stood the test of time, becoming our favorite generic meditation technique, one which uniformly yields excellent results.

This practice will teach you how to bring about a clear feeling of balance and ease in your body very quickly. In studying what makes people feel off-center, we found three commonalities in their experience. First, when people feel off-center, their stomach muscles are usually tense. This is not surprising. All animals tighten their stomach muscles when they're afraid, so this habit probably started for many of us in childhood as a response to fear. Certainly today's business climate has many things about it that trigger fear. Fear is nothing to be ashamed of, and can actually be a useful ally. Fritz Perls, the psychiatrist who founded Gestalt therapy, said that fear was merely "excitement without the breath." Take a few breaths, he counseled, and you will feel your fear turn into excitement.

Second, breathing tends to be shallow and high in the chest. This breathing pattern is part of the fight-or-flight reflex, wired into our bodies over thousands of years of dealing with stressful situations.

Third, people feeling off-center usually tell us that their minds are scattered and overly busy.

We developed the Basic Centering Practice as a way to correct each of these problems directly. You will find that even a short practice of it will quiet your mind and make your body more relaxed.

The Basic Centering Practice

Use it by itself whenever you want a sense of calm well-being. It also can be used as a prelude to each of the other three activities in this section.

INSTRUCTIONS

Get comfortably seated. Arrange it so you won't be interrupted for the next ten minutes. You can do the practice with eyes open or closed; experiment with each way to find out which brings about the deepest sense of ease.

STEP ONE

As you breathe slowly out your nose, tighten your stomach muscles, particularly the ones right around your navel. Keep them tight until all the breath is out of your body, then relax your stomach muscles completely as you breathe in. Take a slow deep breath as deep down into your abdomen as you can get it. As you breathe slowly out, tighten the muscles around your navel again. When all the breath is out of your body, relax your stomach muscles completely as you breathe in. Repeat this procedure several more times, tightening your stomach muscles on the out breath and relaxing them on the in breath. After several cycles, rest and take your mind off your breathing for a few moments.

STEP TWO

Now, return your attention to your breathing. Breathe slowly and deeply, keeping your stomach muscles very relaxed. Count silently in your mind as you breathe in and out:

in-two-three-four, out-two-three-four, making each number equal to about a second. Each in breath will take about four seconds and each out breath will take the same amount of time. Do several cycles with this four-count. When you feel that you can take a longer breath, go to a five-count: in-two-three-four-five, out-two-three-four-five. Do several cycles with the five-count. Always stay in the comfort zone: Keep the breath easy and peaceful.

Eventually, if you are able to do so comfortably, extend the count to six, seven, or eight. Always stay in the comfort zone. The lighter and easier you can make the breath, the more centered you will feel.

STEP THREE

When you feel centered, let go of the counting and the focus on your breath. Just relax for a minute or two, letting your mind and body enjoy the quiet sense of balance and well-being.

> *Meditation is just focus. We all know how to*
> *focus on exterior things in our lives.*
> *Meditation is a focus on the inside. It's trained*
> *my mind not to run away on me. I believe that*
> *90 percent of what most people think is*
> *fantasy created by our runaway minds, and it's*
> *not real. When the mind is focused, you can*
> *concentrate on what is really meaningful.*
> —ED MCCRACKEN

Your Integrity Worksheet: The F•A•C•T Process

The purpose of the Integrity Worksheet is to crystallize all the essential integrity teachings into one concentrated and highly usable form. You can apply the Integrity Worksheet to any problem, large or small. It was originally designed to break up corporate logjams, and it has done so successfully many hundreds of times. It is our hope, though, that you will apply it before the logjam stage is reached. If you use it preventively rather than waiting until a crisis develops, you can smooth out situations in ten minutes that might take months to handle otherwise. The steps in the process are:

- Facing
- Accepting

- Choosing
- Taking Action

Most people find it useful to write down their responses, but it can also be done in the mind's eye.

INSTRUCTIONS

STEP ONE: FACING

The first step is to face the situation as it stands now. Twenty-five hundred years ago the Buddha said, "All human unhappiness comes from not facing reality squarely, exactly as it is." It is a wise, even crucial observation for us today.

The Questions: What is the reality of the situation? How would I like it to be? Are there ways I or others are out of integrity?

- The reality of the situation—the way it is now—is

  _____

  _____ .

- My goal—how I'd like things to be—is

  _____

  _____ .

- Have I communicated anything untrue in the whole course of this situation?
  To myself: _____ .

To anybody else: _____.
•   Have I broken any agreements in the course of this situation?
    With myself: _____.
    With others: _____.
•   If untruths or broken agreements have come to light, the action step(s) I will take to rectify them is

    _____.

    By when? _____.

STEP TWO: ACCEPTING

Once you have faced the issue squarely, you are ready for the step of acceptance. Complete acceptance of a situation, exactly as it is, creates an openness to change.

The Question: What about this situation have I not accepted, exactly as it is?

_____

_____.

•   Is it something about myself?
•   Is it something about someone else?
•   Is it something in the past?
•   Is it something that's happening now?

Take a moment now to accept it, just as it is.

STEP THREE: CHOOSING

Once you have faced and accepted a situation thoroughly, you are in a clear position from which to choose how you would like things to be.

The Question: What do you most want in this situation?

_____

_____ .

STEP FOUR: TAKING ACTION

Once you have faced, accepted, and chosen, the next step is to design the actions that are required.

The Question: What action(s) can you take to support your getting what you most want in this situation?

_____

_____ .

I commit to taking the action(s) by _____ .

Future-Vision

This activity has emerged from our workshops as one of the most powerful ways of getting everyone to become a visionary. The purpose of future-vision is to get comfortable in an imagined future. It is not important that your visions of the future be accurate or feasible. The goal is simply to become conversant with the future, to have the flexibility of mind to "unstick" yourself from the bounds of time. Future-vision teaches this skill by encouraging you to locate yourself in an imagined future and operate as if that future had already happened.

This activity is best done in a team. Three is an ideal number, so that you can have a future-visioner, a facilitator, and a scribe. In our workshops we switch roles so that everyone has a chance to be future-visioner. The job of the facilitator is to read the instructions to the future-visioner and to ask the questions. The scribe's job is to take notes that can be shared later in a discussion. The scribe has an important task, because most people forget half of what they said if they really get into the activity.

The activity can also be done alone, although it may be harder to surrender yourself to it. The following instructions are based on doing it in a team of three.

INSTRUCTIONS

Pick who will be future-visioner, facilitator, and scribe. The facilitator gives the instructions.

STEP ONE

The facilitator says: Choose a goal, issue, or problem that is significant for you. A goal might be something like the successful launch of a new product, while a problem might be something like what to do about an employee who isn't performing well. Pick one and jot it down on a piece of paper.

STEP TWO

The facilitator says: Select a place in the room that you can let represent the future. Get comfortable there, seated or standing. Throughout the activity do your best to stay in the imagined future. Close your eyes and really imagine that you are in the future, when the goal has been achieved or the problem successfully solved. Get the feeling in your body that it was a total, unqualified success.

I'm going to ask you some questions. Do your best to answer them from the future, as if the goal has been achieved or the problem solved. The scribe will keep track of your answers.

- What is it that makes this a total success?
- What is the positive effect that this success is having on people?
- What did you learn about yourself of most value that allowed you to contribute to the success?
- What did other people learn of most value that allowed them to contribute to the success?
- What were the course corrections that might have thrown you and others off-course before that this time you navigated successfully?
- If you had to pick one thing, what did you and/or your team do that created this successful outcome?
- If you were to give one piece of advice to us back here in (name today's date), what would it be?

STEP THREE

Take a moment to relax, then come back to the present and let's talk about what you experienced.

(The scribe reads back the notes from the future-visioner's answers. After discussing these, change roles and do another round.)

The Intuition Practice

This practice is the most reliable way the authors have found for turning on the power of intuition. It is a seeding technique in which you plant a question in your mind, then let go and receive what comes. Sometimes you will get imagery, sometimes words or concepts. Oftentimes you will get nothing at all right away. Be patient, though, because something useful may appear that night in a dream or the next morning while you are in the shower.

INSTRUCTIONS

STEP ONE

Select a goal, problem, or issue to focus on. Phrase it in the form of a question, as in "How could I best handle the GE account?" Jot your question down on a piece of paper. Get comfortable (use the Basic Centering Practice) and arrange it so you will be undisturbed for the next ten minutes or so. This process tends to work better when your eyes are closed, but feel free to experiment to find which works best for you.

STEP TWO

When your mind is quiet, float your question in your mind and then let it go. Let go of any expectation and get receptive. Take any images that come up or any ideas that emerge. Receive them nonjudgmentally; you can sort them out later.

Enjoy your mind and how it works. You might enjoy looking for the open space between and behind thoughts. If you do this for a moment, the open space will actually seem to grow larger. Relax into this space. Accept it.

STEP THREE

When you get to a good stopping place, open your eyes and jot down what you have received. Open the interpretive part of your mind and apply it to what images and ideas have emerged. Look for patterns, metaphors. If nothing you consider useful has emerged, let go for right now and open yourself to something coming along later.

The Last Word

"**A**ny last words of wisdom you can give us?" the student asked.

The mystic thought for a moment. "You can work out just about any difficulty you have by remembering two sentences."

"What are they?"

"Number one: What is, is. Number two: What isn't, isn't."

The mystic continued: "A lot of people waste their time focusing on what isn't—they dwell on things that aren't real. If something's real, if it actually is—whether it's a feeling like anger or a fact like sales are down—it's a waste of time wishing it wasn't. What you do if something is real is accept it just like it is, then decide if you want to put the energy into trying to make it different. Once you decide you want to try to change it, then put your energy into what needs to be done. That's everything you really need to be successful in business and life."

I am one fellow along with you. We are both going to die. We have a common destiny. We're in this together.

—BOB SHAPIRO, CHAIRMAN AND CEO, MONSANTO

Everyone is in the best seat.

—JOHN CAGE

The Seven Radical Rules for
Business Success

H ere they are, the stripped-down essential rules for business
success, derived from over one thousand hours of illuminating interviews and conversation with highly successful
corporate leaders. They are radical for two reasons: They will
produce a revolutionary change in your life and working relationships, and because they go to the root (that is the original
meaning of *radical*) of what is wrong in most businesses.

RULE ONE

Always tell the truth. Especially tell the truth about personal facts and feelings. Make everything possible in your business open book. Teach everyone how to read the spreadsheet, make all salaries public, never hide anything that is not absolutely required to be hidden.

RULE TWO

Always take 100 percent responsibility for any activity you're involved in. If you are in a leadership position, take 100 percent, not 200 percent for all activities. Require that each participant take 100 percent. Equality is possible only through meeting at the 100 percent level.

RULE THREE

Scrupulously attend to all agreements you make and others make with you. Do everything you say you are going to do, and don't do anything you've said you wouldn't do. Demand impeccability of others. If you catch yourself or others in a broken agreement, cop to it immediately and fix it.

RULE FOUR

Never gossip and never get in the middle of communications between other people. Make your no-gossip commitment public, and state your intention to stay out of the middle of conflicts and communication glitches.

RULE FIVE

Set aside daily creative think-time and make it sacred. It doesn't matter if it's five minutes or an hour. What matters is that your intention is to renew your connection with your inner spirit and open to your full creativity. Find your own preferred method: Meditate, deep breathe, sit quietly, doodle. If you miss a day, do twice as much the next day.

RULE SIX

Make a to-do list and update it constantly throughout the day. Put your most dreaded activities first and do them first thing.

RULE SEVEN

Go to the source. Whenever you hear of something that makes you feel uncomfortable, talk to all parties concerned and listen carefully to them. Let people have the ten minutes of clear communication that solves most problems. Listen with as little agenda as you can manage.

About the Authors

GAY HENDRICKS is the author of over twenty books about transformation. After receiving his Ph.D. from Stanford in 1974, he became a professor at the University of Colorado, retiring after twenty years to direct his own consulting firm, The Hendricks Institute, whose fifteen associates have worked with several hundred organizations worldwide. His wife, Kathlyn Hendricks, Ph.D., is also an author and consultant. They live in Colorado Springs and in Santa Barbara, California.

KATE LUDEMAN is an engineer with a doctorate in psychology. An executive consultant, she is the author of the widely used business books *Earn What You're Worth* and *The Worth Ethic*. Among the many clients of the Worth Ethic Corporation, her consulting company located in Austin, Texas, are Motorola, Monsanto, General Electric, Johnson & Johnson, and Silicon Graphics. Her husband, William Miller, is president of Global Creativity Corporation and the author of two books. They live in Austin.

For Further Information

Gay Hendricks is the founder of two organizations. The Hendricks Institute provides training in executive development and the healing professions. The Foundation for Twenty-First-Century Leadership sponsors conferences on innovative business practices. Information on these organizations and their services may be obtained by calling 800-688-0772.

Kate Ludeman offers executive coaching, team building, and keynote speeches through her firm, Worth Ethic Corporation, in Austin, Texas. She has developed proprietary software for conducting 360-degree assessments and corporate culture audits that stimulate greater innovation for long-term transformation. Information on these and other individually tailored services is available by calling 512-794-9270.